DEAD WEIGHT
A Jack Hart Mystery

Rosemary Reeve

Cover designed by 100 Covers
Back cover photograph by Busath Photography: Used by digital and print license to Rosemary Reeve

Please visit my author's page at amazon.com/author/rosemaryreeve

and my Goodreads profile at
https://www.goodreads.com/goodreadscomrosemary_reeve

Printed in the United States of America

First Printing: September 2018
Independently Published

ISBN 9781983066764

The Jack Hart Mysteries:

All Good Things
No Good Deed
Only the Good
Dead Weight

To my grandmothers,
Mary and Sena,
who deserved more.

This book contains adult language and scenes. It includes topics of suicide and sexual assault/abuse.

National Suicide Prevention Lifeline
1-800-273-8255
https://suicidepreventionlifeline.org/

National Sexual Assault Hotline
1-800-656-HOPE (4673)
https://hotline.rainn.org/online/

ACKNOWLEDGEMENTS

"Board Meeting Minutes 4/10" is the best and possibly only rock song ever written about a state insurance commissioner. Many thanks to the great Seattle band Rat Cat Hogan for authorizing use of an excerpt of the lyrics. "Board Meeting Minutes 4/10," Rat Cat Hogan, <u>Don't Call Me Twaddy / Eet Ees Too Koldt to Go Swimmink</u>, Elsinor Records, Copyright © 1998. Reprinted by the kind permission of Robbie Skrocki and Herbert Bergel.

The title and first line of the freelance article in Chapter 10 are from a <u>Stranger</u> article about people who jumped from Seattle's Aurora Bridge. Many thanks to <u>The Stranger</u> and the great Charles Mudede for authorizing this use. "Jumpers: Take it to the Bridge," by Charles Mudede, <u>The Stranger</u>, Apr. 13, 2000. Copyright © 2000. Reprinted by the kind permission of Leilani Polk, <u>Stranger</u> Managing Editor, and Charles Mudede, <u>Stranger</u> Film Editor.

Quote by Nathan Bransford reprinted by the kind permission of Nathan Bransford.

CHAPTER 1

"**A** woman doesn't kill herself when she's losing weight."

A long time ago, I learned never to leave a deposition without first asking the court reporter what she thinks of the witness. A court reporter isn't a machine, no matter how intent she is on taking down every word of every question you ask and every answer you get. She - they're usually shes, even these days - is your first audience, the first impartial person who listens to the witnesses.

So that's why I waited until the silk-clad deponent had glided toward our elevator, handkerchief fluttering but eyes dry. That's why I waited until her lawyer, Boyd Tate, had blustered out behind her, telling Cheryl over his shoulder that he wanted a copy of the dep, "ASAP. Preferably sooner." And that's why I waited until Donald Carter, the cadaverous attorney representing Puget Health Partners, had wished us both a gloomy good night and blotted himself from the room.

I looked at Cheryl over the exhibits, legal pads, coffee cups, and other detritus that accumulates during depositions. She was sorting the paper tapes on which she'd coded the sounds if not the sense of the testimony. It wouldn't make any sense to me until she'd translated it and sent me a copy.

"So, what do you think?" I asked her.

"She's a liar," Cheryl replied. "But by the time this goes to trial, if nothing else, Tate will have taught her how to cry."

Either Melanie Mayer's tear ducts had been surgically removed, or she cared little about her sister's death. True, some people just can't cry, even when distraught. But those people generally don't delay every answer while they daub their stiff, black lashes with stiff, white lace.

"What else?" I asked.

"All that lovey-dovey stuff about her sister was just crap," Cheryl said, snapping rubber bands around the paper tapes. "If she loved her sister so much, why didn't she even have a funeral for her? She just pulled the plug, had her cremated, and scattered her ashes – all in just a couple of days. It wasn't until she heard about the insurance policy that she saw any good in her fat little sister."

"Do you think it was suicide?" That was the critical issue for American Fidelity. If Carrie's fatal, ten-story plunge was an accident, my client was on the hook for the full face amount of her $250,000 life insurance policy - doubled to a cool half-million by her rider for accidental death. But if Carrie had taken her own life, if she had thrown herself over the railing of her apartment balcony, then because it was a fairly new policy, the suicide exclusion would preempt coverage. We would owe her beneficiary only a reserve payment estimated to be a few thousand dollars, if that.

Cheryl didn't answer me right away. "Well," she began, softening the eventual blow, "I'm sure you've got some good solid evidence. She had written that article about suicide for <u>The Stranger</u>. She was still upset because of her mother, and things weren't going all that great at work. So I guess she could have been that desperate, that sad." She stopped.

"But?" I prompted.

"*But*," she said, "she was losing weight, Jack. She had taken off fifty pounds in six months. She would have been down to misses' sizes now. Do you know what that means?"

I shook my head.

"It means she could have strolled into any store and found her size right on the rack. It means she wouldn't have had to walk past all the cute clothes and slink into the Women's World or the Plus-Size Department or even -" she shuddered - "those awful places where they refer to you as a Big Beautiful Woman. She had lost a lot of weight, and she was still losing."

"And, therefore, she could not have killed herself?" I confess to a trace of irritation. Cheryl was seizing on a fraction of the testimony and using it to blow my whole case.

Cheryl gave me an indulgent look of sympathy. "Not could not have, but probably didn't, Jack. A woman doesn't kill herself when she's losing weight. Who has the burden of proof?"

"We do."

Cheryl patted me on the shoulder. "Go with God."

With Cheryl's warning ringing in my ears, I went into my office and called Leah Batson. Leah was American Fidelity's in-house counsel and was, far and away, my favorite client. Leah and I had bonded when we had suspected each other of killing my father. As it turned out, I had been wrong, she had been extremely wrong, and our mutual relief and embarrassment had forged an unspoken trust between us. She had given me all of American Fidelity's Washington litigation, and my fiancée and I were using that cornerstone of business to open our own firm. From a career perspective, it had all worked out very well - except that my father was still dead.

Leah did not waste time. "What's the sister's story on the suicide?"

"She claims she and Carrie were close, that she would have known if something was wrong. She said Carrie was weathering their mom's death pretty well. Sad about it, yes, but not suicidal."

"What's Melanie like as a witness?"

"Right now, she's obviously faking the loving sister routine. But she's still learning her role. Tate will have her in the groove by trial."

"Any other evidence that it wasn't suicide?"

"Well, maybe. Did you know that Carrie had dropped about fifty pounds since last summer?"

"No." Leah sounded surprised and impressed. "That's terrific. How did she do it?"

"I'm not sure. But the court reporter seemed to think that weight loss alone was a reason to live."

Leah was quiet for a while. "To the women on the jury, yeah, it might be," she said. "Unless we can tie it to depression or illness, they'll see it as the most positive thing that could happen to Carrie, something that would make everything better. Anything in the med recs that would account for the weight loss?"

"Nothing. But she hadn't seen a doctor for two years. That's why we didn't know about the weight loss until today."

"Anything in the autopsy?"

"Nope. 'Healthy, well-nourished female.' No tumors, no cancer."

"Any evidence of diabetes?"

"None. The sugar levels were normal."

I could hear Leah tapping the eraser end of her pencil on her desk. That meant deep thinking. She said, "Look, my gut feeling is that the poor girl jumped. She was too short to fall over that railing, even if she was standing on a stool to water her hanging plants. But if it really was an accident, then we'll pay the half-million, Jack. We'll still fight the bad faith claim, but we'll pay on the policy. But first, I need some evidence to take to my boss. I want you to take a week and find out everything you can about Carrie Mayer. Then I want you to come down to L.A. and give us the best case on both sides - suicide and accident. Then we'll go from there. OK?"

"OK," I said, looking at my calendar and starting to juggle my next five days around. "So you just want to know what happened, no matter what?"

"No matter what," Leah confirmed. "Suicide or accident, we want to know - no matter what."

I said goodbye, hung up, and pulled out a new legal pad. I wrote "Suicide" on the first page and "Accident" on the second, then set to work listing the evidence and issues under both. Just before I went home, I read over my plan of attack.

My roommate was a homicide detective with the Seattle Police Department. I don't know whether I was thinking of Mark when I did it, or whether I had absorbed his overall paranoia by osmosis, but for some reason, I turned to a clean page in my notebook and wrote, "Or murder."

CHAPTER 2

started with the easy stuff. Carolyn Anne Mayer had turned 36 a few weeks before she died. She had been born in Ballard, now a somewhat gentrified suburb, then a largely Scandinavian neighborhood northwest of downtown Seattle. Her father had owned a butcher shop on Market Street. When she was thirteen, Carrie won a prize for her aebleskiver during Tivoli Days at the Nordic Heritage Museum. Not counting the news stories about her death, I couldn't find any other mention of her in the public record.

Her older sister Melanie was a different story. She had been a Seafair queen, riding through the hot, dark streets of Seattle's annual Torchlight Parade. The old newspaper photo showed her as a short, busty blonde in a long white gown, flanked by two of the semi-comical Seafair Pirates who swashbuckled along the parade route, kissing women and scaring kids.

"Pretty girl," Mark said, glancing over my shoulder at the Seafair clipping. He picked up one of Carrie's autopsy photographs and compared them side by side. He frowned. "Same person?"

"Sisters."

"Yeah. They look just enough alike."

I hadn't noticed the family resemblance. Carrie's caved-in skull had monopolized my attention. But when I wrenched my eyes away from the gaping wound, I saw that Mark was right. Melanie and Carrie had the same small, regular features.

"What happened to her?"

"She fell ten stories from her apartment up on Capitol Hill."

"*Fell?*" It was his police detective's voice. Mark usually didn't talk like a cop at home, but when he did, he could pack so much suspicion into one sharp word.

"Fell, jumped, or was pushed. I'm not sure which." I was starting to explain to him what had happened, and what I was supposed to determine, when he dropped back his head in mock despair. He raked his hands through his thick, black hair.

"What?"

"I know where this is headed. You'll dig around; you'll ask too many questions; you'll stumble onto something. Someone's going to jump you. Again. I'm going to have to wade in and save your ass. *Again*. I don't know how you do it. Hell's bells, Jack. You're an insurance attorney. Shouldn't your life be boring?"

My life had been anything but boring. I bore a formidable collection of scars - inside and out - as evidence. Since I couldn't really argue with him on that point, I just handed him the autopsy report, the police report, and the police and medical examiner's photographs.

"Mark, I'm not trying to make this into a murder case. If anything, I have an incentive to prove that it wasn't murder, because if it was, my client has to pay on the policy. It comes down to accident or suicide. So far, no one can say whether she jumped or fell. Does anything in there mean anything to you either way?"

He sighed and paged quickly through the documents. "It looks like she had a glass of wine, but that wouldn't be enough to make her topple over a three-foot railing. Lots of lacerations and contusions on her body, though. Did she hit anything on her way down?"

"A big maple tree and the marquee over the apartment entrance. They broke her fall."

"They battered her up pretty good. She's got some marks on her that could be defensive wounds; they might indicate a struggle." He pointed to the cuts and bruises on her hands, arm, head, and shoulder. "But they just as easily could have been from the tree and the overhang."

I made a note. "The medical examiner investigator was really cautious when I talked to her. Even though it was just the two of us, and she wasn't under oath, it sure felt like a dep."

"Yeah, the ME investigators are in court a lot, so that might be why she was formal with you. Except –" He paged through the documents again and tapped the finding on manner of death. "Or that's why, Jack. 'Undetermined.' The ME doesn't like to admit that they can't determine the manner of death. They try really hard to decide whether it's natural, accident, suicide, or homicide. So the ME wouldn't have been excited to talk about a case they couldn't close. Either the evidence just wasn't there, or they didn't trust it for some reason."

"Anything jump out that might have looked weird?"

"No." He started to hand the papers back to me, then paused and pulled back one of the pictures of the dead woman. He held it up to the light, then pushed it toward me. "What do you think that's from?"

There was a shadow at the very edge of the picture. The object that cast it must have been just outside the camera's lens. I blinked at it. The shadow looked like nothing so much as the leg of a cockroach - a huge cockroach. I said as much to Mark.

"It does look like that," he admitted. "But I've lived in some real dumps in my life *and* I was in the Navy, and I've never seen a five-inch cockroach. Three-inch, definitely; four-inch, probably; but never five."

"So what do you think it's from?"

"I'm not sure. The thing is, if it's the earpiece from a pair of glasses, that would mean a lot."

I looked back at the shadow. It could have been cast by a pair of glasses. "Why? Why would that mean a lot?"

"Because almost all suicides take off their glasses before they jump. I'm not sure whether they don't want to see the ground coming, or whether it's the idea of getting the glass smashed in their eyes. If this DOA wore glasses, and if those are her specs there on the ground, she probably didn't jump."

"But if the shadow is from a pair of glasses, and if glasses are so significant, wouldn't the police on the scene have picked that up?"

"Y-e-s." I looked up at the hesitation in his voice. He shrugged and tapped the police report. "I know the detectives on this case. We're working in teams of four now, so I'm getting to know these guys better than I would like. One's right out of the fraud squad. Just a kid. One's been around forever, and he - well, he -" He stopped and chose his words carefully. "Larry Gregerson thinks all crimes are solved within the first couple of hours. If he can't figure them out by then, he decides they aren't really crimes. It's a lot less stress for him that way."

Mark generally didn't criticize fellow cops. Larry must be a complete bozo. "So even if this shadow is from a pair of glasses, you think Larry might have missed it?"

"Missed it, decided not to see it, kicked it out of the way. Whichever, he's good for it. If those are the girl's glasses, there's at least a question as to whether she fell or was pushed. Larry wouldn't have wanted to spend the time trying to answer that question. And he might have pressed the ME to close their investigation fast so he didn't have to. Saying undetermined might have been a way to get Larry off their back."

"Wow."

He shrugged. "Larry and me, we're not great friends. But if you want me to, I can ask his partner what went down. Ed's a nice kid, and I'd rather find out from him what happened than have you going off half-cocked."

"I never go off half-cocked."

"Excuse me. Totally cocked. Completely cocked. Cocked beyond repair."

"I'll just spend a week or so talking to people who knew Carrie Mayer," I protested, "trying to get a sense for whether she was in a state to take her own life.

If American Fidelity ends up paying on the policy, the whole case will probably go away."

There was unease in his eyes, but "I'll talk to Ed," was all he said.

I thanked him and packed away the papers. Throughout the night, Carrie's death nagged at me. After the house was quiet, I pulled out the packet and took the autopsy photograph over to the brightest lamp in the house. My roommate was right - the marks on her face might have been from the fall.

Still, I couldn't help thinking that I saw them there on either side of her nose: two small dents, there at the bridge.

Two small marks from a pair of glasses.

CHAPTER 3

I was trying to convince Donald Carter that he had nothing to fear.

Donald's OK. It's not his fault that he's tall, gaunt, and hollow-cheeked. It's not his fault that his mere presence casts a pall over a room. It's not his fault that he spits a little when he talks, that he smells like an old refrigerator, and that he emphasizes all the wrong words in a sentence. Donald and I get along fine. We have forged a bond of trust by never holding each other personally responsible for the quite appalling positions we have to take on behalf of our respective clients.

In this case, we both had the unenviable position of arguing that Carrie Mayer committed suicide. During the three days she lingered in intensive care before Melanie pulled the plug, Carrie had run up a hefty medical bill. The hospital and the doctors who worked on her were suing Puget Health Partners, Carrie's employer and health insurer, for reimbursement. Like her life insurance policy, Carrie's medical policy excluded coverage if Carrie committed suicide.

Donald at least had the grace to be self-conscious about it.

"Jack, I'm on vulture duty," he had told me, explaining why he wanted to attend my deposition of Melanie Mayer. "I need to protect our interests in the parallel litigation."

Even though Puget Health Partners wasn't actually a party to Melanie's lawsuit against American Fidelity, I understood Donald's position. There were issues common to both cases. Melanie's attorney hadn't objected to having Donald there, so I had let him attend the dep. It wasn't that big a deal to me, and I figured that sooner or later, I'd need a favor in return. Now I was trying to call in that chit.

"Donald, all I want are some interviews with your employees, people who knew Carrie Mayer."

"You can always depose them, Jack."

"I don't want to depose them. I don't want to drag them in front of a court reporter, expose them to Boyd Tate and the Incredible Crying Melanie, and put them under oath. They'll freeze up. They'll get scared."

"So you want to take advantage of them."

"No, I want to talk to them in a place where they'll feel comfortable, where they'll be able to talk freely. I don't need your permission to talk to your non-management employees. I can meet them for lunch. I can take them out to dinner. I can call them at home if I want to. I'm giving you a call as a courtesy, because you and I have always been on the level with each other." I paused for effect. "Until now."

Silence. I was an important ally to Donald, and he knew it. This wasn't the first case we had worked together, and it wasn't going to be the last. After a long pause, he said, "Send me the list. I'll set up the meetings. But I'm going to sit in."

"It wouldn't be any fun without you," I assured him.

"Smart ass," he said, and hung up.

That little argument won, I took a look at my schedule for the rest of the day. My fiancée's plane arrived at noon from Tokyo. I still had plenty of time to visit the nursing home where Carrie Mayer's mother died.

I braced myself for the inevitable smell of urine as I pushed through the wide glass doors of the Evergreen Care Center on Queen Anne Hill. No urine. I sniffed again. Still no urine. The air was cool and clean. Not disinfected, like every other nursing home I had visited. Clean.

The front room was wide and quiet. Couches and overstuffed chairs dotted the soft rugs, grouped companionably around a fireplace, two televisions, and picture windows with drop-dead views of the Space Needle and Elliott Bay. In one corner, two older men in jogging suits were playing chess. By the fireplace, four white-haired women in straight skirts, flat heels, and blazers were deep in what looked like a red hot game of Texas Hold 'Em. There were a whole lot of quarters on that table.

"May I help you?"

A sleek, silver-haired woman was at my elbow. I couldn't tell whether she was a resident or staff.

"I'm Jack Hart," I said. "I have an appointment with Patricia Campbell."

"I'm Pat." We shook hands. "Let's talk in here."

She led me down a hardwood hallway to a small but tasteful office. As I passed the maple wainscoting, the antique tables, and the cream-glass fixtures that bathed everything in a muted glow, all I could think was that this place must have cost Carrie Mayer a fortune. No wonder she had bought a life insurance policy for a quarter-million dollars. If anything had happened to Carrie, her mom would have needed every cent to keep a bed in Evergreen.

Pat settled herself behind the gleaming desk. "I'm not sure I should be talking to you. Usually, I refer all legal inquiries to our attorney."

If that was her usual practice, it was interesting that she hadn't rebuffed me immediately. It meant I at least had a shot.

I explained who I represented and what I was trying to determine. "I'm not trying to make any trouble for you or Evergreen. But Carrie doesn't seem to have had many friends. You probably saw her more than anyone else in the last few months before her death."

She thought about that, then bobbed her head. "Maybe. She was here a lot."

"What was she like?"

"Oh, she was a nice girl. She came almost every night. She'd eat with her mom in the dining room. When Kirstin got too weak to leave her bed, we'd send in trays for them. They kept to themselves, but it was kind of sweet, not snobby at all. They just liked each other's company. They'd sit and laugh together; they'd watch TV, play trivia games. Every now and then, they'd go for a drive. Kirstin liked the milkshakes from Dick's Drive-In down the street."

"How long was Kirstin Mayer in the center?"

"About six months."

"Excuse me for asking this, but how much would that have cost Carrie?"

She named a sum that was twice Carrie's annual salary. When she saw my face, she added, with some asperity, "Quality costs, you know."

I agreed to pacify her and turned back to the topic of Carrie Mayer. "How did Carrie take her mother's death?"

"Very hard. We have hospice counselors here. They meet with our terminal patients every couple of days, helping them get ready to say goodbye. They usually work with the family members, too, but Carrie wouldn't do it. Couldn't do it, I think. She wasn't ready for her mom to die."

From my own recent experience, it occurred to me that perhaps no one was ever ready. "Did Melanie work with the hospice counselors?"

"Who?"

"Carrie's sister."

"I didn't even know Carrie had a sister."

I described Melanie, trying not to sound pejorative. Pat Campbell shook her head. "No. No one like that ever came to see Kirstin. She never mentioned another daughter."

Interesting. "What did Carrie look like?" I had only Melanie's testimony that Carrie had been losing weight. Since it seemed like sudden weight loss was going to be important in the case, I wanted to make sure Melanie wasn't just making it up.

"Look like? Don't you have a picture of her?"

"Only her ID card from work." And the autopsy pictures, I added to myself. "And you can't really tell anything from that."

Pat seemed at a loss to describe Carrie. "Well, she was - she was -" She stopped and thought. "She was just there, Jack. She was one of those people you can't quite see even when you're looking directly at them. And I'm not the only one who thought so. Some of our gentlemen residents are outrageous flirts. Some of them have had strokes. Some just pretend to have had strokes so they can get away with - um, *things*."

She suddenly winked at me, and it changed her whole demeanor. Up to that point, she had been impassive, almost prim. For just a second, the wink made her look alive, sensuous, broad-natured. "Even our most persistent residents never flirted with Carrie Mayer," she continued. "It's not that they didn't like her. They didn't even notice her."

I tried to help her remember. I asked how tall Carrie was, how old she looked, the color of her hair. Her answers were so vague that I was beginning to wonder whether she ever actually met Carrie. Oh, shortish, she said. Youngish. Blondish. Or maybe brownish. No, more blondish. Maybe. She paused, frustrated. Then she brightened.

"I know where we can look."

She led me down the hall to a vast bulletin board covered with snapshots of Evergreen's smiling residents. Some of them were working out in what looked like a very nice gym; some were digging into what looked like very nice meals; some were even dressed in evening wear. Many were surrounded by family - kids and grandkids, I assumed.

"We have a lot of events here at Evergreen: games, movies, parties, family nights," Pat said. "We try to take pictures of everybody, and I'm sure we have a picture of Kirstin. I think Carrie's in it, too."

She searched for a few minutes, then said "ah," and pulled off a photo of a little old lady with pink cheeks, blue eyes, and fluffy white hair. Kirstin Mayer. But Carrie was not in the picture. Pat searched unsuccessfully for a few more minutes.

"Don't you take the pictures down when the residents die?" I asked.

"Oh, no," Pat said. "That wouldn't work at all."

I looked at her in surprise.

"The line between life and death is pretty blurred here, Jack. It sounds callous to say that death is no big deal for us, but in a way, it isn't. It isn't the end. Terminal patients need to know that they'll go on in our thoughts, that we'll still care about them when they're gone. Whatever they believe about God or the afterlife, they need to know that they won't just be blotted out or forgotten when they die. If we took down people's pictures after they died, that would tell our living residents that the same thing was going to happen to them. And it would make it harder and harder for them to meet their deaths with dignity."

I looked at the vast bulletin board. "So how many of these people are gone?"

She paused a few moments before answering. "Sixty to seventy percent, I'd guess," she said.

I stood with her and stared at that wall of the dead. On the one hand, I was touched that Evergreen was so devoted to its residents. On the other, I found that mass of dead, smiling faces incredibly creepy. I was relieved when Pat gave up her search and led me back to her office.

"Our photographer must have missed Carrie. Sorry. We try to get a picture of everybody."

"I had heard - um, I had heard that Carrie lost quite a bit of weight in the last few months."

"Really?" Pat seemed surprised. Then she reconsidered. "Well, yes, now that you mention it, I think she was getting smaller."

"Do you have any idea why?"

She shook her head. "It's very stressful, you know, losing a parent. Sometimes family members gain weight; sometimes they lose weight. Not very many stay the same."

"Did she seem happy to be losing weight?"

Pat paused. She chose her words carefully. "Jack, Carrie Mayer was not a happy girl."

"Why do you say that?"

"I don't know why. But I could sense it."

Now we were getting to the meat of the case. I asked the $500,000 question: "Unhappy enough to kill herself?"

"I'm just an administrator, not a counselor. I'm not qualified to answer that question."

"As a layperson, then. How unhappy did she seem?"

She shrugged. "I can't say. But I wasn't surprised when I read in the paper about her death."

"You assumed it was suicide?"

"Yes, I did. That was the first thing that came to my mind."

"Do you know why she was unhappy - aside from her mother, I mean?"

She shook her head.

"Did Carrie wear glasses?"

She stared at me in confusion. I started to explain the question, but she interrupted me, shaking her head.

"You know, Jack, it's funny. I saw Carrie every night for six months, and I don't have the faintest idea."

DEAD WEIGHT

CHAPTER 4

Harmony's plane was late. I loitered at the gate, passing the time by trying to make myself notice the people I usually didn't. Pat's summation of Carrie Mayer still ran through my mind: She was one of those people you can't quite see. So I stood there in the airport and watched for the people I had been missing.

It was hard. I started out scrutinizing each face as it came at me down the concourse. I'd feel like I was doing pretty well - when suddenly my eyes would zip over to a beautiful woman, or a large, confident man, or a cute little kid. Finally I hit on the best method: I'd let my eyes go wherever they wanted, then I'd make myself look at the person just behind my target. I was amazed by the number of people I hadn't really noticed, the people I would have overlooked.

I was fairly certain that no one was overlooking me. At six-foot-four and considerably more than 200 pounds, I felt conspicuous even when I wasn't holding an enormous bunch of hydrangeas. As it was, just about everyone who passed me seemed fixated on the fluffy mass of violet flowers. They'd zero in on the bouquet I had bought for Harmony, glance up at my face, smirk or smile, and look away.

I was relieved when the plane finally coasted in from Narita. Even though she was on the small side, I spotted Harmony immediately. She stepped off the plane wearing a grey dress and pearls. Her thick black hair was pulled back in a twist. Everyone else - even the flight attendants - looked rumpled and resentful from the seventeen-hour flight. Harmony looked unwrinkled and unruffled.

She saw me and waved. My mother's promise ring sparkled on her hand. Her blue eyes glowed. She had almost reached me when she was suddenly bathed in light, like a saint. As she looked up in wonder, a cluster of men leapt forward, blocking the jetway, and thrust microphones in her face.

"Miss Piper," one of them shouted, "any comment on your father being under grand jury investigation?"

I sucked in my breath. Harmony's father was dead. At least, the man she would always think of as her father was dead. It was only after Humphrey Piper had left for a business trip and never returned that she learned her biological father was Higuro Yamashita, then a foreign exchange student who had lived with her parents while he was going to the University of Washington.

Harmony was a veteran of blitz attacks by the press. She didn't break her stride. She didn't look to the right or left. She didn't say a word. She just slipped past the reporters, her chin level, her eyes fixed on me. Two blue-jacketed airline clerks intercepted the reporters, scolding them for blocking the deplaning passengers. They caused enough of a diversion for me to grab Harmony, block her with my body, and hustle her into the nearest VIP lounge. You never know when college football will come back to help you in later life.

Harmony explained our problem, in the friendly way she had, and the hostess arranged for us to exit to Customs through another door. We got her luggage and hopped into the car before the press picked up the trail.

"What in the world was that?" Harmony demanded, locking all the doors. "Did something happen while I was gone?"

I shook my head. The Carrie Mayer litigation hadn't generated a single story. Although we were handling a couple of high-profile civil fraud matters for a local car dealer, they were in the fallow period between motions to dismiss and discovery cutoffs. I didn't expect them to hit print again until I filed my motions for summary judgment. "Did something happen in Japan?"

"Nothing out of the ordinary. Higuro's still under investigation for paying bribes to *sōkaiya*. But surely that wouldn't justify a grand jury investigation over here."

Probably not. Higuro was engaged in a particularly Japanese scandal, in which companies pay hush money to mobsters who threaten to disrupt shareholders' meetings with allegations of corporate corruption. One of Higuro's top guys had been videotaped offering a bribe to an undercover agent, and Higuro had been battling Japanese government investigations ever since. But there hadn't been any repercussions on the Seattle side of the ocean. At least, not so far.

There was a TV news truck lurking outside our house. I circled the block, parked in the alley, and jumped the fence so I could unlatch the back gate for Harmony. I left her having a joyous reunion with my dog, Betsy, who was 95 pounds of wriggling, panting ecstasy at seeing Harmony. I headed back to work before the reporters figured out that anyone was home. Harmony was going to call Higuro to see if he knew what was going on.

The offices of Piper & Hart - our brand-new firm – were in the Cascade neighborhood, a jumble of warehouses, offices, and apartments northeast of downtown. More and more, downtown Seattle looks like a cookie-cutter version of every aspiring second-rate city in America, all Pottery Barns and Planet Hollywoods and fancy chain restaurants. The Cascade neighborhood looks like the Seattle I remember as a kid. Our new office tower was around the corner from the Greyhound bus station, a lesbian bar, the Boilermakers union hall, a Lutheran church, a methadone clinic, a Scandinavian pancake house, a nightclub in some desecrated chapel, a taxidermist, and an ancient dance school complete with a hardwood ballroom, velvet draperies, and a glittering chandelier.

Mrs. Holbrook was still at her desk. She was wearing a handsome pink suit. She had arrived at work wearing a handsome pink hat, one of her own creations. The vanity plate on Mrs. Holbrook's 1969 Chevrolet Impala read "HATLADY." I had never seen the same hat twice.

She looked up and smiled as I stepped off the elevator.

"Welcome back, Mr. Hart."

"Thank you, Mrs. Holbrook."

At some point, I must have known Mrs. Holbrook's first name. It had hardly seemed worth cluttering my mind with it, however, as Mrs. Holbrook did not countenance the use of Christian names. After reminding her numerous times that everyone called me Jack, I just caved and became Mr. Hart.

"How is Ms. Piper?"

"The flight was OK. But we got jumped by the press at the airport."

"That is disgraceful. I told them this morning that Ms. Piper would be exhausted when she returned from Japan."

Oh, hell. No wonder the press had known where to find us. "Did the reporters say what they wanted?"

"Something about Ms. Piper's father being under investigation by the grand jury."

"You're sure they said grand jury? They weren't talking about a Japanese government investigation?"

"Not unless the Japanese government has grand juries, too."

I was fairly sure they didn't. That meant there was something going on besides the *sōkaiya* scandal. I cussed to myself again, mildly suggested that Mrs. Holbrook stick with "no comment" for further press encounters, and wrenched my attention back to the Carrie Mayer case. I had barely an hour before my interviews with her coworkers at Puget Health, and I hadn't even looked at the documents Donald had sent over.

Carrie Mayer had a thick personnel file. She had worked for the health insurance company almost thirteen years - in the same job. I skimmed through her performance evaluations. She had thirteen long years of being rated "satisfactory." Never "exceptional." Never "distinguished." Just "satisfactory." Even the positive comments seemed impersonal to the point of condescending, like her boss couldn't be bothered to figure out which drone she was evaluating: "Carrie is a team player." "Carrie obeys management directives." "Carrie is dependable."

I wondered: Had Carrie chafed at thirteen years in the same job, working for the same vapid people who said the same vapid things about her every year? Or had she just accepted it? Even worse, been grateful for it? Quite irrationally, I hoped she hated it. I hoped it made her mad.

I turned to the disciplinary section of the file. Until the summer before her death, Carrie had enjoyed a spotless record. But after Kirstin Mayer went into the nursing home, Carrie had been written up for being late, being absent, and being distracted. Her production stats fell; her error rate rose. She was reprimanded for causing a disturbance in the unit. At the time of her death, Puget Health Partners had Carrie on probation and was threatening to fire her.

I shook my head in annoyance. Of course Carrie had been late, absent, touchy, and distracted. Her mother was dying. She had a lot on her mind. She had spent thirteen years at the damn place. Couldn't they have given her a break when she needed it most?

I showed up an hour later at Puget Health Partners, still steamed from Carrie's personnel file. Donald Carter observed me placidly.

"You look loaded for bear," he said, watching me unpack an enormous litigation bag. "I'm not going to regret letting you do these interviews, am I?"

I trusted Donald enough to speak my mind. "I've been reading Carrie's personnel file. Why the hell couldn't you have cut her some slack when her mom was dying?"

"We did."

"You did not. You were threatening to fire her."

"Jack, we did whatever we could for her, even though she may not have thought so. We let her transfer to the early shift so she'd have time in the afternoon and evening with her mom. We let her use all her vacation time whenever she needed to, and we didn't hold it against her. After she exhausted that, we begged her to take Family Medical Leave. You can't count FMLA leave against an employee, and she had a full twelve weeks that she could have been gone."

"But?"

"But she wouldn't do it. FMLA leave is unpaid, and she couldn't afford it. We did what we could for her. We even made it possible for her coworkers to donate some of their vacation time to her. But after she burned through all of that, we didn't have much choice. We have attendance standards, and we have production standards, and we have to apply them consistently. If we don't, then we end up getting sued for discrimination."

I thought that over. "I hear you."

Donald gave me a weary smile. "So you'll behave yourself with our employees?"

I assured him I would, and the interviews began.

All in all, I talked to nine people: Carrie's senior vice president, her vice president, her manager, her supervisor, and five coworkers. The senior vice president and vice president didn't remember Carrie. They told me several times they'd never met her. The manager was almost as vague.

The supervisor knew who Carrie was but struggled to describe her. I couldn't tell whether it was a perception problem or a vocabulary problem. Talking to her, I started to understand why all Carrie's reviews sounded the same. Even in person, she was hung up on business jargon and management buzzwords: Right before her death, it had been hard to keep Carrie "on task," the supervisor said, but she added that she was always sure that Carrie understood "the deliverables of her position." Whatever that meant. The supervisor kept looking over at Donald as she talked. I couldn't imagine why. He was so inscrutable as to be non-existent there in the corner.

Carrie's coworkers were more interesting. They all had a different idea of what Carrie looked like, but at least they had an opinion. Some thought she wore glasses; some didn't. Some said she was blond; some brunette; some were somewhere in between. Everyone agreed that she had been losing weight. Everyone agreed that she was nice. Everyone agreed that she had been brokenhearted about her mom.

I kept as quiet as I could, made myself as small as possible, gave them the time and space they needed to remember. Details started to sift to the surface. Carrie had been in the Medicare claims unit longer than any other claims processor. She was the font of institutional knowledge; she was the person everyone consulted whenever there was a problem. Carrie had a lovely voice. She was too shy to do it in person, but she would sing "Happy Birthday" into her coworkers' voicemail. Carrie volunteered at a local school for homeless kids. Every Halloween, she arranged for the kids to go trick-or-treating from office to office at Puget Health Partners.

I nearly canceled the last interview. It had been a long day, I was worried about Harmony, and Donald was nearly asleep in the corner. But then the door flew open, and in bounded the biggest, brightest woman I had ever seen. Her hair was fire-engine red; her eyes blazed electric green; her lipstick was shocking - and I mean shocking - pink. When I stood to greet her, we were nose to nose. In my entire life, I had met only one woman who was as tall as I was, and she had turned out to be a man.

Kit McCracken gave no indication whatsoever of any male secondary sex characteristics. She curved and surged through an emerald minidress and white go-go boots. I was totally, incredibly, irrevocably faithful to Harmony, but I struggled to keep my eyes riveted on Kit's. If I let myself look any lower, I wasn't sure where I'd stop. Over in his corner, Donald maintained his air of sleepy-eyed calm. I fought the urge to take his pulse.

We shook hands. She sat down, folding her long, long legs in front of her like a challenge. I started to explain what I was trying to do. I got about three sentences into my introduction when Kit suddenly bounced out of her chair. Donald and I started back from the table.

Kit stood there in the middle of the room, all red hair and fury, shaking her head and a lot of the rest of her in despair at our betrayal.

"You're trying to prove she killed herself," she said. "Both of you."

The deep heaving of her chest made it extremely difficult to keep my eyes on her face.

"Well, you're wrong," she said.

"Carrie would never have done that. You're wrong. Wrong, wrong, wrong, wrong, wrong."

CHAPTER 5

After her dramatic entrance, my actual meeting with Kit was something of a disappointment. Donald stirred himself sufficiently to remind her that we were both simply trying to find out the truth about Carrie Mayer, and that we needed to base our conclusions on facts, not feelings. She seemed sobered after his speech. She avoided my eyes as we talked.

I asked her what Carrie looked like, whether she wore glasses, how she had seemed the last few months before her death, what she liked to do. She gave answers similar to her coworkers, albeit more decisively, and with much jangling of earrings and waving of hands. She made two unique contributions: one, she told me that Carrie was clever on the computer and had revolutionized the department's claim tracking system; two, she said that Carrie had been very angry right before she died.

I looked over at Donald. He nodded slightly, in an *I told you so* way.

"Did she say why?" I asked.

Kit shook her head.

"Then how did you know she was angry?"

"Carrie never said a bad word about anyone. But during the last couple of months, she was pissed off at everything."

"What, specifically?"

Kit still wouldn't look at me. "Just everything."

I pressed further but eventually gave up. Donald was growing noticeably restive; I was getting frustrated; and Kit's vivid face was hardening into a stubborn, painted mask. If I needed to, I could always put her under oath and depose her.

As the door closed behind Kit, Donald suddenly grinned at me over the table. "You should have seen your face when she walked in."

"Why didn't you warn me?"

"How was I to know she was your type?"

"She's not."

"Oh, I don't know. You two would make a cute couple."

I glared at him, and he relented. "Anyway, so where are you now on the suicide-accident question?"

"Same place, I guess. I think she jumped. You knew her. What do you think?"

"I barely knew her, Jack. I work mostly with the executives and the managers. The only line employees I know are the disciplinary problems. But in answer to your question, I think Carrie jumped. We're going to keep fighting on the medical claims."

Donald and I said goodnight, and I started the walk back to my office. It was a beautiful evening – cool, clear, and dark blue. I had just turned the corner when someone stepped out of the shadows.

"Buy me a drink, sailor?"

It was Kit. She was smiling at me, one hand on her hip.

"I'm engaged," I blurted out.

She stepped closer. The smile disappeared. She took a firm grip on my arm and backed me up against the wall. I reassessed whether she might, after all, be a man.

"I just want to talk to you," she said. She had an iron grasp on me now. "And I don't want Donald there."

I did a rapid risk analysis. On the one hand, I didn't want to burn Donald. He had been on the level with me, and even though there wasn't any ethical barrier to talking with Kit, I hated the thought of breaking his trust. On the other hand, Kit seemed mighty determined. Unless I pushed her away and ran for it, there was no obvious way of escape. There might still be some intrepid reporters staking out my office. And the last thing Harmony needed was to have her fiancé taped scuffling with a woman. Or a possibly cross-dressed man.

"OK. But let's go back to your office."

"No. I told you. I need a drink."

We crossed the street to the Camlin Hotel, which is as old-Seattle, innocent, and fuddy-duddy as a place can get - all marble, dark wood, worn rugs, and chandeliers ambered with age. As we stepped into the Cloud Room restaurant, our geriatric waitperson took a few moments to size up Kit. She seemed to be debating whether to serve us or throw us out. Once she decided we could stay, however, she was the soul of graciousness. She even brought Kit a saucer of extra cherries, which Kit dunked one by one in her Manhattan and slowly scraped off the stems with her teeth.

"I used to eat Oreos that way," I said, to break the ice.

"In a Manhattan?"

"Milk."

She nodded toward my soda. "You don't drink?"

Not when I was with a witness. Especially not with a witness like Kit. "Not much."

"Wish I didn't." She knocked back the Manhattan and gestured for another.

I watched her warily. My aunt was an alcoholic. I had lived with her until I was eight, and I had far too many memories of her rages, stupors, dishonesty, and abuse. I wanted to get this over with.

"Kit, what did you want to talk about?"

She took a gulp of her new drink. "When I told you that Carrie seemed mad the last few months, you looked over at Donald, and he nodded at you. What was that all about?"

"Nothing. Before you came in, I had asked Donald why Puget Health couldn't have done more for Carrie while her mom was dying. He told me the company had done everything it could, even though Carrie might not have thought so. So when you mentioned she was angry, I guess I looked over at Donald because it just seemed to jibe with what we had been talking about. That's all."

Kit considered that, dispatching a few more cherries.

"Why do you ask?" I prompted her.

"Because Puget Health has been firing people right and left. I need this job. I don't want to give them any excuses to tube me. I don't want them to think I'm badmouthing the place."

"I understand. I haven't heard anything like that."

She paused. "So you're really on the level? You're really just trying to figure out how Carrie died?"

I assured her I was.

She gave me a long, searching look. She had to be wearing contact lenses, I decided. Nobody's eyes were really that green. Finally, she shook herself, took another gulp of her drink and said, "OK. Like I said, Carrie was furious - really furious - at someone right before she died. At first, it was almost funny. I mean, Carrie was so quiet and so gentle. Seeing her mad was like watching a killer rabbit."

"Who was she angry with?"

"I don't know - really, I don't. For a while, I thought it was the nursing home. They had this counselor who was trying to help her mom get ready to die, and it just drove Carrie crazy. She wanted her mom to fight the cancer; she wanted her to fight to stay with her."

"What made you think it wasn't the nursing home?"

"Because even after her mom died, she stayed mad."

"Did you ask her what was going on?"

"Sure I did. Of course I did. She wouldn't tell me. She just said it was better that I didn't know."

The hair rose a little on the back of my neck. "Is there anything you can think of that would have made her mad? Anything at all?"

Kit shook her head, then stopped. "Well, she was upset when they fired some of the folks in the Medicare unit. She didn't say anything in the meeting, but she slammed the door on the way out. She got written up for that."

That must have been the discipline for the disturbance that I had seen in Carrie's personnel file. "Did she say why she was upset?"

"No. We were all upset, though. Can I have another drink?"

I ordered her a Camlin Cosmo - and a turkey sandwich to soak up some of the booze. "What else should I know about Carrie?"

"That there's no way she would have killed herself. She was really religious, and she thought suicide was a sin."

"So she'd actually mentioned killing herself?"

Kit shot me a dirty look. "You're twisting around what I'm saying!"

"Then explain it to me. How did this come up?"

"I can't remember."

"Bullshit."

Kit seemed momentarily stunned by my frankness. Then she let out a drunken little giggle, a sound I knew and loathed. "I really don't know," she protested. "But the point is that she thought it was a sin, and Carrie wouldn't have done anything that would have kept her out of heaven. She wanted more than anything to be with her mom and her dad, and she thought they were nearly saints. No matter how sad she was, she wouldn't have killed herself."

"What religion was she?"

"I don't know. One of the big ones."

After that, I couldn't get many specifics out of Kit. She lapsed into blurred, slurred rambles about Carrie. Carrie was a sweetheart, she said. When Kit had started at Puget Health, it had been hard for her to learn the claims system. Carrie had stayed late night after night, showing her the ropes. Carrie was the best claims processor in the whole Medicare department. Maybe her production stats weren't all that great, but that was because she took the time to make sure each claim went through correctly, that every patient got everything they deserved.

"I think it was because her mom had been sick so long and had had so many problems with Medicare," Kit said. "Carrie was just determined that every claim she worked was going to go through slick as glass."

She fell silent. I decided it was time to get out of there.

"So did you and Carrie hang out outside of work?" I asked while we waited for the check.

She shook her head slowly, almost sadly. "We liked different things. Carrie was really shy. I go to a lot of clubs and parties." She indicated the three empty glasses in front of her. "I like to drink."

"And Carrie?"

"TV, fuzzy slippers, and hot chocolate. That was her idea of a wild Saturday night."

"Come on," I said. "I'll get you a cab."

Kit slipped her arm through mine as she rose unsteadily. I couldn't think of an adroit way to dislodge it. Heads swiveled after her. An open-mouthed elderly gentleman at the elevator looked her up and down with a cheated expression, as if he resented a life lived without encountering such a creature.

The elevator doors slid closed. She turned to me with a rueful smile. "I used to tell Carrie that if we could combine the amount of attention we got and cut it in half, we'd both be better off," she said. "She would have made a great spy. Half the time, she couldn't even get people to wait on her in stores. It was like people didn't even see her."

We stepped out into the dim, plush lobby. Every man at the desk immediately swung to look at her. She half-blushed, half-preened. "Me, on the other hand -" She broke off and nodded toward the gawking men, who seemed unable to look away even though they were clearly busted. "I get way too much attention. Always have. Probably always will."

I asked the gaping desk clerk to call a cab and ushered her outside. We were met with a burst of television lights and flashbulbs. Kit blazed in the sudden glare - her red hair a mass of fiery curls, her green eyes glowing, her pink, pink lips sparkling and parted, and her breaths short and shallow with excitement. She looked around at the reporters with wonderment and turned to me, laughing in delight and disbelief.

"See what I mean?" she said.

I didn't have the heart to tell her they were there for me.

CHAPTER 6

Principal Gretta Berg did everything but genuflect when Harmony and I showed up the next morning at Children First, the homeless school where Carrie Mayer volunteered. The school was south of the Kingdome, a rehab of an old warehouse. Harmony was a donor. A big donor. The principal insisted on giving us a tour, pointing out the lockers big enough for clothes and shoes as well as books, the cheerful cafeteria that served breakfast, lunch, and dinner. Bright beanbag chairs and oversized cushions were scattered around the library, where low shelves of children's books encircled televisions and computers.

"We try to make the atmosphere as home-like as possible," Principal Berg said, showing us a playroom stocked with balls and jump ropes. "We can't control what happens to our kids when they leave at night. Most of them stay in shelters with their mothers; a few, unfortunately, are still on the streets. But at least while they're here, they know that they're going to be safe and warm and fed for the next eight hours. The minute that door shuts behind them in the morning, the wind stops blowing."

The school was snug, clean - and silent. "Where are the kids?" I asked.

"They're in an assembly."

"Oh, dear," Harmony said. "We were hoping we might be able to talk to some of the children who knew Carrie Mayer."

Principal Berg blanched with distress. Harmony noticed her discomfort. "Unless that will be a problem."

Principal Berg waved us into her tiny office. One of the chairs was already occupied by a teddy bear. Harmony picked it up and held it on her lap.

"I'm afraid it will be a problem," the principal said. "The children don't know that Carrie is dead. They face so much uncertainty, so much sadness every day. We just didn't think it was necessary to add a death onto everything else. If you start asking questions about her, they'll get scared. In their experience, when an authority figure starts asking you questions, it means one of two things: You're going into a foster home, or your mom or dad is going to be arrested. Or both. I really, really don't want to expose them to that if I can help it."

"Gretta, we don't want to do anything to upset the children," Harmony said. "But could we possibly talk to some of the teachers? We're just trying to get a sense for what Carrie Mayer was like, and this seems to have been an important part of her life."

"Actually, I'm probably the best person to talk to. Carrie helped us with Halloween, crafts, and story time - and those are all my babies."

"Story time?" I asked. From all other accounts, Carrie had sounded so shy.

"Yes. She was great at it. She'd make up her own stories, bring little finger puppets, weave in all the kids' names. They'd cluster around her like puppies. The longer she talked, the closer they'd get. By the time she said 'the end,' it seemed like she'd have half of them on her lap. She was kind of short, you know, and she had a soft, quiet voice. The kids were just drawn to her. She'd walk in the door, and all of a sudden, there'd be six of them trailing after her."

"How long did she volunteer here?"

"About five years, I guess. The CEO of Puget Health is on our board of directors. He invited us over to trick-or-treat, and Carrie organized everything. It was such a smash with the kids that now they do it every year. All the employees in the Medicare unit dress up in costume, decorate their offices and cubicles, and give out candy as the kids go up and down the halls. Most of our students don't have costumes, so Carrie would always arrange for a face-painter to come and make them look like cats or mice or monsters or whatever they wanted. They always have cookies and a big punchbowl with dry ice, and everyone gets a bottle of vitamins, a toothbrush, and a little tube of toothpaste along with all the goodies."

She laughed suddenly, and I noticed that the smile lines far outnumbered the frown lines on her red, worn face. "They are a health care company, after all. Anyway, Carrie put that together for us every year. She was such a dear."

"What did she look like?"

The question surprised her. "Carrie? Don't you know?"

"No. Not really."

"Well, she was . . . she was . . . unobtrusive. She just got things done and didn't call attention to herself. But when she was telling a story, you couldn't help but watch her. She was short, like I said, and on the round side - although she lost a lot of weight in the last year. Her hair was a very pale brown, she had grayish-blue eyes, and she didn't wear makeup. Her nose and mouth were small, but she had big eyes. Hid them behind big, thick glasses most of the time, unfortunately."

It was the most complete, definitive description yet. When I said as much, Gretta Berg gave me a rueful smile. "A lot of kids come through here, Jack. You have to pay attention and keep on your toes so you'll know whether it was Jim, Jamie, Jake, or

Josh who tried to flush the hamster down the toilet. I guess that eagle eye is just an occupational hazard."

"Do you know why she was losing weight?" Harmony asked.

Gretta slapped an ample thigh. "I never discuss religion, politics, or weight loss. She didn't seem to be enjoying it, though. She wasn't buying any flashy new clothes or bleaching her hair or anything like that. By the end, her clothes hung on her like she was a refugee. In fact, that's what I always thought of when I saw her - that she looked like she was on the run from something, that she was hiding behind those drab, baggy clothes and those big glasses." She shook her head at herself. "What an awful thing to say."

She fell into a sad silence. We couldn't get her to elaborate. We were standing to take our leave when Gretta stopped us. "You know, I probably have some pictures of her from Halloween," she said. "You can have one if I do."

We waited while she sorted through a topsy-turvy file marked "Halloween." Soon pictures of children littered her desk, all with beaming, painted faces, all clutching fat sacks of candy. I recognized some of the Medicare employees from Puget Health - including Kit, who was wearing a positively indecent vampire outfit. She probably pushed the whole sixth grade into puberty.

But there weren't any snapshots of Carrie. Gretta closed the file in exasperation, then opened it and thumbed through some bright drawings on thick construction paper. "Well, here," she said, handing us one of the drawings. "The day after Halloween, we send thank you cards to Puget Health Partners. We always have a couple of drawings that don't make it into the envelope because the kids don't finish them in time. And it looks like Carrie's in this one."

The drawing was signed "Love, Jenny." Jenny was a hell of an artist. Even though almost everyone was a stick figure, I could guess at the main characters. The tall figure with the oblong face and comical feet had to be Donald Carter - even though he seemed to be wearing a dress. The enormous woman with the bright red spiral swirling straight up from her head had to be Kit.

And in the corner, very small, very unobtrusive, was a plump figure that had to be Carrie. She was the only one who wasn't a stick figure. She was rounded. She looked a little heavy. But the drawing left no doubt as to how Jenny saw Carrie Mayer.

In Jenny's drawing, Carrie's whole body was a heart.

CHAPTER 7

I was a stranger in a strange land.

I went to law school and undergrad at the University of Washington - locally known as the U-Dub. I spent seven years in and around the campus and University District - playing football at Husky Stadium, studying in Odegaard Library, doing very occasional laundry at the Lost Sock. I could have found my way around the place blindfolded - just by the resonance of the bricks in Red Square, the roar and mist of Drumheller Fountain, the steam-tray ambiance of the HUB cafeteria. But for whatever reason, I had never had the maturing experience of visiting the Women Studies Program off in Padelford Hall. And from how things were going, that avoidance had been a pretty good idea.

"So you and your corporate figment are taking the position that suicide - the deconstruction of the embodiment - is the heteronormative response for a woman who transgresses the masculinist prescriptions of body size?"

It took a minute to decipher that. *You think Carrie killed herself because she was fat.*

"Dr. Lofton, we're just trying to figure out what happened."

"But I, of course, have no experiential reference point for the actual events of your case. I cannot address them in either situatedness or specificity. All phenomenological or intersubjective analysis - hermeneutic or otherwise - is vitiated by the ungroundedness of the grounds on which you ask me to rely."

If Anastasia Lofton, Ph.D., had not come so highly recommended by my favorite law school professor, I would have taken my leave of her right then. I would not have shaken her hand, however, because unbeknownst to me, handshaking was yet another instrument of male oppression. This had been brought home to me vividly when I had introduced myself to Dr. Lofton and thrust out my hand - which had just hung there in space while she examined it skeptically, then edged around it, then sniffed, and then seated herself on the far side of the desk.

But the fact was, Emma Reynolds - a lawyer and medical doctor and my favorite law school professor - had raved about Anastasia Lofton. Emma had called her brilliant, personable, groundbreaking. If anyone could give me insight into the relationship between suicide and weight loss, Emma had said, Stasia Lofton could. So I gritted my teeth and pressed on.

"Dr. Lofton, I realize you didn't know Carrie Mayer and can't say for sure what happened. None of us can. But we do know that Carrie had some significant experiences right before her death. She lost her mother after a long battle with cancer. She lost a considerable amount of weight. She started getting in trouble at work. I'm just trying to find out whether any of that means anything to you - whether you think it would have driven Carrie to take her own life."

Dr. Lofton looked out the window. "You are seeking to reify the communicative praxis of the act, Mr. Hart," she said. "What you fail to realize, in your phallocentric, hyperbinarial reductivity, is that each experiential embodiment is not simply ambivalent but actually multivalent."

I thought about that one for a long, long time. Dr. Lofton watched me with a resigned professorial impatience, like she was stuck in the classroom giving me a make-up test while she was dying to go outside for a cigarette.

"OK," I said slowly. "What you're really saying is that I'm an asshole."

Dr. Lofton looked at me without change of expression. "You're an asshole," she confirmed.

Finally, a sentence I understood. We were making progress.

"So, in words of one syllable, Doctor, why am I an asshole?"

"'Asshole' has two syllables."

Now I was looking at her with a resigned impatience. Finally she sighed and shrugged. "My research identifies the correlative between female body image and female self-destruction - whether through anorexia, bulimia, liposuction, stomach stapling, plastic surgery, or in the most extreme cases, suicide. My thesis is that the American female's preoccupation with dieting - literally, with *making herself less* - is a gradation of suicide, a step towards suicide. I have spent years studying what I believe to be a public and mental health menace as well as an oppressive masculinist and libidinous construct. I do not take kindly to the thought of my life's work being used to allow your client to evade its financial obligations to the survivors of a troubled and victimized young woman."

"So you believe that Carrie Mayer committed suicide?"

The good doctor's steel-grey eyes hardened into something approaching hatred. "I believe nothing of the kind!"

"Of course you do. You don't want your research used to help us avoid payment on the claim. So if you thought it was just an accident, you'd be falling all over yourself to convince me that it wasn't suicide. And you haven't exactly been falling all over yourself since I got here, have you, Doctor?"

Stasia Lofton glared at me. Her eyes were grey. Her hair was grey. Her face was grey. Her clothes were grey. She looked like an angry wraith. When she spoke, her voice was flat and tense. "Emma told me I'd like you," she protested.

"You will like me. Just stop talking to me like I'm either a monster or an idiot. No one's trying to cheat Carrie Mayer's heirs or get out of paying on the policy. We've already got enough circumstantial evidence to convince a jury it was suicide. My client just wants to be sure. They're paying me a lot of money to give them the best read I can on what really happened. And Emma said you were my best bet to get inside Carrie Mayer's head."

The flattery was not unwelcome. There was an almost imperceptible softening in her eyes. "Are you going to make me testify?" she demanded.

"If it comes to a trial, I may ask you to be an expert witness. But I never make any expert testify."

"Because you want her testimony to be what you've bought and paid for?"

"Because I don't want her getting back at me by using words like 'phenomenological' and 'hermeneutic' on the stand. That would scare the jury."

Dr. Lofton subjected me to a long, appraising look. I wished Harmony was there. Dr. Lofton wouldn't have seen Harmony as an enemy. Unfortunately, Harmony was at that minute meeting with David Mann - the best criminal defense attorney in Seattle - to see whether he could explain our sudden crush of press attention. Higuro had been clueless - and worried - when she had described her arrival at the airport and the photographers outside the Camlin. So I just looked frankly and forthrightly back at Dr. Lofton and waited for her to make up her mind.

When she did, it was as if an armored gate suddenly rose.

"What do you want to know?" she asked.

I quickly outlined what I was trying to determine, and what I had already discovered about Carrie Mayer. "Every woman I've talked to about this case balks at the suicide theory when I tell them about Carrie's weight loss. She dropped fifty pounds in about six months. Even though there were a lot of difficult things going on in her life during that same time - her mom dying, problems at work - the women I've talked to seem to think weight loss alone is a reason to live."

Dr. Lofton's voice was almost soft. "They would."

"Is it?"

"No. Suicide after dramatic weight loss is not that uncommon."

"Why?"

"Survivors tell different stories about their motivations. Some say they tried to kill themselves because they were plateauing or even regaining weight, and they despaired at becoming heavy again. Some say they weren't prepared for the sexual attention their new figures unleashed. Losing weight is in some degree losing protection against men and male sexual demands. If the woman is uncomfortable with her sexuality, suddenly she is exposed in a way she may not be able to handle."

She leaned forward. Her face glowed with intensity. Her eyes looked silvery grey. "At bottom, however, I think that after-loss suicides result from a feeling of betrayal. Constantly, women are told that if they lose weight, they will be loved; they will be accepted; they will be successful. If the after-loss woman finds that to be untrue, she does not fault the lies she was told; she faults herself for not going far enough to destroy the reviled, formerly overweight embodiment. For some after-loss women, this self-destructive drive pushes them into anorexia or bulimia; for others, plastic surgery; for still others, actual suicide."

She broke off and swallowed. She seemed to remember who she was talking to and regret her bluntness. "I suppose you think this is a bunch of sniveling feminist bullshit," she said.

I shook my head. "No. No, it makes sense."

"Because it will help you prove that Carrie Mayer committed suicide?"

The doctor did not like me. "No, because it fits with some things I've experienced." I paused. "With my *phenomenology*."

She caught herself, but she almost laughed. "You find yourself victimized by society's expectations of body size, Jack?"

"Not personally, no," I said, and left it at that, but I couldn't help thinking of my first very serious girlfriend, Betsy. Betsy the girl, not Betsy the dog.

Elizabeth O'Connor was the twin sister of one of my college football buddies. She was a tall, strong girl with freckles and ginger hair, a champion swimmer, an overall athlete. We dated during my junior and senior years of college and lived together while I was in law school. Betsy had been happy, relaxed, and funny, the kind of person who'd go hiking with you, go to a game with you, and sit on the couch and pass the M&Ms back and forth with you. But then Betsy's brother went on to the NFL and married a model, and Betsy dropped thirty pounds. She didn't sleep well; she was snappish; she would burst into tears if I didn't notice her new outfit or hairstyle. Over and over again, she'd ask me, "Do I look fat?"

There is no satisfactory answer to that question.

I wasn't much help. I was finishing up law school and getting ready for the bar exam. I was working at night to put food on the table - which Betsy wouldn't eat - editing the law review, and utterly, completely mystified about what was going on. Just before I graduated, Betsy went to Maui with her brother and his wife and never came back. Within two weeks, she met and moved in with a champion surfer named Wade. They were still together. Every Christmas, Betsy sent me a picture of herself in a bikini at the beach.

"Jack?" Dr. Lofton nudged me from my thoughts. "Are we done?"

"Based on what you know about her, do you have an opinion of whether or not Carrie actually committed suicide?"

"No. I can't go that far. Empirical patterns and theories are one thing, Jack. Individual cases are quite another. I would need to know more - much more - about Carrie's circumstances and psychological stability. The most I can say is that the mere fact of Carrie's weight loss doesn't preclude suicide."

"And you'd testify to that?"

She hesitated. Finally she nodded. "If it came to that, yes, I would. But I'd rather not."

I thanked her and took my leave, being careful not to offer her my hand. I walked through the campus back to my car, enjoying the free, cheating feeling of not having a class to rush to or a paper to write. Back at my office, Mrs. Holbrook - who was wearing a broad blue hat with grey feathers - told me Harmony would be with David the rest of the afternoon.

I called Leah Batson. She had told me to take a week to look into Carrie's death, and I still had a few days to go. But it occurred to me that Dr. Lofton's testimony might put to rest any suspicions in Leah's mind, and if she and her boss were convinced that Carrie committed suicide, I didn't want to run up her bill.

Leah was very quiet while I explained Dr. Lofton's theories of suicide and weight loss. "Bottom line, just because she had dropped some weight doesn't mean she didn't kill herself."

"She'll testify?"

"Begrudgingly, but yes."

"What will she be like as a witness?"

"If I can make her speak in plain English instead of post-modernism mumbo-jumbo, she'll be impressive."

"Is she heavy?"

I was surprised Leah asked so directly. "No. Neither fat nor thin."

Leah was tapping her pencil eraser on the desk. "So the jury won't see her as an apologist or an activist," she mused. "Just a scholar."

"Do you want me to stop now? We've answered the question that got us suspicious in the first place. Women do kill themselves when they're losing weight."

"What else were you planning to do?"

"Visit the scene with the cop who found the body, see if the medical investigator who said the manner of death was undetermined is going to stay on the fence, and get a copy of <u>The Stranger</u> article Carrie wrote about suicide. Other than that, I don't have any leads."

More tapping. "Oh, go ahead and do that, Jack. We'll need all of those for trial anyway, so we may as well get them under control now. But can you come to L.A.

Friday morning to give us your report? It would be nice to get our strategy wrapped up."

It was late Wednesday afternoon. Plenty of time. "Sure," I said, and she thanked me and hung up.

I leaned back in my chair and let out my breath. I was strangely relieved that Leah had given me another day, that I had about thirty-six more hours to make sure we were doing right by Carrie Mayer. Even though Dr. Lofton's testimony seemed to clear up all our questions, I couldn't shake a nagging feeling that I was missing something, that I hadn't assembled all the pieces of the puzzle.

I searched my mind and shook my head. I couldn't come up with anything I had overlooked. Maybe it was just that, deep down, I didn't want this to be a suicide. I hated to think of Carrie standing there on her balcony - bereft, dismissed, overlooked - sad and hopeless enough to throw herself into a final act that finally no one would be able to ignore.

I had started to like Carrie Mayer.

CHAPTER 8

For eight years, Carrie Mayer had lived in a beige-painted, beige-carpeted studio on the tenth floor of First Hill's Melbourne Terrace apartments. The super of the building loitered at the door, unsure whether it was OK to leave us alone. Mark's badge had convinced him to let us into the apartment, but he still seemed skittish.

I tried to draw him out. "Did you know Carrie Mayer well?"

The super shook his head. He had a thick, fleshy neck that wobbled with the exertion. "Only know the bad ones," he said. "She paid her rent, kept the place spanking clean, was real quiet. Nice girl as far as I was concerned."

"Did she have many visitors?"

"Saw her with a friend from work a coupla times. She was a prize at happy hour, I can tell you that."

It had to be Kit McCracken. I got as far as lifting my hands above my head and saying "red hair?" when the super interrupted. "You've met her!"

I was curious. Kit had specifically told me she and Carrie didn't hang out. "Her name's Kit. Was she over here a lot?"

"Naw. Saw her once or twice around Halloween. She was wearing this vampire get-up -" He was cupping his hands in front of his chest and grinning when he caught Harmony's cool, considering eye and started to cough. "And, um, well, maybe she was here at Christmas too."

Interesting that Kit hadn't mentioned that. "What happened to all Carrie's things?" Harmony asked. The apartment was empty. The super was still looking for a new tenant.

"Her sister came by after Carrie died. Took whatever she wanted and told me to get rid of the rest. Made me carry everything down to her car. Nipped at me like a Pekingese."

I liked people who used dog references. "What did she take?"

"Her car, of course. And Carrie had an old typewriter - heavy as lead. She had a coupla nice chairs and a good rug. And a big picture of her mom and dad in front of Mayer's Meats. That's all. Her sister kept saying it was all just a bunch of junk. Pretty girl, but a piece of work. Told me to trash everything else - even her sister's clothes."

"And did you?" Mark slipped the question in so deftly that it seemed to surprise Mr. Sandstrom.

The old man flushed. "Yeah, I got rid of it."

"I asked whether you trashed it."

Mr. Sandstrom looked down. There was a painful, humiliating silence. He was not by nature a liar.

"Mr. Sandstrom, Melanie Mayer told you to throw away everything that was left. At that point, as far as the police are concerned, you were free to do whatever you wanted with it. You're not going to get in any trouble if you sold some of it, or if you kept it. But we may want to take a look at it if it's still around - or we may want to try to track it down if you sold it. Either way, you just need to tell us the truth."

"I - uh, well, I kept a coupla things. Just some kitchen stuff and a little space heater. The furnace goes corky on us sometimes in the winter. I sold the rest. There's a consignment shop up on Pine for big gals. They gave me $150 for the clothes. The junk store up on 11th gave me $150 for the furniture. And they came and picked it up."

He rubbed his thick fingers over his broad, flabby face. "Must sound real gruesome to you, real cold-hearted. But it was nice stuff, and I didn't want to throw it away. And after that sister of hers had ordered me up and down a thousand times, without even a thank you or tip when I was done - well, I just felt like I deserved it. Like Carrie would want me to have it."

He sighed deeply, and I could hear the rattle in his lungs. "I'll send the three-hundred bucks to her sister if you think I should."

Mark shook his head and patted Mr. Sandstrom on the back. "Like I said, once Melanie Mayer told you to throw it away, it was yours to do what you wanted with. I don't see any reason you can't keep the money."

"What about the stuff I took?"

"Up to you," Mark shrugged. "You know her sister doesn't want it."

Mr. Sandstrom left as soon as Detective Ed Perez arrived. The presence of two police officers seemed too much for him to bear. Detective Perez was a compact young man with a baby face screwed tight with worry. The cause of the concern was soon revealed.

"Larry's downstairs. He stopped off to have a smoke. He wanted me to wait for him, but I told him I had to take a leak." He looked at Harmony and flushed. "Sorry.

43

Anyway, I thought I'd better warn you. Good luck, man." Then he dived into the bathroom just as his partner shoved open the front door.

Given Mark's misgivings about his competence, I had pictured Larry Gregerson as a sloppy, balding man with a beer belly and a bad toupee, in my mind the physical shorthand for dereliction and sloth. But the man who barreled into Carrie Mayer's small apartment could have stepped right out of a Marine Corps ad. He wasn't tall, but he was broad-shouldered, hard-muscled, and impeccably groomed. His light brown hair looked razor-cut, his eyes were icy blue, and his suit flowed over his frame as if it had been custom-made.

He got far too close to Mark. "What the fuck are you playing at, Oden?" he snapped. "What gives you the right to horn in on my case?" Before Mark could answer, he spun around and hammered on the bathroom door. "Zip it up, Perez. You and me have better things to do today than stand around holding our dicks."

"Of course you do."

Larry Gregerson hadn't seen Harmony when he burst in. When she spoke, every bit of him seemed to snap to attention. And when she stepped out of the shadows of the little kitchen, he flicked his eyes up and down her in a way that made me want to punch his lights out.

Harmony introduced us. "Detective Gregerson, we know you are a very busy man. We're not trying to second-guess your investigation into Carrie Mayer's death. All we're trying to do is determine whether this was an accident or suicide. We know that the police don't have the time or the resources to waste on situations that don't involve actual crime. We wish you did; you'd do a much better job than we will. But we know you've already got your hands full."

Gregerson preened and swelled. I could swear that Ed Perez was peeking out of the bathroom. "Well, you're absolutely right about that, Miss Piper," Gregerson said. He was so focused on her that I longed to step between them. "Police can't be everywhere. Can't do everything. As it is, it's a 24-7 commitment."

"That's why we so appreciate your coming over to give us some pointers on this investigation. What did the apartment look like the night you found the body?"

Seamlessly, she led him back to the night of Carrie's death:

The door was closed and locked, he said, although the deadbolt and chain weren't set. There was no sign of a struggle, burglary, or forced entry; the building did not have security cameras. The place was neat, but the bed wasn't made. There was an old paperback book in the bathroom, opened face down on the counter, and a wine bottle in the sink, one of the little ones you can get at the supermarket. It was about half full. She had already washed out the glass - just one, and just an ordinary water glass - and set it to drain. They didn't see any evidence of food preparation, but a box of crackers was out on the counter. She didn't look like she missed many meals.

Harmony didn't flinch. "When did it happen?"

"Best guess is 3 a.m. The super's on the ground floor - he heard the pop on the pavement and found her at 3:15. She was wearing pajamas and slippers, like she just got up in the middle of the night to go to the bathroom. A couple of the other residents said they thought they heard something earlier, but it never panned out."

Harmony and Gregerson moved toward the balcony. I positioned myself right behind them. Behind me, I could hear Mark and Ed Perez in a whispered conversation.

"So tell me how you think she may have fallen," Harmony said to Gregerson.

"So any glasses by the body?" Mark asked Perez.

Gregerson was droning on about centers of gravity and torque and thrust. I was a marketing major, and even I knew he was full of crap. "I didn't see any glasses," Perez whispered to Mark. "But Larry told me to go upstairs to the apartment right away. He said he'd handle the scene downstairs."

"So he didn't even come up to the apartment?"

"Nope. He's just cribbing from my report to impress your friend."

"Did you see any eyeglasses in the apartment?"

"No," Ed Perez said. "But I didn't really look for 'em, either."

Finally Larry Gregerson stopped twisting himself back and forth in an apparent attempt to convince Harmony that it was possible for a five-two woman to topple accidentally over a three-foot railing. He pressed his business card on Harmony and demanded one of hers. He saluted her, then summoned his hapless partner with a bark. "Well, come on, Perez. I can't wait around for you all day." Ed gave me a long-suffering eyeroll as the door closed behind them.

Mark locked the door. "Harmony, that was beyond the call," he said.

"I figured you'd intervene if he got out of hand. Anyway, come on out here." She led the way to the balcony. "I think there's something interesting."

During clear weather, Carrie's view must have been magnificent - sparkly, vast, and bright blue - the only luxury of her drab little apartment. She looked out over the Space Needle, the Olympic Mountains, Queen Anne Hill, maybe even a sliver of the Sound. I couldn't tell for sure because it was a dark, close day, when even the 605-foot Space Needle was barely visible through the fog.

I stood on the balcony, looked over the wet, grey south slope of Queen Anne, and felt a sinking in my stomach. The Evergreen Care Center was on the south slope of Queen Anne Hill. I thought I could make out the distinctive shape of the roof.

Poor Carrie. I thought of her pajamas, her slippers, her unmade bed. With her mother dead just over a month, three days after her first Christmas as an orphan, it made perfect, horrible sense that Carrie wouldn't be able to sleep, not even after a glass of wine. That she would read a while, that she would step out into the stinging rain just to feel something - anything - besides her own grief. That she would stand there in the Christmas cold, with the city's Christmas lights disappearing into the

Christmas mist. That she would scour the south slope of Queen Anne Hill, just as I was doing right then, searching for the place where her mother died. That with all of that on her shoulders, Carrie Mayer could have decided - would have decided - that it was just too hard to go on.

"Jack?" Mark beckoned to me. "You ought to see this."

Harmony explained Larry Gregerson's theory of the accidental fall. There was a hanging flower basket at the side of the balcony, now just a web of dead, browned stems. A small stool - no more than six inches tall - and watering can were kicked into the corner.

"Larry thinks she was standing on the stool to water her plants when she got dizzy and fell backward over the railing," Harmony said. "But it can't have happened that way."

"Because she wouldn't have been watering her plants during the middle of a rainstorm?" I guessed.

"Well, there's an overhang from the balcony upstairs, so this basket probably would need to be hand-watered," Mark - who was mad for plants - pointed out. "But it's more what was in the basket that's important." He reached up and twitched off some of the brittle foliage.

"Impatiens," he said. "A soft annual. They would have been flat dead by the end of December, especially with the snow we had last winter. No way would she have been watering a basket full of dead flowers."

He crumbled the leaves in his hand and let the wind scatter the debris.

"She didn't fall over this railing, Jack. She jumped or was pushed. No two ways about it."

DEAD WEIGHT

CHAPTER 9

Mark had to head back to work, but Harmony and I had one more stop up on Capitol Hill. Carrie Mayer had written a freelance article for <u>The Stranger</u>, a weekly newspaper that carries the wildest personals ads north of San Francisco. Donald Carter had mentioned it to me; Melanie Mayer admitted that she was "vaguely" aware of it. But no one had a copy of the article, and no one could tell us what it said. All we knew was that it was about suicide. Even our crack research team - i.e., Mrs. Holbrook, who had come in that morning wearing a black beret - had been unable to locate the article itself. So Harmony and I were heading up Capitol Hill to <u>The Stranger</u>'s offices.

I looked over at Harmony as we waited at the light for the procession of pierced, tattooed kids to skate and strut across Broadway. Most of them tugged along self-conscious-looking dogs. Harmony loved dogs as much as I did, but right then something else monopolized her attention. Her fingertip traced the black satin surface of the aebleskiver pan Mr. Sandstrom had given her.

He had insisted. Before we left Melbourne Terrace, he showed us the heater he had taken from Carrie's apartment and some white plates with blue flowers. Mark told him yet again that he was free to keep it all. At length, Mr. Sandstrom seemed convinced - then rummaged around in his kitchen cupboard and drew out a cast-iron aebleskiver pan with seven deep, round wells and a sky-blue wooden handle.

"You should have this," he had said to Harmony. When she protested, he explained that Carrie used to make aebleskiver for the tenants' New Year's brunches. "She told me it was her grandma's pan. She was fussy over it. Wiped it out with salt; rubbed it with oil. When her sister didn't want it, I couldn't stand to sell it to the junk shop. But it's not like I'll ever use it. You take it, miss."

Harmony tried to pay him for it, but he refused. She hadn't taken the pan off her lap since we left Melbourne Terrace.

"My mother had a pan just like this," she said. "Blue handle and everything. I'd forgotten. She used to make aebleskiver on Christmas Eve."

"What are aebleskiver, exactly?" I remembered from my research that Carrie had won a prize for them at Tivoli Days.

"Scandinavian pancake balls. Delicious. You put powdered sugar on them and serve them with melted butter and preserves."

We turned onto Eleventh Avenue, a mash of apartments, dance clubs, thrift stores, and autobody shops, enveloped in the greasy mist of the Kentucky Fried Chicken around the corner. The Stranger was across from the Bad Juju Lounge.

Before she got out of the car, Harmony slipped the pan under her seat - to guard against all those aebleskiver thieves out there. Down the block from the newspaper was the second-hand shop that bought Carrie's furniture. "I'll just duck in there and see whether they might still have any of Carrie's things," she said. "If I get done first, I'll come to The Stranger. Or you come find me."

Upstairs at The Stranger, the personals ad of the week was posted in large letters over the receptionist's desk: "ISO Daddy for bondage, blood, and water sports. No weirdos."

The receptionist - a pencil-thin kid with a pierced nose and a shaved head - caught my eye and grinned.

"No *weirdos*?" I asked.

He shrugged. "It's all relative. What can I do for you?"

I explained what I needed. Was there any way he could help me locate an article if I knew only the subject, the author, and roughly the year it appeared?

He considered. "How long ago?"

"Five or six years."

It was not the right answer. The newspaper had a new computerized index that could have led me quickly to recent articles. But not from five or six years ago. That would involve filing cabinets and clippings - maybe even microfilm. The receptionist - who looked no more than twenty - seemed intimidated by the sheer prospect of a paper chase. I bet that never once in his life had he used a card catalogue.

"Please," I said. "It's important. I'll pay any research fees for your time."

"Why do you need it so badly?"

"It's for a court case. The author died suddenly - violently."

The kid was thrilled. "Are you a cop?"

"No. Just a lawyer."

He looked me up and down, from my thick, straight, blond-brown hair to my bulging shoulders and big hands. "A lawyer," he said meditatively. "Well, I'll try."

And he did try. But the search was not proceeding at all well when a teddy-like man in a trench coat stepped off the elevator. "Brad!" the receptionist exclaimed. "Can you help this nice man?"

Brad, it turned out, was the managing editor. He remembered Carrie Mayer. I asked why.

"Her article was a knockout," he said, waving me into his office and beginning to rifle through a filing cabinet. "Most of the unsolicited stuff we get is shit. This was sharp, smart - totally clean. I think I ran it without changing a word. After it was published, I called her and asked her to come in and talk to me. She had some ideas for some other stories, and I was really impressed with her on the phone. She wanted to do a feature called 'Table for One,' where she'd go by herself to a bunch of restaurants and report how the waiters treat a woman who's dining alone. I loved it on the phone, but when she came in -" He broke off.

"When she came in?" I prompted.

"Look, it's not that she was heavy, OK? I mean, I'm a big guy, too. I know what it's like. But her angle was going to be that waiters ignore unaccompanied women. And after I saw her, I started to think that maybe they ignored her, well, just because she was her." He grimaced. "That's a rotten thing to say. But she looked - I mean, she seemed - so *squashed.*"

"So you never did the story?"

"No. I gave her some excuse. I think I hurt her feelings. Didn't hear from her again for years."

"When's the last time you talked to her?"

"Oh, I didn't talk to her. But she called here over Christmas, while I was in Wisconsin visiting my folks. I haven't called her back yet." My face must have registered dismay, because he hurriedly added, "But I will. I will." He started to rummage around on his desk. "I think I still have her message."

I had to break it to him. "Greg, Carrie Mayer is dead. She died shortly after Christmas."

He sank into his chair. "Poor thing." He rubbed his pudgy hands over his soft face. I watched the horrified realization dawn on him. "She didn't - did she? It wasn't suicide - was it?"

"We don't know for sure what happened." Reluctantly, I added, "But she may have jumped."

"Off the bridge?"

"No. From her apartment."

Greg shook his head, rifled some more in his filing cabinet, then excused himself. When he came back, he handed me a still-warm photocopy of Carrie's article from six years earlier.

I read the one-word title and grimaced:

"Jumpers," by C.A. Mayer.

CHAPTER 10

G reg was right. The article was a knockout:

"So this is how it happens," the article began, as if the reader was walking into the middle of a conversation. "You jump, and there are three seconds left between you and eternity."

Carrie went on to recount the death of "Jerry," a 54-year-old Green Lake resident who had gotten up one morning, fed the cat, read the paper, kissed his wife, left for work, stopped his car on the Aurora Bridge, and jumped into the cold waters of Lake Union.

No note. No explanation. No money troubles. No women troubles. No men troubles. No fights, no fears. No reason why a middle-aged middle manager would wake up one morning and decide *this was the day.*

Carrie had interviewed Jerry's wife, who said she still dreamed every night of their blue Subaru - just paid off - slowing, then stopping on the bridge, the cars behind honking in aggravation as the driver opened the door, scrambled up the span, and was gone. She was back at work and in grief counseling. She was functioning pretty well. But even during the day, she would start at a sudden pounding of footsteps in her head, feel the jolt of the jump and the journey, the smash of her husband's body smacking the water at more than 55 miles per hour.

"It's like the falling dream," she told Carrie. "The one where you have to catch yourself in time or you'll die. But you can't catch yourself. You can't wake up. You just die."

Why do people jump? Carrie asked suicide survivors. Some were utilitarian: Jumping was fast, it was fatal, it was there. Some were experimental: They had already tried razors or pills, and they wanted something more definitive. Some were mystics: They knew that if they were meant to live, God would stretch out His hand. Some were connoisseurs: There was something about the jump itself that fascinated them, the euphoria of the leap, the moment of flight, the separation - however brief - from the weight of the world where they had suffered so much pain.

Why do people kill themselves at all? Carrie asked a suicide support group. Why does it often seem so inexplicable? So random? Because no one knows or cares what's really going on inside you, said a 27-year-old, married computer programmer. Because you can never tell - you never know - when the hopelessness will suddenly become too much to bear, said a 50-year-old grandmother who had tried to kill herself twice.

"A 30-year-old single woman new to the group disagreed," Carrie wrote. "'I think some of us are born to do it,' she said. 'It's just a question of when.'"

I pushed the article away and looked across our conference table at Harmony. "She would have been 30 when she wrote this," I said.

She nodded.

"Think she's the 30-year-old single woman quoted there at the end?"

"It's an inference the jury can draw. We won't be able to prove it." She paused. "But we won't have to, Jack. I'm sorry. I really am sorry, but I think even the most pro-plaintiff jury is going to find that Carrie Mayer committed suicide."

"Anything I'm missing, Harmony? Anyone else I should have talked to? Anywhere I haven't looked?"

"Anything new from the medical examiner's office?"

"Nope. I called a couple of times. They aren't calling me back. I said in my message that we'd found some potential evidence of suicide that we'd like to share with them, but they aren't returning my calls. The investigator's in, but she's not biting. I think we'll have to depose her to nail down what she'll say at trial."

"Well, that's something to flag for Leah." She thought for a while. "I wish we'd been able to talk to the kids at Children First - although I understand why Gretta wouldn't let us. It's just that children sometimes see things grown-ups don't. It would have been helpful if we could have talked to people at her church - but we don't even know her religion. I'd guess Lutheran from her background, but that still gives us quite a few congregations to check. We can do that before trial. Everything else either was destroyed or never existed. If she kept a journal, it's been thrown away; if she wrote letters, they were trashed. We could do a forensic sweep of her computer at work, but our *subpoena duces tecum* should have picked up anything relevant already." She sighed. "I think we've done the best we could in a week."

"Yeah." I idly sorted through the books Harmony had purchased at the thrift store. Carrie's furniture was long gone, but some of her books had remained, all marked with her name and address on the flyleaf in her girlish, careful hand. She was an eclectic reader: romance novels, murder mysteries, the Bible, children's stories, Medicare manuals, and a couple of tomes on moral philosophy. I picked up a battered copy of <u>The Velveteen Rabbit</u>. It was my cousin Jimmy's favorite book.

"That one really got to me," Harmony said. "I wondered if she had been reading it the night she died, if she was thinking about the way the toy rabbit wasn't real until he was loved. Once her mom died, there wasn't anyone left who loved her. I suppose that's why I bought all her books. They're probably not important; I could have just taken down the titles and had the store clerk certify the list. But I hated seeing her books jumbled up in boxes, marked down to a quarter. That's all that's left of her, and people are still selling her short."

We sat in silence for a few moments. It was almost 7 o'clock. I had to be in L.A. by 10 the next morning.

I started setting up my slides while Harmony logged the evidence we had gathered into our database. She was right. I could convince Leah's boss - a judge, a jury, anyone I needed to - that Carrie committed suicide. I could paint her as someone pallid, cowed, and lonely, someone who lost her only friend when her mother died, someone so insecure about her looks that she avoided every camera, someone you wouldn't even notice if you passed her on the street.

I could make the jury see that shabby little apartment - which she kept painfully neat, as if she was expecting visitors who never came. I could make them see the little kitchen, the glass of cheap pink wine she drank to get up her nerve. I could make them feel the dark December night, the windswept balcony, the stinging rain, the flutters of fear and exhilaration as she stood up on the stool.

I could make Carrie Mayer into a nothing, a nobody, a zero who finally ended her life with her one big splash. I could.

I could kill Carrie Mayer again.

DEAD WEIGHT

CHAPTER 11

B y 8 p.m., we had finished the part of the presentation arguing that Carrie Mayer committed suicide. It was persuasive - verbally and visually. We scanned the pictures and most important documents and worked them into the slides. Next to the clipping showing her sister as an elegant Seafair queen, we put Carrie's blurry ID photo - which looked like a drawing by a distracted five-year-old, just a flat circle of a face and dots for eyes. Over a wash screen of Carrie's Stranger article, we enlarged and highlighted the most disturbing quotes. I headed that slide with Carrie's own title and byline: "Jumpers, by C.A. Mayer." It looked like an obituary, a self-penned epitaph.

We pasted in Stasia Lofton's silvery picture and résumé with bullet points of her eventual testimony about suicide after dramatic weight loss. She looked like an expert right out of Central Casting.

Now for the harder part: making the best case for accidental death. "Factually, there's not much here, is there?" I asked Harmony.

"Factually, no. But if Tate spins it right, he can still give us a run for our money. We've got the burden of proof, and the fact that the medical examiner won't give a manner of death means we've got a rock to get over. They're the expert; it's their jurisdiction, their accountability. And they're saying that they just can't tell. So for the jury to second-guess the medical examiner, they'll be looking to us to tell them facts that the medical examiner didn't consider. Intuitively, the women on the jury will see Carrie's weight loss as a reason to live, and it's not a slam dunk that they'll believe our expert over their own experience. Carrie wore glasses, and there's some evidence - the marks by her nose and the shadow on the picture - that she had them on when she fell. Ed Perez didn't see them in her apartment, and keeping on your glasses is unusual for a suicide. Kit McCracken will testify that Carrie was too religious to have killed herself, and the jury - at least the men - may want to believe anything Kit says."

"What about the dead flowers? Tate's whole theory has been she was standing on the stool to water her plants, and he can't say that if everything was dead."

"He'll probably change his tune at trial. He'll say she was standing on the stool to take down the dead basket, which may sound sort of plausible if it was swinging in the wind and disturbing her. He'll put Larry Gregerson on the stand with his ridiculous torque and thrust theory, and we'll have to bring in an academic kinetics expert to rebut. Larry's very handsome; he's been on the job twenty years; he seems disinterested. In this case, the jury will want to believe the cop."

I shook my head at Harmony. "Not an hour ago, you said there was no way this was an accident."

"It isn't. But proving it is a different thing. That may be why the medical examiner investigator went for undetermined. There's just not a lot of objective evidence. Anyway, we need to tell American Fidelity the best case possible for both sides. We also need to tell them that we'll have a fight over whether The Stranger article comes in - which is probably our most direct, most persuasive piece of evidence of suicide. It's not hearsay because we're using it to show state of mind, not the truth of the matter asserted, but Tate will say it was so long ago and so out of context that it's more prejudicial than probative. Who's our judge again?"

"Shrenk."

Harmony considered. She had tried a complicated employment case in front of Alice Shrenk, a former assistant U.S. attorney. "She's tough. She'll probably let it in, but we can count on a pretty limiting jury instruction. She'll tell the jurors they have to disregard any inference except that at one point, years before her death, Carrie Mayer was interested enough in the subject of suicide to write an article about it. Most jurors will disregard her instructions to disregard, and she knows that, but an instruction like that should stand up on appeal."

I couldn't help smiling at her. She was so calm, so confident, so in her element. I reached across the table and touched her fingertips very lightly with mine. "Good. And I'm glad you're here."

Our fingers shifted into a tight, close clasp. "Me too," she said, and we got back to work.

By 9 p.m., we had finished the part of the presentation that argued the best case for accidental death.

"Do you think we should talk about whether she was murdered?" I asked.

She shook her head. "Tate hasn't argued that, has he?"

"Not yet."

"And Leah hasn't brought it up?"

"No."

"It never hurts to be prepared, so we should at least work up some slides. But I wouldn't bring it up unless they ask. Especially given our . . . well, history, we probably don't want Leah to think that we're looking for trouble."

It was a good plan. We made up two slides summarizing the shreds of evidence of foul play: the possibility that Carrie Mayer was wearing glasses, Kit's certainty that Carrie was too religious to kill herself, Carrie's call to <u>The Stranger</u> right before she died, and Kit's belief that Carrie was angry about something.

"And the locks," Harmony added, looking over my shoulder. "She's a woman alone in a downtown apartment. It's odd that she didn't set the deadbolt and chain."

We saved the presentation to my laptop's hard drive, made two back-up floppies, and printed out hard-copy transparencies just in case. We sat in our darkened conference room, the glittering city at our feet, and did a dry run. It looked good. I e-mailed it to Leah so she could do a last-minute sanity check before I presented it to her boss the next morning.

When I brought up the lights, Harmony was still staring at the screen. I jogged her elbow. "Ready to go home?"

"Oh. Yes." She started collecting the papers around her. "But you know, we still haven't explained why Carrie Mayer was losing weight. We've explained why it doesn't matter - why she still could have killed herself - but we still don't know why it was happening."

"Stress," I suggested. "The lady at Evergreen said a lot of people drop some weight when their parents are dying."

"Maybe. I bet not many of them are women, though. We tend to go the other way when we're upset."

"Should I ask Leah for more time to look into it?"

"No. I don't know where we'd go. It's just one of the loose ends we haven't quite been able to tie up. But let's leave it alone for now."

And we would have left it alone - we really would. In fact, we were all packed and ready to go home when the phone rang.

"Let it go to voicemail, Harmony," I said. "You can pick it up in the morning."

She hesitated. "I can't. It might be David Mann. He was going to talk to Higuro's attorneys. And it's tomorrow afternoon in Japan."

She picked up the receiver. It was Mark. "Hi there!" she said. "Jack and I will be home soon -" I looked up as her voice suddenly died.

"Hang on," she said. She put him on speakerphone. "Mark, Jack's here, too."

Mark's voice was tense. "Stay right where you are until I can get there. Turn on all the lights and lock yourselves in your most secure room. Call the night guard downstairs and tell him not to let anyone up except me or Detective Anthony. We'll be there within half an hour."

"Why? What's going on?"

"The South Precinct found a body in a house fire on Beacon Hill. They think it's Melanie Mayer."

"They *think* it's Melanie Mayer?" I asked. "Is she too burned to be sure?"

"She's burned, but that's not the problem." I could hear other voices in the background.

"Someone cut off her head," he said.

"And her hands."

CHAPTER 12

Mark and his partner, Detective Anthony C. Anthony, arrived within fifteen minutes.

"What's going on?" Harmony asked. "Why do you think Jack and I are in danger?"

"Every time Jack starts looking into something, somebody dies," Mark said. "And then it's only a matter of time before someone attacks Jack. Maybe this will be the case to break the pattern, but we don't want to find out the hard way. It just seems too coincidental - Melanie Mayer being murdered a week after her deposition."

The fire had started on the first floor of Melanie's rented Beacon Hill home, Anthony told us. It gutted the living room, dining room, and kitchen. The headless, handless body was sprawled beneath a sodden, blackened lump that used to be a dining room table.

"How horrible." Harmony sat down. "Thank you so much for checking on us. What do you want us to do?"

"Could you give us chapter and verse about Melanie from your deposition? I know you're kind of hung up with the attorney-client privilege and everything, but just basic information? We've got a headless, handless body in a rented house. The neighbors barely knew her. So anything you could give us – even just a description – would help us out. The fire seems to have wiped out most of the evidence that was in the house. Even the pictures on the wall were burned."

I had no problem sharing basic information with the police, especially with Detective Anthony, who was pretty much a member of my family. He and Mark had stood by me when I was suspected of killing my dad. Unfortunately, I didn't have the court reporter's transcript yet. I tried to reconstruct the most important points of the eight hours I spent with Melanie from the notes I had scribbled on my depo outline.

Melanie Mayer was 38 years old, I told them. She was a graphic artist; she had moved away from Seattle right after college and had lived mostly in the southwest since then. In early December, a few weeks after her mother's death, she had moved back home from Phoenix - to be close to Carrie, she'd said. She was unemployed. She was living on freelance work and the money she got from her Phoenix house.

Mark looked up from his notebook. "Was she married?"

"Single."

"Did she have a boyfriend? Had she ever been married?"

"I didn't ask." I had just needed to know whether there was a current spouse we might need to join as an indispensable party.

"Did she have any friends here? Belong to any organizations?"

"Didn't ask."

"When's the last time she saw her sister?"

"She took Carrie off life support a couple of days after the fall. She claimed they saw each other a lot, but the only recent time she could describe was their mom's funeral in November. She said they were going to spend Christmas Eve together. At the last minute, though, Melanie got a migraine and had to cancel. She said Carrie was fine about it, sounded good. They made a date to get together New Year's Eve and exchange their Christmas presents, but Carrie died before then."

"How did she find out about her sister's fall?"

"Donald Carter called her. You guys found Carrie's ID badge in her apartment and called Puget Health Partners. Puget Health didn't even know Carrie had a sister until they pulled her benefits paperwork and saw that Melanie was the contingent beneficiary on Carrie's life insurance. Donald said it took a while to track Melanie down because she had moved around so much. Melanie went to the hospital, identified Carrie, and pulled the plug."

Anthony sighed. "We don't have a time of death yet, but Melanie's neighbors said they hadn't seen her for days. We have to assume at the moment that it is Melanie, but I don't know who they're going to get to do the ID."

My face must have betrayed my anxiety. I had been in more than my share of morgues over the last few years. Anthony shook his head at me. "Don't worry, Jack. We're not going to drag you down to Harborview and show you the corpse. But it would be helpful if you could give us a general description of how she looked when you deposed her. Height, weight, that sort of thing."

Melanie Mayer was short and blond, I told him. She wore a lot of makeup and very high heels. She had big eyes, kind of a bluish-gray. I couldn't remember any other distinguishing features. I had no idea how much she weighed.

"What's your best guess? Was she thin? Fat? Busty? Flat-chested? Big hips? Good legs?"

The only thing more unnerving than trying to describe a dead woman's body to a police officer is trying to describe a dead woman's body when your fiancée is in the room. It feels like necrophilia and adultery all at the same time. "She, uh, well, I thought she looked like an ex-beauty queen who had let herself go a bit," I said, uncomfortably aware that the tips of my ears were flaming red. "She wasn't thin, but she had on a long black jacket over a black dress, so it was hard to tell how much of it was the outfit and how much of it was her. She looked busty, and she had nice legs. Betty Boop legs - short and curvy, not long and thin."

I glanced at Harmony and was relieved that she appeared neither angry nor amused.

"Squares with our DOA," Mark said. "White female, probably just over 5 feet, around 140 pounds."

A bell rang softly in my mind. That detail sounded familiar. I reached for one of our document binders and paged to the medical examiner's report on Carrie Mayer. "The woman who fell from the Melbourne Apartments was five-two and 141 pounds."

We looked around the table at each other. "Well, I guess that could be an explanation for Carrie's weight loss," Harmony said. "I guess it's possible that Carrie could have been dieting down so she could pass for her sister."

"Arrgggh." It was Anthony. "That would be an absolute pain in the butt. It's a long shot theory, but Jack, do you know anything about Melanie's estate?"

I did not. Melanie's attorney might know, but it was past midnight, and Boyd Tate worked out of his house. I was looking at the telephone, wondering whether I should call Boyd, when the phone rang.

"Good evening, Piper & Hart," I said.

"It is not evening any more, Jack." I could hear the accusatory note in Leah Batson's voice. "It is not even night. By my clock, it is seven minutes into the new day, and you had better not be billing me."

"We're not billing you, Leah. What's up?"

Leah was calling with feedback on the slides, which she generally liked.

"Um, Leah, Mark and Detective Anthony are here and would like to talk to you."

I put her on speakerphone just in time for them to hear her say, "Oh, hellfire."

Leah knew Mark and Anthony from our mutual mistaken suspicion re: my father's death. "Who died?"

There was a pause.

"Oh, hellfire and *damnation*," Leah said. "You don't know. And what does this have to do with American Fidelity?"

Leah was my client. It was my job to tell her.

"There's been a development, Leah. When it comes to Carrie and Melanie Mayer, there's at least a question about which sister went over that railing."

CHAPTER 13

"Let me get this straight."

Leah was trying to sort out what we were telling her about the headless, handless woman in the Beacon Hill housefire. I didn't blame her for any confusion. Reality was starting to seem a bit shifty.

"It's possible that Carrie took out $250,000 of life insurance with her sister as the contingent beneficiary, invited her sister over for a post-Christmas shindig, pushed her over the railing, and then pretended to *be* her sister so she could collect on her own policy?"

"It's possible," Anthony confirmed. "It's only one of many options at this point, but given just the height and weight – and the fact that this killer seems to have gone to some significant trouble to disguise identity - it is possible."

"If Carrie was pretending to be Melanie, why would Carrie have ended up headless in Melanie's burned-out house?"

"If Carrie faked her own death to collect on her life insurance, she probably would have needed a confederate to push her sister over the railing," Mark said. "She wasn't big enough to do it herself. And Jack's been going around asking questions that would have made any confederate nervous. Or, the confederate could be the beneficiary of Melanie's will or insurance policy. Do you know anything about Melanie's estate? Does she have a life insurance policy with you?"

"About her estate, no idea. She's not a policyholder. That's one of the first things we look for in conflicts checks. How are you going to identify the woman in the fire?"

"Just old-fashioned police work – step by step. Melanie seems to have gotten rid of Carrie's car, but we'll try to track it down. It may still have some prints. We'll show Carrie's autopsy photographs to her coworkers and friends and ask them whether there's any reason to believe it's not actually Carrie. We'll look for any inconsistencies with medical records. And with the permission of the kind partners of Piper & Hart, we're likely to want to dust this conference room for prints – see if we get a match to anything we can lift from Melanie's house."

Harmony and I both removed our hands from the conference table with a start, trying not to muddle any existing prints of Melanie/Carrie. Anthony put the phone on mute. "Believe me, the department already has your prints on file. I think we have a special wing dedicated to you two by now. We'll be able to exclude your prints from everything else on this table."

"Why can't you just exhume the body and get the fingerprints from the original corpse?" Leah asked. "And DNA samples and the whole bit?"

"Because Melanie had Carrie cremated," I told her. "And she scattered the ashes."

"Thorough." I heard the tapping of a fingernail against the phone. Leah must be lacking a pencil.

"Do you still want me to come today, Leah?"

"No. I'll walk through your slides with my boss and let him know about the *development*. Always interesting with you weirdos up there. Keep me posted."

She hung up without saying goodbye. Anthony's beeper buzzed. He ducked into my office to make a call. I heard him say, "Son of a bitch, Larry," as he closed the door.

I looked over at Mark. "What's up with our friend Detective Gregerson? Why is he calling Anthony?"

Mark yawned and stretched. He had been up as long as I had. We had gone running together at 5:30 a.m., and his day had included nipping home to feed Betsy and pulling a headless body out of a burnt-out house. But Mark looked like he had just gotten ready for work. His black hair was perfect; his suit was pressed; he looked, as always, extremely handsome in an Elvisy way. Every one of my four sisters had a serious crush on Mark - even Marianne, who was married and had two kids.

"Larry's been calling everyone. He's worried that having the sister turn up dead night make people wonder whether he did everything he should have on Carrie's investigation. So he's on full-time CYA. He even told our sergeant about our visit to Carrie's apartment, made it sound like I had been trying to undercut him somehow."

"I am so sorry." I was sorry. I was starting to appreciate that the police department was almost as political as my old law firm. I should have been more careful about asking Mark's advice on a case.

"Oh, it's fine. Only a small amount of shit approached the fan. We all just got a highly motivational speech about teamwork. And – silver lining, I guess - it means you're probably right about the Carrie Mayer thing being more than it appeared."

Anthony walked back into the conference room in time to hear Mark's comment about Carrie Mayer. "Jack, the ME and the department haven't reopened Carrie's death yet. Larry's doing his best to make sure they don't. But just so Mark and I have the context, did anything strike you as strange when you talked to people about Carrie Mayer? Anything at all?"

I reflected. Now that I looked back on it, in almost every one of my interviews, there had been a moment when the hair stood up on the back of my neck.

In Melanie's dep, it was when she had gone out of her way to tell me about scattering Carrie's ashes at Golden Gardens Park.

At the Evergreen Care Center, it had been when I stood in front of that bulletin board plastered with snapshots of people who were dead.

At Puget Health Partners, it had been when Carrie's SVP and VP had told me over and over that they had never met her.

At the Camlin, it had been when Kit told me Carrie was angry about something that it was better Kit not know.

At Children First, it had been the eerie resonance of our footsteps echoing up and down the silent, kid-free hallways.

At Melbourne Terrace, it had been the moment I stepped out on that balcony and realized that Carrie Mayer wouldn't have been watering her hanging plants.

"Of all the people you talked to, who's big enough to chuck a 140-pound woman over a three-foot balcony?" Anthony asked. "Even if there were two people, it might have been a struggle."

I pulled out my interview binder and looked over the list of witnesses.

Donald Carter was thin but tall. He had the leverage that would have been necessary.

Carrie's senior vice president, Jim Hunter, was short but muscle-bound. He easily could have picked her up and thrown her over.

Gretta Berg of Children First was a hefty woman with large, capable hands. She looked like she could handle anything or anyone.

I looked over the list again and winced. There was one more witness big enough to toss a small woman off a tenth floor balcony. She was tall; she was strong; and she was the only person who had insisted - over and over - that Carrie hadn't killed herself, that we should pay on the policy.

Kit McCracken.

67

CHAPTER 14

Betsy lunged at me when we got home around 1 a.m. – something that hadn't happened for more than a year. Then she realized it was me and sat down in mid-snarl. She looked disappointed.

She padded next to me as I took inventory of the day's destruction. On our answering machine were four voicemails from two neighbors, all complaining about her barking. Our fan club. She had scattered my socks – in varying stages of annihilation – throughout the house. A roll of quarters I was going to take to the bank had disappeared from my dad's rolltop desk. Let's hope she had just buried it somewhere. If she had eaten it, those coins would soon resurface in unspeakable ways. There was a notice from the Post Office suspending our home delivery. Again. Betsy's barking, growling, and slavering through the mail slot were triggering PTSD flashbacks of all the times she had chased our postman down Aurora. No wonder the neighbors were always calling the police.

I entered the damage in the list we kept on the fridge. It was the vet's idea. Always arguable, Betsy's socialization was regressing as we worked longer and longer hours, and she spent more and more time alone. The list had become a veritable Day-Timer of canine misbehavior – *Bad Things I Did Today*, by Betsy Hart.

Betsy would not go to sleep, for reasons that were not apparent. She didn't want to play. She didn't try to grab my pajamas or run away with my pillow. That was odd. Keepaway was Betsy's favorite – and only – game. But she was restless and distracted. She trotted back and forth between me and Harmony a dozen times, pushing a cold, anxious nose in my face and making small sounds of concern. Even when I let her up on the bed - which normally would have sent her into a relaxed, *move over* sprawl, she remained tensed and fretful beside me, swiveling her ears at the slightest noise.

Maybe it was more reporters, I tried to tell myself. Even at three in the morning, I didn't buy it. Betsy didn't so much dislike reporters as disdain them. She barked at them the same way she did my neighbor's cat - *you, there, get the hell out of my yard.* They didn't frighten her; they didn't upset her. They certainly didn't unnerve her. And Betsy seemed like all three of those things. She was not my usual intense, challenging, but happy dog.

Her restlessness was contagious. It didn't help that every time I did drift off to sleep, Carrie's flat, round face flashed before my eyes and dissolved into flames. I felt the thwack of the axe on Melanie's neck, saw her cunning, painted face go slack and staring, spattered with blood. I dreamed of deposing Melanie, only to look up from my outline and realize it was Carrie – fat and forgotten – looking at me reproachfully from across the conference room table.

By 4 a.m., I was out of bed. I checked on Harmony, who was asleep in the sunroom. I checked downstairs; Mark still wasn't home. I checked all the doors. Locked.

Betsy's thick orange scruff lowered slightly, and she leaned against my leg. I rubbed her taut shoulders. Maybe this was stupid, I told myself. Maybe I was freaking her out instead of the other way around. As her muscles softened, and her tail twitched into a tentative wag, I began to feel foolish.

I got Betsy a biscuit from the kitchen. She took it eagerly - then dropped it. The thunk on my maple floor sent a shudder up my back. Betsy loved Mr. Barky's vegetarian dog biscuits. I had never seen her refuse one.

She went rigid. The growl came all the way from her tail. Her scruff rose; her ears came up; she bounded toward the living room and started barking.

I was right behind her - just in time to see why she was so agitated.

I saw a shadow slide across the fence.

There was a tall, thin man caught in profile from the glow of my back porch.

Then I saw a back, then a butt.

He scrambled over my fence and was gone.

CHAPTER 15

Two years ago, I would have gone after him. I would have jumped the fence myself, hunted him down, thrown him on the ground, and demanded to know what in the hell he was doing in my yard. But I was older and wiser - and I wasn't going to leave Harmony alone. I did what a rational person would do and called the police.

Two cars arrived within five minutes. The older policeman - Officer Johnson - stayed behind with me while the others fanned out through my neighborhood. Betsy stalked around the yard – sniffing, snarling, and growling. She barked in every corner, re-establishing her perimeter. I was going to get some seriously constructive feedback from my neighbors over this.

"Any idea who you might have seen out there?" Johnson asked.

I hadn't seen a face. I had seen only the shadow of a tall, thin man. And the only tall, thin man involved with the Carrie Mayer investigation was Donald Carter. And I liked Donald Carter. With a sinking feeling of disloyalty, I told Officer Johnson about Donald.

"But I can't imagine he'd be skulking around my house," I said.

"One way to make sure. You have his home phone?"

"Yes. But it's 4:30 in the morning."

"Better to call him and wake him up than have him be a suspect unnecessarily." When I started toward the phone, he shook his head and handed me his cell. "Might have Caller ID," he said. "Don't make a sound. Just give me the thumbs-up if it's his voice."

The phone rang six times. I was beginning to worry that Donald wasn't home - which meant he might have been skulking around my house - when a dazed, worried voice came on the line. "Yes? Yes? Hello?"

It was foggy with sleep but definitely Donald. I gave Officer Johnson a thumbs-up and handed him the phone.

"Sorry, sorry, man, wrong number," Johnson said. He clicked the phone closed. "Well, that's helpful. We can cross your friend Donald off the list."

Good. I relaxed a little and petted Betsy while Officer Johnson looked around the house. He went in every room except Harmony's; I checked on her myself, then closed her door.

"So Oden lives downstairs?" The question was suspiciously casual. Mark's fellow police officers seemed inordinately interested in the relationships between the three of us. Apparently, it was strange enough for a cop to live with two lawyers. Judging from the care Johnson took to make sure I didn't notice that he noticed that Harmony and I had separate bedrooms, it was even stranger for a cop to live with two lawyers who didn't sleep together even though they were engaged.

"Yeah. We're building him a bachelor pad down there."

"Looks good. I like the wood floors."

I had exhausted my store of early-morning small talk. Apparently, so had Johnson, because he radioed his fellow officers. "Find anything?"

It took a few minutes for the answers to arrive - by radio and in person. The officers on foot had found prints of large men's running shoes in the flower beds on both sides of the fence. It looked like the man had entered from my neighbor's yard, jumped the fence, and started toward my house. Then there was a skid of flattened grass that probably meant he dived for cover when Betsy started barking. He had trampled some of Mark's favorite plants in his haste to get back over the fence and snagged some shreds of purple fabric on the top of the posts.

The police couldn't tell how he left my neighbor's yard. The footprints stopped at the edge of the lawn; he could have cut across the front and hopped into a car parked on the street out of sight of my house, or he could have gone around the back and jumped the fence to a car waiting in the alley. Either way, he could have disappeared onto Aurora within seconds. The officers in the patrol cars had found no suspicious vehicles in the area.

The police were talking about whether or not it was worth making a plaster cast of the footprints. The consensus was, it wasn't. In fact, now that the four of them were congregated in my living room, it was obvious that they were more interested in me, Mark, and Harmony than they were in our mystery visitor.

"Nice place," one said. "But kind of, um, small for the three of you, isn't it?"

"Oden lives downstairs," Officer Johnson explained glumly, to which they all replied, equally glumly, "Oh."

They were about to leave when the sunroom door opened and Harmony stepped out, shading her eyes.

"Jack, what is it? What's going on?" she said, then froze when she saw the four policemen. She was wearing a black silk nightgown that my sisters had sent her for

Christmas. She crossed her arms. I stepped in front of her, blocking the view of the disappointed policemen. Betsy jumped beside me.

"There was someone in our backyard. Betsy scared him off. I called the police to make sure he was gone."

What else aren't you telling me? her look said. But over my shoulder, she said, "Thank you very much for coming. Please just give me a minute to get more presentable."

The policemen - who had been just about to leave - all sat down and eagerly awaited her return.

When she came back, she had knotted her matching robe tightly over her nightgown. She looked stunning, with her glowing black hair melting into the glowing black silk, making a lustrous outline of her shape, her face, her skin.

She shook hands. She sat with her arm around Betsy while each of the policemen repeated - in much greater detail, and with a new emphasis on the risk and daring on their parts - what they had already told me. They really should make a plaster cast of the footprints in our flower beds, they decided. It would only take an hour or so. They hoped we wouldn't mind?

We did not mind.

Then, because they obviously weren't going anywhere anytime soon – and because we had to get to work and hadn't eaten in twenty-four hours - we invited them to stay for breakfast.

"You know, I do buy groceries," Harmony said, as we inventoried the fridge. To my eye, it was not predictive of wild success in the breakfast department: hot dogs, buttermilk, two eggs, the apparently mandated baking soda, and half a can of pumpkin, left over from Betsy's birthday cake. "This house just seems to inhale food."

"That would be me, Mark, and Betsy," I confessed. "We believe that if it can be eaten, it must be eaten."

"We could make *huevos con weenies*."

I shook my head. "It's not as fun without Mark here to tell us we're doing it wrong."

"Well, he remembers his mom making it. It's important to do it like she did. And in that spirit, let's christen our new pan." She rummaged around for flour and pulled the buttermilk, eggs, pumpkin, and baking soda out of the refrigerator. I was astonished that the baking soda might have an actual purpose. "How about pumpkin aebleskiver with buttermilk syrup?"

There was a lonely stick of butter in the freezer. Mark had had Carrie Mayer's pan dusted for prints, so I washed the fingerprint powder off it while Harmony made the batter and put the stuff for the syrup over a low flame. When she added the baking soda, everything bubbled and fizzled spectacularly. Powerful stuff. No wonder it was mandated. I stirred the syrup into a thick brown caramel while Harmony rotated scoops of the batter in the sizzling wells of the aebleskiver pan until they were perfectly round. We put a platter of them on my coffee table, with a pitcher of syrup, a pan of melted butter, and powdered sugar.

The policemen mellowed over breakfast. One of them even got up the courage to take on Betsy.

"So that's your infamous and fantastic orange dog," he said, admiring the delicate way she licked powdered sugar off her whiskers. "Will she let me pet her?"

"Sure," I said, hoping it was true. "She likes policemen."

Betsy proved surprisingly amenable. She even favored him with a very small lick of her startlingly purple tongue. Suddenly, her ears pricked, and her scruff rose. The police officer snatched back his hand but soon realized that she was paying him no attention whatsoever. She was riveted on the front door. Growls exploded from her throat.

"Right. Sounds like our midnight caller's back." If I hadn't been so worried, it would have been amusing - four policemen with powdered sugar around their mouths suddenly reaching for their sidearms and taking charge.

Through the peephole, I could see a young, tall man wearing a dark suit. "Open the door quickly and step to the side," Johnson told me.

I did as I was told. Johnson and the visitor were face to face; I was almost hidden behind the door.

Our visitor had a square face, short brown hair, and shrewd brown eyes. He stuck his hand inside his coat.

"Don't be reaching anywhere!" Johnson ordered him.

The visitor affected a nonchalant expression that annoyed me - and cut no ice with Johnson, either. He raised his hand in a reproving manner and pulled out a badge before Johnson could stop him.

"Special Agent Rich, FBI," he said.

"I'm here for Harmony Piper."

CHAPTER 16

Betsy may have liked policemen, but she didn't much care for the Fan Belt Inspectors - which is what Detective Anthony called the FBI. She bared her teeth at Special Agent Rich. The wrinkles that indicate imminent attack appeared on her nose. I took a tight hold on her collar and felt the power gathering in her body.

"Control your dog," Rich snapped. He pulled a canister of pepper spray from his pocket and aimed it at Betsy. "Don't make me mace her."

In two minutes, Rich had threatened my fiancée and my dog. He was not scoring any points. But I wasn't letting any harm come to Betsy, so I renewed my grasp on her collar and told her to sit. She responded with an outraged glare in my direction - *are you out of your mind; we've got real trouble here* - but, amazingly, sat.

Rich turned his charms on Officer Johnson. "What are you guys doing here?" he demanded. Is SPD sitting on them too?"

Too. I didn't like the sound of that. Neither, apparently, did Officer Johnson. It's the rare local policeman who can abide the feds.

"So it was you guys!" Officer Johnson exploded. "Skulking around here at night, scaring these poor folks to death. They should have set their dog on you. What were you trying to do, hook in a wiretap?"

Rich's square face settled into a smug expression - but not before I saw the flash of surprise in his eyes. I couldn't tell whether it was surprise that we had been visited in the night or surprise that his cover was blown

He ignored Johnson. "Harmony Piper," he said to me. "I know she's here. I need to talk to her."

"She's not dressed."

"If she's dressed enough for the SPD, she's dressed enough for the FBI."

"Beat it, Rich," Officer Johnson intervened. "We're in the middle of an investigation here. Whatever you've got going, it can wait until we're done."

"Looks to me like you're done, Officer. Just wipe the sugar off your mouth and move along. You can always follow up with these two later. Believe me, they won't be going anywhere anytime soon."

Johnson cussed at him and started to slam the door. Harmony's voice stopped him.

"What do you want, Agent Rich?" she said. She was standing at the end of the hallway, flanked by two police officers, a third standing protectively behind her. Their arms were crossed, their mouths grim and sugar-free. Rich took in the scene.

"Why, Ms. Piper," Rich drawled with a malicious smile, "I knew you lived with one police officer. I didn't realize you entertained them in groups."

"Get out." The words were out of my mouth before I could stop them. "Get out of my house before I let go of the dog."

Rich ignored me and shrugged. "I'm giving you a chance to do this the easy way, Ms. Piper. If I have to, I'll get a subpoena and take you in front of the grand jury. At the moment, I don't have any proof that any of this was your fault, and until I do, I'm willing to believe you were just following orders. We can probably resolve this now, just with a signed statement. You choose. Either we have a quiet, informal conversation over -" he shot a mocking glance at Johnson - "*doughnuts,* or I come back here with a subpoena and a U.S. Marshal."

Harmony moved forward. The policemen followed her.

"Give me a little credit, Agent Rich," she said quietly. "If I know anything relevant to whatever you're investigating, you'll take me to the grand jury anyway, regardless of how cooperative I am. And we both know that you want to talk to me beforehand so there won't be any surprises when I testify. So let's not trouble the Marshals. And let's not waste time with threats."

Rich looked self-conscious. I suspected that the policemen behind me were smirking at him. "My attorney is David Mann," Harmony said. "He's in Rainier Square. Please call him and tell him what you want to talk to me about."

Rich recovered some of his composure. "A criminal defense attorney?" he said. "Why would a nice little girl like you need a criminal defense attorney?"

"You obviously haven't researched us very well," Harmony said. "Good day, Special Agent Rich." And she shut the door in his face.

Betsy barked for good measure at the door. The policemen shuffled their feet and cleared their throats, suddenly uncomfortable. Loitering over breakfast was one thing. Loitering over breakfast with someone who might be mixed up in something strange was apparently another.

"Are you in, um, any trouble, Harmony?" Officer Johnson asked.

"Not that I know of. But that may be the worst kind of trouble."

That was enough for our friends from the SPD. They shook our hands and left, thanking us sheepishly for the aebleskiver. Harmony and I looked at each other.

"I better call David," she said.

I washed up the breakfast dishes while she talked to David Mann. Per Mr. Sandstrom's instructions, I scoured Carrie's grandmother's aebleskiver pan with salt and rubbed it with oil. It had a scalloped finish at the bottom to let air circulate to the burner. I blotted it dry with paper towels and thought about all the thin winter mornings that pan must have warmed.

"Oh, no!"

The distress in Harmony's voice yanked me back to reality.

Mark and Anthony were standing in the entryway, one on either side of Harmony.

"But you said you didn't need it," she protested. "You said it didn't have any useful prints. You said I could keep it."

Mark looked perplexed. "We'll bring it back, Harmony."

"No, no, you don't understand. I've used it. I cooked breakfast with it." She glanced behind her and saw me standing at the kitchen door with the pan in my hands. "We've even washed it. Whatever evidence was on it, we've - *I've* - ruined it."

Harmony was such an interesting girl. An early morning visit from the FBI didn't noticeably unnerve her. The thought of messing up Mark's and Anthony's investigation - however innocently – did.

"It's OK, Harmony," Mark said. "Anthony noticed something on Carrie Mayer's autopsy that I didn't pick up. We'll show you."

I handed over the pan. The four of us clustered around the kitchen table while Mark and Anthony pulled and perused autopsy photographs and X-rays from a large envelope. I recognized the dead face of Carrie Mayer - or the person I had assumed to be Carrie Mayer.

They lined it all up on my kitchen table: the pan, with its satiny scalloped edge, an identical scalloped bruise on the left side of the dead woman's head, and a dark flooding inside the corresponding X-ray of Carrie's skull.

Or Melanie's skull.

Or whoever it was who went over that railing.

Anthony rubbed his eyes.

"I'm sorry, honey," he said. "But it looks like you may have cooked breakfast with a murder weapon."

CHAPTER 17

Murder would mean we would pay on the policy – unless the person was murdered while committing a crime. Leah and I started working through all the possible scenarios, which got weirder and weirder as we considered whom we would pay if Carrie had passed herself off as her sister and then ended up murdered by her confederate. No one, we eventually concluded: In that scenario, Carrie would have been engaged in insurance fraud, if not murder – both unacceptable behavior under the Revised Code of Washington.

But as it turned out, neither the Seattle Police Department nor the Medical Examiner's Office seemed in any hurry to reclassify the original death as a homicide. I blamed our friend Larry Gregerson. As Mark put it, somewhat more shit had approached the fan, and Larry had been doing his best to dodge and deflect.

Strangely scalloped-shaped bruise on the dead woman's head? Larry scoffed at the pan as the cause. In a ten-story fall through a tree and an apartment marquee, Larry said, there were all manner of obstacles that could be responsible for that sort of trauma. For now, the ME's office was sticking with "undetermined" for the manner of Carrie Mayer's death.

So the only clarity we had was that we had two short, dead women who weighed about the same and who both fit the basic description of the Mayer sisters. The first had jumped, fallen, or been pushed from the balcony of Carrie Mayer's tenth-story apartment. The second was headless and handless in Melanie Mayer's burnt-out rented house.

I left Boyd Tate a message asking whether he intended to press the lawsuit in the face of his client's ostensible death. It was simply a courtesy call; I didn't really expect him to withdraw - or even to call me back. Tate didn't win much; he needed the money. He was not a man to drop a case for the trifling reason that his client was dead. Or presumed dead.

If Mark and Anthony dispositively identified Melanie as one of the dead women, I would move to dismiss, unless Boyd came up with an heir to step in as plaintiff. And if Boyd ever did produce Melanie's heir, I knew he or she would be Suspect Number One for Carrie's and Melanie's deaths.

Mark and Anthony set about trying to clear up the confusion the only way they could: old-fashioned, painstaking police work, including questioning Carrie's coworkers at Puget Health Partners. Things did not go particularly well. One woman fainted; another threw up; Kit McCracken fled the office in tears. Or so I was informed by Donald Carter, who waylaid me later that morning when I darted out from work to buy a bagel.

Donald had dark circles under his eyes. His face looked wrinkled and creased, as though he had neglected to hang it up the night before. When I asked him if he was OK, he grumbled about the wrong number that had rousted him from bed at 4:30 that morning.

"What in the hell is going on, Jack?" he demanded, sinking his teeth into his own lunch. A pesto bagel with peanut butter, I noticed with a queasy feeling. "Carrie's been dead for months. Now all of a sudden the cops are shoving the most awful photographs under our noses and asking everybody whether they're sure it's her. Who else is it supposed to be?"

Donald and I had a tacit understanding. We didn't lie to each other. When we couldn't say, we didn't say, but we never lied.

"Donald, even if I knew anything, I couldn't tell you."

His red eyes rested on me in a long stare. "So it's like that, is it?" he said, sitting down at one of the bagel shop's tiny tables and nodding for me to join him.

"It's like that."

"Oh. OK then." Genuine concern suddenly focused his tired eyes. "But if it wasn't Carrie, then where is she? Is she OK? Is she hurt?"

I tried again. "Donald, even if I knew anything -"

He waved his hands in interruption. "Got it, got it. Heard you the first time. It's just that - damn. I know you can't tell me anything, but if Carrie is OK, we'd sure as hell like to know. Kit especially. She was so upset, I offered to give her a ride home, call her a cab, whatever. But she just ran out sobbing."

We were both quiet for a moment.

"Did she think the woman in the photograph was Carrie?"

"Sure of it. She couldn't stop crying. Up to that point, she'd sort of been flirting with one of the cops -" Mark, I assumed - "but as soon as she saw that picture, she couldn't even say goodbye to them."

"What about you? Did you think it was Carrie?"

Donald paused. "Jack, you have to understand that I barely knew the girl."

"But?" I prompted.

"But I'm not so sure that was her." He shifted uncomfortably in the answering silence, spreading the peanut butter round and round the second half of his bagel. "It could have been; I'm not saying it wasn't. But I'm not sure."

"Why?"

Donald gave me a lopsided grin. He had a speck of basil caught on one of his teeth. "You sound like your cop friends, Jack. And I can't give you any better reason than I gave them. I don't know why. I'm just not sure. And neither were most of the other people they asked. Kit's the only one who was positive it was Carrie."

I let the matter drop and said goodbye to Donald, who was casting longing glances at the Emerald Downs racing paper on the table next to us. On the walk back to my office, I thought over what he had said. Kit's tearful insistence that it was Carrie made me uneasy - and a little suspicious. Nobody looks the same in an autopsy picture as they do in life, especially after a ten-story plunge to the pavement. If Kit and Carrie had been in it together - if they had lured Melanie to the apartment and thrown her body off the balcony - Kit would be sure to stick to her story that it was Carrie in those photographs.

On the other hand, I chided myself, Kit was Carrie's best – maybe only - friend. Maybe her emotion was genuine; her certainty, heartfelt. I wanted to believe that. I really did. But there was something forced about it.

As the days passed without a break on the identification, the case shuffled to the back of my mind. There wasn't anything I could do to protect American Fidelity until the bodies were identified, and I had plenty of other work to keep me busy. We also had plenty of other things to worry about, most involving Harmony's biological father, Higuro Yamashita.

We no longer had to wonder why the press had been waiting for us at the airport and the Camlin. The Seattle media had been bursting with stories about Higuro's new scandal. Among his many other ventures, Higuro had recently purchased a Seattle-based sporting goods store that supplied tents, ropes, canteens, and crampons to the U.S. military. Or theoretically supplied them to the U.S. military. There had been a slight problem in the billings.

According to the stories - which all featured photos or footage of me and Harmony - Rockface, Inc., had been charging the government for shipments to military bases that no longer existed - and in one case, had never existed. One reporter who was particularly good at math led with the allegation that Rockface had billed the government for twice as many canteens as there were enlisted personnel.

David trolled his vast network of sources – reporters, clerks, bailiffs, cops, lawyers, looky-loos. Everyone agreed on one point: The prosecutor saw the case as a colossal opportunity. There was an open spot on the federal bench, and Todd Poehl – an intense, humorless Assistant U.S. Attorney with a small, soft body and a disproportionately large head – had picked the Rockface scandal to make his judicial career.

The Rockface indictment seemed open-and-shut: the company was clearly in the wrong. But Poehl wasn't going to be satisfied with a guilty plea from, and a Corporate Integrity Agreement with, a relatively small and much-loved local subsidiary. He wanted the huge parent company, Yamashita, Inc. More specifically, he wanted Higuro Yamashita himself. He wanted the headlines and prestige of prosecuting a formidable, international billionaire in the fusty old Western District of Washington.

Poehl had been thrashing around for months, David said. He'd been searching for evidence that Rockface was a mere instrumentality of Yamashita, Inc., so he could charge the parent company. He'd been searching for something - anything - that would link Higuro to the misbehavior at Rockface so he could indict Higuro personally.

Word on the street was he'd been unsuccessful - until now.

Poehl thought he'd found the missing link to Higuro.

It was Harmony.

CHAPTER 18

"**N**o offense, gentlemen, but I was hoping to be facing someone significantly more attractive this morning." Assistant U.S. Attorney Todd Poehl steepled his hands and tapped his fingertips together – a judicial gesture he no doubt practiced in the mirror. "Ms. Piper had a pressing social engagement?"

Harmony's presence had been cordially requested for an interview with the federal prosecutor. David Mann and I had checked in with the unsmiling woman behind the bullet-proof glass at the old Seafirst Building, passed our briefcases and ourselves through the metal detector, and clipped our numbered visitors badges on our jackets. It was like going to a tastefully understated prison.

It was feeling like a prison interview, too, sitting across from Todd and Special Agent Rich from the FBI. Sometimes, even with opposing counsel, there's a sense of collaboration, of working something out together.

Not today.

"No immunity; no Ms. Piper," David said.

"Come on," Todd said. "We confirmed that Harmony's not a target of the investigation – she may not even be a subject. Why would she need immunity?"

"Why would you be concerned about granting her immunity if she's not even a target – and *maybe* not even a subject? No immunity; no Ms. Piper. That's the bottom line."

This went on for a while. David was protecting Harmony against a possible Section 1001 charge. Next time you hear about someone being convicted of obstruction of justice for making false statements during a federal investigation, try telling the same story exactly the same way multiple times. Or even just twice. Chances are, you'll change something. It's just the way memory works. And it makes everyone – even the most honest person – vulnerable to a Section 1001 charge for obstruction by an over-zealous federal prosecutor.

So David had been painstakingly clear with us: Until he was satisfied with the immunity deal, he wasn't bringing Harmony anywhere near the old Seafirst Building. She was keeping the firm afloat while David and I scoped out what was going on.

"What's Harmony got to offer in exchange for immunity?" Todd asked. Finally, we had moved off the posturing.

"We have no idea why you want to talk to Ms. Piper, and we have no idea whether she can talk to you in the first place. Mr. Yamashita hasn't waived the privilege, so she can't divulge anything where she was legal counsel. Give us the high level of what you're looking at so we can start trying to get all these pieces together."

There was a lot more back and forth, but eventually Todd and Rich gave us the high-level outline of their case. They even showed us a few documents – one that worried me. A lot.

It looked like a memo that Harmony would have written. In fact, it probably *was* a memo that Harmony had written. Most of it sounded like her – a careful, precise summary of a wage and hour investigation she had done for Higuro at Rockface.

I remembered that wage and hour investigation. It was real. But there were three or four paragraphs in the memo that had nothing to do with wage and hour, and that I was sure Harmony didn't write. They had spelling errors and usage errors. Those paragraphs – and only those paragraphs – said that one of the witnesses had reported during the investigation that Rockface was defrauding the government. They said the witness – Hugo Bogaty, an offshore Finance analyst in Poland - had tried to talk to his supervisors in Poland and Seattle, but that they had shut him down. They said he had contacted The Seattle Times, the P-I, and the King, KOMO, and KIRO news stations for help in stopping the fraud. And they said he wanted Harmony to tell the company's new owner – Higuro – about the fraud so Higuro would take steps to put it right.

"Well, we've got their link to Higuro now," I said, as we debriefed afterwards over lunch at the Union Square Grill. We had called Harmony on the way over to the restaurant. She had stepped out of a mediation long enough to confirm that the memo itself was real, but the paragraphs on the fraud allegations were not.

David nodded. "And unless Higuro waives the privilege, it won't be that easy for Harmony to convince the grand jury that the memo's forged. They won't see the real memo or her investigation work papers. If all she can do is deny she received problematic allegations against Higuro, she won't look credible."

It was a sore spot. Higuro had dug in his heels at exactly the wrong time, on exactly the wrong issue. It was in his best interest to waive the privilege, to let Harmony – who was charm incarnate – demystify and personalize him for the grand jurors. It was in his best interest to launch a transparent and trustworthy investigation of the Rockface allegations, to show the prosecutor and the press that he was part of the solution, not part of the problem. But beset by investigations and increasingly suspicious, Higuro had done a total lockdown on all communications, including and especially privileged communications. Yamashita, Inc., was a fortress.

The waitress brought our lunches. David was recovering from a massive heart attack. He had ordered the crab Louie salad with no dressing – just crab and lettuce. We were in a steakhouse, and David was paying. I had ordered steak. And mashed potatoes.

"Enjoy your arteries while you can, Jack," David said, eyeing my plate. Like Carrie Mayer, David had dropped about fifty pounds really fast. Unlike Carrie Mayer, David was flaunting his new physique. He was wearing a beautifully tailored, close-cut black suit. From the neck down, he looked twenty years younger. Neck up – twenty years older. His eyes and cheeks were sunken, with deep grooves carved around his mouth.

I had been watching David a moment too long. He glared at me. "Let's see how good you look after someone cracks your ribs open and takes indecent liberties with your heart. It won't be long if you keep eating like that."

I was already apologizing when he shrugged. "I realize that I may have lost a bit of my *je ne sais quoi*." He tugged back his slumping cheeks. "Whoever said black doesn't crack never had a quadruple bypass. People who see me from behind or from a distance come up all excited and full of compliments because I've dropped so much weight. And then they take one look at my face and say, 'Was it . . . um . . . *intentional?*' But even after I tell them about the heart attack, they all tell me how great it is that I've lost weight, like I should be marketing a massive coronary as a trick to go down a pant size. It's nuts. *And Jack, will you get those damned potatoes out of my sight.*"

It was not a request. It was an order. I asked for a to-go box.

Offending potatoes under wraps, David refocused. "I need you to start preparing Harmony for the conditions Todd Poehl will put on any immunity deal. He only gives something if he gets something. He'll want her to testify that Bogaty 'may have' reported those fraud complaints to her, and that if he did, that she 'would have' told Higuro about them."

I thought that over. Legally, it was a good strategy. It would let Poehl preserve the credibility of all his witnesses and his evidence against Higuro. There was just one small problem.

"But that's not true."

"If she had received the fraud complaints, Harmony would have told Higuro." David didn't look at me.

"But she didn't receive any complaints about the fraud, David. I've talked to her about this investigation. No one would tell her anything, not even about the basic wage and hour issue she was investigating. Higuro had just acquired Rockface. Everyone was afraid for their jobs. Even the offshore billing and Finance people in Poland just gave her a bunch of excuses – not my fault, just following orders, blah, blah, blah. She had to reconstruct everyone's pay history and timecards through the paper trail. She's not going to lie and say that Bogaty might have reported fraud allegations to her when she knows he didn't."

"It's not lying - exactly," David protested. "She could have forgotten about it. Or if it was very upsetting to her, she could have blocked it out."

"Being told your dad's new company is defrauding the government isn't the sort of thing that just slips someone's mind. Especially not someone like Harmony. She's not going to lie, David."

He groaned rubbed his temples. "Higuro is in deep shit, Jack. There's going to be an indictment of Rockface, and since Higuro is kind of a - oh, let's say, *high-directive* boss - everyone still at Rockface is pointing fingers at him and his company for anything that occurred there since the takeover. Realistically, CEOs get indicted when there's evidence that they knew about the fraud and didn't do anything about it. So unfortunately, that puts Harmony and that memo right in the crosshairs: They're the link between the allegations and Higuro. Harmony needs to get as far away from this as she possibly can."

I didn't answer. He wasn't wrong. But Harmony wouldn't go for it.

"Just work on her. I will too. Higuro may not be someone to go to the stake for. His lawyers don't return my calls. Even before he lawyered up - and then his lawyers lawyered up, and then I was dealing with all of Martindale-Hubbell - Higuro never even asked me about Harmony. He's certainly not going out of his way to help her. She needs to think of herself, not him."

We walked out of the restaurant in silence. As I turned to head back under the Convention Center, David stopped me. He slipped two tickets into my breast pocket.

"Jack, you two need a break. Bring Harmony to the CareForKids auction tonight."

David knew that Harmony did not like charity auctions. As I started to shake my head, he said, "Take it from the guy with the quadruple bypass. You've got to give yourself some mental space. And I guarantee you: This will be just the thing to take your minds off Yamashita, Inc."

He had no idea how right he was.

CHAPTER 19

Sequins and cleavage glittered and heaved against a sea of identically penguin-suited men. The air was thick with chatter and alcohol. A lockjaw blonde wearing a blue satin "Chairperson" sash clamped a proprietary hand on Mark's arm and led him away - apparently to be catalogued with the rest of the merchandise. He nodded at Harmony over his shoulder before he disappeared into the crowd.

Harmony had agreed to attend the auction when she learned that Mark and Anthony would also be there. Ever since the press had gotten a good look at Mark the year before, the police chief had been donating ride-alongs with Mark and Anthony to charity auctions. Anthony told Mark it fell under the part of the job description called "other duties as assigned."

It was not Mark's favorite thing to do. Rich women got handsy when they had plunked down ten grand, but the chief had warned Mark about giving offense to big donors. So since we were all going to be at CareForKids anyway, Harmony had offered to help.

The two of them had worked out their system on the way downtown. Harmony would stand just to the side of the dais during the auction - paddle at the ready. If Mark wanted her to rescue him from the highest bidder on their ride-along, he would turn and look right at her on the "going once." Sometimes it's darn useful to live with an heiress.

Waiters plied us with tray after tray of appetizers: salmon mousse in pea pods, icy raw oysters, crab cakes baked on silver spoons. A gaggle of women clustered around the bar, stirring their drinks with their fingers and giggling.

"Diamond cocktails," Harmony whispered. "There's a real gemstone in one of them, and they're probably charging a couple hundred dollars a glass. It's a way of raising a lot of money and making sure everyone's blitzed before the bidding begins."

It sounded like a potential lawsuit to me. *Socialite chokes on diamond-doctored drink.* Being a lawyer changes you. It really does. Everyone else sees a party, and all you see is a tort.

I got us sodas from the bar. No diamond danger there. Harmony and I wandered around the ballroom, admiring the blown-glass Chihulys that were the centerpiece of the charity auction. Wearing his trademark eyepatch and paint-spattered sneakers, Chihuly himself held court between a constellation of shimmering blue-green shells and a chandelier that belonged in a bordello – pendulous, nippled balloons of blown glass, softly lit from within. I wondered who would buy such a thing.

David, apparently. He had his arm around Chihuly and was admiring the suggestive chandelier. If David did end up with it, I predicted that his wife would make him hang it in the basement - casting its pale pink, salacious glow over his rowing machine, his big-screen TV, and everything else that clashed with her beige and blond decor.

Harmony and I said hello to Gretta Berg from Children First, who seemed nervous but hopeful about the auction. The school got half its budget from the CareForKids donations and bids, she said. I suspected that Harmony made up a lot of the other half. The directors of every one of the ten charities represented seemed to know Harmony - or want to. They shook her hands, kissed her cheeks - did everything but reach into her purse.

I put my arm around her. We avoided the glad-handers and television cameras and slipped around the perimeter of the room, taking in the items up for bid: an American Quarter Horse; a yacht named "Decompression"; Home Plate Suite tickets and sushi with Ichiro; oysters from "a secret inlet in the San Juans"; an original Tom Robbins manuscript; studio time to record your own album at Orbit; a ruby bracelet that allegedly belonged to Mother Damnable, who ran Seattle's first brothel/courthouse, and who could swear in six languages; a Guy Anderson painting; organic produce delivered weekly from P-Patch community gardens ("actually, that's a good idea," Harmony said, circling the lot number); and a vasectomy. The minimum bid for the vasectomy was $250 - "anesthesia not included."

I edged away from the doctor offering the vasectomy - right into a magnificent, pure-white German shepherd. It was Snow, the SPD's new drug-sniffing dog. She was sitting straight and proud next to her partner, waiting for the bidding on the K-9 ride-along. I introduced myself to the dog, then to the cop - who laughed as he shook my hand.

"I figured you must be Jack," he said, nodding to Snow, who was leaning against me and furiously wagging her tail. "Oden told me you and Snow would hit it off. Believe it or not, she's usually pretty shy."

Snow took that as a cue to stand up and lick my face. What the hell. The tux was a rental, and the lights were low.

"Where's Mark?" Harmony asked the officer.

"Her royal highness sent Mark and Anthony home to change," he said, nodding toward the blonde in the sash, who had draped herself all over Dale Chihuly.

"Why?"

"She wanted them in dress uniform. Thought they'd fetch a higher price. They're not actually supposed to wear dress uniform except for ceremonial occasions, but the mayor backed her up. So they're off putting on the epaulets. They'll be a while."

We were moving toward a table to wait out Mark's return when someone hailed Harmony from across the room. The blonde with the sash was bearing down on us.

"Harmony Sweetie-Pie Piper!" she squealed, air-kissing her in the general vicinity of both cheeks. "Don't you look splendid!"

The blonde was clearly waiting for a return compliment, which Harmony delivered with all indicia of sincerity: "I love your sash." She let the blonde blink at her uncertainly for a moment, then went to her rescue: "You've worked so hard on this evening, Didi. You put so much of yourself into it. You must be so proud of how beautifully it's going."

Didi beamed. Suddenly, we were bosom friends. Not only did she give us both a real hug, but she paraded us around the ballroom, showing off Harmony. She also introduced me to her husband, Chuck - a bluff, rangy man with a crushing grip - who turned out to be the CEO of Puget Health Partners. I was trying to think of an adroit way to bring up Carrie Mayer when someone sidled up and whispered in Didi's ear. Before I knew exactly what was happening, she was spiriting Harmony toward an excited group of women just outside the door. Someone was showing off her engagement ring.

The CEO had disappeared. I was torn between trying to find him and trying to keep tabs on Harmony. The auction was starting, and I couldn't see her any more. As the crowd thronged the dais, I found myself suspended in a sea of rich people, unable to move. Harmony was just going to have to find me.

"Now, here we have a sharp little item," began the auctioneer. "It's sweet revenge for those ladies whose husbands bought them the boob jobs at last year's CareForKids. For the man who has everything, the gift that stops the giving, the ideal Father's Day present - a vasectomy!"

Dead silence.

I listened with half an ear while the auctioneer whipped up the bids for the vasectomy. "$500?" he said at one point. "You ladies can't come up with more than five hundred measly dollars? Don't get me wrong; we'll do it for that, but I'll have to use my 9-iron."

The vasectomy finally went for $1,700. The crowd was starting to warm up. The oysters - a dozen a month for six months - brought in $3,400. The summer produce - which I had considered buying for Harmony - finally closed at an even $5,000.

Five-thousand dollars for carrots? I stuck my paddle through my cummerbund, to prevent any twitches that might be misinterpreted as a bid. This was definitely not my scene. I looked around the ballroom, at the liquor flowing in and the money flowing out, like osmosis. I had spent ten years in foster care. I could have been the poster kid for any one of these children's charities. I couldn't have conceived of a scene like this when I was in foster care - the plumage, the preening, the grave waiters pressing oysters and martinis on giddy, anorectic women and haughty, impatient men. I still could barely get my mind around it, even while I was looking right at it.

I knew what it was like to be poor. I knew what it was like to be cold. I knew what it was like to eat nothing but macaroni and cheese and then to eat nothing at all. I couldn't reconcile the two worlds in my head. It didn't seem possible that the grim subsistence I had grubbed out as a ward of the state had been funded in part by the largess of a bunch of similarly self-satisfied nincompoops, all brandishing their cash like a peacock's tail. They must have had charity bashes like this when I was a kid. So why hadn't I ever seen any of this alleged charity money? I totted up the take so far - already pushing a hundred grand, and the night was very, very young. Where did all this money go?

A stir on the stage snapped me out of my reverie. The auctioneer had his arm around a little girl, who was standing next to a red wagon heaped with stuffed animals. "So why are you donating your Beanie Babies to the CareForKids auction, honey?" the auctioneer asked, thrusting the microphone in front of her.

The little girl shied away from the mike, then rallied and spoke in a small, firm voice. "Because my friend has leukemia, and I want the hospital to find a cure to make her better."

An audible "ah" rose from the crowd.

"Is your friend here tonight?" At the child's nod, the auctioneer walked to the edge of the dais and helped another little girl climb the stairs to the stage. She was bald and beanpole thin. She went to her friend and took her hand. They shuffled together, uneasy under the spotlight, the only children at an event ostensibly devoted to Seattle's kids.

Harmony. Where was Harmony? At the only other charity auction I knew Harmony had attended, she had paid an outrageous sum for a puppy just so she could give him back to the little boy who led him out on stage. She would not stand by while a little girl made a bigger sacrifice than anyone else in the whole damn place. She would buy those stuffed animals and return them to their rightful owner. At least, she would if she were in the room.

I could not get through the crush of the crowd. Craning my neck, I could just make out a cluster of women outside the door. Harmony was standing at the far side of the cluster - well out of earshot of the ballroom. I couldn't call to her. I couldn't wave to her. She wouldn't hear a thing about the bidding for the Beanies until it was too late.

The auctioneer was gearing up for the bidding, touting the quality and completeness of the collection. I took one look at those little kids clinging to each other in the glare of the spotlight and decided that if Harmony wasn't going to be able to do it, I would.

I was going to buy those stuffed animals for that little girl.

After all, I thought, how much can a bunch of Beanie Babies cost?

CHAPTER 20

The opening bid was half the payment on my house. I was sure I must have misheard - until the next bid topped it by five hundred dollars. After that, the bids came fast and furious. Women pressed toward the stage, paddles fluttering like fans. The auctioneer's patter distilled into unintelligible adrenaline, pushing the crowd into all-out war.

My paddle was still firmly wedged in my cummerbund. There was no way I could scrape up the sums that were being bandied about. I had a sizeable mortgage; I was trying to get my own firm off the ground. My dad had left me some property in Bellingham, but I didn't want to sell, and the taxes threatened to pull me under.

"Going once," said the auctioneer.

The little girl flinched. I twitched my paddle up, and the bidding was off again. I stared at the paddle in horror. As the bids raced upwards, I almost dropped the damn thing in sheer surprise.

Finally there was a pause. I steeled myself against the sight of the two little girls, so small up on that stage. *It's not my money; it's our money*, Harmony always said, but we weren't even married yet. I had accepted gifts from her - sometimes lavish gifts - but I had never spent a penny of her inheritance. And I wasn't going to start by paying the equivalent of the gross national product of a small Latin American country for a bunch of beans and thread and felt.

"Going once," the auctioneer said again.

The little girls shuffled their feet. I was sweating, and it had nothing to do with the heat and crush of the room. It was obscene. The whole thing was obscene. That little girl thought she could save her friend by giving up her stuffed animals. You could see it in her sober, expectant face, the way she clutched the other kid's hand. No child should have to lose what those kids were losing: their toys, their hair, their health, their friends. There was just altogether too much sacrifice up there on that stage.

"Going twice."

I shut my eyes and brandished my paddle. Somehow, it was easier that way. I held my breath in the silence that answered the auctioneer's *going once . . . going twice.* Then the word that I was simultaneously hoping for and dreading - *sold!* - and the auctioneer was off on something else. I could pick up my Beanies at the end of the evening.

I was queasy with relief, excitement, and anxiety. I was not quite myself. "Did you get those for your daughter?" the tight-faced matron next to me asked with a cold smile.

"They are all for me," I replied reprovingly, before I could control my tongue. She edged away.

The auction was clipping along. There went Mother Damnable's ruby bracelet; there went the Quarter Horse; there - unfortunately - went the ride-along with Snow. Having seen the trouble it could cause, I decided not to touch my bidding paddle for the rest of the night. The compression of the crowd gradually pushed me to the fringes of the room. I caught glimpses of Harmony down by the stage, poised for Mark and Anthony's big moment, but I couldn't get to her. I just sipped my watery Coke and waited for it all to be over.

When Anthony stepped onto the stage, you would have thought the Beatles had entered the Ed Sullivan Theater. The spotlight caught the gold braid and brass buttons on his dress uniform, and all the women in the ballroom - debutantes to dowagers - sighed. Then they realized Mark was right behind him, and they started screaming. And whistling. And jumping up and down. When Mark and Anthony removed their caps and tucked them under their arms, the shrieks were piercing. They snapped into parade rest, and the bidding began.

"These gentlemen are officers, ladies," boomed the auctioneer. "The cream of the Seattle Police Department. For a modest donation, you can spend eight full hours watching these detectives - going to crime scenes, interviewing witnesses . . . checking out the handcuffs." Squeals from the women in the audience.

"If you stumble over a body together, the detectives will help you up." Oooohs. "If you faint, they're highly skilled in mouth-to-mouth." Absolute hysteria.

An elf-like old lady wearing a bright purple dress finally bought the ride-along for $18,000. She pumped her scrawny arms in the air and shouted, "yes, yes, yes." Mark never looked over at Harmony; she didn't try to top the winning bid. I guessed he figured that if he and Anthony couldn't fend off an 80-pound, octogenarian admirer - when they were armed with Glocks, pepper spray, nightsticks, and a 20-gauge shotgun - they really didn't deserve to be policemen.

The crowd around the stage was still too thick for me to fight my way through to Harmony. Mark and Anthony had disappeared. As the auction shifted into the big-money items, the air of riotous frivolity hardened into steely-eyed resolve. Up to this point, it had been mainly a ladies' game. Now the men were bidding on boats, cars, sports, and booze. They did not like to lose. I retreated farther and farther from the stage, got myself another Coke at the bar, and sat and watched the spectacle with a sort of morbid fascination.

I finished my soda and crunched a nugget of remaining ice. At least, I thought it was ice. I bit down, and suddenly my tooth exploded. The pop reverberated throughout my body. I grabbed a napkin and spat out shards of shattered enamel - and a blood-smeared diamond. In the soft light of the ballroom, it glittered red like a monstrous, reptilian eye.

Well, this was just peachy. I packed the napkin into my mouth to stop the bleeding. At least now I would be able to afford the Beanies. If the diamond didn't cover them, the lawsuit sure as hell would.

The napkin was not helping. Probing tentatively with my tongue, I realized that the diamond had not only crushed my molar but slashed my gums. I headed for the door to find a bathroom.

Framed in the magnificent entrance to the Spanish Ballroom, Chairperson Didi and her CEO spouse were having an intense conversation with two men in dark suits. I slowed as I approached them. Didi's husband was stabbing his index finger into the chest of the larger man, while Didi - sash slipping a bit on her shoulder - desperately tried to quiet him. I couldn't make out his words, but I could hear the spitting sounds of vicious whispers. One of the dark-suited men turned slightly toward me, and I recognized him from my periodic visits to the police station. He was a detective, like Mark and Anthony, although I didn't know which squad he worked.

I have a tendency to wander into trouble. Sometimes I know what I'm getting into - most often I don't - but even I could tell this was not a scene I should interrupt. Unfortunately, given all the auction exhibits arrayed around the room, there was only one available exit. As I paused, wondering if I could swallow all the blood that was gushing into my mouth, Didi caught a glimpse of me and stretched out her hand. It was a beseeching gesture, jarringly at odds with the peremptory waves, beckons, points, and tugs with which she had ruled the evening. Still immaculate in her long cream dress, she looked shrunken and scared. If you had torn off her sash, stomped on it, and thrown it in her face, I didn't think you could have wreaked such a transformation.

"Jack, you're a lawyer," she pleaded when I reached her. *"Do something."*

She couldn't have chosen a worse introduction. Attorneys are not popular with the boys in blue. I set about trying to repair the damage.

"Jack Hart," I said, shaking hands. "Mark Oden's roommate."

A flicker of recognition crossed their faces. "What happened to your mouth, Jack?" asked the detective I had seen before.

"Uh, rough crowd," I said, biting back the blood. "What's going on here?"

The detectives just exchanged glances, but Didi couldn't contain herself.

"They say we have to come to the police station with them," she said, taking my arm in her pincer-like grasp.

Then tears flooded her eyes, and I almost turned away as she crumpled into sobs.

"They say Chuck molested a little girl at Children First."

CHAPTER 21

An SUV honked and swerved around us. In Ballard, no less.
Long known for poking along with their left turn signals on and their seat
belts shut in their doors, now Ballard drivers were just like the rest of the
gas-guzzling speed freaks crowding the streets of Seattle. The SUV driver paused
long enough from his cellphone conversation to give us the finger as he roared off
down Market Street. Seattle used to be a city of lovable losers. Now it's a bunch of
pissed-off people who didn't quite win.

I looped back to retrace our route. We were searching for the house of the
Beanies' rightful owner, and we were having no luck at all. Beside me, Harmony
reached back into the enormous box.

"They're sure cute," she said, holding up a velvety black puppy. "Such sweet
faces."

"Wish we were keeping them after all?"

"Oh, no. I'm glad you bought them for the little girl. Besides, I don't want any
souvenirs of last night."

I was with her there. After Didi dropped her bombshell, I very nearly turned on
my heel and strode away. Only the slim possibility that her husband was innocent
kept me from washing my hands of them right then.

Instead, I swallowed hard, told Didi that I wasn't qualified to advise her on a
criminal matter, and went to pry David away from Dale Chihuly. Just as I reached
the sculptor and his throngs of admirers, an auction staffer decided to present me
with my mammoth box of stuffed animals.

David had looked me over - the blood trickling from the corner of my mouth, the
Beanie Babies in my arms, the dog hair all over my tux - and said, almost sadly,
"Jack, I cannot take you anywhere."

I had introduced David to his new clients and sought out Mark and Anthony -
also thronged with admirers - with the scoop. It was a hell of a motive for Carrie's

murder. Chuck was Carrie's CEO; he had started the Halloween parties in the Medicare unit; he had chaired Children First's board of directors for years. If a kid at Children First told Carrie she was being molested - or if Carrie even suspected it - Chuck might well have killed Carrie to keep her quiet. Who knows what he might have done to silence the kid. Mark and Anthony had set off to follow the new lead. We hadn't seen Mark since.

"There it is," Harmony said, pointing up a narrow street overhung with trees. We parked and threaded our way through a comfortably overgrown garden to a royal blue door.

A brown-haired woman with a long, dancer's body opened it before we knocked. "Hannah's in there," she said, nodding toward the front room. "Like I said on the phone, it's up to her."

We had called Hannah's mother to make sure it was all right to return the Beanies. We didn't want her to be uncomfortable or think that her sacrifice had been rejected. Her mother had said, "Only Hannah can tell you how she'll feel about it. Why don't you stop by for breakfast and ask her yourselves?" So after my early-morning date with the dentist, Harmony and I had headed out to Megan and Hannah Swenson's house in Ballard.

"Honey?" Megan reached over and switched off the Saturday morning cartoons. "This is Mr. Hart and Miss Piper. They're the folks who bought your Beanies at the auction last night."

Hannah clambered up from the floor. "Is something wrong with them?"

"No, no. They're wonderful. Really cute. But the thing is -" I paused. When I was in the midst of my bidding frenzy the night before, returning the Beanies had seemed like the easy part. But now that it came down to it, I wasn't sure what to say. Hannah was a miniature version of her mom, with serious brown eyes. She deserved total honesty. So I sat down on the couch and tried again.

"I bought your stuffed animals because I wanted to give them back to you. I'm sure you gave this a lot of thought, and I respect what you did to try to help your friend. But if you feel OK about it, I would very much like you to have your Beanies back. You obviously love them, and I don't think anyone else would care about them the way you do."

Hannah's face was anxious. "Does that mean you won't give all that money to Children's Hospital?"

"Absolutely not. They'll still get every penny."

"And it won't make it any less likely that your friend will get better," Harmony put in.

Hannah considered for a moment. "Then I think I would feel OK about taking them back," she said. She extended a small hand. "Thank you."

"You're welcome." We shook hands gravely, then she suddenly surged at me and wrapped her arms around my neck.

"Thankyouthankyouthankyou," she said, hopping up and down. Her face shone. "Where are they?"

I carried the box in from the hall, while Hannah bobbed around me, chattering at top speed, hoisting toys out of the box by the scruffs of their necks and rattling off their names and birthdates. Her favorites were Pugsly the pug and Prickles the hedgehog. And of course, her Princess Diana bear. Did I want to play with her Princess bear?

Indeed I did. I held the purple teddy while Hannah lectured me about her toys and Harmony helped Megan set the table. In deference to my temporary crown, breakfast was toast, scrambled eggs, and bowls of tiny strawberries that smelled like roses. Harmony and I both looked up in surprise at the first spoonful.

"Wild strawberries," Megan explained, with a pleased blush. "*Fragaria vesca*. From our garden."

"You have wild strawberries growing in your garden?"

"We have wild *everything* growing in our garden," Hannah announced proudly.

It turned out that Megan's grandfather was Snoose "Wildman" Nelson, an immigrant naturalist who had roamed the woods and mountains around Seattle. "He picked up wild seeds and cuttings and planted them around the house," Megan said. "It wasn't illegal back then." She pushed aside the curtains, revealing a densely green backyard.

Harmony squeezed my hand. In his spare time, Mark was a self-taught botanist and landscaper who had mentioned Snoose Nelson's name. I was sure he had no idea that Snoose's experimental nursery survived in the heart of Ballard. I was equally sure he had no idea that Snoose's granddaughter was extremely pretty. I looked around for evidence of a male presence. Nothing obvious. The TV in their front room was tiny. But they might have a basement.

Harmony was going the more direct route: asking. "Megan, our housemate loves plants. He'd be fascinated by your garden. Would you mind if he came over sometime?"

"Not at all. I love to show it off. Just tell him to give me a call."

Good job, Harmony - and she wasn't done. "So how long have you lived in Ballard?" she asked Megan, beginning to clear the table.

"Three generations strong. Granddad was born in Sweden, but he came to America when he was ten. He and my father built this house."

"Do you remember Mayer's Meats down on Market Street?"

"Of course. The Mayers lived on the corner, where that big apartment building is now. Carrie Mayer and I used to play together. We'd take my cocker spaniel on walks to the butcher shop, and Mr. Mayer would always give Sophie a hotdog to take home. He'd wrap it up in white paper and tie it with string, and she'd strut along with it in her mouth - just so proud." She laughed a little at the memory. "How do you know the Mayers?"

Harmony drew Hannah aside with a request to meet her cat, and I picked up the last dishes from the table and nodded Megan into the kitchen. I waited until she had set down the plates before I answered her question. There wasn't any gentle way to do it. I explained about the insurance policy, the apparent suicide, the confusion over the identification.

"I can't believe it," Megan said. "I can't believe I didn't know. I read about Carrie's mother in the newspaper, but I didn't see an obituary for Carrie."

"Did you know her well?"

"Not really. Not anymore. We were friends in elementary school. I mean, she just lived down the block, and we were the same age. But after that, we didn't spend much time together. We liked different things, had different friends. I haven't seen her since we graduated from high school."

"You didn't go to her mom's funeral?"

She shook her head. "Couldn't get off work."

"Did Carrie or Melanie ever get hurt? Break an arm or leg?"

"I don't think so. Why?"

I explained about trying to identify the bodies from old fractures. Megan swallowed hard. She couldn't think of anyone who was close to Carrie and Melanie Mayer, she said. She was willing to look at Carrie's autopsy pictures if she had to, but she hadn't seen her for fifteen years. She didn't think she could identify her. I was about to change the subject when she started up.

"I probably have some old pictures with me and Carrie in them," she said. "Would those help?"

I assured her they would, and she set off to look for them. Hannah and Harmony were hand-in-hand out in the garden. Hannah had her cat slung over one shoulder like a stole.

Megan glided back into the kitchen. She couldn't find her high school yearbooks, but she had found a tattered brown album. She paged through the stiff, crackling sheets.

"Here it is," she said finally, extracting an orangey Polaroid from beneath the cellophane. "This is one of me and Carrie. We're probably about seven."

I blinked at the picture. It was easy to identify Megan. She looked just like her daughter. But things were not adding up with Carrie.

"Um, isn't this Melanie?" I asked, holding it out to Megan.

"No, that's Carrie all right," Megan said, handing it back. "That's me, that's Carrie, and that's my dog Sophie. We're playing in Carrie's backyard."

I sat down at the kitchen table and stared at the picture. Carrie Mayer had been a beautiful little girl, all dimples, bright hair, and a melting, sidelong smile. She had her head on one side and was holding Sophie up to the camera, waving with her paw.

It wasn't just Carrie's beauty that surprised me.

It was her familiarity.

I had seen that deeply dimpled face before - and not in the autopsy photographs. I had seen that face alive, across from me in my conference room, crying carefully and tastefully as I asked question after question about the alleged accidental death of the late, unlamented Carrie Mayer.

I looked at that snapshot and felt sure of it.

Carrie had passed herself off as her sister.

That meant the woman in the autopsy photographs was Melanie Mayer.

CHAPTER 22

I was convinced of it until we got back home to Green Lake. School photographs littered my coffee table. Mark was asleep on the couch, a Ballard High School yearbook open over his chest. He was still in his dress uniform.

Harmony fetched the comforter from her bed. I was trying to maneuver the yearbook from Mark's hands so she could cover him up when he suddenly grabbed the book and started up with a warning shout. We all needed to get more sleep.

To the degree he could, Mark filled us in on the allegations that Didi's husband had molested a little girl. The police had received an anonymous letter the afternoon of the CareForKids charity auction. The writer claimed to be the father of a little girl who had gone to the homeless school at Children First. Three times, the letter said, Chuck Thomas had touched the child. The little girl had finally told her father. The writer said he had taken his daughter away from Seattle because he was afraid that someone with Chuck's wealth and influence could have his parental rights terminated - leaving the child vulnerable to foster care or even adoption by the Thomases. The letter closed with threats so specific and vitriolic that the police worried the father might be planning violent revenge at the CareForKids auction that night.

That was one of the reasons why the police had shown up at the Olympic Hotel instead of going quietly to Chuck and Didi's house the next morning. The other reason, of course, was to put as much pressure as possible on Chuck, in hopes that he would crack and confess from fear and humiliation.

"So do you think he's guilty?" Harmony asked.

Mark paused. "Well, he was such an asshole to us last night that all the cops are hoping he's guilty," he said. "And they're trying to think of a reason to lock up Didi, too."

"But?"

"But there's something hinky about the letter. The tone's right, the background facts are right, but it's way more explicit than you'd expect from a pissed-off dad.

Most parents can't even talk about someone abusing their kid. They go right to the bottom line: *I'm gonna kill him.* This one goes on forever. It doesn't necessarily mean it's a fake; the dad could just have been afraid we wouldn't take an anonymous letter seriously. But it's hard to picture a dad - especially a dad as mad as this one claims to be - writing down every graphic detail about what happened to his daughter. It just smells wrong."

"What's Chuck's story?"

"Flat denial. He doesn't have an alibi for the specific dates in the letter. He doesn't have an alibi for the night Carrie Mayer - or whoever it was - was thrown over her balcony. You know, that's another thing that's weird. Chuck actually held up pretty well during questioning about the little girl. But when we threw Carrie into the mix, he started losing it. Of course, it was really late by then - we'd been at him five or six hours - but still."

I was incredulous. "David let you question him for six hours in the middle of the night?"

"Not David. Between the hotel and the police station, Chuck and Didi decided to switch attorneys."

"They dumped David?" It was inconceivable. "Why?"

Mark threw me a sardonic look. "Why do you think?"

A racist *and* an alleged child molester. What an unbeatable combination. "Is David OK?"

"He's fine. He said, 'Have at them, boys.' Then he went back to the party. It was Palmer Worthen who got to sweat it out with us all night. And Palmer's, well, you know."

We knew. Palmer was the attorney rich people called to resolve relatively minor but embarrassing offenses, like drug possession and no-injury DUIs. He had been best man in the mayor's third wedding, and he was rumored to play an excellent game of golf, which meant he always lost to the most important person in the foursome. He was the wrong guy for a serious crime.

"What happens now?"

"We try to identify the alleged victim. From the description in the letter, you'd think it would be easy, right? Just find out which kids don't come to school anymore, track them down, and figure out why. But this is a school for homeless kids. It's not like any of them stick around for long. Gretta Berg said we're talking thirty or forty little girls. And she has no idea where they've gone."

"How's Gretta taking this?" Harmony asked.

"Rough," Mark said. "She thought she was making a safe place for the kids. And maybe she did - but she admitted that Chuck Thomas dropped in *a lot*."

Betsy strolled in from the kitchen, making a conspicuous show of ignoring me. She had been giving me the cold shoulder since I had come home the night before smelling of Snow. She had bounded toward me - then stopped dead when she smelled the other dog on my hands and tux. I tried to reassure her - *it was just a casual pat; it meant nothing to me* - but she had turned with an injured sniff and stalked away. We'd see if she could hold out the sulk until dinner time.

"Tell us about all these pictures," Harmony said.

Mark walked us through the school portraits. Detective Ed Perez had been busy collecting every available picture of the two sisters, pestering the Department of Motor Vehicles and poring through the archives of photo studios that had contracted with Carrie's schools. I added the snapshot Megan had given us to the collage.

Growing up, Carrie and Melanie both had the same sweet, dimpled faces and bright hair. Around fifth grade, Carrie got glasses - the thick, distorting kind used for lazy eye. Then she got braces. And then she started gaining weight. Each year, her face seemed more and more out of focus as the added fat blurred her features. Her senior yearbook photo looked just like the picture on her Puget Health ID badge: a flat, round face with dots for eyes. I would not have believed the transformation if it hadn't been spread out so clinically before me.

Melanie, on the other hand, got prettier in every school portrait, especially as she filled out and made up. By her senior year, she was a ready-made Seafair queen, with huge blue-gray eyes and hair the color of melted butter. Her stated weight on her driver's licenses never varied, but if her Arizona DMV photos could be believed, Melanie had packed on a few pounds when she reached her thirties. She still looked like a beauty queen, but one who had let herself go a bit. I squinted at the grainy image of the last photo - already three years old. I don't know why the Department of Motor Vehicles even bothers taking ID pictures. It could have been the woman I deposed. Or not.

I rubbed my temples in frustration. I had been so sure when I saw Carrie's childhood face, so hauntingly like the adult Melanie I had met. Now I was back at the beginning. I still didn't know who I had deposed. It could have been Carrie, who had dieted down to her sister's weight to pose as the beneficiary of her own death benefit. Or it could have been Melanie, come to collect the blood money on her little sister. And we still didn't know who had gone over that railing.

"Any other leads on the identification of the body?" Harmony asked.

"Nothing solid. Gretta Berg was sure the woman in the autopsy photographs was Carrie. She seems to have a good eye, but it's not something we can bank on. We don't have any forensic comparisons. Since Carrie's sister identified her body, the ME didn't keep DNA or blood samples or take dental impressions or X-rays. Ed's called Melanie's attorney about ten times - even stopped by his house - but we can't even get him to return our calls, and Ed can't catch him home. It's maddening."

We were silent a moment, considering the problem. Betsy was curled next to Harmony, sniffing her hands and growling a little at the imagined cat that had dared to attach itself to her mommy. Her nose roamed over Harmony's hands like a palm reader, identifying the cat, the breakfast, the kid, the garden - everything we had experienced since we left her that morning. Dogs are amazing critters.

"What about using one of your sniffer dogs?" I asked Mark. "You've got one body. Give one of your trackers that scent and see if he picks out anything that belonged to Carrie. It wouldn't be dispositive, but it's hard to fool a dog."

Mark looked up. "Not a bad idea," he allowed. "But what have we got with Carrie's scent?"

"We've got her aebleskiver pan and her books. And Mr. Sandstrom still has her heater and her kitchen stuff. Did anything else survive the fire at Melanie's place? The Mayer's Meats picture? Her typewriter?"

Mark shook his head. "Her books might do it if she'd read them recently, but it's been months. Her car, definitely, but there was no vehicle at Melanie's house. We've got a BOLO out in case it's stolen. There's no title transfer record, but since she'd only had it a few months, she might have sold it recently and just not gotten around to filing it yet. Her typewriter was upstairs; it's fine. But that stuff wouldn't carry a scent. You'd really need something she'd worn."

Mr. Sandstrom said he'd sold Carrie's clothes to a Capitol Hill consignment shop for "big gals." If the store took them on consignment, they might still be around. Even if they'd washed them, a dog might be able to pick up a scent, especially if we put them with the books. It was worth a shot.

Harmony found the store in the phone book while Mark changed clothes. On the way over, we filled him in about our trip to Ballard. Harmony told Mark that Megan and Carrie had been childhood friends, that Megan was willing to look at the autopsy photographs, and that Megan was the granddaughter of Snoose Nelson. She told him just enough about the garden to get him interested. And then she changed the subject, but not before Mark asked her for Megan's number.

Up on Capitol Hill, we circled the block three times before we spotted the address. The sagging, tarnished numbers were wedged in a crevice between a bar and a tattoo parlor. We parked and inspected the literal hole in the wall. The alley between the buildings yawned alarmingly into a steep flight of rough, creosote-soaked stairs. Black walls shot three stories on either side of the staircase, which seemed to narrow as we descended. With every step, I felt increasingly vulnerable and furtive. There was no daylight visible at the bottom. At some point, it seemed, we were simply going to step off into nothingness.

Suddenly, there it was, alongside us. The steps kept going, but to our left, set back from the staircase on a little landing, was a bright pink door flickering in the weak glow from a single, dangling bulb. An enormous red lip-print splashed all over the bottom, while the top was swathed in six-inch, swirling letters: *Hello, Gorgeous.*

Inside, I blinked in the rush of light and space. The room unfurled before us: orderly rows of clothes, groupings of mannequins, shelf after shelf of shoes, and an immaculate cosmetics counter complete with a tall, white-coated *artiste* surrounded by brushes. On first glance, it looked like any high-class department store. It took me a minute to realize that the ladies' shoes seemed unusually large. It took me a little longer to absorb the significance of the unusually extensive wig display, the black and white diva shots surrounding the cosmetics counter - Garbo, Garland, Minnelli, Monroe - and the giant-size poster of RuPaul touting MAC Cosmetics: "All ages. All races. All sexes. All MAC."

How Mr. Sandstrom mistook this place for a consignment shop for "big gals" was beyond me.

"Hello, Gorgeous!"

A white-coated person wearing high heels and a curly blond confection that would have made Dolly Parton proud swept up to Harmony. He – or, I guess, she – pulled Harmony into an embrace and kissed her soundly on both cheeks.

"I'm Tonie! Sedrique is doing free makeovers this whole weekend. A new summer palette would just brighten you right up. Or are we looking for something for your gorgeous friends? All our shoes and clothes are marked with both women's and men's sizes, so if someone is transitioning, the new measurements can be a natural progression. So tell me, what can Hello, Gorgeous do to make you three even more beautiful today?"

Mark drew his badge.

"Seattle Police Department."

Tonie's welcome came to an abrupt halt.

"We're not doing anything illegal here," she snapped. "This is a completely legitimate business. The hairstylist, masseuse, and manicurist are all licensed, so don't even think about trying to close us down because of that. And we meet every provision of the fire code, so you won't trip us up there, either."

Mark held up his hands to stem the flow. "I got no problem with your store, Tonie. I just need some information."

"We don't talk about our customers. That is private and confidential. You've got no right to harass them."

"I'm not harassing anybody," Mark said. "Is there somewhere we can talk privately?"

With an anxious glance at the nearby shoppers, Tonie pointed to a small, spare office behind the shoe display.

"Look, around Christmas, a young woman died a few blocks from here," Mark said. "When the super in her building cleaned out her apartment, he sold you her clothes. If you've still got them, we need to see them. And if you've sold them, we need to track them down."

"I can't release the names of our customers. This is their safe place. Sometimes their *only* safe place. Where else can a father of four from Bellevue get fitted for a girdle?"

Fair question. Mark explained that he was willing to rely on the store manager to get in touch with the customers - so long as they promptly called him back. "I don't want to make any of your customers uncomfortable. But if you won't help me, then I'm going to have to come back here with a search warrant. And after that, everything I do is pretty much in the public record."

Tonie finally admitted that she remembered Mr. Sandstrom. "He was adorable," she said. "He obviously had no idea where he was. He just saw our ad in the paper."

"Can you tell whether you still have any of the clothes you bought from him?"

She tapped magenta-painted nails over her computer keyboard. "Most of it, no. I just gave him a $50 flat fee for the three boxes he brought in. The clothes were clean and in good shape, but they didn't have any style. I just priced them and put them out on the racks. I've no idea whether any of them are still here."

We leaned back, disappointed. But Harmony prompted, "You said, 'most of it.' So was there something you can track?"

Tonie nodded reluctantly. "Two complete outfits," she said. "Beautiful. Brand new. They still had the tags. Two suits with silk blouses and matching scarves. I took them both on consignment and sold them right away. All her other clothes were size 20, 22. They were so dull, so shapeless. The suits were size 12."

She shook her head. Her wig rustled. "I do that too, sometimes - buy something beautiful in hopes I'll diet into it. It never works, of course. I wish this poor girl had come to see us. We'd have gotten her into something that fit and had some style, no matter what size she was. Sedrique would have given her a makeover; Jasmine would have done her hair. She would have walked out of here looking like a million bucks. At Hello, Gorgeous, we can find the large, lovely lady in everyone."

She was quiet for a moment.

"I mean, it's sad, isn't it?" she said. "She never got to feel beautiful. She never got to have her big day."

CHAPTER 23

Tonie's words came back to me Monday morning, as I watched Mrs. Holbrook step off the elevator. She was wearing a straw hat with a navy dress. Mrs. Holbrook is on the ample side, but she would be impossible to overlook. And it isn't just the hats. Hatted or hatless, Mrs. Holbrook always looks perfect. Her clothes are always pressed; her shoes always shine. Every now and then, she'll brush off my shoulder or straighten my tie. I am certain that no one has ever had to tidy up Mrs. Holbrook.

I wished Carrie had had a Mrs. Holbrook to spiff her up. The school pictures still bothered me - Carrie's slide into pale obscurity. It was as if the larger she got, the harder she worked to make herself disappear.

Except for those two suits. I thought of them hanging unworn, untouched in Carrie's closet, so carefully matched with silk blouses and scarves. All weekend, we had asked ourselves the same questions: Why did Carrie buy those outfits? What was she saving them for? She seemed to have been getting ready for something - losing weight, buying new clothes. But ready for what? If she was planning on passing herself off as her sister, why didn't she take and wear the new suits she had bought?

We didn't have answers. We just had questions. And the more we learned, the more questions we had. We had cleaned out Hello, Gorgeous' inventory of size 20 and 22 used clothes, all of which matched Tonie's description of Carrie's clothes as dull, shapeless, and style-free. The tracker dog didn't alert on any of them, even when we grouped them with Carrie's books. We didn't know why. Maybe the clothes and the body were Carrie's, but the scent on the clothes wasn't strong enough to attract the dog. Maybe the clothes weren't Carrie's but the body was, which was why the dog didn't find the match. Or maybe the clothes were Carrie's but the body wasn't. Or maybe neither the clothes nor the body belonged to Carrie Mayer. Round and round and round.

My head began to ache with the remembered frustration of the tracking test. We had tried every possible combination, with a mounting sensation of failure. The dog had been great, though - a genuine bloodhound with ears like mud flaps and eager, liquid eyes. After thoroughly sniffing and considering all the items we presented, he had loped back to us with an embarrassed expression, as if apologizing for his inability to find a match. I had been overcome with empathy and rubbed his ears and belly until he cheered and licked my face - which earned me yet another day of silent treatment from Betsy. My dog was more possessive than my fiancée. A troubling situation.

Tonie was going to contact the man who had bought Carrie's suits. When we got them, we'd try the test again. Even though she hadn't worn them, they might have picked up her scent by hanging next to the rest of her clothes in the closet. Until then, I couldn't think of anything else to do on the Carrie Mayer case. I pushed Carrie to the back of my mind and settled down to work on my other matters. American Fidelity's Washington litigation was heating up. If the pace proved steady, Harmony and I might have to hire associates. It was sobering to think of someone detesting me the way I had hated the partners at my old firm.

By noon, I was starving. Harmony was defending a deposition at a downtown firm, and Mrs. Holbrook had already left for lunch, so I dashed across the street for a bagel.

Donald Carter was sitting by himself in the corner, one of his horse racing papers arrayed before him. I wasn't going to disturb him, but the counterman greeted me loudly by name and bagel of choice - *HiJackPoppyseedLightCreamCheese$1.55. ThankYouNextPlease* - and Donald started and waved me over.

Donald mustered a wry smile as I sat down across from him.

"Your cop friends are back. They're over there searching Chuck Thomas's office."

Mark and Anthony had served the search warrant at 7 o'clock that morning. I was surprised Donald had left them alone. I couldn't imagine he'd let two cops paw through his company's confidential records without being there to supervise them.

"They're looking at his board of directors files on Children First," Donald said, as though reading my mind. "The school's counsel is with them, so I told them I'd leave them to it. No need to have two lawyers sweating blood."

"You doing OK, Donald?"

"No. No, I'm not, Jack. I've worked for Chuck Thomas for ten years. He hired me. I'm not saying he's a good man. He's difficult, and he's demanding, and no one knows that better than I do. I wouldn't buy a used car from him, and I don't know many people who would. But I'm just stunned to think that he would hurt a little girl. I just cannot bear to think that."

A reporter attending the CareForKids auction had overheard Didi's outburst. The allegations of sexual abuse at Children First had been front-page news ever since. I had been grateful that for the time being at least, the media seemed to forget about Higuro and Harmony.

"What does this mean for you and Puget Health, Donald?"

"I don't know yet. The board of directors is meeting tonight. They might fire him, suspend him - anything. It's something else, isn't it? One day you're the CEO of a billion-dollar company; the next day somebody writes an anonymous letter, and you might as well be dead. Even if he's never charged, he'll never clear his name."

"How are your employees taking it?"

"They're stunned. Chuck Thomas *is* Puget Health Partners. They all know him; most of them have been involved with his Children First activities one way or another. We do the Halloween party in the fall, a Sub for Santa tree at Christmas, and a fun run in the spring to raise money for books and computers. It's the only way Chuck shows his human side to the employees. They put up with the way he barks at them at work because they know how much he gives to the kids. They figure it shows his heart's in the right place. Now they're not just appalled; they're betrayed. We've got counselors from our employee assistance plan coming on site. We've got talking points for them to use with irate callers. But the company's never going to be the same. How would you like to spend hours on the phone, trying to convince your customers that no matter what the newspapers are saying, your CEO is not a pervert?"

"Do they think he did it?"

"They don't know what to think. None of us do."

There was a quaver in his voice that worried me. "I thought you said you believed he was innocent."

"I said I couldn't bear to believe he was guilty. And I can't. I just can't bear it. But -" He stopped and put his hand over his mouth, as though he was going to be sick.

"But?" I prompted.

"It doesn't mean anything. It really doesn't."

"*What* doesn't mean anything?"

Donald hesitated, then caved. "Last Halloween, we took the kids trick-or-treating up on the top floor. Most of the executives dress up and really get into the spirit of it. Our CFO is always a vampire; our junior vice presidents put rubber knives in their backs and joke that they've been there all along; and I usually come as the state insurance commissioner, which is the scariest character I can think of. Chuck Thomas never wears a costume, but he always likes to see the kids. After the kids had gone door to door getting their candy and showing off their painted faces, we did a nose count at the elevator and came up one kid short. The executive secretaries and I split up and searched the floor until we found her." He swallowed.

I was dreading the worst. Donald's eyes were so troubled; his mouth so pinched. "Where was she?"

"Underneath Chuck's desk. I mean, that's not all that strange. I have days when I'd be happy to hide under my desk, too. But she was way back there, and she had her hands pressed on the sides of the cubbyhole, like she was holding on. And when I said, 'Honey, it's time to go downstairs for cookies and punch,' she pulled the chair back to cover herself and said, 'No, I won't.' Gretta Berg finally had to coax her out." He let out a long, slow breath. "It doesn't mean anything. Children like to hide. But ever since I read the paper on Saturday, I've been worrying about it. It's been all I could think of."

I was worried too. The father's letter said that Chuck Thomas had touched his daughter on Halloween. But I couldn't share that with Donald.

"Donald, you have to tell the detectives about this," I said. "Maybe it's nothing, but they'll need to check it out. You have to tell them now."

Donald looked, if possible, even more disconsolate than when I had sat down across from him. "Children like to hide, Jack," he protested.

"I know they do. But even when they're hiding, they usually don't turn down cookies and punch." I paused to let that sink in. "You have to tell them, Donald."

He finally agreed and stood to go. I told him I'd accompany him, which brought a wry smile to his drawn face.

"You want to make sure I'll follow through?"

Actually, yes, but I wasn't going to tell him that. "No, I'm going to take some bagels to the guys. They've been skipping meals since this broke."

Mark and Anthony were still in Chuck Thomas's office, bent over reams of files with the attorney for Children First, a firecracker of a woman I had met during some of my own pro bono work. Larry and Ed were nowhere to be seen.

Chuck's office was enormous, with floor-to-ceiling windows and a sweeping view of the Sound, the Space Needle, and Lake Union. It was furnished with leather and dark wood, with glass art in glass boxes, and with a large, framed portrait of Didi as a Seafair queen. That must have been where she picked up the taste for a sash.

I loitered by Didi's picture while Donald told his story to Mark and Anthony. They played it cool. You couldn't even see their ears prick up. But I knew them, and I knew they were interested.

"What was the little girl's name?" Mark asked casually. The police were already overwhelmed with trying to identify the alleged victim.

"I don't know," Donald confessed. "I just show up for the trick-or-treating, and it's not like I'm a kid magnet. Especially not dressed like the insurance commissioner."

Despite the gravity of the situation, I had to hide a smile. Donald was tall and shaped like an L, with enormous feet and almost no flesh on his bony frame. He wore dark, conservative suits that flapped on him like the wings of flying squirrel. Our insurance commissioner was a short, belligerent woman who rode a Harley and had a taste for tight leather miniskirts. For future Halloweens, I wondered if I should tell Donald about Hello, Gorgeous.

"I know, Mr. Carter," an elegant older woman said from the doorway. I hadn't realized she was there. Donald started and quickly introduced us to Lorraine Rhodes, Chuck Thomas's executive secretary.

"Her name is Jenny Walton," Lorraine said. "She's in first grade."

Jenny. There must be a lot of Jennys in the world, but the coincidence disturbed me.

Jenny was the name of our little artist, the one who drew the picture Gretta Berg had given us.

Jenny was the name of the little girl who had drawn Carrie's body as a heart.

CHAPTER 24

Jenny Walton's father had a history of drug dealing and two warrants out for his arrest. That fit with Mark and Anthony's theory of the case. If the father's letter was legit, they figured, he must have had a major reason for not going to the police. Staying out of prison was a major reason. As the police looked into it further, everything they learned about Jenny Walton dovetailed with the details in the letter. She had been in school on the dates of the alleged touching. She had disappeared a few days after the last alleged assault. She was small for her age, shy, and behind in school. She kept to herself. An easy child for a predator to cut from the pack.

The more Jenny fit the profile sketched by the letter, the more horrible it all became. It was bad enough when we were thinking of the allegations of sexual abuse as a hypothetical motive for Carrie Mayer's murder. But as bits and pieces of the puzzle fell into place, Jenny Walton began to take center stage. There was nothing more we could do for Carrie except find her killer and – once we knew who killed whom – resolve her life insurance policy. But if Chuck Thomas had molested Jenny, there was a little girl out there somewhere who needed help. She needed food, shelter, stability, counseling - maybe medical care. No matter how much her dad wanted to protect her, he couldn't do much for her while he was on the run.

Mark and Anthony were especially frustrated. The way cases were assigned was not helping them get work done. But Mark's boss had gone to some conference or hired some consultant, and the new team-based system was sacrosanct. "We are all accountable" was the catchphrase of the day for the homicide squad. In reality, that meant that no one was accountable, that it was as confusing for the detectives who wanted to do a good job as it was it was concealing for those who wanted to slack off. Exasperated, Ed Perez transferred back to the fraud squad. Instead of filling the vacancy on homicide, Mark's sergeant pushed some of their work to other detectives. This caused no end of grousing – as Mark put it, all of the shit approached the fan – but the far greater problem was additional delay.

The molestation allegations were being handled by the sex crimes squad. Those detectives were fierce and dedicated – the guys I had met at CareForKids were legendary for taping mugshots of rapists over the cutouts at the firing range – but they were drowning in other, more immediate cases. It was difficult to find time for an anonymous, possibly faked letter when every day there were newly traumatized, flesh-and-blood victims who needed help.

The lack of evidence didn't keep the Puget Health Partners Board of Directors from asking Chuck Thomas to step down as CEO. Officially, it was a leave of absence, Donald told me, but the Board had changed the locks on Chuck's office and taken his electronic keycard to the garage and outside doors. Unless someone publicly cleared him of suspicion - and it didn't look like that was going to happen any time soon - Chuck's career was over. The state crime lab had dusted under Chuck's desk, and there were ten tiny prints where Jenny had braced herself in the cubbyhole. For days afterward, Donald told me, the little prints glowed a strange grey-green in the dark office, like stars struggling in a muddy sky.

I glanced at my watch. I had been cooling my heels outside Judge Shrenk's chambers for twenty minutes, waiting for Boyd Tate to show up for a status conference on the Carrie Mayer case. Never my favorite person, Tate was progressing from a general irritant to a complete pain in the ass. He hadn't bothered to return my courtesy call about whether he intended to press the case in light of Melanie Mayer's ostensible death; he was perilously late on some discovery I had requested; and now he was making me look bad in front of Judge Shrenk - one of the least forgiving judges on the Superior Court bench. Every now and then, her bailiff would glare at me over half-glasses. Finally, Shrenk pushed open her door and waved me in.

"Still no Tate?" she asked.

"No, Your Honor."

"Talked to him recently? Was he planning on squeezing us into his crowded social calendar?"

"He hasn't been returning my phone calls lately."

"Is that unusual?" I wondered why she even bothered asking. Tate was notoriously sloppy and disorganized. For all the years I had known him, he had bumbled around the King County Courthouse with a briefcase tied closed with a piece of rope.

"No, Your Honor."

"I didn't think so. The man's a disgrace." She glowered at me, as if I were to blame for not keeping better track of my opposing counsel. Even on her best days, Alice Shrenk cut a fearsome figure, with her jutting chin and penetrating black eyes. In her current mood, she looked like she ought to be off worshipping Satan instead of meting out justice in Superior Court. She hadn't invited me to sit, so I stood uncomfortably before her, like a kid in the principal's office.

"Well, we can't have the conference without him, so you'll have to reschedule." She called out to her bailiff. "I'm sanctioning Tate $250, to be paid to the charity of his choice. And remind him that the charity of his choice cannot be him. Damned idiot has tried that a couple too many times."

She turned back to me, and for the first time, seemed to thaw, marginally. "How's Harmony?"

"She's OK. It's been a hard couple of weeks."

"I hear she's got the Tadpole after her."

It took me a moment to translate that. "Tadpole" = Todd Poehl. Wow. I had forgotten that Judge Shrenk was a former Assistant U.S. Attorney. And now I would never be able to shake this new image of Todd.

"Todd's talked to us," I evaded.

Shrenk gave me a not-unsympathetic smile - which sent shudders up my back. Sympathy seemed so foreign to her nature that the display made me think that Harmony must really be in trouble.

"Todd never talks to people. He either threatens them or flatters them. No middle ground. And I'd lay money he hasn't been long on flattery lately."

"Well, no."

Shrenk nodded grimly. "I like Harmony. She's a good attorney, and she's remarkably sane for someone as rich and good-looking as she is. I don't believe the bullshit people are saying about her."

"Saying about her? What are people saying about her?"

"Just some insanity about hushing up some fraud complaints. Stupid for anyone who knows Harmony. But she should watch out for the Tadpole. A couple of the AUSAs are interested in the open judgeship, and they're all trying to outdo each other to show they're tough on crime. Even if Todd doesn't have anything against Harmony personally, he'll run right over her if she gets in his way."

Judge Shrenk came around to the other side of her desk. She put her hand on my arm. She didn't look angry. She looked worried. I had never once, in five years of appearing before her, seen Alice Shrenk look worried.

"Jack, tell Harmony to be careful."

CHAPTER 25

After an almost silent dinner, Harmony excused herself and went to bed. Betsy barreled after her.

David had accurately predicted Todd Poehl's immunity offer, and I had accurately predicted Harmony's reaction. Todd had called David that morning: full immunity if Harmony testified that she "may have" received allegations of fraud against the government during her Rockface investigation, and that if she had, she "would have" told Higuro about them. Harmony had pointed out that claims of defrauding the government were not a little thing that a girl would just forget.

I poked my nose around the sunroom door. Harmony was lying on her back under the covers, but her eyes were open. Betsy was snuggled beside her, applying small, reassuring kisses to her cheek.

"Do you ever have that dream where all the spiders you've flushed down the toilet come back up the drain to seek their revenge?" Harmony asked. "That's what's happening to me right now. Every trick I've used in depositions, every clever cross examination - I feel like it's coming back to haunt me."

"I don't flush spiders. I squash them."

Her voice was so soft I barely heard her. "That's what's happening to me, too."

I settled down next to Harmony on the futon and smoothed her hair back from her forehead. I kissed her until Betsy felt neglected and pushed her nose between us. I thought - not for the first time - that when Harmony and I finally got married, Betsy was going to sleep with Uncle Mark.

We laid side by side in silence. I had my arms around her, but she made no move to inch away. This by itself was unusual for Harmony, who was uncomfortable being prone and alone with me. I was wondering whether this was a sign of progress or just a symptom of how miserable Harmony was, when she spoke directly to the ceiling.

"I'm really, incredibly sorry about this, Jack."

Elliptical. The woman was elliptical. "Sorry about what?"

"Sorry that you're going to get mixed up in all this mess." She turned toward me. "You're going to get hit with the smear, too, if Todd indicts me. Our firm's going to tank. We'll lose our clients. They won't want a lawyer with a cloud over her head. And it's terribly unfair, but they won't want a lawyer who hangs out with a lawyer with a cloud over her head, either."

She stopped, and I could tell that the next words hurt her. "I'll pull out of the partnership if you want me to. The two of us are pretty closely allied in people's minds, but if we split up now, there might be enough time for you to separate yourself from any fallout that's going to come with me."

I was so surprised I couldn't respond right away. Piper & Hart was our baby. We were 50-50 partners: Thanks to American Fidelity, I had brought half the work to the firm; the rest had followed Harmony from Piper Whatcom, where her grandfather had been the founding partner. We had both sweat blood to get the shop off the ground; we both put in even longer hours than we had at Piper Whatcom, trying to keep the place afloat. And it was afloat. Better than afloat. We were bringing in new clients and new matters every month, just based on our rates and reputations.

I indulged myself in one short thought about how much I loved our little firm and how much I would miss it if it were gone. Only a few months out on my own with Harmony had proven something I hadn't dared believe: stripped of the internecine warfare, bureaucracy, bullshit, and backstabbing of a big firm, practicing law is kind of fun. I had loved being my own boss. I had loved having full control of a case. I had loved Mrs. Holbrook. I had loved her hats. I had loved my clients - even and maybe especially the odd ones.

I thought of the sexual harassment defendant who had tried to hug Harmony goodbye at the end of our first meeting ("Ted, I think I see the problem here," she had said, disentangling herself), the used car dealer under investigation for odometer turnbacks who was, most unfortunately, an involuntary winker. He had winked the whole way through his deposition: "I can guarantee you that each and every car on my lot has its original mileage - WINK WINK." Harmony and I had been thinking of buying him an eyepatch for trial.

Had been.

I was already thinking of it all in the past tense, I realized sadly. Then I realized that it was taking me far too long to respond to Harmony, who was looking even more unhappy than when I had come in to cheer her up.

"So the firm tanks," I said firmly. "So what?"

"You've worked so hard. You enjoy it so much."

"So what?" I asked again, with a bravado I didn't quite feel. "First of all, it's not going to tank. And second, it doesn't matter if it does. We went out as Piper & Hart, and we'll stay out as Piper & Hart. You didn't do anything wrong, Harmony. You did an investigation for your dad, and you did a good job. I'm not going to run away from that. And if Poehl does anything that hurts our business, then we'll just have more fire for our malicious prosecution claim."

She regarded me gravely. "Do you mean that?"

"Yes, I do," I said, and by this time, I truly did.

"I have to ask you something else."

"Shoot."

"It's going to hurt your feelings."

"Then shoot *carefully*."

She sucked in her breath, and once again, I could tell it hurt her just to form the words. "If everything was gone - if it all went away, Jack - not just the firm, but the money, and the property, and everything else - because the fines in this case, they could take pretty much everything I have. And Todd can tie it up for years. And that's best case – that's assuming I stay out of jail. If it was all gone, would it make a difference to you?"

It took me a moment to unravel that. Harmony was usually so fluid, so eloquent that at first the broken syntax concerned me more than the question itself. Finally, thanks to the gift of tongues that had helped me survive my meeting with Anastasia Lofton of the UW Women Studies Program, I burst out, "Do you mean, would I still love you if you weren't rich?"

She nodded, but she looked away.

"Well, of course I would!" She was right. She had hurt my feelings. "You can't think that that's what we're all about," I whispered in her ear, committing my own offenses against the English language as I struggled with the pinprick of her mistrust. "I don't give a damn about your money, Harmony. Except when you're rescuing Mark, when it is super-useful. I don't want your money, I don't need your money, and if it all goes away, if even the firm goes away, then we'll just think of something else to do together."

She looked at me with relief, but still some lingering doubt. "Like what?"

"Well . . . ." I thought for a moment. "Well, we'll turn my dad's house up on Orcas Island into a bed and breakfast. Mark will flirt with all the lady guests. We'll have a waiting list a mile long. We'll get four stars from every guidebook from here to New York."

That made her laugh - a strangled, sad little laugh, but a laugh nonetheless - so I pressed on, spinning ever more fantastic tales about all the ways we could keep the wolf far from the door. We'd call our bed and breakfast Hart Harbour House, milking every ounce of elegance out of that extra "u." We'd sell souvenir postcards of Mark. And if business dwindled during the dark, wet winter months, we'd rent a

Winnebago and hit the highway. Harmony would go blond and wear little halter tops and start calling me "Sugar"; I'd get a wooden-bead seat cover and a CB.

"Stop," Harmony said, laughing for real this time. "That's enough."

"But I haven't even told you about the cult we could create. We'll have our headquarters in the airport meditation chapel. It's public property; they can't kick us out. I got a trespassing case dismissed that way. And if things get really rocky for us, we could probably live in the airport for a couple of months before anyone noticed. If someone asks, we'll just tell them our flight's delayed. If we say we're on United, everyone will believe us."

I rattled on for a few more minutes, hoping I could make her smile, gratified when I did. Still, her eyes had that hunted look. I thought I understood. Mark and I had grown up with nothing - we had met in a foster home - so the prospect of complete ruin scared us but didn't paralyze us. We knew what to do, how to start again. But Harmony had grown up swaddled in wealth and influence. She was an heiress in her own right; her father - both her fathers - were rich and powerful men. Now the Tadpole threatened to rip all of that away. And she didn't know what to do. She didn't know how to respond. She couldn't quite believe that she'd earned her success and her reputation by herself, and that she could do it again, with or without an influential daddy and a quarter billion in the bank.

"And if the worst comes to worst," I summed up, "I can always work construction to support us, although I'd rather try a career in interpretive dance before I do. But the bottom line is, we're going to be OK. No matter what Todd does, it's not going to mess us up. I love you, and I'm going to stand by you. And while there is breath in my body, we are not going to starve. This is America, Harmony. We'll get another job."

She studied me for a moment or two, then reached up and stroked my face, letting her fingertips play along my jaw. "You're quite something, you know that, Jack? You really are something else."

I allowed as how other people may have mentioned that, although generally not in that context.

"Will you come to the courthouse with me for my testimony? I know it's a pain; you can't come into the grand jury room. You just have to wait outside. But it would mean a lot to me to know you're there."

"Of course I'll come," I assured her.

"And will you stay with me tonight? Just to sleep?" she added hastily.

Harmony and I had been engaged six months. This was my first invitation to spend the night with her, however platonically. Once again, I considered: Progress or misery? Misery, I decided, looking at her tense, drawn face.

I slipped one hand under her back and turned her over on her stomach, just like flipping a fried egg. I spooned her up against me and put my other hand on the warm, bare skin at the base of her hair. Instantly, she went rigid.

"Just relax," I told her. "Don't worry about a thing. I'm going to rub your back."

And I did, pressing in slow, small circles with the heel of my hand, working up each side of her neck, across her shoulders, and down her spine until I reached the soft, black silk of her nightgown. After a few moments, her stiff muscles softened. I kept rubbing until her breathing slowed and deepened. I slid under the covers and held her tight.

"Good night, sweetheart," I whispered.

"Good night," she whispered back. There was a sleepy pause and a little twitch of her mouth.

She breathed out the word so I barely heard it: "Sugar."

CHAPTER 26

I couldn't go to sleep. I was worried about Harmony. I was also intensely aware of her presence. Even with Betsy glaring at me from across Harmony's small, still figure, I was still luxuriating in the fact that I was actually in bed with Harmony - and that I wasn't too incapacitated to enjoy it. Up to that point, Harmony had permitted such nearness only when I was strapped into a hospital bed, and preferably sedated.

Betsy did not relax her guard. At midnight, she was still keeping a wary if heavily-lidded watch on me from the other side of the bed. I reached over and tousled her ears. She licked my hand. It wasn't that Betsy didn't like me. She did. In her own crazy way, Betsy adored me. And it wasn't that Harmony didn't like me. She really did. But Harmony had an ugly incident in her past, and at sixteen, she had just shut down as far as boys were concerned. I was the only man she had ever dated, and it had taken almost a year for her to risk even that. She loved me; she wanted to marry me. But the thought of actually sleeping with me made her profoundly anxious, and Betsy hated anything that upset her mom.

I lost the stare-down with Betsy and finally sank into sleep. I woke disoriented just after two o'clock, to find that Betsy had wedged herself between me and Harmony and was burrowing and stretching in the narrow space, working me away from Harmony and toward the edge of the futon. Caught in the act, she grinned up at me, her purple tongue lolling out in delight at her own cleverness. She was so proud of herself that I couldn't help but smile back at her, even as I rolled my eyes in exasperation.

I worked my fingers into the soft scruff of Betsy's neck and wished I could wedge myself between Harmony and the Tadpole. I wished there were some way I could protect her from the fight looming on the horizon.

It was three o'clock in the morning before the ideas started to flicker in my mind, before the suspicions that had been nagging at me finally shifted into focus.

Maybe I could.

"Gentlemen, you are, if possible, even less attractive than last time," Todd Poehl said when David and I walked into his conference room at the federal prosecutors' office the next morning. "You asked for an immunity deal; I gave you an immunity deal. Where is the beautiful Ms. Piper?"

"And we appreciate the deal, Todd; we do. There is just one small problem: I cannot in good conscience permit Ms. Piper to agree to anything that would require her to lie."

For the next half hour or so, Todd and David tussled over the deal, with Todd taking the position that David had tried on me: How could Harmony possibly be so sure Hugo Bogaty had never raised the whistleblower allegations? Couldn't she have just forgotten?

I kept out of the fray, kept focusing on the 360-degree view. Beneath his sarcasm and aggression, Todd seemed genuinely disappointed. He kept trying to convince David to get Harmony back to the table. Beside him, the FBI guy, Special Agent Rich, was stolid and silent – but every now and then I saw that smug, malicious smile from his early morning visit.

In mid-sentence, David broke off and turned to me. We had debated who was going to try to get the Tadpole alone. I had been bested in our sophisticated decision-making of rock-paper-scissors on the way to the Seafirst Building.

"You doing OK, Jack?" David asked sharply.

"Um, no. I'm sorry. Just not feeling so great. Todd, could I use your restroom?"

Yes, it's embarrassing, but it's a guaranteed way out of a meeting. No one wants to be thrown up on. Todd jerked his thumb toward the door. "Down the hall."

I paused at the door, looking desperate and confused. "I'm sorry – which way?"

Todd cussed, said, "Let's take five," and headed down the hall with me. David intercepted Special Agent Rich with a casual, "Hey, just walk me through this one more time." The conference room door clicked closed behind us.

Todd turned into his office. Without looking over his shoulder, he said, "End of the hall. On your left. Leave it decent."

He swung down at his desk and tapped his keyboard. As he spun around to grab a document, he realized with a start that I was standing in his office. "Shit! Jack! This is not the bathroom!"

I sat down in one of his guest chairs.

"I just need five minutes, Todd."

"You fucking asshole. Get out of my office before I have you arrested."

"Look, I think you'll be a good judge. I think there might be something going on here that could blow up on you. And if there is, I don't want any of us to be in harm's way. "

Todd absorbed that. He and I had worked together a couple of times over the years, on civil forfeitures and insurance fraud. He knew I wasn't a total flake.

"You've got four minutes. And I still might have you arrested."

Fair enough.

"Todd, for those four minutes, just start from the premise that the memo you've got was forged – that someone took one of Harmony's real memos and added paragraphs about the fraud allegations."

"Three-and-a-half minutes. And closing fast."

OK. I barreled on. "There's only a couple of reasons why someone would add paragraphs about government fraud to a memo about a wage and hour investigation. Obviously, it could have been the prosecution -" Todd looked up from his watch long enough to cuss at me. "- But I don't believe that. The most likely person is someone at Rockface or Yamashita. Someone who's trying to support a *qui tam.*"

A *qui tam* is an unusual sort of lawsuit, where a person sues for fraud committed against the government and can get up to 30% of whatever the government ultimately recovers. It started out as a way to police rapacious Civil War contractors. Now it's kind of a nationwide game of Lotto, with really strict rules.

One of those rules is that *qui tams* are filed under seal, so the government has time to investigate and decide whether to intervene. That's why Todd responded, "You know very well I can't confirm or deny whether there's a *qui tam* lawsuit against Yamashita's company. Even if there is, then it just sucks even more to be Higuro right now."

"Might suck to be you, too, Todd."

"You do know what a *qui tam* is, don't you, Jack?"

I did. Another one of the very strict rules of *qui tams* is that the plaintiff can get part of the government's recovery only if the allegations they bring to the courthouse haven't been previously disclosed. If there's been a public disclosure, the plaintiff has to have been the "original source" of that disclosure, or the case will be dismissed. The theory is that the government wants to reward only the people with unique and valuable information.

I thought Hugo Bogaty had falsified Harmony's memo to keep his *qui tam* hopes alive. When news stories broke about the fraud at Rockface, any *qui tam* lawsuits about those allegations would have been foreclosed - unless the plaintiff could show he was the one who told the media about the fraud. That's why I thought the added paragraphs in Harmony's memo spelled out the media sources in such strange and specific detail, saying Hugo Bogaty had gone to the <u>Seattle Times</u>, the <u>P-I</u>, and KING, KOMO, and KIRO TV news – all the reporters who had ambushed us at the airport. He was creating a paper trail to try to prove he had been the original source all along.

So how to make the Tadpole care? He was glaring at me and tapping his watch.

"You can't introduce falsified evidence before the grand jury, Todd. It's unethical."

"I don't *know* that the memo's false." He half-rose.

"You better find out now, before your confirmation hearing."

Todd sat down hard. "You threatening me, Hart?"

"I'm not the threat. It's everyone else who wants the judgeship and everyone who'll be against you because you're not in their political party. They'll go through everything you've done trying to find the smallest reason to knock you out of the running or embarrass you during the hearing. You know how poisonous all the confirmation battles have been. All the insults, and accusations, and . . . name-calling. You don't want to give them any ammunition. You don't want to lose your place on the bench because of something like this. You need to get to the bottom of it now. "

Todd groaned and passed his hand over his light, smooth hair. "So there are what, ten thousand people in Yamashita's companies, maybe a couple thousand more with all the subsidiaries and the vendors? And I'm supposed to come up with the one person who might have – mind you, *might have* – messed with Harmony's memo?"

"We may be able to help you narrow it down."

"Hart, if you have been holding out evidence on me, I will crucify you."

Alice Shrenk was right. Todd really was a two-speed bicycle. He was going to be hell to deal with as a judge, when lawyers before him would get only his threatening side. But that was a future problem.

"I don't have evidence. I have a hunch. But if my hunch is right, it means you've got someone on your team that you need to worry about – someone who gave information about your investigation to someone in Yamashita, Inc."

Poehl turned away, but not before I saw the flash in his small gray eyes, the flush across his neck, the tightening of his jaw. I had scored a direct hit. Todd Poehl had already been worried about leaks or disloyalty or both.

"Who?" he demanded.

"My hunch is that we're dealing with relatives: One working for Yamashita; one working for the government. My hunch is the person working for you gave intel about your investigation to their relative, but the relative didn't get the *qui tam* filed before the media started picking up on the story. The person I'd look at in Yamashita is the alleged complainant – Hugo Bogaty."

"A trifle retaliatory, isn't that, Jack?"

"Not if you check it out, no. Then it's just part of your *qui tam* investigation."

There was a trace of humor in his face. "Assuming one exists?"

"Assuming so, yes. Hugo Bogaty works for Yamashita in Poland. Higuro has a lot of his back office stuff done there – IT, billing, Finance. Bogaty's in Finance now

– that's why Harmony called him during the wage and hour investigation – but he used to be in IT. My hunch is that Yamashita isn't tight on their security profile controls, that Bogaty still has the access to the system he had in IT, and that's how he got Harmony's memo."

Poehl considered that. "And the relative you think works for us?"

"I've worked with the FBI a couple of times," I told him. "Every time, with every client, the FBI would send two agents for witness interviews. But Special Agent Rich showed up alone at my house before six in the morning and wanted to talk to Harmony 'informally.' He was trying to get her to sign a statement. He said he'd come back with the Marshals if she didn't."

"It's called a dawn raid, Jack. You've seen pressure tactics before."

"Have you seen Hugo Bogaty before?"

I pulled a paper from my coat pocket, unfolded it, and handed it to him. Harmony had printed out Hugo Bogaty's security photograph from Yamashita, Inc.'s online directory. Bogaty was a stolid, square-faced young man with brown hair, brown eyes, and a smug smile.

"Remind you of anyone?" I asked.

Poehl's expression shifted from incredulous to suspicious to alarmed – then back to suspicious. "You are absolutely shitting me," he said. "You're accusing the freaking FBI of leaking information?"

I shook my head. "It's just a hunch," I reminded him. "But when Special Agent Rich came to our door, he said something like what Harmony heard from the offshore witnesses in her wage and hour investigation – 'maybe you're not at fault; maybe you're just following orders.' That's not something you hear very often from witnesses who grew up in the United States."

I nodded down the hall.

"If you've got a leak, he might be sitting in your conference room. Todd, in Polish, 'Bogaty' means 'Rich.'"

CHAPTER 27

"Wait for me by the Good and the Bad. I'll find us an open room."

Since David and I had left him three days earlier, Todd Poehl had served a search warrant on Yamashita, Inc., for all records relating in any way to Hugo Bogaty, Special Agent Rich, or the Rockface billing. As they scrambled to respond, Higuro and his army of attorneys had become increasingly skeptical that David and I were in any way improving matters. As David put it, we had at least managed to unite Higuro's defense counsel – by now, bicoastal if not international. They all agreed we were idiots.

But we would see.

Todd had called us. He wanted to talk. He was in trial on another case but coming up on a recess. We had fifteen minutes to get to the lobby of the federal courthouse, where we waited for him under the two big allegorical paintings on the effects of good and bad government – "the Good and the Bad."

Todd led us through the courthouse with the suave confidence of premature ownership. He already thought of himself as a federal judge.

"No Special Agent Rich?" David asked, as the door closed behind us.

"Don't be a smart ass. Here is the new deal. Do not expect another one."

The offer was complete immunity for Harmony, with no direction or limitation on what she could or could not say. But there was one big condition, which was not within Harmony's control. Todd wanted her to do a non-privileged investigation of the allegations that Rockface had overcharged the government – with all her work product shared with the government and all her findings conveyed to the grand jury.

"You understand that this is Mr. Yamashita's call, not Harmony's, right?" David said. Higuro was still not willing to waive the attorney-client privilege. There wasn't much Harmony could say about her work for him until he did.

"He should be grateful for the shot at it," Todd said. "Thanks to Jack and his hunches, I am light on investigators at the moment. So Yamashita can demonstrate good faith to the government while the FBI brass is busy pointing fingers and covering their butts."

"What about the memo?"

"There's certainly reason for concern. But without what you say is the real memo and the notes from Harmony's interview with that asshat in Poland, it's hard to be sure. Tell Yamashita to just drop the whole attorney-client privileged nonsense and let the girl talk about what she did."

David said he would pass the offer and conditions along to Harmony and Higuro. Todd nodded, his mind already back in the courtroom. He was halfway out the door when he looked over his shoulder.

"And Jack?"

"Yep?"

"*Dzięki.*" He headed down the hall.

"'Thanks' in Polish," I translated for David, closing the door.

"Since when do you know Polish?"

I didn't. But American Fidelity had started outsourcing shared services and back office functions to Eastern Europe. I had learned enough Polish and Hungarian phrases to demonstrate respect, but with atrocious enough pronunciation that people still responded to me in English. Very slow, kind English, like they were concerned that I might need some assistance even with my native language.

David called Harmony and outlined the terms of the deal. She was on board – it was the right way to handle the fraud allegations. But waiving the privilege would be a tough sell for Higuro.

"He'll see it as being disloyal to him," she warned David. "And loyalty is everything."

I checked my messages while Harmony and David discussed who would talk to Higuro and how to approach him. Mark had called while we were with Todd. He wanted me and Harmony to stop by the police station as soon as we could.

As I clicked my phone closed, David was assuring Harmony he would take point to get Higuro on board. Harmony would meet me at the courthouse in fifteen minutes.

Then she said, "And Jack?"

"Yep?"

"*Jestem ci wdzięczny za wszystko.*" Her pronunciation was, if possible, even worse than mine. She added, "I'm not sure if I've got the agreements right. I probably don't. But that's what your phrase book says."

I said goodbye to David and sank onto one of the wooden benches outside the magistrate's chambers to wait for Harmony. I was exhausted. But I was also feeling the warming flickers of hope. The prosecutor had just called his formerly star complainant an asshat. That had to be a good sign. And Harmony had said *jestem ci wdzięczny za wszystko* to me – roughly, "I am so very, very grateful for everything."

My second-hand Polish phrase book cautioned that this phrase packed a lot of emotion; it wasn't something to throw into a random e-mail on a document production. The page she was reading from said something like, "Use this phrase wisely – and only in the right settings!" The book's previous owner had drawn a big red heart around it.

I leaned back on the hard wooden bench – eyes closed, smiling, thinking of Harmony. I was just on the edge of dozing when I realized that I was not alone.

The door to one of the interview rooms was opening. I glanced up at a pastiche of people coming toward me through the door: a somber-suited man with brown hair, a tall, thin man with black hair, and a small woman with silver hair. Sleepy and still distracted with my fuzzy thoughts of Harmony, I didn't actually see who they were. I just registered shapes and colors. I was too deep in my own thoughts to spare enough mental space to recognize them. But I was relaxed and hopeful for the first time in days. I favored all of them with a wide, warm smile.

It did not have the intended effect. Instantly the three faces dissolved in a scuffle and a scramble to get back into the interview room. I couldn't tell who was being pushed or pulled, but the tall, thin man pivoted around the woman, who disappeared abruptly after him. The brown-haired man spun around and slammed the door. I was left with the echo, the empty hall, and a suddenly thudding heart.

What the hell?

Who were those people?

Why had they panicked at seeing me?

The most logical explanation was that the brown-haired man was Special Agent Rich – the FBI agent I had accused of conspiring with an apparent relative, probably a brother, in Poland. But from what Todd had said, it had sounded that Rich was at the very least, out of favor. I had not expected to see him at liberty in the federal courthouse. Then again, it appeared that he hadn't expected to see me, either.

If it had been Special Agent Rich, who were the others? The woman and the tall, thin man had to be witnesses he didn't want me to see, witnesses he thought I would recognize.

It was clear that when I so much as smiled at them, they had panicked because they thought they were busted.

But busted for what?

My relief was shattered. Anxiety was gnawing at me again. I went outside and sat on the courthouse steps, waiting for Harmony, going over and over it in my mind.

Busted for what?

CHAPTER 28

"**W**ow," Harmony said as we approached Mark's desk in the big cubicle he shared with the other detectives on his team. "Is that Prada?"

Tonie from Hello, Gorgeous had obtained and returned Carrie Mayer's size 12 suits, and Mark wanted a woman's opinion.

Carrie's suits looked out of place up on the fifth floor of the Public Safety Building. They might have looked out of place in any office building.

When I heard that Carrie had two new suits, I thought of the outfits Harmony wore. I thought of power suits – black or dark blue, conservative, tailored, severe. I had watched Harmony getting ready for work in the morning. She buttoned up her jackets like they were armor.

Carrie's suits did not look like Harmony's. At all.

Harmony stopped a few inches away from the clothes, probably remembering the fracas with the aebleskiver pan. "Can I touch them?"

Mark gave her the go ahead. They'd already brought in the bloodhound, who hadn't alerted on either of the outfits. Their new owner favored a strong, floral perfume.

Harmony methodically inspected the first outfit, scanning labels and seams, tugging at the lapels. It was dark chocolate with a dull sheen. The jacket was short, nipped in at the waist. I had the sudden, strong impression of a spider's articulated body: *The Brown Recluse.*

Harmony replaced the suit and examined the matching blouse and scarf - a narrow tube of sullen gold and a shimmery wisp of copper. She turned back to the suit. "It's not actually Prada, but it's a good knockoff," she said. "It probably cost her three or four hundred dollars. And a couple of hundred more for the blouse and the scarf." She shook her head. "It's not what I was expecting."

"In what way?" Mark asked.

"I was expecting work clothes, suits that would give her confidence, that would make other people sit up and take her seriously. But this is short and sexy. It's something you'd wear out to dinner, or on a date. I don't think it's something you'd wear to work at a health insurance company."

Unless you're Kit McCracken, I thought, remembering her bright green minidress and white boots. But Harmony had a point. Kit's flamboyance had been the outlier among the witnesses at Puget Health.

"What about the other one?" Mark asked.

Harmony turned to the other outfit with something like a wince. It was electric blue with a sheer white blouse and a bright pink scarf.

"I don't know what to make of that one," she said. "I'm not familiar with the label. It's not a copy of any particular designer. It's nicely put together - all the seams are finished, and the buttonholes aren't frayed at all. So she probably paid quite a bit of money for it, but - and I'm not trying to be mean here - I can't think why." She let her hand play over the Prada knock-off. "I mean, she obviously had good taste. The first one is beautiful. If she lightened her hair a little, the colors would have been stunning on her. I don't care how shy she was. She would have stopped traffic in that suit." She pondered over the electric blue outfit. "She probably would have stopped traffic in this one, too, but not for the same reason."

"Maybe it wasn't for her," I suggested. "I think the blue one would be on the conservative side for Kit McCracken. Carrie could have got it for her as a Christmas present."

"Would Kit wear a size 12? She looks so - um - healthy," Mark said.

"I've never met her. But from the reporters' footage outside the Camlin, she looks, well, gifted. So she might need a 12 on top," Harmony said. "But if Carrie bought this suit for Kit, why didn't she give it to her? The apartment super said he saw Kit at Carrie's place around Christmas."

"Good question." Mark maneuvered plastic bags over the outfits. "Let's go ask Kit. I need to finish my interview with her anyway. She got all weepy on me last time."

But Kit had called in sick, and her supervisor wouldn't release her home address. Mark called the DMV and got a Capitol Hill address for Kit McCracken. The three of us piled into an unmarked car and headed up James Street.

It was a soft June morning in Seattle. The sea and sky were a new, milky blue, and - in the local vernacular - the mountains were out. The sharp peaks of the Olympics etched across the northwest. Mt. Rainier hovered like a cloud-swathed ghost to the south, all 14,000 feet looking fragile as an eggshell against the sky. It seemed like a fine time to hang out with Mark, drop in on Kit McCracken, maybe have lunch. There are times when it's great to be your own boss.

Kit lived just off Broadway in a brick building that had seen better days. The chipped front stairs were marble, and there was an arch of leaded glass over the peeling brown door. We rang the apartment several times without response.

Harmony dialed the number from the phone book on her cellphone. No answer. Then Mark led us on a hunt around the apartment building, scoping it out, peering in windows, rifling through the dumpster, getting the lay of the land.

Kit seemed to live in the back basement apartment. Unfortunately, the curtains were drawn, and the deep window wells were covered with cage-like iron bars that kept him from getting close enough to see through a sliver between the drapes.

"What are you looking for?" Harmony ventured, when he lay down on the ground and tried to wedge his face between the bars.

"Let me put it this way: If I see feet, I'm kicking in the door," he replied, only to swing himself up with a groan a few minutes later.

"No feet?" I asked.

"No nothing. Can't see a thing."

He brushed himself off. "It just bothers me," he said. She's not at work. She's not at home. It's 11 in the morning. It ought to be one or the other." He frowned at the window. "There's something hinky about it."

Hinky is a word you pick up from living with a cop. It means something undefinable is not quite right. I had great faith in Mark's instincts. But I was also hungry.

"Let's get burgers and park over there." I pointed down the street. "Maybe Kit will come home, or someone else will let us in."

Which is how we ended up in line at Dick's Drive-In on Capitol Hill. Around us, goths, street kids, students, suits, and Jesuit priests sunned themselves in the rare warmth of the day, played with the stray dogs that own Broadway, and waited for their burgers and fries.

We were almost to the front of the line when someone grabbed my arm. I whirled to face Greg, the news editor from The Stranger. Beside him was the pencil-thin receptionist who had approached the paper files with such alarm.

"It is you!" Greg exclaimed. "I've been hoping I'd run into you again. I lost the number you gave me, but I found something you might want. I've been carrying it around with me ever since."

From an apparently cavernous front pocket, he excavated a ring of keys, a pack of gum, a band aid, a compass, three crumpled dollar bills, a condom, a monocle, and a tattered slip of pink paper.

"I was pretty freaked out about what you told me," he said, repacking his pocket. "About how Carrie Mayer died. I mean, she tried to talk to me just a couple of days before she, um, fell. If she really killed herself, then, well, it's kind of like I was the last person she reached out to before she died. And I wasn't there. I don't know what I could have done to help her even if I had been there, but I would have tried. I really would have tried."

I nodded to keep him talking. I wanted to see that pink paper.

"It got to bothering me so much that I started looking for the message that she left me, just to see whether there was anything, you know, that I should have picked up on. And I found it." A wry flicker crossed his face. "You probably noticed that I'm not too tidy. It was in the second-to-last layer on the edge of the desk, between a petition to legalize marijuana and a press release from the mayor's office about light rail."

He held the message out to me. "Anyway, I don't know whether you're still trying to figure out how the poor kid died, but from the looks of that, I'm not so sure she committed suicide."

I unfolded the pink paper and deciphered the receptionist's scrawl:

"Call ASAP. A scoop. Huge scandal."

CHAPTER 29

W hat scandal?

Mark questioned the receptionist, who seemed thrilled with the attention but bereft of any useful information. He verified that it was his handwriting on the message, but he couldn't remember Carrie or the call. We eventually said goodbye to him and Greg and spent the next hour or so keeping a watch on Kit's apartment building, munching our Deluxe burgers, and trying to figure it out.

The obvious answer was that Carrie knew or suspected Chuck Thomas of child molestation. That would have been a huge scandal. It would also have given Chuck a dramatic motive for tossing Carrie off her balcony. But it didn't feel right.

"If you really thought a child was being hurt, you wouldn't go the newspapers," Harmony said. "You'd go to the police. You'd go to someone with the power to stop it." She turned to Mark. "And Carrie *didn't* go to the police, did she?"

"Not that we know of." He took a large bite of his burger. "But there are always anonymous complaints about schools, Children First included. Last year, we had three anonymous female callers who said something was going on at the school. Nothing specific, and nothing about Chuck Thomas. When dispatch started asking questions, the callers hung up."

"Why didn't the police tell the school about this?" Harmony demanded.

"We did. Each time we got a call, a detective went out and talked to Gretta Berg. She always gave us the same story - no complaints from her end, no reason to worry. There wasn't much else for us to go on."

"Gretta never mentioned that to me," Harmony said, suspicion gathering in her voice. "I suppose it's not exactly the sort of information you want to tell your donors, but it's also not the sort of information you want anyone else telling your donors - or the media. That could be a motive for murder. If something terrible happened at the school, there won't be a Children First anymore. The child's family could sue; the school would lose any public funds. And their donors would just move on to the next good cause." She nibbled one of her fries. "But still, it seems that Carrie – that *anyone* - would have gone further than an anonymous call if she thought Chuck Thomas was molesting a little girl."

"Maybe Carrie didn't really know. Maybe she just suspected something was wrong," I said. "If she went to Gretta Berg, and nothing happened, and then she called the police, and still nothing happened, her next stop might have been The Stranger. She was awfully shy, and she needed that job at Puget Health. You don't keep your job by accusing your CEO of being a pervert. Greg could investigate it a lot easier than she could. And for sure he could light a bigger fire under the cops."

We all fell silent, wondering what might have happened. Our burgers lay half-uneaten in our laps. Sitting there in the sun with my best friends, a perfumed June breeze wafting through the open car windows, it was almost impossible to envision that stinging, bitter night a few days after Christmas. Assuming it was Carrie who had gone over that railing, I couldn't imagine why she would have let her CEO into her apartment in the middle of the night - especially if she suspected him of molesting a little girl.

Maybe that's where we should focus. If we knew who could have been in that apartment, maybe then we could figure out their connection to the scandal - the *huge* scandal - they would have killed to cover up. I considered, reviewing what we knew about Carrie Mayer. She would have let in her sister. She would have let in Kit. And - I was fairly sure - she would have let in Gretta Berg. I pictured the bluff, hearty woman with her flushed face and engaging smile. And her large, capable hands. Hands that easily could have pitched Carrie into oblivion.

"Does Gretta Berg have an alibi for the night Carrie fell?" I asked.

Mark shook his head. "No. But you'd be surprised how few people do have an alibi for anything that happens at three o'clock in the morning. Even if they live with someone else - and Gretta doesn't, unless you count her five cats - the witnesses just say they were asleep. No way to prove it, no way to disprove it. In fact, the only person who does have an alibi is the person who probably shouldn't. The night Carrie fell, Didi Thomas was on the red-eye to New Orleans. Chuck gave her the trip as a Christmas present. They were supposed to go together, but at the last minute, Chuck says, something came up and he insisted Didi go on ahead. Kind of makes you wonder why he wanted his wife out of the way so badly."

He broke off. "Hello," he said. A frail elderly woman was struggling down the street, pulling a two-wheeled aluminum cart with a single bag of groceries. She stopped at the door of Kit's apartment building and tried to tug the cart up the chipped marble stairs. She dropped her purse and dislodged her hat in the tussle, and she was flustered and muttering to herself when our shadows fell across her.

She looked up in alarm. Mark instantly whipped out his badge. "I'm a Seattle Police detective, ma'am. May I help you get your groceries up those stairs?"

The old lady looked him up and down. He gave her his most stunning smile, which she suddenly returned. She had small, square, gray teeth. "Why, thank you. That would be very nice," she said, and put up her hand to smooth her hair. A flicker of chagrin crossed her face. Harmony picked up her hat and purse and handed them to her.

While Harmony helped the old lady reseat her hat on her dull gray curls, Mark carried her groceries, and I tugged her cart through the front doors and down the basement stairs. Mark chatted with her along the way, and she beamed back at him. By the time we reached her apartment door, down the hall from Kit's, the exchange was very close to full-out flirting.

Our new friend did not approve of her neighbor – particularly Kit's overnight guests. "Men, women, and what have you," she said. "Sometimes you can't even tell." She had never seen a woman fitting Carrie's description. She didn't know the names of any of Kit's friends. But Kit did have one frequent guest – a tall, thin man with short, bristly black hair.

The blurred image of a tall, thin man with black hair flashed into my mind. If only I hadn't been so distracted in front of the interview room. I had no idea who I'd seen.

"When's the last time you saw Kit? Or heard her?" Mark asked.

The old lady paused and set down her keys. "Oh, it's been quite a while. I complained to the apartment manager about a month or so ago." She sniffed. "I haven't seen or heard her since then."

Another dead end. Our only progress was the telephone number of the apartment manager, who would have a master key. Harmony tried him twice on the way downtown, but there was no answer.

Mark dropped us off at our office and headed back to the police station. Harmony and I greeted Mrs. Holbrook – who was wearing a thin, flat hat that looked like a lime green communion wafer – and tucked into the day's paperwork. I shuffled through my in-box and ground my teeth. Boyd Tate was three weeks overdue on answers to interrogatories on a wage and hour case against American Fidelity. I had sent him one polite, one crisp, and one borderline-caustic reminder, culminating in a request for a Rule 37 conference. No answer. Tate was one of those attorneys you just couldn't be nice to, one who would delay, deny, and obfuscate until his back was against the wall. It was time to bring in the big guns: the fearsome Judge Alice Shrenk.

I was deep in my motion to compel when the phone rang.

"Are you free on October 9?" Harmony asked.

I looked up in surprise. Harmony was all of ten feet away, tapping away in her own office. I could see her reflected in the conference room door. She could have wandered over – she could have shouted through the wall. So why was she calling me on the phone?

Sometimes, with Harmony, it was better not to ask. I just brought up my electronic calendar and toggled to October. "All clear on October 9," I said, clicking on the date to add an appointment. "What's up?"

"Do you want to marry me that day?"

I almost dropped the phone. "What?"

From her conference room reflection, I could tell that Harmony's eyes were closed. She said, "Do you want to marry me that day? The pastor called from Japanese Presbyterian. They had a cancellation on October 9. We can have the chapel that day if we want it."

"I would love to marry you on October 9, Harmony." I highlighted and reserved the whole weekend. "It's on my calendar."

"It's on mine, too," she said, and I couldn't keep the grin off my face. We were as good as married. When Harmony made an appointment, she kept it.

"I love you," I said into the phone.

"I love you, too," she said from the doorway. I jumped. I hadn't heard her hang up. She didn't quite look me in the eyes. More like in the eyebrows. "I'm going over to Presby to give them our deposit."

"I'll go with you," I offered, but she stopped me.

"Actually, I'd rather go by myself. I've been talking to Pastor Riki about Higuro. That pesky commandment to honor thy father. He said he had some books for me to read."

I followed her toward the elevator. "Can I tell people? "

"Tell people what?" Mrs. Holbrook's head bobbed up from her keyboard.

Harmony paused. Then she smiled at Mrs. Holbrook. "Are you free on October 9?"

I left them chatting, went back into my office, and got on the phone. I reached Mark and Anthony at the police station, interrupted David in the middle of a mediation, and woke my sister Emily from a nap - and then had to try to talk her out of planning my bachelor party. I was not going to Vegas with my sisters.

After an hour on the phone, I ran down to the jeweler's on Fifth Avenue. Underneath all the blood, the diamond that had crushed my tooth turned out to be one carat of white fire. I had reached a gentleman's settlement with the Olympic Hotel's insurance company: I didn't sue them or talk to the press; they let me keep the diamond and paid my dental bills, the Beanie Babies donation, and the cost of putting the diamond in an engagement ring. Fair enough.

On the way back, I ducked into Torrefazione for a celebratory latte. Over in the corner, a tall, thin man with a black buzzcut was bent over a grande and a sheaf of papers. My pulse quickened when I realized it was Donald Carter. He fit the description of the mystery man at the courthouse *and* Kit's most frequent overnight visitor. I tried to imagine Donald and Kit together and failed utterly. Not just failure. Catastrophic failure.

"Hey, Jack!" Apparently I had been staring at Donald for quite some time. "Earth to Jack." I loped over, embarrassed, and joined him. He seemed ticked off. "What's the matter? You look like you've never seen me before."

I had an iron-clad excuse. "Can you keep a secret?"

He nodded warily.

"Harmony and I just set a date – October 9. Japanese Presbyterian on the west shore of Lake Washington. She's over there right now, giving them our deposit. Details to follow. Are you free?"

The announcement and the invitation broke any tension between us. He insisted on buying my latte. As we headed back uptown, he suddenly darted into a florist, his black suit jacket flapping behind him like a cape, and emerged with a dripping bundle of roses – "for the blushing bride."

By the time we reached my office, I was feeling reconciled enough to inquire after Kit. "Is she sick? Mark tried to call her today, but they said she wasn't in."

"What did he want?" There was defensiveness in Donald's voice, so I played it cool.

"He's got to finish his interview with her. She got all hysterical on him last time."

There was an awkward pause. I made myself look as innocent as possible. Finally he said, "I'll call her supervisor and check on her. But I really don't like exposing our employees to the police."

"It's just routine, Donald. Mark can't file the report until he finishes the interview. And his sergeant's on his back to wrap up the paperwork."

I had touched the inner bureaucrat that lurks inside every corporate lawyer. "Oh, OK then," Donald said. He gave me a stiff pat on the back – rather like being whacked with a stick. "Congratulations again. I'll be in touch."

On the way up to my office, I couldn't help fingering the small velvet box in my pocket. I was whistling when I stepped off the elevator. Mrs. Holbrook silenced me with a look. "There's a *lady* waiting for you in the conference room. She wouldn't give her name."

A tall blonde in an immaculate cream-colored suit was standing with her back to me, looking out the conference room window. She turned as I opened the door. My smile of professional greeting froze.

She was impeccably dressed. Pearls glowed at her throat. Her pale blond hair curved in a perfect newsbunny bob. Her suit was almost the same color as her hair, hose, and shoes. She looked like she was carved out of bone.

But her face! Under the sheen of makeup, her cheeks were sunken and deeply lined. Lipstick sketched the hard, joyless slash of her mouth, and her eyes were shadowy blue, like a new bruise. Didi Thomas – the beautiful chairperson of the CareForKids Auction, the former Seafair queen, the lady with the taste for a sash – looked like she had aged thirty years. Thirty long, hard, miserable years.

And she knew it. And she didn't care. I'm sure my face betrayed what I was thinking, but she didn't flinch. She gave me a horrifying smile – merely a baring of long, creamy teeth – and said in a cold, dry voice, "It's been a difficult few weeks for me, Jack."

She cut across my apologies. "Don't worry about it. I know I look like hell. But I'm here on business. And my money looks just as good as it ever did."

"What can I do for you?" I asked, motioning for her to sit down.

She remained standing. Every muscle of her body seemed tensed. "You heard that Puget Health threw my husband out?" she demanded.

I nodded.

"Leave of absence," she fumed. "That's what they're calling it. Like he can come back. Like it's going to end. It's not ever going to end. The police aren't doing anything. Chuck can't clear his name unless he can actually confront his accusers, unless there's actually a trial. That's not going to happen. Not unless you help me."
She fell silent. Slowly and jerkily, like she was thawing limb by limb, she sank into a chair.

"What do you want me to do?"

"I want to hire you," Didi said. "I want to hire you to find that little girl."

151

CHAPTER 30

I tried to talk her out of it. I pointed out that I wasn't a detective, that the police were doing everything they could, that there was no way I could justify taking her money for a wild goose chase. Nagging at the back of my brain was the fear that she and Chuck were trying to trick me into witness tampering. If I found the kid and her father, what was to stop Chuck and Didi from trying to buy them off – or even from trying to make them disappear?

"I can't do that, Mrs. Thomas," I protested. "I wouldn't even know where to start."

"Precisely!" Didi hit the table. On the other side of the glass door, Mrs. Holbrook raised an eyebrow. "That's exactly the trouble. No one *knows* anything. The police, the media, Puget Health – they just assume that it's that little girl, that poor little Jenny Walton, because she and her daddy disappeared. And the only way to prove them wrong is to find them and figure out why they left, figure out what really happened."

"Mrs. Thomas -" I protested.

"*Didi.*"

"Didi, I can't possibly do what you're asking."

She whipped out a folder and handed it to me. "But you have such a good reputation for finding things out. And I have all sorts of leads."

In spite of myself, I was curious. I opened the folder and started to skim the contents. There were pay stubs and work orders from the Millionair Club, a job assignment service for day laborers. There were logs from a couple of downtown shelters, and sign-in sheets from a methadone clinic.

"Where did you get all this?"

"I'm a member of the boards of the Millionair's Club and the homeless shelters. I've raised more than a hundred thousand dollars for drug treatment centers like this methadone clinic. So when I called and started asking questions, people were more than happy to help me. They want to make sure that the money keeps coming. All of that will tell you where Jenny's father worked, where he ate, where he slept, and where he got his fix up to the day he disappeared."

I was weakening. I'm like a big dog. I love to follow a trail. "Mrs. – um – Didi, I'm not saying I would take this on, but if I did, we'd have to agree on certain ground rules."

There was a flicker of amusement in her sad blue eyes. "And exactly what might those rules be?"

"Number one, that there would be no attorney-client privilege between us. Number two, that I would share all developments and information with the police, as they occurred or were discovered. Number three, that if I did locate Jenny and her father, neither you or your husband – nor any representative – would try to talk to them without a police officer and a caseworker present."

The flicker of amusement was gone. Her voice was dry and dangerous. "That's what you think I'm all about? You think I mean this child harm?"

I looked her right in the eye and spoke slowly and distinctly, a trick I had picked up from Harmony. "I think," I said, and paused for effect, "that neither of us can afford to be misunderstood."

She held my gaze for a moment – hard and tense with offense and frustration. I stared directly back at her. This could have gone on for the rest of the afternoon, but suddenly, she looked away. When she raised her eyes to mine again, the bruised cast had returned. "You're right, of course," she said, and I bristled at her placating tone. Then her voice sharpened. "I agree to your ground rules. But just so there is no misunderstanding between the two of us, I want you to know exactly what I want – and why."

"Fair enough."

"I want to know exactly what happened. If Chuck really did abuse Jenny Walton – or any other child – I will leave him, I will denounce him, and I personally will testify against him. We've never been able to have children. I've gone through all the fertility treatments. I've taken the pills; I've had the shots; I've even tried *in vitro*. I got pregnant once. For fifty-seven days. And I miscarried in the bathroom of the Columbia Tower Club during a fundraising ball for Save the Children."

She stopped and swallowed. "That was two years ago. I've tried everything else since then. I take my temperature about twenty times a day; I switched Chuck from briefs to boxers; I even went to a psychic. I'm 45. The doctors say it's time to stop trying to have one of our own. So Chuck and I are – were – trying to adopt. Twice we've gotten clear up to the actual delivery, and the birth mothers backed out. This has been the hardest, saddest, most painful thing I've ever done. It's been the thing that kept me and Chuck together – the only thing we both wanted. And if I find out that he's a monster, that the only reason he wanted a child – the child I struggled for, for so long – was to . . . to . . . abuse her –"

Her voice failed. Her eyes brimmed with furious tears. "I'll kill him," she said flatly. "If he did it, I'll kill him. If he didn't, I will go to my grave defending him, because whatever else Chuck deserves, he doesn't deserve this. But I have to know, Jack. I can't live like this. I have to know."

She pressed graceful, manicured hands to each side of her face, as if embarrassed by how much she had revealed. "So is that enough? Do we understand each other?"

I hadn't expected to like Didi. And I didn't – not exactly. But she wasn't the vain, empty-headed society matron she had seemed. I looked at her lined, sunken cheeks and felt sorry for her.

"I'll need to talk it over with Harmony. And I'll need to make sure the police are okay with my getting involved. But I'll review the file tonight, and I'll call you with an answer."

A faint, hopeful color rose in her face. I felt a burst of panic at how much she was relying on me – and how desperate she must be to do so. "Oh, thank you, Jack," she said. "Thank you so much."

"I haven't said yes yet," I reminded her.

She gave me her best fundraising smile. It was easy to see how she'd earned her Chairperson sash. "But you will."

"Maybe." There was one last question I had to ask her. "You said that if Chuck actually did it, you'd testify against him. What is it that you'd say?"

She patted my arm. "That's why I want you to help me on this, Jack. Nothing gets by you."

I was not deterred by the flattery. "What is it that you'd say?" I asked again.

She stood up. She straightened her suit. Her fingers strayed to her pearl choker. "I'd say that Chuck was interested in adopting Jenny Walton," she said.

"And is that the truth?"

She gave me a grim, ghostly smile.

"It's the truth."

CHAPTER 31

I was itching to talk the whole Didi business over with Mark and Harmony, but we were having company that night. Mark had been suitably impressed by Snoose Nelson's beautiful garden – and by Snoose Nelson's beautiful granddaughter – and had invited Megan and Hannah over for a barbecue so they could admire our yard. I walked into an abnormally spotless house, was slobbered over by an abnormally spotless dog, and said hello to my normally spotless roommates, both of whom were bustling about getting ready.

I changed my clothes, shut the door to my room as my contribution to our house beautification, and had the grill blazing hot by the time Megan and Hannah arrived.

Megan was wearing a loose black dress; her long, silky brown hair was pulled back with a heavy gold clip. Hannah had on pink shorts and a unicorn T-shirt with a matching sweater. She presented Harmony with a bunch of daisies and a basket of tiny strawberries. I knelt down beside her and introduced her to Betsy, whom she greeted solemnly and with great respect. She held her little hands in front of Betsy's enormous nose, giggling as the sniffing tickled her. She squealed with delight when Betsy licked her face.

"She loves you," I told her, and she wrapped her arms around Betsy's neck and said, "I love her, too."

Over dinner, Megan confirmed that she was, indeed, a dancer. For eight years, she had performed with the Pacific Northwest Ballet. When a broken foot sidelined her, she got a job as a reservations agent for Alaska Airlines. She was trying to carve out a reputation as a choreographer. She was divorced. Hannah's dad worked for the governor's office in Olympia.

After dinner, Megan strolled around our yard with Mark, admiring our six-foot hostas and all Mark's heirloom veggies. Hannah played Frisbee keepaway with Betsy while Harmony and I washed the dishes.

"Everything's going very well," she whispered to me over the suds.

"*Excellent,*" I returned, conspiratorially. I winked at her, and she winked back. I was firmly in favor of whatever Pastor Riki had said to her about honoring – or possibly about not honoring - Higuro. Whichever. I didn't know. I didn't care. Harmony had been relaxed, happy, and smiling all night, and whatever church stuff got us to that place, I was all for it.

Harmony and I had finished the dishes and were smooching in the kitchen when Mark, Megan, and Hannah wandered in. "That reminds me. We've got something to celebrate," Mark said, drawing two tall green bottles from the refrigerator. "Jack and Harmony are getting married!"

Megan gave us both a hug, and we toasted with the champagne - fizzy cider for Hannah.

After Megan and Hannah had gone home, bearing a bouquet of weird-shaped and strange-colored lettuces from our garden, I sat Mark and Harmony down in the living room and recounted my conversation with Didi Thomas. Even after I showed them Didi's signed agreement to the ground rules I had established, reactions were less than supportive.

"You'll get killed," they said together.

"What?"

"This always happens," Mark said. "You go wandering off looking into something, and – bam – someone takes a shot at you. Or bashes you over the head. Or sets you on fire. Or all of the above. Please, please don't do this, Jack."

"I'd just be looking for a six-year-old girl."

"Who's disappeared. Which means someone doesn't want her to be found. Which means someone's going to jump you if you start sniffing around."

They had a point. Life had been eventful over the last two years. But those attacks had been personal – threats to me, to Harmony, to Mark, to my family. I didn't know Chuck, Didi, or Jenny. There was no reason for anyone to connect me with them or target me.

"If Jenny is the little girl in the letter, and if it happened like the letter says, then she's hurt and she needs help," I argued. Both Mark and Harmony were suckers for kids. "And Mark, if she told Carrie Mayer about it, then you've got a motive to go at Chuck Thomas for murder. But if it's not true, then Chuck Thomas needs some way to clear his name. He can't do that unless someone starts tracking down the people who might have written that letter."

"What do you care about Chuck Thomas?" Mark asked. "He's a gold-plated asshole."

"I know what it's like to be falsely accused of something. And so do you." I looked over at Harmony. "Both of you. No one deserves that. Not even gold-plated assholes."

They were saved from responding by a knock at the door. Megan was standing on our front porch.

"I'm sorry. But did we leave Hannah's sweater here? We got halfway home before she started shivering. Do you mind if I take a look in the backyard?"

"Where's Hannah?" Mark asked.

"Oh, she's waiting in the car."

"*Alone?*" Mark's cop voice. At exactly the wrong time. So much suspicion in one sharp word.

Megan didn't take offense at first. "Well, of course alone," she said in surprise. Then she bristled as the suggestion sunk in that she was a neglectful mom. "She's locked in," she protested. "She's perfectly safe."

"She shouldn't be out there alone," Mark insisted.

Megan took a deep breath. I think she was about to tell Mark to mind his own business – or words to that effect – but Harmony interrupted.

"I'm sure Betsy will want to say hello to Hannah. Mark, will you take her out to Megan's car? Jack, will you help Megan find Hannah's sweater?"

Separating the combatants. A good strategy. I flipped on the deck lights and drew Megan outside. After a pause, during which he seemed to be considering going after Megan, Mark whistled for Betsy and disappeared through the front door.

Megan searched for Hannah's sweater in stiff, offended silence. Looking at her set jaw and hurt expression, I thought furiously for any way to repair the damage.

Hannah's unicorn sweater was dangling on the outside of the deck, fluttering above the garden like a small pink ghost. Megan took it from me with an awkward nod. "Thanks, Jack. We'll get out of your hair."

"Megan –" I couldn't stand to let her just walk out. "Please, wait. Just a minute."

She rounded to face me. She was clutching the sweater to her chest, and the unicorn's horn was aiming right at me. "It's OK, Jack. You're not responsible for him."

"He's working on a case that's really gotten under his skin. A little girl might have been molested. She's disappeared, and the police can't find her. He can't help it, Megan. He just sees danger everywhere right now."

"Oh."

"It doesn't have anything to do with you. You didn't do anything wrong. We were talking about the case when you came to the door, and when Hannah wasn't right there beside you –" I broke off and shrugged. "It's one of those things that's hard to get out of your mind."

She nodded. With her face half-shadowed, it was difficult to gauge how much impact I was having, but I thought she looked slightly mollified.

She rubbed her temples. "How do they know the little girl was molested if she's disappeared?"

The information had already hit the papers, so I didn't mind telling her. "The police got an anonymous letter accusing some mucky-muck of molesting a little girl at a school where he volunteers. The cops aren't even sure who the alleged victim is, but one particular little girl disappeared from the school right after the dates in the letter. So you really have to wonder."

Megan sank down on one of our deck chairs. She shivered and hugged the sweater closer to her chest. The soft June evening had turned into a cold, damp night.

"That's weird," she said. Her voice had a hollowness, as if she were far away.

"I know."

"No, I mean that's really, really weird, Jack." She swallowed hard. "This has something to do with Carrie Mayer, doesn't it?"

I sat abruptly on a chair beside her. "Why would you say that?"

"Because when Carrie and I were in grade school, the principal got an anonymous letter saying one of the teachers was getting too friendly with a student. A counselor came in and talked to all the girls – to me, and to Carrie, too. They never did find out who wrote the letter, or who the student was supposed to be. But one of the teachers left really suddenly – just there one day and gone the next. There were so many rumors." Her voice trailed off. "So *many* rumors," she repeated, in that same distant, hollow voice.

The hair on the back of my neck was prickling. "Were there rumors about the student, too?"

"Oh, yes. Yes."

"And?"

She looked me straight in the eye, summoned back from the sad, strange past.

"Well, some of the boys said it was Carrie."

CHAPTER 32

I t was just too much of a coincidence. Even Mark and Harmony agreed that I had better try to find the little girl. I took Didi's file to bed with me, and by the time I fell asleep, I already had a plan.

Jenny's father had worked at three different construction sites before he disappeared: a new apartment building just off Broadway, an expanded hospital wing on First Hill, and an office complex over on Queen Anne. Didi had listed the jobs still outstanding at each site – drywall, framing, landscape, mudding up. My back started to ache in dread. Didi also included directions to the Millionair Club and instructions for getting a job assignment "just in case" I wanted to pass myself off as a day laborer.

So that's why Didi had chosen me. There were thousands of lawyers in Seattle – and probably thousands of private eyes. But I actually looked like a day laborer. I was big and built, with the size, scars, and broken nose of a washed-up football player. Opposing counsel – and even some clients – looked me over with apprehension when we first met. And that's when I was stuffed into a suit and tie. In worn blue jeans and a T-shirt, I looked like nothing so much as a guy down on his luck.

Before setting my alarm for 4 a.m., I spared a moment to be ticked off at Didi. All that crap about my reputation. She just wanted someone who looked rough and battered enough to go undercover. Still, it would be helpful to find out what Jenny's father did and said during the last few weeks before he disappeared, and the day laborers were more likely to talk to a fellow worker than a police officer or even a private detective. A good idea was a good idea.

It didn't seem like all that good of an idea when the alarm went off at four in the morning. I left Mark and Harmony a detailed note about my plans and destination, pulled a scruffy jeans jacket over my scruffier jeans, and headed downtown.

I parked at my firm and walked the rest of the way. The streets were dark and empty, but shadows moved at the edges of the glaring yellow pools beneath the street lights. At the Millionair Club, a line of silent, bleary-eyed men stood with their heads bowed, hands sunk in their pockets against the stiff wind off the bay. Didi's instructions had noted that jobs were assigned first-come, first-served, so I was dismayed to see that I was twenty-third in line. I pledged to get up an hour earlier the next morning.

As it turned out, it wouldn't have mattered. Didi had neglected to mention that the laborers had no say in where they worked. The curt man in charge took my name, asked me whether I had any skills, and gave me bus fare to a demolition site in Georgetown. "You can have breakfast before you go," he said, jerking his thumb in the direction of another sullen knot of men. "Be back before 4:30 for your pay."

Which is how I ended up spending ten solid hours at the bottom of a Georgetown demolition pit, loading up and carting off the rubble that escaped the wide swath of the heavy equipment. Within two hours, I had burned through my breakfast of scalding coffee, donated meat sauce, and a slice of venerable Wonder Bread. Four hours in, my muscles were screaming.

I had thought I was in good shape. I ran at least five miles a day, Mark and I lifted weights together a couple of times a week, and our constant improvement projects kept me hopping around the house. But it had been years since I had put in a full day of non-stop, merciless, hard labor. My shoulders jarred again and again as my shovel hit hidden, hateful clumps of uncrushed concrete. My back felt like it would snap with the wrench of tossing each spadeful into the wheelbarrow. My knees and arms shook with the strain of pushing the damn thing over the broken, pitted ground.

There was nowhere to buy food, and I hadn't brought a lunch. I had two swigs of tepid water all day, and my eyes and throat burned with the heat and the dust. To rub my nose in it, the whole day was an absolute bust as far as collecting information about Jenny's dad. No one talked to me except to order me around. The union guys took breaks and shot the breeze. The day laborers kept their heads down and worked straight through. I survived by inventing ever more creative curses about Didi.

My mood did not improve when I returned to the Millionair Club to get my pay. The going rate for a broken back and blistered hands was seven bucks an hour. I walked out of the Millionair Club with $65 in my pocket – after taxes.

I was seething; I was starving; and I couldn't wait to get home, call Didi, and tell her to shove it up her ass. Preferably from a cold bath with a cold beer and a cold compress on my hands. The presumption, I fumed. Waltzing into my office, giving me a big song and dance about wanting a baby, tricking me into busting my body busting rocks. Well, she could damn well get another pigeon to carry her water. Or whatever. I was too tired to care if my metaphors made any sense.

I had worked up a fine head of steam by this time, and I easily could have stomped away and called the whole thing off. Would have, in fact, if I hadn't turned at a noise behind me. I faced a stream of smiling men pouring out of the Millionair Club. I heard their fervent, repeated thanks to the stone-faced man doling out the pay: *thank you, grazie, muchas gracias, arigato, spasibo, dziękuję, God bless.* I saw my fellow workers folding and refolding their bills and checking their coins in delight, counting and calculating how much they had with the desperate precision of the desperately poor.

I was suddenly, shatteringly ashamed. Ashamed of the whole day. Ashamed of my assumption that I could pass myself off as a working man when I was obviously nothing more than a pampered corporate lapdog. Ashamed of showing up so unprepared that I didn't even think to pack a lunch. Ashamed of bitching to myself non-stop. And – this is what really stung – ashamed of being ashamed of the day's work. Because when I got right down to it, that was what had infuriated me. I was a lawyer. A big-time lawyer. I had my name on our door, on our stationery, on our tasteful ad in the Bar Journal. I thought I was too good to chuck rocks for seven bucks an hour.

I looked around at my fellow workers, at their happy, relieved faces. They had worked just as hard as I had, sweated just as much if not more. They were just as dirty, just as tired, a hell of a lot hungrier. But they were grateful. Grateful for the below-subsistence pay. *Grateful for the work.*

A lot had happened to me since I had been abandoned by my aunt at eight years old and spent the next ten years in the foster system. I had gotten a football scholarship to the University of Washington. I had graduated from college, done well in law school, passed the Bar. I had bought a house, adopted a dog, bonded all over the place with four sisters I hadn't known I had. I had spent five bruising but educational years at a big firm, survived a couple of attempts on my life, and found the girl of my dreams. I had a checking account, a savings account, and a 401(k). All that changes you. It really does. I knew I was different. But I never, ever thought I was this close to becoming yuppie scum.

To make me feel even worse, the curt man came out and pressed a voucher in my hand. "Forgot to give you this," he said. "It's enough for some work gloves or boots at the thrift store. You'll get another one next week." He looked me over critically. "You been inside, right?"

I started and nodded, thinking that my indoor pallor had betrayed me for the white-collar wuss I really was. Then his meaning sunk in and I flushed and shook my head vigorously, realizing I had just admitted to being incarcerated. "Oh, no. I mean, yes, but not like that –" I began to stammer.

The curt man misunderstood my panic. "Don't worry about it. So long as you work hard, no one gives a shit about what you've done. Only what you can do. See you tomorrow, kid." And then he patted me on the back.

After that, I didn't have a choice. Wearing my new - to me - work gloves and carrying a PB&J and a Coke in a tattered paper sack, I was fifth in line for the job assignments the next morning. And so began one of the most surreal episodes of my life. I busted rocks, framed walls, dug trenches, cleared mammoth blackberry brambles, and - in one day of almost mythological torture - carried fourteen pallets of concrete blocks up forty-seven cement stairs, block after block after block.

After a week or so, my muscles stopped screaming. I still ached everywhere at night - and my back still could not fully admit this was happening, or that it had any sort of important role to play - but once you've got the muscle of a college football player, it just waits to snap back into action. In five days, I dropped fifteen pounds. My arms, chest, and neck bulged with new definition. I was below my playing weight. The whole thing reminded me of playing college ball - the sweat, the dirt, the smells, the ever-present threat of serious injury. The only real difference was that nobody cheered.

Nobody paid me any attention whatsoever. The story seemed to have gotten around that I was fresh out of prison, and no one wanted to be my friend. But gradually, I was becoming a familiar face, someone to speak in front of if not to. After paying my dues for a couple of days, I began following a group of the guys after work. They drifted to the grocery store across the street, where they bought malt liquor and fortified wine under the owner's suspicious watch. I bought a 40-ouncer and - with some hesitation - followed them into Regrade Park on the corner of Third and Bell. It's illegal to drink in a public place, but even the cops won't go into Regrade Park. Night after night, I'd wedge myself in what seemed to be a neutral spot near the cinnamon-roll-shaped concrete sculpture and just listen.

I caught bits and pieces of slow, slurred conversation. A lot of it was your basic locker room bullshit: who was getting it; who was giving it; whose mother was a *puta*; who was a *maricón*. As the bottles emptied and the shadows lengthened, the talk turned wistful as they compared notes about what they would do once they saved up a little money. Go back to Arkansas. Buy a share of a fishing boat. Get married. Get divorced. Get a food cart down by the Kingdome. Everyone agreed that was a good idea. They laughed and teased and toasted each other in the dying light.

After ten days, I was ready to call it quits. I had yet to be sent to any of the job sites where Jenny's father had worked prior to his disappearance. Even if I ended up there someday, I had a greater appreciation for the transience of day laborers. A month was an eternity to last on a job, and no one had seen Clifford Walton since November. Work was piling up for me back at the office; the few questions I had ventured during our nightly drink-off in Regrade Park had yielded no useful information; and no longer in good conscience could I bill Didi $200 an hour for whacking down blackberries - much as she richly deserved it.

I showed up for my last day of work prepared with a story about having saved up enough money to get to my family in Spokane. The gruff supervisor seemed to have taken a personal interest in my rehabilitation, and I didn't want to sour him on future good works by disappearing. I was all ready to launch into my tale when I looked at my job assignment and realized where I was going: the new office complex on Queen Anne. Clifford Walton's last job site.

It was still half-dark when I stepped off the bus on Queen Anne, the Sound glinting black under the sinking moon. The foreman set me to work hammering wooden molds for a concrete wall. I measured and squared and cut and swung until the sun was high, and the foreman signaled that I could take a break.

I got myself a drink of water, washed my face, and looked around the job site, getting my bearings. The actual construction was almost done. Glazers and painters were finishing the insides of the complex; all that was left outside were a couple of dividing walls, a walkway, and the landscaping. If there was anything to find, I would have to work fast. There were only a couple of days of unskilled labor left. Assuming they asked for me again, I could expect a week there, tops.

I heard my name and snapped out of my reverie. Break time was over, and I wanted to make a good impression. I took a shortcut around the other side of the complex instead of going back the way I had come. As I rounded the corner, I stopped dead, disoriented. The distinctive slope of the roof opposite me was at odds with the building I remembered. Then the boss bellowed my name again, and everything snapped into focus. The building looked different because I had seen it only from the front, and now I was looking at it from the back.

I had no doubt what it was. The shape of the roof, the frail figures at the windows, the silent ambulance stationed at the back door - they all added up.

Right across the street from the job site was the Evergreen Care Center, the nursing home where Kirstin Mayer spent the last six months of her life, the nursing home where she died. Between us was the lot where Carrie must have parked on her daily visits to her mom. Clifford Walton had spent a long time on this job site. Carrie worked the early shift at Puget Health. She would have been arriving to visit her mom just as Clifford was leaving the site to get his pay. They would have walked right by each other, night after night.

I stood on the rocky, trampled ground that soon would be sodded over and pristine. The glare of the sun on the glass distorted the shapes, but I could still see movement in the residents' rooms. On a dark morning in November, with a light burning in those windows, what could Clifford Walton have seen?

A third bellow. The foreman was royally pissed. I went back to work and measured and squared and cut and swung the rest of the afternoon, but my mind was far away.

In my mind, I was all the way back in November.

In my mind, I was watching those windows, watching out there in the dark.

CHAPTER 33

I couldn't imagine that Carrie would have spoken to him - not a dirty, sodden construction worker on a muddy construction site. By all accounts, she had been far too shy. It was true that my fellow workers and I had drawn a few whistles and giggles from passing girls. But Carrie didn't seem like that type of woman, and even that type of woman wouldn't have whistled at Clifford. Mark had shown me the mugshot from Clifford Walton's last arrest. His eyes were small and close together, and his nose slumped in the middle like someone had notched it with a knife. He looked trampled and rat-like - not, to be blunt, a babe magnet.

But he might have spoken to Carrie. He knew her, Gretta Berg confirmed - at least he knew who she was. A couple of times a month, until her mother's final illness, Carrie held after-school story times, keeping the children occupied while they waited for their parents to pick them up at Children First. Clifford would come in early and wait for the story to be finished, hovering in the shadows of the library until everyone lived happily ever after. If he saw the story lady from his daughter's school going into or coming out of the rest home across the street, he might have said hello, especially if she seemed upset.

And if he had broken the ice with Carrie, what would they have talked about? I couldn't envision the two of them chatting through the wire fence about the possible molestation of Jenny Walton. It was a busy street, a busy site. If that concern ever passed between them, I was sure it had happened somewhere else. But they could have made a date to meet at a neutral place, or Carrie could have given Clifford her number at Puget Health.

How do you tell someone you think his kid's being molested - assuming you do? Or was it the other way around? Did he seek her help - and end up sending her to her death when Chuck Thomas tried to silence her suspicions? Or maybe it had nothing to do with Jenny Walton. Maybe Clifford saw something bad through the uncurtained windows of the rest home - a slapped patient, a sexual assault, a light-fingered nurse - and mentioned it to Carrie when he saw her going to visit her mom.

I shook my head. There were so many possibilities and so few facts. I was going to have to put it squarely to Didi: I'd been working for her for two weeks, and I had nothing solid to show for it. But I kept putting off that day of reckoning. It had to mean something, a voice inside me kept insisting. It had to mean something that Jenny Walton's father was working right next to the nursing home where Carrie Mayer's mother died.

Work on the Queen Anne jobsite that day was surprisingly easy - breaking down scaffolding, unrolling sod, sweeping up debris, planting trees. We were reaching the end of the build. A couple of hours in, the foreman called me over.

"Sorry, kid, I'm going to cut you loose. I can't justify the rest of the day."

Disappointment hit me like a punch in the stomach. I felt so close to something. Close to what, I didn't know, but I felt there was something waiting to be unlocked on that job site – and I had yet to find the key.

"Please," I said. "I really need this job. Could I just I stay to the end of the day? Maybe for six dollars an hour?"

"Nope. I don't set your pay. If you're here, it's seven bucks."

I was trying to come up with another way to stay on the site when one of my Regrade drinking buddies interrupted.

"Oh, come on. Let him stay. At least until he gets his little girl."

I jumped. I had told no one about Jenny Walton. The few questions I had ventured had been careful and oblique - *did anyone have custody of their kids? did they know anyone who had kept custody even though they were looking for another place to stay?* - and I had received no leads and raised no eyebrows. Until now, apparently.

"What girl?" the foreman snapped.

I was saved – sort of – by my Regrade drinking buddy, who might possibly still be drunk from the night before. "Our friend here, he's had all the ladies lining up to watch him," he told the foreman. "Even the old ladies from the rest home. It's hilarious. But there was one particular little girl - one of the waitresses at the café across the street. She watched him all day yesterday. And whenever he looked up, she'd wa-a-a-ve." Here he did an eye-fluttering imitation of a Betty Boop yoo-hoo and dissolved into laughter.

Everyone was snickering by this time. I could not get any redder. I mentally added another zero to Didi's bill.

But they let me stay – for the entertainment value. The foreman assigned me to load a truck right across from the café. He sauntered by to see how I was treating my public. The café waitress was nowhere to be seen, but - sure enough - old ladies were peeping out of their rest home windows at me, and some black-clad sophisticates kept a rapt watch from the Starbucks across the street.

"Any luck?" The foreman had a detestable grin.

The blood rushed into my face. "She's, uh, well, she hasn't shown up yet. The girl I wanted to see."

"It's too early. They don't open until lunch. But if she doesn't come, you could always go for those three," he said, nodding toward the three women at Starbucks. "'Course, three at a time, all revved up on caffeine. Think you could handle that?"

Yet another zero on Didi's bill. I mumbled an embarrassed demurrer, which he ignored. "Regular singles bar around here," he said. "In fact, last year some bitch lifted one of my guys right from under my nose. All of a sudden he comes up to me, says he needs a break, and goes off down the street with this broad. And he never comes back. Asshole left a whole section of concrete that needed to be leveled out. We had to dig it up and start again."

"What happened to him?" I said, trying to sound casual.

"No frigging idea. The cops came around a couple weeks ago asking about him, so I figured he might have gotten the shelter-shave." He drew his finger across his throat. "He's probably this broad's pool boy over in Bellevue. She looked rich enough - like she got whatever she wanted. And she wanted him. Stood right there talking to him through the fence, insisting he come with her."

"How did you know she was from Bellevue?"

He looked at me pityingly. The consensus on the site was that I worked fast but thought slow. "Just looked like that type, I meant. All spiffed up and snippy. I didn't mean she was actually from Bellevue, you understand."

"Oh. I understand." He looked like he might respond with, "yeah, right," and tell me to get back to work, so I tried another gambit to keep him talking. "Was she hot?"

He threw back his head and laughed. "Noooo. Face like an old tire - with a lot of miles on it. But it's not like Cliff was any big prize himself." He laughed again. "They would have made quite a pair. Anyway, get back to work. If your little friend shows up, you can take five and see if she wants to play - or just likes to watch."

He elbowed me in the ribs and swaggered off. I bent back over my work, mentally reviewing the women I had encountered in this case. I was searching for someone who fit the description of the woman who had lured Clifford Walton away from the construction site on the day he disappeared: spiffed up, snippy, ugly, and old.

Carrie Mayer? By all accounts, she was not attractive, but no one ever said she had looked old. Or spiffy. According to Mr. Sandstrom and the folks at Hello, Gorgeous, the only spiffed up clothes Carrie owned were brand-new, unworn, and still had their tags.

Melanie Mayer? Spiffy and snippy, with the look of having been around the block. But not old. Not yet. And not ugly. With her bright hair and heavy makeup, Melanie still had the cast of a beauty queen.

Gretta Berg? She had a red, worn face that my foreman might have considered both ugly and old. She seemed neither snippy nor spiffy. She seemed nice, and at the CareForKids auction, she had worn a plain black pantsuit. But Clifford Walton would have gone with her. If Gretta had said something was wrong with his daughter, Clifford probably would have left even fresh-poured concrete to get to Jenny.

Kit McCracken? I dismissed her out of hand. I couldn't imagine anyone, anywhere describing Kit as having face like an old tire. She seemed like everybody's type. And if she had so much as beckoned to a man like Clifford Walton, he probably would have dropped dead of pure joy - right splat in the concrete.

So who else was there? I could barely remember what Carrie's manager and supervisor looked like, although I was fairly certain that they had not seemed spiffed up in the least. Most of her co-workers were younger. I loaded pipes and scrap lumber and racked my brains.

When the answer came, it was chilling, not just because I had started to like her – or at least respect her - but because it might mean I was working for monster. There was another woman in this mess. She was both spiffed up and snippy. She had been a beauty queen too, but she was twenty years past her prime. I pictured her ravaged face and wondered. I had thought her haggard look came from worry over the accusations against her husband, but I had seen her only once before, in the flattering half-light of the Spanish Ballroom. Maybe she always looked like that. Like a spoiled Bellevue housewife who always got what she wanted. Like an old tire with a lot of miles on it.

Didi Thomas.

My client.

The woman who had hired me to find Clifford Walton.

The woman who desperately wanted me to find his little girl.

CHAPTER 34

I spent the rest of the morning on autopilot, pondering why Didi would have hired me to find Jenny Walton if she had had a hand in her disappearance. The only explanation I could come up with was blackmail. If Didi and Chuck had paid Clifford to drop out of sight and keep silent, they would want to track him down pretty fast if he doublecrossed them by alerting the cops after he and Jenny safely disappeared. But if Didi had lured Clifford away from this construction site, why encourage me to go undercover at a place where her role might be remembered? Maybe to check out whether she *was* remembered?

I sighed, stretched, and sank down on one of the brand-new concrete walls to eat my peanut butter sandwich and drink my Coke. I was amused to see that Harmony had snuck an apple into the bag. She was sure I was going to die of scurvy during this experiment. Higuro had finally agreed to waive the attorney-client privilege and to let Harmony do the investigation of the Rockface fraud claims. So she had been super busy too, especially since she was keeping our practice afloat single-handed while I was busting rocks – but she was still thinking of me.

I crunched my apple, smiling a little, thinking of Harmony. I completely missed the waitress's approach. Suddenly, someone shoved me in the back - causing me to choke on my bite of apple - my foreman hissed "go get her," and she was right in front of me, separated only by the cyclone wire fence.

I was trapped. I had had no intention of pursuing the waitress - or allowing her to pursue me - but that was how I got to stay on the jobsite. And I had a grinning audience to make sure I followed through, who had been waiting all morning for just this moment. I ambled up to the fence, wondering what in the hell I was going to say, trying as much as possible to block her from the view of the snickering guys behind me.

"Hi." She had blond hair and big brown eyes. She was wearing her zippered waitress uniform and dark red lipstick. If she was over twenty, I would eat my apple core.

My apple core. Dammit. I was still holding the half-eaten fruit. There was no choice but to gesture with it carelessly, as if it were a cigarette. *Mr. Suave.*

"Hi." So far, so good.

"I'm Tara."

"Jack."

"Hi, Jack." She giggled.

"Hi, Tara." Oh, boy. It was a good thing I was getting married. I had completely lost my ability to chat up a girl.

Or maybe not. She was still looking at me with that expectant expression on her face, that secret little smile girls get when things are going very well.

"Look, Jack," she said and stopped. She giggled again, as if my very name were amusing to her. "I never do this, but when you were here a day or so ago, and I was waiting on the outside tables, I noticed that you kept looking at me."

Lies, I thought. I wasn't looking at her. She was looking at me. Then I wondered how I could have known she was looking at me if I hadn't been looking at her, and I started to worry.

"Anyway," she said, "I can tell that you guys are getting ready to leave, and if I didn't say something to you, I'd regret it forever. Would you like to have a bite to eat with me tonight? I have two hours off between the lunch and dinner crowd. I thought we could go over there." And she pointed to the nice Italian restaurant down the street.

She misread the anxiety that must have flashed in my eyes. "My treat, I mean," she said hastily. "I'd like to take you out to dinner, to, to . . . celebrate your finishing this building."

I was not going to let a hardworking little waitress waste her money on me. I couldn't refuse her flat, not with my cheering section behind me and that nervous, hopeful look in her face. But I could let her down easy and keep up the facade with the guys.

"I don't want you to do that," I said, hating myself when her eyes dropped in disappointment. "But I'd like to buy you a cup of coffee instead."

Her pretty lashes came up immediately. The spark had returned to her eyes. "No, I mean it. It's fine. I'd love to treat you to dinner."

I shook my head. "Please. I wouldn't be comfortable." When she looked unconvinced, I reached for a clincher that was more or less the truth. "I'm an old-fashioned guy."

For whatever reason, that charmed her. "OK, then," she said, lifting her hands in a gesture of mock defeat. "You win. *Indulge me.*"

We arranged to meet at Starbucks at 3 p.m. She glided back to the café, turning around twice to make sure I was watching her pert retreat. I was. Not, I assured myself, for the obvious reason that her uniform was tight and shiny and outlined her every curve. I was just making sure that she was out of earshot before I went back to the guys.

The predictable chorus of cat-calls and rooting greeted my return. I suffered through three more hours of ribbing - particularly about being an old-fashioned guy - collected my final pay directly from the foreman, and prepared to leave the construction site for the last time. "Don't do anything I wouldn't do," the foreman said.

I looked at him with sober, respectful interest. "What wouldn't you do?"

It was a good thing I had cultivated such a solid reputation as an idiot. Otherwise, he might have taken a swing at me. As it was, he just puffed out his breath in exasperation and said, "Have a good time, kid."

Tara was already at Starbucks when I arrived. I bought her a caramel macchiato and - I insisted - a ginger molasses cookie, and settled her in a comfy chair by the window. She was flushed and smiling. I liked the way she drank her coffee. Instead of sipping through the absurd little hole, she took off the lid and bent over the cup, eyes closed and breathing deep, letting the steam curl and curve around her face.

"It's good for the skin," she said, blushing, when she saw I was watching. "Keeps wrinkles away."

I had to agree with her on that one, because Tara did not have a single wrinkle. Then again, she was all of nineteen years old. I learned that - and apparently, everything else about her - as we sat together and drank our coffee. She talked quickly and eagerly, like she didn't get to very often. Her mom and dad both worked at Boeing; she had graduated from high school a year ago; she had taken the year off to earn tuition money for the Brenneke School of Massage. She was starting in the fall. She had good hands. She flexed her fingers at me. Did I want a demonstration?

I was trying to think of one good reason why I wouldn't want a demonstration - why any heterosexual man alive wouldn't want a demonstration - when she gave me a wide, warm, trusting smile. "Or are you just too old-fashioned?"

"Definitely too old-fashioned," I replied, and she dissolved into giggles. When she suddenly stopped and sucked in her breath, I thought she was choking and half rose to help her.

"You OK?"

She was staring over my shoulder. Her forehead puckered in concern. "Oh, that's so sad," she said. "Another one."

I turned in the direction she was looking. Across the street, two men in blue uniforms were loading a sheet-draped figure into the ambulance that was always on alert behind the Evergreen Care Center. They jostled the gurney. They seemed in no particular hurry. A small, silver-haired woman signed something and handed it to the men, who slammed the back doors and climbed into the front. Without lights or sirens, the ambulance made a slow and silent turn into traffic. It inched right by us. I had never realized how creepy a dark and dawdling ambulance is before.

When I looked back at Tara, she was shaking her head. "That's three in the last two days. They must feed them a lot of fat or salt at the beginning of the month."

"What do you mean?"

"I have a girlfriend who's a dietician. When I get my massage certificate, we're going to open a clinic together. She says you're like three-hundred-times more likely to die after a heavy meal than a light one. They've done, like, studies and stuff."

"What was that you said about the beginning of the month?"

"It's like clockwork. And I'm not the only one who's noticed. There are always at least a couple of deaths over there in the first week of every month."

"Don't people die all the time there? It's a rest home, right?"

"Not like this. Not all in a clump. Someone ought to tell them. They're probably serving a lot of meat this week because they get it in fresh early in the month. That's how we do it in the café with our specials. We start out with pot roast and chops and end up with stir fries and hash. But they're cooking for old people. People who are sick. They ought to be more careful. For heaven's sake, it looks like they're killing people over there."

A chill slipped down my back. As Tara talked on earnestly about her theories of health and wellness, I couldn't help wondering whether something more serious than menu planning might be awry at the Evergreen Care Center.

Kit had told me how angry Carrie was at the center staff, how furious she was that they tried to get her mother to prepare to die instead of encouraging her to fight the cancer that took her life. I thought of that vast and unsettling wall of the dead, the smiling snapshots of patients who had passed on. And I thought of the center manager, the sleek Pat Campbell - a small woman with silver hair - who had told me that the line between life and death was pretty blurred there at Evergreen.

How blurred? I wondered. I sipped my coffee and nodded at Tara and made appropriate noises at appropriate intervals and couldn't keep my thoughts off the rest home, on what seemed to me to be the very clear and very important line between life and death.

Just how blurred did they think it was?

CHAPTER 35

My mind was full of mercy killing and those news stories about nurses with a penchant for poison. If there were signs I should have seen, I completely missed them. Tara glanced at her watch, gulped her coffee, and said, "Oh my gosh, I've got to get back to work." She thanked me for the chat, planted a peck on my cheek, and gave every indication that our date - if you wanted to call it that - was at an end. So I was totally unsuspecting when she said, "Jack, would you mind walking me back to work? I have to go in through the kitchen, and sometimes there are creeps hanging around the alley."

Chivalry demanded no less. We were right in the middle of the alley, which as alleys go, was fairly clean, when Tara pushed me against the wall. I thought she was falling and flung my arms around her. I opened my mouth to ask if she was all right, but she obviously was. She was kissing me. I mean, really, really kissing me - deep and hard and hungry. Her tongue was pierced, and there was an exquisite flicker of metal through my mouth. I was so stunned that I just held her and kissed her back.

Kissing Harmony - doing anything physical with Harmony - was like engaging in a delicate, high-stakes negotiation. There was always forethought, planning, and a detachment strategy on her part. Sometimes I could feel her thinking of ways to initiate the endgame, of ways to get away from me. Tara wasn't thinking at all. She just wanted me. It had been two years since I had kissed anyone like this, two years since anyone had just wanted me.

Her skin met mine. Her uniform was unzipped; my shirt was half off. She was not wearing a bra. The jolt that went through my body knocked me back again. She pressed harder on top of me, straddling me, wriggling her arms out of her uniform. I was trying - at least I thought I was trying - to push her away, but she felt so good. Everything about her felt so good - so generous and eager and shudderingly alive. This was the difference between a wary girl who had been hurt and a wild girl who didn't even realize she could be. No one had ever taken advantage of Tara.

Until now. The acid words reverberated through my skull as though someone had thumped me on the head. Even though I felt more like the hunted than the hunter, there was no question that I was the grown-up here. She was nineteen. I was twenty-nine. I was engaged. And I had been lying to her since I met her. Lying just by appearing to be something I wasn't.

She was tugging at my belt. I brushed her hands away. I zipped up her uniform and held her at a distance, breathing hard, until things returned more or less to normal. "No," I said, realizing how unconvincing I sounded. "I can't do this."

"You could have a minute ago."

"I won't do this."

"You don't like me? I'm not pretty?"

I assured her that I did, that she was. "I'm not going to take advantage of you."

She stuck her tongue out at me. An adorable little tongue. "I'm not a little girl, Jack."

"I didn't say you were. But you deserve a lot more than this."

There was more in that vein, but that's what it came down to. I was an old-fashioned guy. She seemed a little confused, but also strangely flattered, when she finally said goodbye. She went through the kitchen door smiling and turned back two times to wave. Or wa-a-a-ve. Or whatever. At least she didn't blow me a kiss.

I stumbled out of the alley, tore the telephone number she had given me into bits and tossed them in a dumpster, and high-tailed it back downtown. I didn't wait for the bus; I didn't hail a cab. I just hustled. I was by turns elated at my escape, aching for what I had left behind, and sick to my stomach with guilt. I didn't know where to go. I couldn't go home - not with remorse stamped all over my face. I couldn't go to work. I definitely could not go to Regrade Park. I couldn't stand to see anyone who knew - or thought they knew - what I had done.

I ended up on Boren at Four Columns Park, a cluster of ruined church columns, overgrown with greenery. I sat on the rickety wood bench in the shadow of the trees, watched the heavy summer night draw across Queen Anne Hill, the city lights begin to glitter. The Space Needle sprang to life with its ethereal green glow. One by one, the windows of my law firm went dark. First Mrs. Holbrook's, then the conference room, then - much later - Harmony's. *Harmony.* I put my head in my hands and wondered how - or if - I was going to explain to her what had happened.

I'd give it a couple more hours, I decided. Mark and Harmony were used to my staying out late in Regrade Park. If I timed it right, they would both be asleep when I got home.

I was settling in for a long wait when I realized I was not alone. A lighter spluttered below me in the tangle of moss, vines, and brambles between the park and the drop-off to I-5. As he sucked in on the cigarette, I caught a glimpse of the stubbly face of the man bedded down about fifteen feet away from me. Reluctant as

I was to go home, it struck me that it wasn't smart to sit out there alone in the dark. I could go to a shelter, I thought. I could sleep in my car. I knew I was over-dramatizing, but both seemed preferable to facing the music at home.

I bit the bullet. I drove home slowly, took my time in the garage. Betsy bounded to greet me, but Mark and Harmony were nowhere to be seen. So far, so good. The kitchen light was on, and a small covered pot was on the stove. It looked like a few mouthfuls of some sort of stew - a much more modest dinner than usual. Since I was queasy with anxiety, that was probably for the best. I took a spoonful, chewed - and pitched over to the sink to spit it out. It was beyond awful. It was disgusting: metallic, slippery, and sickeningly sweet, like a beefy, rotten apple. I rinsed out my mouth and spit again. I wondered - madly - if Harmony had somehow found out about my afternoon and had decided to poison me.

"There you are!" There she was, framed in the doorway, smiling, looking pleased to see me and not in the least murderous. Then she glanced at the pan in my hand and shook her head. "Your dinner is in the oven, Jack. That's not for you, that's -"

"For Betsy?" I interrupted, horrified. Maybe she had gotten it into her head to heat up Betsy's canned food. I took another gulp of water.

"For me," she responded, with an edge to her voice.

"For you?" I tried to backpedal. Harmony was a wonderful cook, but even the best cooks have occasional failures. "Is it, um, a new recipe or something?"

She laughed. I relaxed. "Well, you could say that." She opened the cupboard and extracted a bevy of small tan boxes, boxes I recognized and detested on sight. "You see, I've started this diet -"

"You *what?*"

The intensity of my reaction startled her, but she tried again. "This diet," she said, trying to show me the boxes, which I knew all too well contained the bits of sawdust and modified food starch that a nationwide diet chain peddled as prepackaged meals. "This one is the beef bourguignon. I've already lost two pounds."

"What in the hell are you on a diet for?" My voice was sharp and hot in the quiet kitchen. I was scared, and that fear was starting to bleed into anger. I wasn't even really seeing Harmony. I was seeing Betsy - Betsy the girl - my old girlfriend, who had dropped into a funk, dropped thirty pounds, and then dropped *me*. Suddenly, I was furious at Harmony. After I had been so worried and so guilty about Tara, it was an intense relief to decide that Harmony had also been in the wrong. For two years, she had strung me along with little dabs and scraps of affection. I was tired, I was hungry, and I was horny as hell. This diet thing was just another way to get away from me. Two pounds here; two pounds there. Pretty soon, she would just disappear.

"Oh, no," I said, picking up the saucepan and heading for the sink. "You're not going on a diet. That's final."

Her voice was calm and low, her words spaced evenly, firm and deliberate as headstones. That meant she was seething. "Do not tell me what to do. Do not ever tell me what to do."

It was her cobra's voice. I ignored it. I started scraping the "bourguignon" into the sink. She grabbed my wrist. "What has gotten into you?" she demanded, coming close. "What on earth is the matt -" And then she broke off.

She was staring at my neck. My hand flew guiltily to the spot, right behind my ear. Everything after that was just a blur of searing impressions: the hurt in her face, the stink of argument and infidelity, the dark red smear of lipstick that trailed off on my fingers. Shame and rage and longing churned through me. I hated myself for hurting her. I resented her for being hurt, for reminding me what I'd done.

She turned and walked away from me. Didn't say a word, just dropped my arm as if it were unclean and turned around. I waited for the slam of her bedroom door, but it closed with a whisper, the kind of unnerving click that wakes you, sweating, at 3 a.m. It seemed more final and more terrible than anything else she could have done, as though there were nothing else either of us could do or say.

Mark found me twenty minutes later, sitting on the back steps, looking out at the dark garden. "Well," he said, sitting down beside me, "I guess now you know why undercover cops get divorced."

"Don't start with me."

He handed me a beer. "You either need to get drunk or get beat up. And because I generally like you, I'm going to go with drunk."

I took a swig. It tasted terrible. I squinted at the label: a fancy microbrew. Great, just great. I'd spend the rest of my life drinking Olde English 800 and making out in alleys. I put down the bottle. "No thanks."

"You want to tell me what happened?"

I shook my head. I didn't want to talk about it. I didn't want to think about it. We sat in silence for a little while.

Mark rolled the beer bottle between his hands. "You know, when I was undercover, every now and then Brewster would pull his guys back in and put us on desk duty for a couple days. It was his way of reminding us who we really were. After you've been under for a while, you can forget that. He'd pull us off before we got into trouble, before we started thinking we were players."

"So?"

"So, I think you could use a break. You go be a lawyer again for a while. OK?"

It wasn't like I had anything else to accomplish as a day laborer. "OK."

He clapped me on the back. "Good. David Mann invited us over day after tomorrow to watch the fireworks. Think you'll be sane by then?"

"Who says I'm not sane?"

"I've never known you to come home with lipstick on your neck, pick a fight with Harmony, and hit the roof when you find out she's on a diet. Most guys cheer when their girlfriends go on a diet, Jack."

"Most guys don't get dumped whenever their girlfriends start losing weight."

"Come again?"

I told him about Betsy. Betsy the girl. When I was finished, he gave a long, low whistle.

"Harmony is not planning on dumping you. At least, she *wasn't*. She's been so excited to tell you what she found while you were off being Mr. Millionair. She had an appointment up at Virginia Mason last week and noticed one of those diet places a couple of blocks away from Carrie Mayer's old apartment. She went in, asked them if they gave credit to customers who brought in new clients, and told them that she had been referred by Carrie Mayer. The clerk looked her up, and sure enough, Carrie had been going to that diet center. That's how she lost all her weight. Harmony signed up on the spot. She's gone every day to be weighed and measured; she's trying to get in good with the counselors, trying to find out if they know why Carrie wanted to drop some pounds. She says they gab like a beauty shop up there."

"Wow." I couldn't think of anything else to say. I felt in equal parts relieved, stupid, and intrigued. So Carrie was intentionally losing weight. It wasn't depression or stress from her mom's illness. She was purposely dieting down.

But why? The question brought me right back to where our initial investigation foundered. We still didn't know for sure who had gone over that railing. If Carrie had planned to pass herself off as her sister to collect on her own insurance policy, she would have had to shed fifty pounds to match Melanie's weight. That was clear. But if Carrie was our first victim, the woman who was bludgeoned with an aebleskiver pan and thrown to her death, we still didn't know why she would have gone on a diet. When I added up the weight loss with the new clothes, it still seemed like she had been preparing for something, repackaging herself so she would be ready.

Ready for what? I asked myself, staring out at the dark yard.

Ready for what?

CHAPTER 36

woke to a silent, sundrenched house. A terse note on the fridge said that Harmony had gone plant-shopping with Mark. There was a P.S.: "I am not that mad at you." And a P.P.S.: "But Betsy is."

Betsy *was*. I made myself some toast and tried to read the paper, but it was hard to eat or read with her constant glowering a few feet away. Sometimes I could jolly Betsy out of a glower, but right then I was in no mood to even try.

I pulled on my pants and almost fell over as the fabric pooled around my feet. I pulled them up and watched them fall again. I folded the fabric over at my waist and measured with my hand. Amazing. In my two weeks as a day laborer, I had sweat off about five inches. Getting dressed at 4 a.m. in my grubbiest clothes, I hadn't noticed the change. I had figured that my grubby clothes were stretched, not that I had shrunk. That's just what belts were for.

None of my real clothes fit. In a pleasant sort of exasperation, I went downstairs and helped myself to a pair of Mark's shorts. They fit perfectly.

I needed new clothes. I needed a haircut. I needed to reorient myself to being a lawyer. I threw my uneaten toast to Betsy - who was not too mad to snap it up - and headed downtown.

I spent three interesting hours alone in my law office, catching up on my cases. Judge Shrenk had granted my motion against Boyd Tate to compel discovery - but Tate still hadn't come through with the documents and answers to interrogatories. I looked at the order and raised my eyebrows. Tate hadn't even responded to the motion; that's why Shrenk hadn't called me in for oral argument. She had assessed cumulative sanctions: all my fees and costs, plus $200 for every day the discovery was outstanding. I checked the date on the order and did some quick math. Tate was already into this $1,400. Tate was a bozo - a certified, certifiable bozo - but even he usually didn't get this deep in Dutch with a judge. Not because he had any ethics or any scruples, but because he just couldn't afford $1,400.

Unease fluttered through my stomach. I couldn't offhand remember the last time I had seen the man. Melanie Mayer's deposition, I decided finally. Eight weeks before. Eight very, very long weeks before.

I punched in his office number. Boyd Tate worked out of the downstairs bedroom of his ramshackle house in the Central District. I had been there once for a document production and still remembered the greasy, clammy feel of the air, the generalized impression of nearby silverfish.

His machine picked up. "You have reached the office of Boyd Tate, Attorney at Law," his voice informed me. He droned through his office hours and invited me to leave a message at the tone.

It was the longest tone I had ever heard. His messages must have been backed up for weeks. The unease in my stomach ripened into full-fledged anxiety. I almost hung up when the tone finally stopped and the machine clicked into record. Then I shook myself. Tate was a screw-off. He was notoriously sloppy and disorganized. The backed-up messages, the failure to appear - all totally according to character.

"Boyd, Jack Hart," I said firmly. "July 3. Look, you have to call me about this outstanding discovery. You need to get out from under these sanctions, and I need the documents. I'm in the office all next week. If I don't hear from you by Friday, I'm going to move to dismiss."

I hung up, worried about it for a moment longer, then turned to the next pile of paper on my desk and was soon lost in other cases. I worked happily and steadily until I felt I had a good grasp on what had happened while I was gone. I reviewed our receivables and sent out June billings before I left: a fantastic month. Harmony had brought in three new clients and four new matters while I had been out busting rocks. Didi Thomas's bill was going to be delightfully, alarmingly large, but it was no more than either she or I deserved.

I walked downtown in the sunshine, enjoying the bright blue weather, the rare warmth of a Seattle summer's day. I bought lunch at the Pike Place Market and ate it relaxing on a bench in Victor Steinbrueck Park, looking out at Mount Rainier and Elliott Bay. As I tucked into my halibut sandwich and box of raspberries, I became increasingly aware of the attention I was getting.

A perky suburban blonde gave me a bright, appreciative smile.

A goth girl with black lipstick unfurled her velvet cape as she strolled by me, revealing a black body stocking that revealed pretty much everything else.

A trio of giggling Japanese girls approached with their camera out, in the universal "take our picture" gesture. I tried to shepherd them into a pose, but it soon became apparent that they wanted their pictures taken *with* me, not *by* me. So I complied, posing with them one by one, as they giggled ever more furiously and chattered to each other. When I tried out the few words of Japanese I had learned from Harmony, you would have thought I was the smartest performing bear in their personal zoo. They beamed at me and clapped their hands.

It was like that everywhere I went. I had barely stepped into the men's department of the Bon Marché when the saleslady bustled over to help me. The teenage clerk at the Levi's store insisted on measuring my waist, smiling and suggesting the whole time. The extremely attentive lady barber kept running her fingers through my hair, admiring the streaks from the sun. Then she spent almost an hour clipping little bits of it, her face bent close to mine, before she finally spritzed me with some musky-smelling spray and proclaimed me perfect. This was the same place where I usually got a five-minute whack job for $10 bucks. When I wished her a happy Fourth, she asked me if I had plans for the holiday. And when I told her that my fiancée and I were going over to a friend's to watch the fireworks, she couldn't hide her disappointment.

I was loving every minute of it. I was an ordinary-looking guy blessed with an exquisite girlfriend and a roommate with a strong resemblance to Elvis - young, thin Elvis. Whenever we went to Green Lake Park together, the men fixated on Harmony, the women (and not a few men) fixated on Mark, and all the dogs in the place trotted up to me to wag hello. I was used to being the average one, the solid one, the one who was just a nice guy. It was fantastic to step into the heartthrob role, to walk down the street warmed by the soft, inviting glances of passing girls.

How could Carrie Mayer not have loved this? How could she have dropped fifty pounds and kept on wearing her same old, shapeless clothes? They must have sagged on her, hung on her, flapped on her, even. I thought of the way Gretta Berg described her: as a refugee. Why hadn't she bought a few new clothes to wear to work, clothes to fit and flaunt her new figure? Why hadn't she gotten rid of the thick, ugly glasses that hid her big eyes and delicate face?

I didn't like the obvious answer: She was dieting down so she could pass herself off as her sister. If she had plotted to murder Melanie and collect on her own policy, she would have wanted to keep the family resemblance well under wraps. It explained the weight loss. It explained the old clothes. It even explained why she avoided every camera.

"Makeover, ma'am?"

The Nordstrom Clinique girl was right at my elbow. It took me a moment to sort out that she was talking to the blond, leather-faced matron beside me. I watched as the smooth-haired attendants in short, white coats daubed and powdered the older women perched on high stools around the makeup counter. There was something in equal parts scientific and sacramental about their attentions: the lab assistants at the altar of youth. I wondered if Carrie Mayer had come to a place like this for help in turning into Melanie.

Then I blinked at the scene in front of me, struck by a sense of omission. There was a witness we had neglected to question, a witness I had seen in a setting almost - though not quite - like this, a witness who would have known a thing or two about makeovers, if not transformations. A witness who would have been the soul of discretion.

It took me five minutes to get back to my firm, grab a couple of pictures of Carrie and Melanie, and pick up my car. Ten minutes later, I was clattering down the alley stairs to Hello, Gorgeous.

The place was an alternative universe version of Nordstrom and the Bon, mobbed with just as many holiday shoppers and with an even more festive air. They were having a 50-percent-off shoe sale. Nothing says independence like half-price, jumbo pumps.

The cosmetic counter was relatively quiet - still guarded by the giant-size picture of RuPaul, still ringed with black and white diva shots. One white-coated attendant was demonstrating the fine points of eyelining and eyeshadow to a bald man in blue sweats. I waited until the customer had completed his purchase of what seemed like an astonishing number of little pots and brushes. The attendant turned to me with a warm smile. "Yes, sir? What can Hello, Gorgeous do to make you even more beautiful today?"

Sedrique's eyes were lined and shadowed, and his complexion was as waxily perfect as any Clinique girl's. It was hard to see the face behind the makeup.

I gave him my card. "Sedrique, I was in here a couple of weeks ago. I'm a lawyer, and I'm working on a case where a young woman died - just a few blocks from here. Your boss helped us get back some of the clothes her super brought here after she died."

He nodded warily. "I remember. The two suits."

"Right. Look, I realize that it's really important for you to keep your clients' confidences. I understand, and I respect that. But I need to know if this lady ever came in here, if you ever helped her do her makeup."

Reluctance shuttered his eyes. "I do hundreds of makeovers every week," he protested. "I couldn't possibly remember."

"You don't do many young women, do you?"

He was silent.

I pressed. "You'd remember a young woman?"

More silence.

I pressed harder. "Please, Sedrique. She's dead. No one knows who killed her. If she was in here, you won't be doing her any favors by keeping quiet."

He shrugged. "Maybe."

"Will you at least look at her picture?"

A long pause. Finally he held out his hand. I withdrew Carrie's blurred ID badge from my envelope and a copy of the picture from her senior yearbook. "Ever see her before?"

He nodded slowly. "Yes. She was here. Just once. Around Christmas, I think."

"What did she want?"

"Just a makeover. She was sweet - real shy. She didn't wear any makeup. I had to show her how to do everything, like one of my regular clients. It was like I had to teach her how to be a girl. I told her to go home and practice, but she never came back."

"Did she want to look like anyone in particular?" I nodded at the diva shots. "Marilyn? Madonna?"

"No one like that. I think she had a picture with her, but it wasn't of anyone famous."

"A blonde?"

"Everyone wants to be blond, darling." He glanced at my sun-bleached hair, amused. "You should know that."

I flushed with embarrassment. "Could you make her look like the woman in the photo she brought?"

Again the amused look. "Darling, with a little work, I could make *you* look like the woman in that photo."

I pulled out a copy of Melanie's senior picture and the clipping showing her as a Seafair queen. "This woman?"

"That's her. It wasn't hard." He put the pictures side by side and pointed with the end of one of his makeup brushes. "It's almost the same face, just a little fuller and a little older. So I evened out her skin with a beige foundation, toned down the puffiness with a jade powder, and contoured in her cheekbones. I put a dab of slate gray at the corner of her lashes - it just opened up her eyes. I plucked her brows - they were a disgrace - and filled them in with pencil. And then I curled her lashes and swiped on three coats of an espresso mascara and filled in her lips with a terracotta plum. It's my own blend. She walked out of here looking like a million bucks."

I was staring at him in astonishment. He smiled at me. "It's like painting a picture. Each one's a little different. And when you see the face again, it all comes back."

"And she looked like the girl in this photo?"

"Not just like her, no. But like an older, more sophisticated version of her. She wanted it contemporary, not retro."

"Can you remember anything else she told you?"

He shook his head. "I'm surprised I remembered that much."

"What did you sell her?"

"Probably small sizes of everything I used on her. Like I said, I told her to go home and practice."

"You're sure she didn't tell you why she wanted the makeover? Why she suddenly wanted to start wearing makeup?"

"If she did, I couldn't say."

"Couldn't say, or don't remember?"

He shrugged. "Don't remember. Really."

I let it drop. "About how much would that kind of makeup cost?"

"Well, let's see." He walked around to the opposite counter. I had to circle the display to keep up with him. He was checking his display case and ticking off the prices on his fingers, but I was distracted.

The diva shots continued on the other side of the counter. One was of a beautiful, bountiful woman in a Farrah Fawcett pose, back arched, head back, one hand in her hair, smiling for the camera.

The picture was in black and white, but I knew that her hair was fire-engine red, and her eyes were impossibly green.

I knew that she was six-foot-four, give or take high heels.

And I knew that no one had seen or heard from her since she had insisted that it was Carrie who went over that railing.

I just didn't know what Kit McCracken's picture was doing there at Hello, Gorgeous.

CHAPTER 37

The Fourth of July was long and dark – in more ways than one. Harmony and I were polite to each other, but that was all. Mainly, she stayed out of my way. She left for church that morning without waking me to issue her usual invitation to come along. I never went. But she had always asked.

There seemed to be no anchor to the day. There was no delicious Sunday dinner, no gathering around the table in my warm, snug kitchen. I made myself some toast; Harmony heated another noxious diet packet and repaired to her room with a black binder and a stack of legal pads. Mark told us we were both nuts and took Betsy out for pizza. I munched my toast in my silent house. I listened to the sound of my own jaws and the rain cascading down. Then my toast was gone, and there was just the rain.

It was still pouring when we arrived at David's house just before 10 that night. David lived on the western shore of Mercer Island, with a jaw-dropping view of Seattle across Lake Washington. We admired his new chandelier in the basement, huddled on his deck in the rain, sipped cocoa, coffee, and hot buttered rum, and watched the fireworks over Lake Union. The Fourth of July, Seattle style.

The stiff wind elongated the explosions into parabolas of flame, streaking light across the sky; the raindrops refracted the light into multicolored billows of mist. It all reflected crazily on the black, glinting surface of Lake Washington. Standing there drenched and cold on David's deck, I felt like I was underwater, like everything was upside down.

Harmony went right to bed when we got home. When I woke up the next morning, she had already left. I rubbed my eyes and squinted at the kitchen clock. It was only half past six.

"What in the hell is going on?" I demanded of Mark, who was sitting at the kitchen table, munching a Pop-Tart.

"It's called eating. You ought to try it sometime."

"Where did Harmony get off to this early? Why didn't she wait for me if she was going into work?"

Mark stared at me. He actually put down the Pop-Tart. "Harmony's not at work, Jack," he said. "This is her first day before the grand jury. They start at seven because Poehl's fast-tracking the case. I thought you knew."

The world turned upside down again. "No, I didn't know." My voice sounded flat and thin. "She didn't tell me."

I sat down heavily at the kitchen table, reproaching myself for not noticing her preoccupation over the weekend, for not asking what she was doing all day with that big black binder and that stack of legal pads. I had promised her I would be there for her, promised her that I would sit outside the grand jury room until she was done. "She doesn't even talk to me anymore."

Mark gave me an even look. "What are you going to do about it?"

"I don't know what to do. I've tried. I've apologized. She said we were OK, but you know that's always a true lie." I jumped up. "I can still make it down there if I hurry. I can still see her before she goes into the jury room."

Mark shook his head. "You won't be able to get in. The courthouse is closed for the holiday. The grand jury's in session just because Poehl's pushing for a quick indictment. Harmony and David had to meet him at 6:15 to get into the courthouse with the grand jurors. Other than that, everything's going to be locked up tight."

"Oh." I sat down. I couldn't think of anything else to say.

"Just do something, Jack. If you two split up, who gets custody of *me*?"

I had to stop this conversation. It was making me way too nervous. I decided to deflect. "What about your love life, Mark? Have you called Megan Swenson?"

Mark looked at me with a trace of pity, but he answered anyway. "No. And I'm not going to."

"Why not? She's probably not mad at you anymore."

He took another bite of Pop-Tart and chewed it slowly. "Not meant to be, Jack. The whole stepfather thing. Better this way." Then he shoved in the last bite of the Pop-Tart and whistled for Betsy. "Race you downstairs." And the two of them were off in a blur of black hair and orange fur.

Alone in the kitchen, I resolved to be a good little lawyer for the rest of the day. If I acted like everything was normal, I reasoned, maybe it would be. And there is nothing more normal for a lawyer than going to work on a holiday. So I went for my run, gobbled a Pop-Tart, dressed in my new skinny clothes from the Bon, and headed downtown.

Mrs. Holbrook had the day off for the observation of the Fourth, and the phones were still. I was soon lost in an appellate brief for one of my shipping clients. I printed it, proofed it, cite checked it, and e-mailed it to Mrs. Holbrook for service the next day. I answered some interrogatories and finished up a set of Rule 26 disclosures on one of our employment cases. I didn't stop for lunch - I just worked and billed until the piles on my desk were satisfyingly small and my timesheet was satisfyingly long.

I reviewed Harmony's to-do box to see whether there was anything she would need covered while she was before the grand jury. I had to smile as I paged through the files. Everything was organized in sections - discovery, motions, correspondence, research, witness interviews. Each file began with the court schedule and a flow sheet documenting every time she touched the case. One note actually read, "Lost temper. Told Boyd he was being a jerk."

Boyd Tate. The Incredible AWOL Boyd Tate. The date of the note was a few days after I had deposed Melanie Mayer. That was the last time I had seen or talked to Boyd Tate. I skimmed through the rest of the flow sheet. Harmony had tried to contact Tate six times since then - each time without success. On the last entry, she had written, "Called LAP. Something wrong? Even for Boyd, bizarre. Intake said several calls."

I put away the file with an uneasy feeling. "LAP" was the Lawyers Assistance Program, a bar service where lawyers or judges could report anonymous concerns about fellow members of the bar. If the LAP received enough input about a particular lawyer, it would send out a letter saying that people were worried and listing several places where the lawyer could get help. If a couple of people had already called, that meant Tate probably already got a LAP referral. And knowing Tate, that could mean anything. He could be ignoring it. He could be in the drying-out place. He could have tried to sue the LAP for defamation. Or he could be . . . dead.

That was the puzzle with a guy like Boyd Tate. He was such a fruitcake to begin with, it was hard to tell where general dereliction left off and ominous silence began. But even for Boyd, two months was just too long to go totally incommunicado. He didn't make enough money to go underground for two months. Besides, he had a built-in stupidity clock. Every few weeks or so, he pulled a major boner. It had been months since I had heard a good Boyd Tate story being bandied around the courthouse. And more than anything else, that scared me.

I looked up Boyd's address in the bar directory, programmed my home and office numbers to ring through to my cellphone in case Harmony tried to reach me, and headed out to the Central District.

Boyd lived in a shabby wood house just off Cherry. I rang the doorbell and knocked. Silence. I walked around to the back door and knocked. Still more silence. I punched in his number on my cellphone and listened to the muffled ring reverberating through the house. When his machine picked up, I waited for the tone. If anything, it was even longer than before.

I tried the neighbors on either side of Boyd, but if they were home, they weren't answering. I peeked through a crack in his garage door. His beat-up Dodge was there. I tried to look through the letter box, but something seemed to block my view. All I could make out was a corner of a dusty hallway.

I circled the house, trying to catch any glimpse through the curtained windows. The damp summer air sagged on me like a wet wool scarf, and there was a strange, faint humming in the distance that made my ears feel thick and prickly. Sweat stung my eyes as I bent down and tried to peer through two squat basement windows. But it was no use. Boyd seemed to have covered them inside with black plastic, and I couldn't see a thing.

I straightened up, cracked my back, and thumped the wall in frustration. Abruptly, the humming stopped. Before my eyes, the black coating on the windows dissolved. And then I had to grab the wall, because suddenly I knew what was covering the inside of Boyd Tate's basement windows.

Not plastic.

Flies.

CHAPTER 38

"**B**reathe through your mouth," Mark told me, leading the way into the house. I had called him on my cellphone, and now the place was swarming with cops. "And don't touch anything."

The first breath wasn't so bad - just foul like a gust from the dump. The second hit me right in the gut. The stench was overpowering, and it was sickly, raw, and primitive.

Mark gave me a sharp look over his shoulder. "You OK?"

"Yeah. Sort of." I took another breath and felt a shudder deep inside me. "He's in the basement?" I hazarded.

"Someone is."

I wasn't going to view the body. I had already made that clear. Mark had given me a one-word description of the state of the corpse - "*advanced*" - and I had no desire to see what that meant in the flesh. But I had been to Boyd Tate's home office once before for a document production, and Detective Gregerson – the lazy detective who was now part of Mark and Anthony's team - wanted my opinion on whether anything looked out of place.

Or to be more accurate, whether anything looked *in* place.

"You mean it's always like this?" Gregerson demanded, looking around him in disgust.

"I was only here once," I reminded him, taking in the tottering stacks of outdated lawbooks, the sagging boxes of files, the calcified plates of old food, the dog-eared piles of papers slipping over the desk. "But yes, this is the way it looked. Just normally, I mean."

"Shit," Gregerson said. "We thought there'd been a search."

If there had been, it was impossible to tell. Gregerson dismissed me with a nod.

On the way out, I stumbled over the mail mounded in the dusty hallway. Mostly bills, I noticed, but also a couple of padded packages from the King County Law

Library. Right there at the top was the letter from the Lawyers Assistance Program. Not exactly in the nick of time.

I leaned against my car and gulped the heavy air. The clouds were low and lowering, all red and black from the collision of the coming storm and sinking sun. My nose and throat still burned. An absurd thought came to mind: If the body was Tate's - and I had to believe it was - who was going to go to his funeral? Who was even going to *have* a funeral? I couldn't think of anyone who liked the man. Even his clients seemed to count their fingers after they shook his hand. What a perfect murder victim - someone no one cared about enough to check up on, someone no one missed. He could have lain there forever in the basement of his ramshackle house, lain there until the bank or the tax collector foreclosed.

Mark walked over. "Can I have a ride home?"

"Sure. But don't you have to stay?"

"Gregerson's case. Unless he wants help, I'm the third wheel."

On the way back to Green Lake, Mark shared what he had gleaned from the crime scene. The body was in a basement closet. The cause of death wasn't obvious, but it was almost certainly murder. There was blood on the other side of the room, a drag trail to the closet. The victim was probably male, but it would take the ME to make sure. They'd have to rely on insect infestation to determine time of death.

"My guess is a couple of months ago," Mark said. "But they'll have to see what kind of flies were hatching then. You see -"

I was saved by the ring of my cellphone. Maybe it was Harmony.

It wasn't. It was, to my great surprise, Megan Swenson.

"Hi, Megan!" I said, trying to drive, greet her, and hand Mark the phone. "Mark's right here -"

"No, Jack, it's you I want," she interrupted. "Listen, I thought of something. I know how you can tell whether that girl is Carrie Mayer."

"How?"

"When we were in grade school, everyone in our class put something in a time capsule that we buried on the playground. Carrie and I had both lost our front teeth that week, so that was our contribution. The school building's still there, although they've made it into condos. But they just paved over the playground to make a parking lot; they didn't dig it up. So I bet that time capsule is still in the ground!"

"Where's the school?"

A bell rang in the background. "Just a second, Jack. I've got to get the door."

I am not a psychic person. The aunt who raised me made her living reading tea leaves and peering into crystal balls – or saying she did - which instilled my contempt for the paranormal. But when I heard that doorbell, foreboding struck me so hard that I struggled to keep my hands on the wheel. I still don't know whether I was just reacting to the accumulated horrors of the day - the body, the flies, the glowering red and black sky - or whether I actually sensed something out there, some menace encircling Megan Swenson. But whatever the reason, I blurted, "*Don't open the door!*"

There was a pause. "Why not?"

"Don't open the door. Please. Not until we get there." I swerved off Linden onto 65th. "Is Hannah with you?"

"Of course." Her voice was sharp. The doorbell rang again. "Jack, this is silly. I have to get the door."

"Do you have a peephole? Can you tell who it is?"

"Well, no -"

"Then *please*, please don't. Just make sure all your doors and windows are locked and stay on the phone with me."

Another ring. Threat and terror seemed to be filling the car, pouring out of the phone.

"Jack, what on earth -"

"Look, we just found Melanie Mayer's attorney dead in his house. I don't know who's at your door, but I don't like the coincidence. Please, Megan. Take Hannah and lock yourselves in the bathroom or something."

Another long pause. Then she said, "OK." I heard knocking in the background - getting fainter as I waited. "All the doors are locked. Hannah and I are in the basement. But I still don't understand what's going on."

Just so long as they were safe. I was about to hand the phone to Mark when she suddenly hissed, "Jack, she's coming around the side of the house."

"Who?"

"I don't know. Somebody. I can only see her legs.

"Get away from the window. Make sure she doesn't see you."

Beside me, Mark was hissing into his own cellphone, ordering a patrol car to go to Megan's address, a police escort to join us as we fought the traffic on 65th.

"Jack, she's trying to open the window." Megan's voice was a thin, grey thread of fear.

"Can you get back upstairs?"

"We'd have to go in front of the window. She'd see us."

"Hide the best you can. Keep quiet. Just tap the phone receiver so we know you're still there. We're on our way." I handed the phone to Mark because I needed both hands on the wheel. The police escort met us at the corner of Cleopatra Place - one blue-and-white ahead of us, another behind - and we were screaming down 65th toward Ballard.

Beside me, Mark was talking to Megan in smooth, soothing tones, like one long, slow caress: "It's OK, just keep quiet, stay with me, no one's going to hurt you, we're almost there." Whenever he paused for breath, Megan's tapping on the receiver throbbed through the car like a heartbeat. I glanced over at him once and wished I hadn't. His eyes were screwed shut. Maybe it was my driving, maybe it was Megan, but Mark – tough cop Mark – was scared shitless.

Lightening ripped the sky. A thunderclap cracked above us like a gunshot, and the phone went dead. "Fuck!" Mark roared, hammering the phone against the dashboard. He stabbed at all the buttons, he tried to get a signal on his cellphone, but we were right in the middle of an electrical storm. There was nothing we could do but drive.

Just a few blocks later, the cellphone buzzed to life. The sound of shattering glass broke the sweaty silence. Megan's voice was a squeak, but I could hear her clearly from the other side of the car. "Mark, Mark, she's coming in."

"Scream. Scream 'Fire.' Scream that the police are coming. Scream anything." For seconds that seemed like hours, we listened to Megan and Hannah scream. It was like the phone itself was a trapped and tormented animal, pleading for help in a tiny, terrified voice. Finally, we started to hear sirens mingled with the screams. We heard ourselves arriving before we actually arrived.

Mark was out of the car before it stopped. He hurtled up the stairs and hammered on the royal blue door, simultaneously talking on the phone to Megan and ordering the patrolmen to go around both sides of the house. When Megan flung open the door, she still had her phone in her hand; she was still talking to Mark on the phone as if she couldn't believe they were face to face.

I stood at the bottom of the stairs and watched them framed against the bright blue door. They ran right into each other. They met with a sort of click, like magnets or the last pieces of a puzzle. Megan was leaning against Mark's chest, her arms around his neck. Hannah hung on his waist, her face buried in his side. Mark had one arm around Megan and the other resting on Hannah's shoulders. Still holding onto each other, they all suddenly stepped inside the house and closed the door.

They did not look back.

Mark, in particular, did not look back.

I stood there in the rain, staring at the door, trying to sort out what had just happened.

Megan was safe.

Hannah was safe.

Whatever was out there, whatever had been coming toward them, we got there in time.

And Mark was my best friend.

I loved him.

I wanted everything in the world for him.

I just never thought he'd get it all that fast.

CHAPTER 39

The police recovered the time capsule. It was in a concrete-lined vault three feet under the paved playground. The top of the vault was decorated with tiny handprints pressed in the cement - all the kids in Megan's and Carrie's class. The police tugged it out and took it back to the police station to crack it open.

Megan Swenson - who still hadn't let go of Mark - gave a blood sample to the paramedics so her baby tooth could be separated from Carrie's. She and Hannah sat on each side of Mark, both leaning against him, while they gave their statement to a sympathetic policewoman. The woman who tried to break into their house seemed tall and slender. She was wearing expensive-looking, low-heeled pumps, black stockings, and a knee-length black skirt. They never saw her face, just her legs and hands.

"What race was she?"

"I don't know. She was wearing gloves."

That let out the possibility of fingerprints. Footprints were also a bust. Whatever impressions she made were washed away by the downpour. But Megan's neighbor across the street had seen a tall, well-dressed blonde in a black suit knocking on Megan's door just before the rain started. She had been wearing a black hat with a broad brim. I remembered my foreman over on the Queen Anne jobsite. He had said that a well-dressed woman with a face like an old tire had lured Clifford Walton away from the job site. It was the last time anyone had seen Clifford or his daughter, Jenny.

"Who knew that you had remembered about the baby teeth in the time capsule?" the policewoman asked.

"I ran into my old grade school principal this afternoon at Fred Meyer," Megan said. "I told him that Carrie had passed away, and we were reminiscing about old times. That's when I remembered the time capsule."

"I'll need his name and number. Did anyone overhear you?"

"Oh, there were people all around. Everyone was shopping for the holiday, and it was just a zoo. So I guess we were talking pretty loud. Anyone could have heard." She turned to Hannah. "Did you see anyone, sweetie?"

Hannah shook her head and hugged her cat. Megan squeezed her daughter's knee and nodded the policewoman into the next room, where she opened her address book and copied down the contact information for her old principal.

Mark drew me aside. "I'm going to stay here tonight, just to make sure they're OK."

"Do you want me to bring you some clean clothes or something?"

"No. I'll swing by tomorrow and pick up what I need. I mean, I will if I'm going to stay here again."

There wasn't anything else for me to do. I drove home slowly. I wasn't sure what if anything was waiting for me there.

The house was still. No Harmony. No Betsy. There was a message on my office voicemail from Harmony, telling me she would be spending the night at David's house because the grand jury was convening early again the next morning. I stood and puzzled over it for a few moments, wondering why the call hadn't automatically transferred to my cellphone, the way Megan's had. The answer hurt. She must not have actually called the office. She must have dialed into our office voicemail and sent me the message from there. That meant she didn't want to risk even the slightest chance of talking to me.

I went in search of the canine member of the household and soon discovered why she had disappeared. She had had an accident on the kitchen floor. I didn't even swear as I cleaned it up. It had been a dogshit sort of day anyway, and we had left Betsy by herself for hours. Hardly her fault.

I found her hiding in the laundry basket, cringing and embarrassed. None of us had ever spanked her for anything, but her prior family must have been the devil when it came to housetraining. She hung her head and whimpered as I approached. I rubbed her, hugged her, and carried all 95 pounds of her up the stairs.

While Betsy took a much-needed break in the back yard, I walked through the house, assessing the damage of the day. There was a collage of toilet paper twining from the bathroom and down the hall. Most artistic. Harmony's wastebasket was overturned, and shreds of crumpled pages from her legal pads were scattered all over the sunroom. Mark's bed had been torn apart, with sheets tossed on one side of the room and pillows and comforter on the other. Or maybe not. Sometimes it was hard to tell where Mark left off and Betsy began.

My room was untouched. I wasn't sure how to feel. Flattered? Insulted? Was I no longer even a member of the pack, no longer someone Betsy missed and sought?

Betsy padded into the kitchen and watched me, with a gratified expression, as I entered the damage in the *Bad Things I Did Today* list on the fridge. I took her for a run and bought toilet paper and a box of Mr. Barky's biscuits at the PCC. I also bought myself a sandwich, because with Harmony dieting, I knew there would be no discernible food at my house. We sat together on my deck and munched.

It was almost midnight, but we were bathed by a fat, silvery moon. Betsy thrust her nose in my hand and wagged her tail. I was touched by her forgiveness until I realized she was inching toward my sandwich.

I tossed it to her and got ready for bed. One of us might as well enjoy it. It had been a long, sad day, and I felt like I wasn't going to be hungry again.

The phone rang just as I was drifting off to sleep. Betsy was already snoring next to me. I almost ignored the call. Almost.

"I'm sorry. Did I wake you?" It was Harmony's voice, very soft and low.

I sat bolt upright. "No, no, you didn't. I'm awake."

"I just wanted to hear your voice before I went to sleep."

"How did it go today?"

"It was hard. I don't really want to talk about it."

"I'm so sorry I wasn't there for you. I didn't realize it was today."

"I'm sorry I didn't tell you. It was silly of me." There was a pause. "I love you, Jack."

"I love you, too. I'll be there tomorrow. Bright and early. I'll stay all day."

"You don't have to."

"I want to."

"Really, it's not worth it. Todd only gave me two breaks today, and each time, he had me work through them reviewing documents."

I spared a bitter thought for the Tadpole. "Then I'll meet you at the courthouse before you go into the grand jury," I promised. "I miss you. I at least want to see you."

"That would be nice," she admitted. She sounded so tired.

"Here, talk to your dog. She misses you, too." I held the phone to Betsy's ear. She twitched and started up at the sound of Harmony's voice, sniffed the phone, and tried to lick it. Harmony was laughing softly when I took it back.

"Did she swallow it?"

"She tried."

We said a few other kind things to each other, then said goodbye. I closed my eyes feeling better than I had in days.

I was at the courthouse an hour early, just in case. The edges of the sky were beginning to glow. Across the street, a few slumped figures were already waiting for the public library to open its doors.

Harmony seemed to have dropped several more pounds since I'd seen her last. Her cheekbones looked sharper than usual, the hollows beneath them even more pronounced. I didn't broach the topic of her diet. But when she excused herself for a moment, I turned to David.

"Will you make sure she eats lunch today?"

David didn't look up from the documents he was reviewing. "She brought some protein bars with her yesterday. That's all she wanted."

"That's not enough! She's wasting away."

David glanced up curiously. "You've dropped a fair bit of weight yourself. What's going on with you two?"

Harmony was walking toward us from the restroom. "It's nothing," I muttered. I sat with her and filled her in about Tate and Megan until Todd came to take her into the grand jury room. I watched her go, hating his proprietary hand on her shoulder. She looked back at me just as she went through the door. I gave her the thumbs-up, and the door closed on her smile.

I waited a few more hours, until it became clear that she wasn't going to reappear anytime soon. "Go to work," David said. "You can't do anything here. I'll call you if something happens."

As I headed back to my firm, I noticed a crowd of homeless people waiting in silence for the library to open. I wondered why. The morning was warm and bright; there was no need to seek shelter from the weather. I stopped for a moment, feeling that I was missing something important, then gave up and started down Fifth Avenue.

I was almost to my firm when it struck me. E-mail. Internet access. Computers. Seattle has some of the most wired homeless people around. The downtown library is stocked with Web-linked terminals; a non-profit service provider offers free e-mail addresses to every library patron. That meant we might find Jenny Walton's father somewhere on the Web.

Mrs. Holbrook was already at her desk, resplendent in a bell-shaped, sky-blue hat that perfectly matched her suit and shoes. After we had admired each other's new clothes, I outlined my theory that Clifford Walton might be reachable on the Internet. She pulled up an on-line e-mail directory and found him within five minutes.

Or, at least, she found his e-mail address. He was registered with the Seattle Community Network, but the Internet address gave no hint of his physical location. He could be in Seattle. He could be in Tibet. There was just no way to tell from the screen.

Mrs. Holbrook and I puzzled over it for a few minutes. "Can you subpoena his e-mail records?" she asked.

"Probably not. There's no current litigation going on."

"Can the police get a warrant?"

"I don't think they have probable cause. Clifford Walton's daughter might be a crime victim, but I don't think that's enough."

"He might respond to an e-mail."

"Not from us."

"No," she mused. "Not from us." A most unladylike gleam came into her eyes. "But it wouldn't have to be from us, you know. Why don't I work up a few options for us to try?"

The hidden depths of the HATLADY. I raised my hands in surrender and left her to plan our Internet approach to Clifford.

I was deep in a motion on our odometer turnback case when Anthony called. "Could you swing by the police station? I'd like to show you something."

"Sure," I said, "What's up?"

"Just come."

Mark met me at the elevator on the fifth floor of the Public Safety Building.

"How are Megan and Hannah?"

"Feeling a lot better, thanks. But there's something hinky in that concrete box." He led the way to a conference room, where the time capsule reposed on a table covered with blue plastic. The concrete vault was cracked in two beside it.

Two officers in rubber gloves were unpacking the time capsule, sorting and cataloging its contents. I had to smile when I saw some of the kids' contributions: Tang and Space Food Sticks, which no doubt would taste exactly the same as the day they went in the ground; vintage comic books probably worth more than my car; a petrified egg of Silly Putty. And a small plastic box, opened to show two tiny teeth. One had split in two, revealing the heart-shaped darkness inside.

One of them was Carrie Mayer's. Either we were about to match it up with her decapitated body, or it was the only bit of her that was left, the only physical evidence that she had ever existed.

I shook off a sudden chill.

"So what's hinky?"

Mark nodded to one of the gloved officers, who handed me a stiff, black and white picture of children, posed in rows on what looked like the bleachers of a gym. "That was at the top of the box. We didn't put it together at first."

I scanned the faces of the children, searching for Megan and Carrie. They were in the front row, both with Minnie Mouse hair bows and gap-tooth grins.

"See anyone else you recognize?"

I started to shake my head - and then I spotted him. There were two adults in the picture, bookending the children. One of them had a black buzzcut and was, if possible, even thinner than he was now. I whistled.

I was looking at the innocent, open face of Donald Carter, thirty years ago.

CHAPTER 40

"Yes, I talked to Meg Swenson yesterday," Donald told Mark. He looked calm and slightly puzzled. "I ran into her at Fred Meyer."

I kept my eyes on Donald's face as Mark led him through the conversation. Mark had put me on the business side of a two-way mirror, and Larry Gregerson and I were watching for cracks in Donald's facade.

None so far.

"Could anyone have overheard your conversation?"

"Oh, anyone. We were standing right in the middle of the store. And it was packed. We almost had to shout."

"Did anyone seem to be listening in?"

"Not that I noticed."

"Did you see anyone else you recognized there?"

"Sure. I met the couple behind me over by the meat counter. They were throwing a party."

Mark took down the neighbors' name, just in case. "Did you tell anyone about the conversation you had had with Ms. Swenson?"

"Oh, yes. As soon as I got home, I called Chuck Thomas. I left a message about it on his answering machine."

Mark and Anthony looked up. I sensed the charge that passed between them.

"Why did you do that, Mr. Carter?"

"Chuck and Didi have been so worried about this case. Meg said you weren't positive that the woman who fell up on First Hill was even our employee. I knew they'd want to know there was a way the police could tell for sure. So I just said I'd run into Megan Swenson, an old student who was friends with Carrie Mayer, and she'd remembered something that would help the police clear everything up."

"I see." It was the first time Anthony had spoken. His voice was cold.

"Detectives, if I shouldn't have told Chuck and Didi about the time capsule, I'm very sorry. Did I do something wrong?"

"Someone tried to break into Megan Swenson's house less than an hour after she met you in Fred Meyer," Anthony said. "It just seems like too much of a coincidence."

"Oh, no. Poor Meg. She's OK, isn't she? And her little girl?"

Anthony inclined his head.

"I'd better call her." Donald pulled a shabby leather calendar from his breast pocket and made himself a note. "I've got a couple of extra bedrooms if she needs them. She must be terrified."

"You seem very fond of Ms. Swenson," Anthony said.

"I taught Meg in second grade. I've known her family forever."

"You were a teacher? I thought you were the principal."

"First a teacher, then the principal. A couple of years later."

"I didn't think a lot of men went in for teaching at elementary schools," Anthony said. His words were mild, but his tone was not.

Donald didn't bristle. "I started teaching to stay out of Vietnam. And I found out I liked it."

"But not enough to keep with it?" Again, there was an edge to Anthony's voice.

"If possible, Detective, teachers are even more underpaid than the police. The worst lawyer makes more than the best teacher."

"Are you the worst lawyer?"

This time Donald absorbed the gibe. His stance and smile stiffened. "I beg your pardon, Detective," he said, half-rising.

Mark made a placating gesture and jumped in with another question. Over the next half hour, I watched Detective Anthony driving Donald closer and closer to Mark. It was a wrenching game. Mark usually played bad cop in interrogations. Detective Anthony looked like a football coach. Most of the time, he seemed too by the book to instill serious fear. But Anthony was the father of daughters, the grandfather of granddaughters, and scorn and fury poured out of him for the men who killed women, the men who hurt little kids. Looking at him glaring at Donald, I felt guilty for being a guy.

"How come you didn't tell us you used to teach Carrie Mayer?" Anthony demanded. "When we talked to you about that poor girl going over her railing, you pretended you hardly knew her."

"I did hardly know her." Donald was sweating. "Until Meg told me that one of my old students had been murdered, I never put them together. I never knew she was my old student. The Carrie Mayer I knew from school was a beautiful little thing. Just blond, and sweet, and sparkly. She didn't look anything like that grown up. She wasn't, she wasn't -"

"A beautiful little thing anymore?" Anthony sneered. "You only like them when they're little?"

Donald stared at him, open-mouthed. "Now just a minute here -"

Anthony barreled right over him. "We know that a teacher was driven out of Carrie's school when she was a little girl. Someone sent an anonymous letter saying he was getting way too close to a student. Was that the real reason you left teaching?"

Donald suddenly laughed out loud. "Is that what all of this is about? Detective, I don't know why you're interested in all of this. It's ancient history, but you are barking up the wrong tree. I was still teaching second grade when the principal got that letter. Within a week, one of the fifth-grade teachers had resigned. None of it had anything to do with me. And if you don't believe me, you can get the investigation records from the school board."

Anthony demanded and received the name of the fifth-grade teacher who had resigned. Jerry Iverson. "This better check out," he said, scraping back his chair. "I do not like wasting my time." He slammed the door behind him.

Donald turned to Mark, flushed with strangled indignation. "What in the hell was that? I'm here voluntarily, as a good citizen, trying to help you out, and he just as much accuses me of being a child molester."

Mark apologized. "Detective Anthony has a soft spot for kids, Mr. Carter. Sometimes it gets the best of him."

"That's outrageous. It's criminal to go around treating people like that." Donald swept up to his full, gangly height. "This is the last time I will talk to either of you."

"Mr. Carter, please." Mark stood up too. "Right now, that's the worst thing you could do. If you stop cooperating, Detective Anthony is sure to think you've got something to hide. And that will just make him even more suspicious. If you stay in the loop, he'll check out the information you gave him and get turned around the right way. Believe me, I wouldn't want Detective Anthony after me - whether or not I'd done something wrong."

"I haven't," Donald snapped.

"I didn't mean to imply that. But as you know, the only thing worse than a true accusation is a false one."

Donald sat down. "You're right. I'm sorry. I just have never been spoken to like that before."

"I understand. Let me get you my card. If you'd feel more comfortable, you can call me directly."

Donald nodded. Mark closed the door quietly but firmly behind him. Donald looked straight at the fake mirror and let out his breath. I had the weird sensation that he was staring right into my eyes, that he knew I was there.

Mark and Anthony walked into the observation room and stood side by side in front of the glass, looking at Donald. He was still staring at the two-way mirror, breathing deeply. There was a flush of red over his sharp cheekbones.

"So, what do you think, Larry?" Anthony asked Detective Gregerson.

Gregerson shrugged. "Seems pretty cooperative. If his info checks out, I think we're looking at the Thomases. The wife - that blond bitch - she matches the description of the gal who tried to break in. And of the gal who was over at the construction site talking to the father of the little girl that's missing. This mope here," he jerked his thumb toward Donald, "I think he's a dead end."

Anthony nodded slowly. "What do you think, Jack?"

I had known Donald for years, and I liked him. I had always liked him. He hadn't said or done anything strange in the interview. His story made sense. Everything pointed to Chuck and Didi Thomas. But there was something, there was just something, that made my throat go dry as I looked at him through the glass.

"Jack?"

"Er, I'm not really sure," I said. "I mean, it does seem like Chuck and Didi are in on this some way."

"But?" Mark prompted. Larry Gregerson rolled his eyes. Civilians observing an interview. I could feel his contempt.

"But Donald just seems too all over the place to count out entirely. He was Carrie's teacher, her principal. He lives in Ballard, just about a mile from Megan. He never told us he knew Carrie Mayer. Mayer's Meats was a big deal in Ballard until Carrie's father died. It's just hard for me to believe that Donald wouldn't have remembered that name, that at some point, he wouldn't have put two and two together. And I didn't like what he said about asking Megan and Hannah to stay with him. It just seemed, I don't know, creepy."

"Oh, *that's* enough to go on," Gregerson interjected. "We arrest people all the time for felony creepiness."

"What do you think?" I asked Mark and Anthony.

They both looked back at Donald. They both spoke at the same time, as if with one voice:

"I think he did it."

CHAPTER 41

They didn't have a reason. They didn't have evidence. They just had a hunch. Donald was hinky; there was something about him that made them wonder.

But the evidence pointed the other way. Everything Donald said checked out. He had left Chuck and Didi Thomas a telephone message. Neither Chuck nor Didi had an alibi for the time someone tried to break into Megan's house, and Didi owned a whole wardrobe of black suits - plus a broad-brimmed black hat. They both swore that they hadn't even listened to Donald's message, that they had gone out for a long drive to enjoy the Fourth. But no one had seen them; no one could vouch for them; and as far as I could tell, no one believed them.

Donald's story about the fifth-grade teacher checked out too. There had been an anonymous complaint when Carrie was in fifth grade. Her teacher never admitted doing anything wrong, but he resigned abruptly after being confronted with the letter. The letter didn't identify the child, but Carrie fit the description - blond, blue-eyed, the teacher's pet. I thought back to her collection of school pictures. It was around fifth grade that she had started gaining weight.

The DNA evidence came back from the lab. Carrie's tooth did not match the only body we had - the headless, handless woman found in the rubble of Melanie Mayer's burnt-out house. But it was close. The lab estimated "first degree of consanguinity." In other words, sisters. That meant Carrie Mayer had gone over the railing. That meant Melanie Mayer had been killed, mutilated, and set on fire.

The way it looked had been the way it was. Why, then, had Melanie's killer gone to the trouble of hacking off her head and her hands? Was it just a misdirect to make us think Carrie might have passed herself off as her beauty-queen sibling? If so, it had worked - for a while.

Duty first. Knowing who died first – and how - meant we knew whom to pay. Sort of. Even though the Medical Examiner still had not reclassified her death as homicide, American Fidelity now believed that Carrie Mayer had been murdered. That meant we would pay Melanie Mayer Carrie's $250K death benefit – except for two small problems. One, Melanie Mayer was dead. Two, there was still a possibility that Melanie had been involved with Carrie's murder.

The second problem was more difficult than the first. If Melanie was innocent, we would just pay her estate, and then the money would pass to her heirs, whoever they might be. If Melanie was implicated, she would be disqualified from taking under the policy, which would leave Carrie without any beneficiaries. When there are no beneficiaries, the government gets the money. We would end up escheating the $250K to Washington State. But at least we were a step closer to resolution.

It was a relief to know for sure that Carrie was a victim, not a victimizer, that the bitchy beauty queen at the deposition had been her sister. We were back to our original theory, slightly modified by the discovery that Carrie had purposely been dieting down, had acquired two flashy new suits and Hello, Gorgeous make-up tips, and had contacted Greg at The Stranger right before she died. It seemed that Carrie had stumbled over something that made her furious and was going to use it to get another shot at writing for The Stranger. Greg had brushed her off because she was heavy and shy. But he wouldn't be expecting a slimmed-down, glammed-up blonde in a fake Prada suit, offering him an exclusive shot at a scandal. A *huge* scandal.

So what was the scandal? And who would have killed her to keep her from revealing it?

"Maybe her fifth-grade teacher worked at Children First," I suggested to Mark over our dinner of Michelob and macaroni and cheese. We were roughing it while Harmony spent yet another night at David's, in preparation for yet another day in front of the grand jury. "Or at her mom's nursing home. Maybe she thought he was abusing the patients."

Mark shook his head. "We looked into that. He's dead. He committed suicide six years ago."

"Oh."

"But I think you're heading the right direction. If she was molested as a child - and it looks like she may have been - she would have picked up on the danger signs way before anyone else. So that's why we're looking really hard at Chuck Thomas."

"Even though your gut tells you it's Donald?"

He paused. "I just feel like Donald's involved someway. I don't know how. Maybe just trying to cover up for Chuck. He's known him ten years."

"But I don't think he even likes Chuck. He told me he's shifty and mean - that he wouldn't buy a used car from him and doesn't know anyone who would."

"Maybe he's covering for Didi, then. Maybe there's something going on between the two of them."

After dinner, we sat out on the deck with Betsy and made lists of the possible scandals Carrie could have uncovered - and the possible suspects who would have wanted to shut her up:

Scandal	Suspects
Child molestation	Chuck and Didi Thomas
Student abuse/ molestation	Gretta Berg
Patient abuse/ mercy killing	Pat Campbell

"The girl got around," Mark said.

I recalled what Kit McCracken had said about Carrie - *she would have made a great spy.*

"Something could have been going on at the insurance company," I suggested. "That might explain why Kit McCracken's taken off."

Mark nodded and added "insurance scandal" to our list. He wrote "Chuck Thomas, Donald Carter, and Kit McCracken" under "Suspects."

"I didn't mean that Kit might have done anything wrong," I protested. "Just that she might be afraid that whoever killed Carrie would come after her, too."

"It could go either way," Mark said. "She went missing right after Melanie was murdered - and even though the ME can't be too specific, probably right around the time Boyd Tate was murdered, too. If she knew something, she had lots of opportunity to tell us. If she was scared, she could have asked for police protection. She didn't. She's one of the few people Carrie would have let into her apartment. I don't think we can count her out."

I mulled that over. I hated the thought that Kit might have been involved. But Mark was right. We couldn't count her out - not yet. "Any progress on finding her?"

"Zip. Since she's got her picture up at Hello, Gorgeous, we checked around the clubs up on Capitol Hill. There's someone up at Foxxes who kind of fits her description, but Kit's a lot taller – even accounting for heels. Kit's never gone back to work. As far as we can tell, she's never gone back to her apartment, either. Her landlord's trying to evict her."

"Do you know whether she's a he or a she?"

"No. That makes it harder. No one would forget seeing Kit McCracken as a woman. But if she's a man, we just don't know what he looks like. It's not much of a description - 'white male or female, about six-four, possibly black or red hair, eye color possibly green.'"

He checked his watch. "I've got to get over to Meg and Hannah. I'm staying with them again tonight. And I almost forgot. The search warrants came through on the Boyd Tate investigation. Would you take a look at some of the mail we took from his house? We weeded out the obvious stuff - bills and ads. And all the intervention letters from the Lawyers Assistance Program. Nothing looks suspicious to us. But maybe you can give us a read on all the legal shit."

Jack Hart, Reader of the Legal Shit. "Sure," I said, and he fetched a plastic wrapped package from his trunk, waved and drove away. Betsy stood on the porch looking after him, barking and wagging her tail. When his car turned the corner, her ears and tail drooped, and she moped into the house.

The stench of decay had permeated the envelopes. I took the package to the deck and spread out the letters, hoping the throat-clogging rot would dissipate in the still, warm air.

It didn't. Finally I got tired of waiting - and of shooing a fascinated Betsy away from the mail - went into the garage, and hunted down the particulate mask I had used when I refinished my hardwood floors. Wearing the mask and breathing hard through my mouth, I could at least edge near enough to read. It probably looked like I was engaging in some unnatural practice, but it helped me get through it without gagging.

I sorted the mail. I set aside the handful of letters that seemed to be from Tate's clients. I couldn't risk breaking any of their confidential communications. Most of the mail was from other counsel and the courts. By far the largest stack was vitriolic letters from attorneys whom Tate had screwed in one way or another. My own increasingly irritated reminders about late discovery and threats to file motions to dismiss went into that pile. I winced at the thought of him lying dead in his basement while I pounded out those nastygrams. Court sanctions imposed against Tate for his various pre- and posthumous blunders went into the next largest pile. I skimmed the litany of malpractice, misfeasance, and misconduct: forging a critical affidavit, failing to disclose a conflict of interest, destroying documents, lack of candor with the tribunal, discovery abuses, Rule 11. And then the pattern started, right around the time the medical examiner had fixed as the probable date of death - failure to appear, failure to appear, failure to appear.

All that was left were the mailers from the King County Law Library, each containing books Tate had requested before he died. I pulled them out one by one. A hornbook on civil procedure, an elementary treatise on the rules of evidence. A collection of pre-written demand letters for the use of litigious non-attorneys. That explained a lot. And then I pulled out the last book and was so surprised that I forgot to breathe through my mouth. I sat there with my eyes watering and stared down at the book: *Qui Tams and Whistleblowers*, by Eugene Levy. *Successful Private Prosecution Under the False Claims Act.*

I leaned back and looked out at the garden. Boyd Tate wasn't one to pursue knowledge for its own sake. If he had requested the book, that meant he needed it for a case. And that meant that one of Boyd Tate's clients wanted to file a *qui tam*, to prosecute a fraud action on behalf of the federal government. A fraud action that would give him or her a stake of up to 30 percent of the government's recovery.

Maybe it was Melanie Mayer.

CHAPTER 42

rs. Holbrook spent a couple of hours the next morning trying to determine whether Tate had represented anyone in a *qui tam* lawsuit. She searched the computerized court dockets, reviewed recent district court decisions, and plied her wiles with the federal clerks' office. Nothing. But that didn't rule it out. *Qui tam* cases are filed under seal to give the government a chance to investigate and decide whether or not to take over the individual's fraud prosecution. Even though nothing showed up on the docket, the U.S. Attorney could right then be reviewing allegations made by Melanie Mayer - or any of Tate's other clients.

"Here's something," Mrs. Holbrook said, bursting into my office. "I called my friend at the law library. She told me when Mr. Tate requested the book on how to represent a client in a *qui tam*." She proudly handed over a legal pad. "The book was checked out - that's why they mailed it to him when it came back. But he asked for it February 28. That's just about two months after someone threw Carrie Mayer off her balcony."

I thought back over our conversation with the super at Melbourne Terrace. When had Melanie Mayer shown up to clean out her sister's apartment? I couldn't remember. If it was sometime in February, that might mean that Melanie had stumbled over evidence of the scandal - the *huge* scandal - in Carrie's effects, and had taken it to Tate to see if she could make some money from it. And Tate might have known just enough about *qui tams* to realize that he needed a hornbook.

I called Mr. Sandstrom at his office at Melbourne Terrace. He couldn't remember exactly when Melanie Mayer had come to cart away her sister's stuff, but February made sense to him. Carrie had paid her January rent before she died, and her first and last month's rent when she leased the apartment. Mr. Sandstrom had had the unit on the market, ready to rent, by March 1.

"Did Melanie take any papers or books from Carrie's apartment?" I asked, wondering how Melanie would have figured out what scandal Carrie was planning to expose.

"Nope. Nothing like that. Just her car, and the rug, and the typewriter, and a coupla chairs. Oh, and the picture of her mom and dad in front of Mayer's Meats."

"What about when you helped Melanie load up the car? Did you see any papers or books in there?"

There was a pause while the old man thought. "I don't remember any papers. There was something under the seat, though - one of those thin leather things. It slipped out when I had to move the seat up to get the chairs in the back."

"Was it a briefcase?"

"No, thinner."

"A binder?"

"No."

"A portfolio?"

It wasn't the word he wanted, but he knew what I meant. "I guess. You know, it folded over. It had a gold clasp. Looked new. Her sister liked it."

"Did she open it?" My pulse was picking up. Mark had described the evidence the police had taken from Melanie's burnt-out house, and a leather portfolio had not been present.

"Naw. Just looked it over and stuffed it in her bag. Why? Is this about the letter I gave the police?"

"What letter?"

"Carrie got a letter from the government a coupla weeks ago. I've been throwing most of her mail away, but this looked official. So I gave it to that cop who was here the day you and your girl came over to see the place."

"Detective Oden? Tall, black hair?" I was puzzled. Mark wouldn't have kept something like that from me.

"The other one. The one who looked like a Marine."

"Detective Gregerson." I should have known.

"Yeah. I called the police station, and he said to bring it over to him." He paused. "Guess I hadn't oughta told you."

I assured him he hadn't done anything wrong and hung up. Just like that idiot Gregerson to mangle the evidence. If Carrie was getting letters from the government, that might mean she was the one with the *qui tam*. And accusing someone of defrauding the federal government is a pretty good motive for murder.

I let loose with a well-chosen epithet before I remembered that Mrs. Holbrook was still sitting across from me, benign and encouraging as a kindergarten teacher.

I apologized and explained about Gregerson and the letter.

"That must be very frustrating," she replied. Then she tactfully introduced another topic. "I have a plan for the e-mail we should send to Clifford Walton. I think we should tell him we want to buy some drugs."

"Excuse me?" She seemed like such a prim sort of person. I was sure I misheard.

"I looked up some of his priors when I was down at the courthouse. One of his running buddies went by the street name of Robbie B. I've already opened up an e-mail account for a 'RobBB.' And I've already put together the message I think we should send."

Priors? Running buddies? RobBB? I must have looked as dumbfounded as I felt.

"My late husband was an undercover police officer," she said. "I picked up the lingo from him."

It was the first time she had mentioned her husband. It was also the first time she had mentioned that he was dead. "Oh, I'm so sorry," I said in confusion. "I'm sorry about that."

"Sorry that he was a police officer?"

"Sorry that he was, uh, late."

She gave me a Mona Lisa smile and looked away. I rushed in with words. "Mrs. Holbrook, it's illegal to solicit drugs over the Internet. Or anywhere. I mean, I'm fairly sure about that. Let's try something else. Maybe a sweepstakes or something."

"We wouldn't actually say we wanted drugs," she pointed out. "You see, you do it like this." She handed me a typed e-mail message: *"My man - anywhere I can find some joy?"*

Joy. Not drugs. Joy. Really, who isn't looking for joy? But it was close enough to the line that I wanted a professional's opinion.

Mark burst out laughing when I read him the message over the phone.

"OK, which one of you has been watching *Kojak* reruns?"

It was not the time or place to explain about Mrs. Holbrook's apparently very late husband. "It's a little dated?"

"*A little*," he said. "And since you're trying to get him to offer you drugs, it's probably illegal, too. What the hell are you two playing at?"

I explained about the return receipt to our e-mails, the plan to send another message that Clifford Walton wouldn't be able to ignore.

"Not a bad idea," he allowed. "But you're going at it wrong. Cliff Walton isn't a big-time dealer. He sells a little to support his own habit, but he'd rather take a drug than sell it. If you really want him to respond, offer to *get* him drugs, not the other way around."

"Wouldn't that be even more illegal?"

"Not if I'm using you as a confidential informant. Which of you wants to be my snitch?"

Snitch is such an ugly word. Fortunately, Mrs. Holbrook volunteered. Her eyes and cheeks were shining. She and Mark collaborated on the message while I looked over the list of scandals and suspects Mark and I had compiled the night before. If Melanie and Carrie had been killed because they were considering a *qui tam*, that narrowed the list. Only people and companies that do business with the government are vulnerable to a *qui tam* challenge for making fraudulent claims. I was pretty sure that Children First didn't have any government contracts.

That left the nursing home and the insurance company still in the mix. The nursing home billed the government for Medicare patients, and the insurance company paid the claims out of the government's Medicare trust fund. Either one of them could have fiddled with the books some way. And Carrie's mother had lived and died in the nursing home, and Carrie herself had worked in the insurance company's Medicare claims unit. Whichever one was at fault, Carrie would have had a chance of stumbling over the fraud.

Mrs. Holbrook and Mark were still debating the fine points of the message to Cliff Walton as the thoughts went round and round in my head. Where did he and Jenny fit into this? Cliff had spent a couple of months working at the construction site right across from the Queen Anne nursing home. As she passed him each day to visit her mother, Carrie could have told Clifford her concerns about the home. Or - and here I actually felt a flash of insight - Jenny could have overheard something when she was hiding under Chuck Thomas's desk on Halloween. It was a huge, executive desk. Donald had told me how far back she was. We had all assumed that she was hiding because she was afraid, because Chuck Thomas might have done something to her. But maybe she was just hiding for fun. And maybe she heard part of a closed-door meeting that Chuck did not want spread around.

I fetched the box of Carrie's books that Harmony had bought from the thrift store. The Medicare Carriers Manual was at the bottom of the box, a rusty black binder that seemed to weigh twice your average medicine ball.

It was gobbledy-gook to me. But as I paged through it, I noticed clusters of highlighting and underlining on certain topics: claims appeals, performance incentives, and - pay dirt - nursing home coverage. I marked the sections with Post-its so Mrs. Holbrook could copy them.

The message was drafted. It was a thing of beauty: "Out and about. Anything you want? Got some good shit cheap." Mrs. Holbrook beamed at me, scooped up the Medicare manual, and went off to assume her electronic identity as RobBB.

Mark was still chuckling when she handed back the phone. "She's something, isn't she? Your HATLADY seems like she's living a double life."

I told him about her late husband. That sobered him immediately. Mark was nearly killed when he was undercover.

"What was her husband's name? Did he die on duty?"

I told him I didn't know, that it would probably be a while before Mrs. Holbrook allowed me any further glimpse into her personal life. And then I asked him about the letter.

"What letter?"

I explained about the letter Carrie had received from the government, how Mr. Sandstrom had given it to Detective Gregerson. Mark responded with the exact epithet I had used when Mr. Sandstrom had described the situation.

"I'll get it. I'll call you," he said. He hung up without saying goodbye.

When he called back about an hour later, he sounded more puzzled than annoyed. "Gregerson had it all right, but, you know, he may have had a point about this one. I can't figure it out. It doesn't really seem to say anything."

He faxed me the letter and a photocopy of the envelope. I saw what he meant. The envelope and letter were addressed to Ms. Carrie Mayer. The upper left corner of the envelope said "Health Care Financing Administration." Underneath that was a return address for something calling itself "PRO-West." The letter itself was even more impenetrable. It said that PRO-West had investigated Carrie Mayer's August complaint and taken appropriate action.

Complaint about what? What appropriate action? It didn't say. But then I looked down at the bottom of the letter and sucked in my breath. There was a small typewritten summary: the date of the complaint, the name of the complainant, and the company about which she had complained. There it was in black and white:

The Evergreen Care Center.

DEAD WEIGHT

CHAPTER 43

It still didn't smell like urine.

The air at the Evergreen Care Center was still cool and fresh. The floors and wainscoting still gleamed. Well-dressed residents still lounged around the lobby, like superannuated extras from a J.Crew catalogue. In fact, the only difference was in the director herself. Pat Campbell was still sleek and silver-haired, but her air of Zen-like equanimity was gone. Her face was flushed, her hands shook, and her voice was thin and sharp. She kept swiveling her head around, as if searching for a friendly face in the crowded conference room.

She wasn't finding one. Anthony was impassive; Mark was grim; the hectoring lady from the State Department of Health was approaching apoplectic. Mark and Anthony had brought me along to kick them under the table if Pat contradicted anything she had told me before.

"Ms. Campbell," Mark insisted. "The file. We need to see Carrie Mayer's complaint against the nursing home."

"Care center," she snapped.

"*Nursing home*," he replied. It was his cop's voice.

"As I've explained several times, Detective, Medicare complaints are confidential. Medicare refers all quality of care complaints to PRO-West, and unless the care provider chooses to waive its confidentiality protections, neither the substance of the complaint nor the resolution is ever disclosed."

"Ms. Campbell, this is a subpoena. It's not an invitation to a party. You either give up the file now, or we come back here with a search warrant and twenty cops and start carting all your records right through your front door. And that can't be something you want your residents to see."

Pat had a whispered conversation with her attorney, an overgrown frat boy with a fake orange tan and small, piggy eyes. "And I assume that if Ms. Campbell elects to turn over this file, this ridiculous witch hunt will be at an end?"

"That depends on what we find in the file. And whether or not the Department of Health still has concerns."

Judging from her guttural *tsk* of disgust, the Department of Health investigator still had concerns. She had graphed patient deaths at the center over the past two years, and it turned out that Tara the waitress was right on target. Even though patients died at various times, there was an unmistakable clustering in the first week of every month.

We couldn't find any monetary motive - residents paid by the day, not by the month, so it was actually in the center's financial interest to keep them alive as long as possible. The Department of Health was working the euthanasia angle. The investigator found the wall of grinning dead patients just as unsettling as I had. She thrust the damning graph across the table with a grim expression.

"Ms. Campbell, your death rate in the first week of each month is more than two standard deviations greater than industry norms. Now unless I hear a plausible explanation, I'm going to have to assume the worst. What happens here at the beginning of each month?"

Pat didn't answer.

"Do you have different staff? Different services? Is that when your hospice counselors come in?"

"We have hospice counselors every week," Pat said, "not just at the beginning of the month."

The health investigator started to ask another question, but I interrupted. "The *same* hospice counselor every week?"

Pat shot me a dirty look. "I don't know," she said. I could hear the lie in her voice.

I excused myself while the interview continued. The crowd in the living room had thinned. A small, white-haired woman was sitting alone and straight-backed on the leather couch, staring out at the Sound. I went up to her.

"Pardon me. I'm trying to get in touch with the hospice counselors who come here at the first of the month."

"Why on earth would you want to talk to Bruce the Snooze? That man is so damned boring I've seen people double up on their meds just to make sure they'd sleep through his visits."

She looked up at me, gauging me. She had a sweet, powdery face, but her keen brown eyes were still and watchful. She knew. I swear as I looked at her, she knew. She knew why we were there. She knew what we were going to find. And she was trying to fob me off with a ridiculous tale of accidental overdoses to explain the trail of death that followed Bruce the hospice counselor. Bruce, the Permanent Snooze.

I stood and stared at her. Just stared at her. She stared back, her eyes steady. "You don't believe me, Jack?"

I rocked back on my heels. "How did you know my name?"

"Oh, I recognized you from the telly. I've kept up with you over the years. I've got a soft spot for people who go blundering in where they don't belong. I was a bit of a muckraker myself - forty years rattling the city's cages at the P-I. Wrote under the name Ian Lark. And Trudy Hooks. And Tommie Pekins. Every now and then, my editors would make a big show of firing one of me - whenever I'd get the mayor good and lathered up - and I'd just start right up again with another name. Gads, it was fun." She looked at me with her head on one side. "Ever hear of me?"

I shook my head, regretfully.

"Whippersnapper," she said, without offense. She patted the couch beside her. "Sit right there, and I'll tell you stories about Seattle that'll make your hair go as grey as any one of us old codgers."

She was trying to distract me. I shook my head again and answered her earlier question. "No, I don't believe you."

"*Rude* whippersnapper." She considered. "When I saw you here with Patty a few months ago, I figured you must have stumbled on it somehow. Then I saw you keeping an eye on us from across the street, pretending to be a construction worker." She fluttered her eyelashes. "By the way, we all thought you looked *divine*. We actually put you on the Events Calendar. For days, no one played any Bingo. When you walked in this morning with two of Seattle's finest and that nervous Nellie from the Department of Health, I could tell the gig was up. But it's not what you think, Jack. It really isn't."

I sat down beside her. "OK, then what is it?"

"It's a good death. People come here looking for a good death. They've lived well; they want to die well. And this place has it all. You've got your water aerobics. You've got your shuffleboard. You've got your big band music every Tuesday. And if everything gets a bit too much - if even morphine doesn't stop the pain, if you can't eat, or sleep, or carry a coherent thought from your mind to your mouth, if you soil yourself whenever you sneeze, and if it's only a matter of time - well, then, you've got your good death to look forward to. It's better than Mexican Fiesta night and those damned little kids who come to screech to us at Christmas."

She looked at me sadly. "You're too young to understand. It's all perfectly innocent. There's no pressure, not even a suggestion. Bruce is just very careful about warning you about your medication. Hell, half the stuff we take around here would kill cockroaches if you sprayed it on them. When you're getting near the end, and if you're inclined that way, Bruce will come by and look over your meds. And he'll tell you to be sure *not* to take more than a certain number of the little blue pills. Because if you did take more than a certain number of the little blue pills, your breathing might get slower and softer until it just stopped, and you might die -

quickly, and gently and painlessly - in a deep and peaceful sleep. And wouldn't that be too bad."

She shot me a level glance. Something about her reminded me of Harmony - her stillness, her sharp eyes. She seemed to sense that she was winning me over. "And even though I like raking up muck just as much as the next person, Jack, I'd hope you could see your way clear to leaving this one alone. If you can corral those three in there beating up on poor little Patty Campbell, I think all of us would be obliged if you would just go away and right some real wrongs. Because we're very happy here with our shuffleboard, and our big band music, and our good deaths."

I thought about Carrie Mayer, Melanie Mayer, and Boyd Tate. Three very bad deaths. Had Bruce the Snooze sacrificed them so his wealthy patients could die in ease and comfort? I didn't know. But I had to find out.

"I'm sorry. I can't do that."

She nodded and looked away. It was the gesture of someone who has seen all the stupidity, cruelty, greed, and downright boneheaded behavior the world has to offer and doesn't expect people to get any better. "Well, it was worth a shot."

"I really am sorry."

"You'll be sorrier someday. It may take sixty or seventy years, but someday you'll wish you could come here."

The front door swung open, and Detective Gregerson led a dozen uniformed officers across the plush carpets. "The Cavalry," she said, and rose.

I stopped her. "What's your real name?"

She smiled at me, a pink-cheeked little old lady with dark eyes that could nail you to the wall. "I forget, Jack. I'm 92. Sometimes I think I'm a Russian countess. Sometimes I'm sure I'm a Paris chorus girl. And sometimes, I tell the most outlandish lies." Leaning heavily on her cane, she limped slowly and painfully toward the elevator.

"Then what's Bruce the Snooze's last name?"

She looked down the hall, where Pat Campbell was engaged in an intense, hand-waving confrontation with Gregerson and Anthony. She sighed. "Oh, what the hell. It would take you two minutes to find out. It's Campbell. His name is Bruce Campbell."

I looked back at Pat Campbell, who was now shaking a perfectly manicured finger in Gregerson's face.

"Is he -" I began, but my new friend cut me off.

"He is," she confirmed. "He's Patty's son."

CHAPTER 44

The story of the mother and son mercy killers knocked the afternoon soaps off the air - thanks to Detective Gregerson. He had the TV cameras waiting outside the nursing home to catch him emerging with Pat Campbell in handcuffs. He arrested Bruce Campbell at his modest office on the other side of Queen Anne. Bruce was a serious, shaggy-haired young man who had prepared a statement for the cameras: "I have broken no laws. I have merely advised patients about the possible adverse effects of an overdose of their medications. In every case, I have warned the patients to avoid such overdoses. That is all."

"Larry's really good at the arrest part of the job," Mark said as we waited in line at Starbucks later that afternoon. Larry had told the excited TV reporters that the Campbells were under arrest for 137 murders – all the Evergreen patients who had died within a few days of Bruce's visits. "It's the investigation part that he finds unnecessary."

Anthony and Gregerson were at that moment meeting with an aggravated prosecutor, arguing over whether there was any basis to charge the Campbells, and if so, with what. Mere advice about potential lethality of medications did not seem to violate state law. Even if Evergreen had screwed up its Rx dispensing so patients had an opportunity to hoard and then overdose on medications, that seemed more like negligence and a licensing issue, not murder.

Anthony had suggested that Mark and I take a break. Mark knew it was to keep him from criticizing Gregerson in front of the prosecutor. He seemed to no longer care. He seemed tired and resigned. It wasn't for lack of caffeine.

"Double shot in the dark," he told the barista. Black coffee with a couple of shots of espresso.

"It might be cheaper and perhaps even safer just to do crack," I suggested.

"Latte for the kid," Mark told the barista, who wrote "The Kid" on my cup.

"Do you see any connection with Carrie or Melanie?" I asked, as we drank our coffee at a tiny table in the back of the store.

He shrugged and sighed. At this point, he said, anything was possible. If – and it was a big if - there was mercy killing, it was possible that Carrie had learned of it, and that the Campbells had killed her to cover it up. And it was possible that Melanie had stumbled over the information in Carrie's effects, and that she and Boyd Tate had tried to bleed the Campbells for hush money. And it was possible that the missing Clifford Walton had cottoned to the pattern of patient deaths across from his construction site, and that Pat Campbell had paid him to disappear.

But there wasn't any evidence that Carrie even knew about Bruce's extra-curricular advice. Mark and Anthony had seized the care center's files on Kristin Mayer, but they seemed innocuous. Carrie had written several letters of complaint about billing issues – not hospice services. The complaint she had made to Medicare was about wound care. Hardly something to kill over.

"Does it seem like we're getting nowhere?"

There was a long pause – longer than I would have thought physically possible for someone who had just downed a double shot in the dark. "No, no, it doesn't, Jack. It feels like we're close."

I looked at him curiously.

"There's that feeling of brushing by something – like we've clipped it. Maybe it's something at the care center; maybe it isn't. But as much as Larry doesn't want to admit it because he knows he screwed up the original investigation, Carrie Mayer was murdered. This girl knew something, and it got her killed. It's just a matter of rewinding the last few months of her life to figure out what."

I thought about Carrie Mayer as I walked back to my firm. The problem was, Carrie seemed to know so many things.

I checked my voicemail as I walked over and changed course. Harmony was done with the grand jury and wanted me to meet her in Magnolia. I grabbed my car, swung by Green Lake, picked up Betsy, and headed over to Magnolia. I couldn't help wondering why. Harmony avoided her parents' vast, empty mansion, even though it was perched high on the edge of Magnolia Bluff overlooking the bay. Her stepmother had been killed there; her father - the man she would always think of as her father - had left there for a business trip and never returned. After their joint funerals, Harmony had covered everything in canvas and plastic and locked the door. And then she had moved into my sunroom. We had never talked about it, never negotiated the rules of cohabitation. It had just happened.

I punched in the security code. The heavy metal gate swung open. Harmony's house was silhouetted against the sunset, casting long shadows across the lawn.

I averted my eyes from the formal drawing room - now just a collection of plastic-draped lumps and bumps - and headed up the marble stairs to Harmony's wing of the house. Betsy stuck close beside me, her orange exuberance quashed by the strange white moonscape.

It wasn't any better upstairs. The bookshelves in Harmony's study were cloaked under canvas; her living room looked like an operating theater; and the dishrack in her kitchen - still holding dishes - was wrapped in plastic. Even the floors were covered with canvas, so we walked slowly to keep our footing.

I stopped at the door to Harmony's bedroom. Everything was draped with white. The only spot of color in the whole room was Harmony herself, small and still, stretched out on the bed. She was wearing a dark blue suit. One arm was flung over her head, one shoe half off her foot. Her eyes were closed, and from where I was standing, I could not see her breathe.

For one horrible second, I thought she was dead. She was so still. Fortunately, Betsy lived by her nose, not her eyes. With an ecstatic bark, she launched herself onto the bed, landing right on Harmony's stomach. Harmony let out a most unladylike *ooof*, and suddenly, the bed was alive with color and sound.

Harmony arced up and threw her arms around Betsy's neck. Betsy barked and danced, trampling Harmony in her zeal to lick her all over. Then she slipped onto her back and rolled back and forth over Harmony, as if she could not get enough of her, as if she wanted to immerse herself in her scent. She leapt up, licked her again, and danced so vigorously that the canvas tarp slid off the bed. Both Betsy and Harmony abruptly disappeared.

I waded around to the other side of the bed and started to untangle them from the canvas - a soft, furry, wriggling mass. Harmony was warm, glowing, and roaring with laughter. Her jacket had popped open, and a few buttons on her blouse had come undone. I looked at her, she looked at me, and suddenly I was kissing her there on the floor. I had her jacket off, and then her blouse completely open, and then I encountered her slip beneath. She wore so damn many clothes.

I don't know how long we were down there on the floor. Betsy kept trying to intervene. I kept pushing her away. When Harmony finally stopped me, it was much sooner than I wanted but much later than I expected. I had actually gotten within shouting distance of the exciting territory between third and second base. I was amazed. Grateful, and amazed. Progress. Progress. It was definite progress.

We were both flushed and out of breath. I had unaccountably mislaid my pants. We dressed quickly and without speaking, with shy glances in each other's direction. Betsy ignored us both, captivated by the fun of pulling the canvas off everything in reach. *Whoosh*, there was Harmony's black leather armchair; *whoosh*, there was her lacquered table; *whoosh*, there was her marble mantelpiece. It looked like the room was waking up.

When we were covered and the furniture was not, we heaped the tarps in the center of the floor and piled onto the bed. Betsy wriggled between us and would not budge. I filled Harmony in on the events of the past few days. She was interested to hear about the Evergreen Care Center, but like me, not sure how to apply it to Carrie Mayer.

"Everything points in different directions," she said, shaking her head. "If Melanie was threatening to file a *qui tam*, it can't have been because of this alleged mercy killing. The False Claims Act only covers defrauding the government, not dispatching Medicare patients."

"It's Boyd Tate. He may not have known that."

"Well, true," she said. Harmony had loathed Boyd Tate. "But it doesn't explain the anonymous letter about Chuck Thomas. Or the blond woman who tried to break into Megan Swenson's house. I mean, Megan doesn't have anything to do with the care center, does she?"

"Not that I know of." We puzzled on it a few more minutes, and then I turned the conversation to the grand jury. Todd Poehl had finally released her at 7 o'clock, after a week of 13-hour days. The grand jury panel had only a few more days of existence. If they didn't return an indictment before they broke, Todd would have to start again with a fresh panel.

"What's your sense? Do you think they'll indict Higuro?"

"I've no idea. They don't like Todd. It's amazing how oblivious he is to that, but they don't. But he presented his case against Rockface intelligently. And the jury was interested."

Harmony had been the Tadpole's star witness against Rockface. Her investigation had confirmed most of the allegations of fraudulent billing – but primarily pre-acquisition by Higuro. Rockface's prior management had been overbilling the government to goose its stock price, so Higuro had paid a premium for the company. Even though Yamashita, Inc., was the new corporate parent, both Higuro and his company were also victims of the fraud.

"Did Todd introduce the memo that says you knew about the allegations?"

"No. He believes that it was falsified. He never even mentioned Hugo Bogaty or Special Agent Rich." My hunch had been right. Todd's search warrant had turned up e-mails and voicemails between Bogaty and Rich, who were indeed brothers. Rich had told Bogaty that the FBI was investigating Rockface for fraud, and Bogaty had been trying to capitalize on that leaked information by filing a *qui tam* lawsuit. Rich had been suspended from the FBI. He and all the other cases he had worked were being reviewed by the Office of the Investigator General.

"What were the grand jurors like?"

"Well, the most startling thing is that they can ask you questions. And they do. They wanted to know all about my investigation; who had verified what I'd found; how we'd worked with the AUSA and the OIG and FTC." Todd had had an alphabet soup of federal agencies looking over Harmony's shoulder. "Their questions were actually really good. They wanted to make sure we were paying back the money to the government, and that there would be better controls in place to make sure it didn't happen again. It's just surprising when you're not used to an investigative jury. David warned me, but it's still disconcerting when you're used to a jury just sitting there quietly. Or sleeping, or whatever."

She smiled at me. In our first trial together, one of the jurors could barely stay awake for the "all rise." We had resorted to all sorts of shenanigans - dropping the biggest books we had, sneezing vehemently - just to wake him up.

"They seemed to like me. Two of them hugged me when Todd sent me on my way. But I don't know how they feel about Higuro. I did my best to try to give them a sense for him as a person. It's dangerous, because you don't want to give up anything more than you have to. But on the other hand, there's no one there to do direct examination. So very sparingly, I'd slip things in here or there. They know that Higuro recruits all over the world, that his company is the most diverse in all of Asia. They know that he was here going to the University of Washington when he met my mother. The women seemed to think he's quite a dashing figure. So alone. So rich. So misunderstood."

There was a flatness in her voice. "Have you heard anything from Higuro?"

"David called him tonight, to let him know my testimony was over."

"Did you talk to him?"

She shook her head. "He didn't want to talk to me." She pressed her lips together. "I guess that's why - I don't know. I guess that's why I wanted to come back here. I just really needed to come home."

I held her tight. We kissed some more, much to Betsy's annoyance. I was to the point of contemplating another toss-off in the clothes department when Harmony pushed me away. "Besides, I wanted you to help me look for something. My mom's wedding dress is down in the basement. I think I've lost enough weight to wear it. If it doesn't fit, I'm going to have to have one made. I'm too short for most of the styles out now. They make me look like a chandelier."

That was such an appealing image that I almost asked her to forego the search. But she wanted to try on her mom's dress, so Betsy and I traipsed down to the basement with her. The locked room was at the end of a long, dark hallway.

The wedding dress was over in the corner. As I got closer, I could see that there were four wedding dresses, each preserved on a dressmaker's dummy so they looked like a procession of headless brides. Harmony had had three stepmothers, each younger than the last. I fought a revulsion at touching the dresses. I did not want Harmony to wear anything that came from this room.

Harmony pivoted the last dress toward me. "This is my mom's."

It looked like a dress a Disney princess would wear right before she ate the poisoned apple. White satin sprang from a tiny waist and pooled to the floor.

"Do you like it?"

"Um, yeah."

She looked at the waist. "I'm still probably a bit too fat."

I told her that was bullshit - or words to that effect - and tried to maneuver the dummy out of the crowded corner. It was not easy. The figure stood on a leaden base, the dress was voluminous, and the whole shebang was wrapped in a plastic bag that also held a gross of mothballs. When I tried to pick the mannequin up by the waist, the figure detached from the stand. When I tried to heft it from the base, the damn thing toppled over. I tucked it under my arm and headed for the door.

Or tried to, anyway. As I tried to angle it out the door, the base swung wide and knocked a hulking electric typewriter off a plastic-covered table.

The typewriter seemed to explode as it hit the concrete floor. The ribbon went one way; the keys popped off. "Don't worry," Harmony called, bending down to address the damage. "I'll get it."

I wrestled the dress out the door, then turned back and saw Harmony kneeling beside the broken typewriter, staring down at the tangled black ribbon in her hands. "Stupid," she said, almost to herself. "So stupid."

That was a bit harsh. But she had been in grand jury all week. "I'm sorry, honey," I said. "I'm sorry I knocked it off."

She looked up like she barely heard me. "What?"

"I said I'm sorry I broke it."

She shook her head. "No, no. That's not it. Didn't Mr. Sandstrom tell us that Melanie Mayer took a typewriter from her sister's apartment?"

"Yes."

"And didn't Mark find it in Melanie's burnt-out house?"

"Yes. It was upstairs."

"Was it damaged?"

"I don't think so, but -"

"We've got to see it," she said, brushing past me. "We've got to call Mark."

"Harmony, it's a *typewriter*. It's not a computer. It doesn't have any memory."

She held up the unspooled typewriter ribbon. Clear, perfectly formed letters were etched on the inky filament. With each strike of each key, the typist had left a reverse, run-together record of her manuscript. All her manuscripts. Everything ever typed using that ribbon.

"Oh, there's memory," Harmony said. "So long as Carrie's typewriter ribbon wasn't burned, her typewriter remembers."

CHAPTER 45

The typewriter ribbon was fine - just a little smoky. And it took us only nine and a half hours to decode Carrie Mayer's last story - the story, I was sure, that she had slipped into her new leather portfolio to take to Greg over at The Stranger. The story, I was sure, that got her killed.

One of the criminalists unspooled the ribbon with gloved hands and read out the letters. We wrote the letters on legal pads, reading them backwards until we could identify the word. Then we wrote the word at the bottom of a large piece of white paper we had tacked to the wall. And then the next word to the left of it. And then the next. Gradually, very gradually, Carrie's last story took shape there on the wall.

I don't think any of us were expecting what she said. Even when Harmony finally wrote her byline and story slug at the top of the paper, we had to read it over a couple of times just to let it sink in:

Slug: Medicare Fraud

By C.A. Mayer

Over the past thirteen years, Puget Health Partners has cheated the federal Medicare trust fund out of almost $100 million.

I know.

I helped them do it.

As a Medicare carrier, Puget Health got hefty performance incentives from the government if it processed claims within a certain number of days and if it answered calls within a certain number of seconds. And according to Carrie Mayer, the insurance company met those standards by outright fraud:

> I'm just a claims processor. I do what I'm told. Whenever we had claims show up on our aging report - claims even a day over standards - my supervisor would have us delete them from the system.
>
> No old claims, no problems. The providers would rebill eventually, and in the meantime, we'd look great for the government auditors.
>
> Whenever we weren't getting to the phones quickly enough, my supervisor would call each of us six or seven times on an outside line and hang up once we answered. So we always met the very highest standard of the average seconds to answer.

According to Carrie's calculations, the insurance company had pocketed more than $93 million in unearned incentives over thirteen years – government money that should have gone to patient care. She hadn't recognized the fraud - hadn't even known that what she was doing was wrong - until her mother fell ill. The Evergreen Care Center was a stickler for prompt payment. They didn't have many Medicare beds. Most of their patients paid their own way.

When Kirstin Mayer's Medicare bills were not paid on time, the nursing home illegally pressured Kirstin for payment. Kirstin was terrified that she would lose her place at the center. She asked her daughter to intervene. And that's when Carrie Mayer started reading up on the standards for Medicare claims processing. And that's when she realized that for thirteen years, she had been a pawn in Puget Health's scheme to defraud the government.

The realization had not sat well. Her mother was dying, her last days consumed in worry about the unpaid bills. Carrie herself was pouring every penny she had into her mother's treatment. Her mother's drugs were outrageously expensive; the care center, astronomically so. And while she and her mother were struggling just to stay afloat, she learned that Puget Health was looting the Medicare trust fund - and had no intention of stopping.

> I went to my supervisor. She told me it was none of my business. I went to my manager. I got written up for causing a disturbance in the unit.

I tried to get an appointment with my vice president and senior vice president. They were too busy. I sent them an e-mail. I got put on probation.

Finally, I went to see our general counsel. Before he became a lawyer, Donald Carter used to teach elementary school in Ballard. I had him for second grade. I didn't think he'd remember me - but he did.

If there's a hero in this story, it's Donald Carter. He listened to me. He looked at the documents I brought. And he promised me he'd take care of it.

And promised.

And promised.

And promised.

It wasn't his fault. He tried. He tried as hard as anyone could have. He even took on our CEO, Chuck Thomas.

The story closed with a line that was so eerily prescient, so disturbing, that it made me feel sick.

My mother died November 24. To her last day, she worried about the bills that were piling up. I promised her I would take care of it. And this is the only way I can.

I won't have a job when this is published. I know that. It's a miracle I've been able to hold on this long.

I don't know what I'll do. I don't know where I'll go.

But to get to a new life, sometimes you need a push.

After we had read it through a couple of times, we all sat around the table in drained and saddened silence. It was such a waste. Such a waste of a kind and conscientious person who just wanted to do the right thing.

"Well, she told <u>The Stranger</u> receptionist the truth," Mark said. "It would have been a huge scandal."

"And if Melanie found this story in Carrie's car, it explains why Boyd Tate was reading up on *qui tams*," Harmony said. "Some of this would have been time-barred, but there are treble damages for defrauding the government. Melanie would be eligible for up to 30 percent of the recovery if she brought the suit."

"So Chuck Thomas gets wind that Carrie's going to blow the whistle, and he throws her over the balcony?" Anthony said. "Why would she let him in?"

"I've been thinking about that."

To his credit, Larry Gregerson had hung out with us all night. "Carrie knew Chuck's wife from that school for homeless kids, right?"

Mark nodded. "Well, they both volunteered there. But Didi Thomas flew to New Orleans that night. Carrie was tossed off her balcony around three in the morning, and Didi was tucked up in the French Quarter by then."

"But not before then," Gregerson said. "We know when Carrie got thrown off her balcony, but not when she got hit over the head. It could have been hours before. So Didi Thomas goes to see Carrie on some Children First business, maybe has a glass of wine with her, smacks her over the head with the pan, puts her in her PJs, messes up the bed, and waits for her husband. Didi lets Chuck into the apartment and heads to the airport. While Didi's having chicory coffee in New Orleans, Chuck Thomas waits until everything's quiet, throws Carrie off the balcony, and slips away. Just their damn bad luck they forgot to search her car."

We all looked at Gregerson with a newfound respect. He smiled grimly. "Told you I couldn't stand that blond bitch. I've known it was her ever since she tried to break into that little girl's house over in Ballard."

"But why would Didi Thomas want to hurt Megan and Hannah?" Harmony asked. "They don't know anything about any insurance fraud."

Gregerson tapped the passage where Carrie had described Donald Carter as a hero. "This mope left Chuck and Didi a voicemail telling them he'd run into an old friend of Carrie's and Melanie's, and that she'd remembered something interesting. That was probably enough for them to assume that Carrie had told Megan about what was happening at Puget Health."

Harmony still didn't seem convinced.

"Well, hell, let's ask them then," Gregerson said.

There was a long, tired pause. Anthony broke the silence.

"Let's bring 'em in."

CHAPTER 46

Donald Carter caved five minutes after walking into the police station. Anthony had only to push Carrie's last story across the table to him, and Donald started to cry - big, splashy tears that ran in rivulets down his long face. He admitted that Carrie had come to him in October with the evidence of the Medicare fraud, that he had fought Chuck Thomas for months to get him to stop, and that Chuck knew Carrie was reaching the end of her patience.

"I kept trying to calm her down," Donald sobbed. "I know what it takes to change Chuck's mind. Sometimes, I've worked at it for years. But she was so determined. She was so angry." He covered his face. "And I told Chuck. Oh, God forgive me, I told Chuck that she was going to take it to the newspapers if he didn't make some changes fast. And the next thing I knew, she was – that poor little girl – she was dead."

"Why didn't you tell us this before?" Anthony's voice was acid.

"I couldn't. I couldn't, Detective. It was all attorney-client privileged communication. And I couldn't believe - I still can barely believe - that Chuck could have hurt poor little Carrie Mayer. She was so upset about her mother, so lonely. I guess I just wanted to believe it was a suicide."

"So what changed your mind?"

"What you told me. How someone tried to break into Meg Swenson's house right after I left that message for Chuck and Didi. I would have never have done it if I thought they meant anyone any harm. And since that night, Detective, since you brought me in here and told me what happened, I haven't been able to sleep."

"What about Melanie Mayer? What about Boyd Tate?"

"Boyd called me a few days after Melanie's dep. Somehow, Melanie had found out about the way we were handling Medicare claims. Boyd said they'd go to the U.S. Attorney unless we paid them off. They wanted $10 million. I told Chuck we had to go to the government, that we had to get out in front of this, but he said he wanted me to try to settle with Melanie and Boyd. I set up a meeting for the four of us, but Boyd and Melanie never showed up."

"And that didn't concern you?"

Donald spoke the unvarnished truth: "Boyd was, well, he was unpredictable. I've had lots of cases against him. Still have one, in fact. It wasn't unusual for him to forget meetings - even hearings. I had a case against him once where he left the courthouse before he gave his closing argument. So no, it didn't concern me."

"Did you kill Carrie Mayer?" The question was low and deadly. It seemed to come from a place in Anthony that I had never sensed before.

Donald looked at him in horror. "I did not. I absolutely did no such thing. I agreed with Carrie. I was glad she had reported what was going on. She and I were on the same side. I took on Chuck Thomas for her, and believe me, that is not an easy thing to do." His defiance faded. "But I did fail her, Detective. She came to me because she trusted me. She trusted me to do the right thing. And I tried. I swear I tried. I felt we were getting somewhere. But just not fast enough."

Donald dropped his head in his hands. Beside me in the observation room, Harmony made a small sound. I couldn't tell whether it was out of pity or revulsion. Maybe a little of both. Donald seemed so truly wretched.

"He could have done something," she said. "He could have reported the Medicare fraud. Once Chuck Thomas refused to stop it, everything Donald learned would have been in furtherance of a future crime or fraud. That isn't privileged." She paused, studying Donald's haggard face through the two-way-mirror. "Of course, that's a lot to ask of an in-house attorney. You can put yourself out of a job and your only client in jail in the same breath."

Chuck Thomas was as disdainful as Donald was defeated. Flanked by graying attorneys in $3,000 suits, he broke his silence only to deny - with an icy indignation - that he had anything to do with Carrie's, Melanie's, or Boyd's death. He refused to answer questions about the Medicare allegations, but I saw the muscle pulsing in his cheek as he clenched his jaw and glared at the two-way mirror. It was almost a relief when Gregerson placed him under arrest and took him out of the room.

The worst - for me and Harmony - was the interview with Didi. She was immaculate - and ashen. She spoke before Gregerson closed the door.

"So you must have found her then," she blurted. Her attorney - a tall brunette with the look of a steely weathergirl - placed a warning hand on her arm, but Didi shook her off. Her blue eyes burned in her drawn face. "Is she all right? Does she say Chuck did something to her?"

"Where were you on December 28 last year?"

Didi gave Gregerson a blank stare. "I don't know. What does that have to do with Jenny Walton?"

"You deny you left for New Orleans that night?"

She considered and shook her head. "I went to New Orleans last Christmas on vacation. Chuck caught up with me after a couple of days. I don't know exactly when we went."

"But he was sure to send you on ahead?"

The look in her eyes was pure horror. "What are you saying? Did Chuck do something to Jenny Walton while I was in New Orleans?" She surged up toward him, and on instinct, both Gregerson and Mark reached for their guns. That was enough to tick off her attorney.

"If you have questions for Mrs. Thomas, ask them," she snapped. "Or we're out of here."

"When is the last time you saw Carrie Mayer, Mrs. Thomas?" It was the first time Mark had spoken.

"Who?"

"Carrie Mayer. She worked for your husband's company. She was the story lady at Children First."

Didi shrugged. "I'm sorry. I don't remember anyone named Carrie Mayer."

Mark fleshed out the description, but Didi still shook her head. "I don't remember seeing anyone like that at the school," she said. "Does this Carrie person know where Jenny is? Does she say Chuck did something to her? Please tell me - have you found little Jenny Walton?"

Gregerson leaned toward her. "We haven't found the little girl. No one knows where she is. Thanks to you."

"What do you mean, thanks to me?"

"We tracked down the foreman at her dad's last worksite," Gregerson said, taking credit for all my backbreaking undercover sleuthing. "He'll testify that you came to the site and lured Clifford Walton away. And no one ever saw him or his daughter again."

"What? That's preposterous. I never went near any construction site."

"Since you're making this ridiculous accusation, I assume that this foreman positively identified Mrs. Thomas?" The weathergirl attorney was looking tense.

"No need, ma'am. He described her to a T. He said she was tall and blond and beautifully dressed - and had a face like an old tire."

Didi slapped him. She started back as her hand hit his cheek, as if she was shocked by what she'd done. Gregerson didn't move, but there was an awful smile on his face. "Assault on a police officer," he said, pulling out his handcuffs. "We'll add that to the list."

Mark's eyes closed as Gregerson snapped the cuffs around Didi's wrists. I couldn't tell whether it was in anger, empathy, or just exhaustion. It turned out to be almost entirely anger.

"What in the hell is he thinking?" Mark hissed as he burst into the observation room. Gregerson had taken Didi and her attorney to booking. "We only have a couple of days to charge them now, and we'll need most of that to coordinate with the feds on the Medicare fraud. We don't have any physical evidence, we still haven't found Clifford Walton to confirm that it was Didi who approached him, and Meg never saw the face of the woman who tried to break into her house. We'll just have to let them go and do our investigation with the press and their attorneys all over us."

"So you don't think she did it?" Harmony asked.

"It looks bad for them both - for Chuck, especially, and I guess the prosecutor can argue that Didi would have killed to keep her husband's fraud from being exposed. But that's all circumstantial."

"Will Donald be charged with anything?" I asked.

Mark shrugged. "Up to the federal prosecutor, I guess. They may go after him on the Medicare fraud. But there's nothing to tie him to the murders. He really does seem to have been on Carrie's side. Our guys have pulled more stuff off that typewriter ribbon. Carrie wrote Donald at least two letters thanking him for standing up to Chuck."

He rubbed his eyes. "I've got to get back to work. Thanks for everything - for thinking of the typewriter ribbon, and for staying with us. It helped a lot." He gave Harmony a bear hug. "And glad to hear you beat the rap in front of the grand jury, Baby Face."

His cellphone rang, pealing out between them. He snapped it open. *Mrs. Holbrook*, he mouthed, and then covered the phone with his hand. "Cliff Walton responded to her message about the drugs," he said. He spoke into the phone. "Mrs. Holbrook, can you read it loud so everyone can hear?"

The three of us crowded around the phone, ears together. Mrs. Holbrook boomed out the e-mail in a ringing voice.

"No need, bro," Clifford had written in response to her e-mail. "I'm telling you, it's true. *The grass is greener.*"

What in the hell did that mean? The three of us sank down on the hard chairs of the observation room and rubbed our temples. We had been up all night, we were each running on a single slice of pizza - eaten hours before - and I couldn't remember the last time any of us had had a decent, sit-down meal. And now Clifford Walton was blathering on about the grass being greener, and we were in no mood.

Maybe Clifford had gone straight.

Maybe Clifford had moved away from the city.

Or maybe it was just a private joke.

"Oh, screw it," Mark said, stretching and cracking his back in frustration. "I'm going to call the prosecuting attorney's office. This has to be enough for them to get a warrant."

"Wait." Harmony had been puzzling quietly over the message, which we had written across the top of the pizza box. "Maybe it's kind of a play on words. Mrs. Holbrook asked him about drugs, and he starts talking about 'grass.' And the rest of that saying is 'on the other side.' Like he's talking about the other side of the border."

The "border," for Washingtonians, means the Canadian border. And just over the Canadian border is Vancouver, British Columbia, one of the most beautiful cities in the Northwest, known for its dazzling views of sea, sky, and mountains - and its permissive approach to marijuana. Harmony's nutty cousin Charlie had moved to Vancouver – "Vansterdam," he called it - a year earlier. She hadn't heard from him since. Even his regular appeals for money had stopped.

"You think he's in Vancouver?" I asked.

"I'm not sure," she said. "But it's worth a shot."

CHAPTER 47

I t took them less than a day.

Mark and Anthony had helped the Vancouver police solve a gang slaying the year before, and the cops up there were happy to return the favor. They posted Cliff Walton's picture in the squad room; they personally contacted the officers who patrolled Vancouver's Pot Block. Within hours, they had a positive ID.

Cliff Walton was living with his daughter in a room over the Mary Jane Café, which dished up platters of munchies through a pervasive blue haze. He had never been in trouble in Vancouver, but he didn't have a visa to stay in Canada, and it wasn't clear how he had entered the country given his criminal record. More than enough reason to bring him in.

It's a three-hour drive from Seattle to Vancouver - unless Mark Oden is at the wheel of a Seattle police car, in which case it's a shade over two. He had called ahead to the border crossing, and Customs waved us through the Peace Arch at Blaine.

The sun was setting as we pulled into Vancouver. The city glittered and glowed against the violet sky, slung like a bright lattice between the mountains and the harbor. The Vancouver detectives greeted Mark and Anthony warmly - and shook Harmony's hand without looking her over, not even a little bit. I liked them immediately.

Clifford Walton had gained weight in Canada. He looked less like a rat and more like a chipmunk. Even his nose was fatter.

He was not, at first, cooperative. "What's this all about?" he demanded as the police walked into the interview room. Once again, Harmony and I were behind a two-way mirror. "I haven't done nothing. And where's my little girl?"

"You're in the country illegally; these two gentlemen have warrants for your arrest in the U.S.; and if you don't change your tone, you're going back with them tonight." Canadian detectives evidently took no shit.

Clifford eyed Mark and Anthony. "What do you want?"

"Right now, just some information," Anthony said. "If you're upfront with us, it's not going to be worth our time to extradite you. If not -" He shrugged eloquently. *You choose.*

Clifford considered. He was not a stranger to the system. "OK, maybe I got some info. What do you want to know?"

"Why did you leave Seattle?" Mark's tone was mild.

"Hated the weather."

"I'm going to give you one more chance to answer that question. And before you do, I want you to think long and hard about what I might already know."

Clifford was silent.

"Say, for example, you had tried to blackmail someone," Mark continued. "Keep in mind I wouldn't be here unless I was a lot more interested in nailing that person instead of nailing you."

Clifford nodded slowly. "OK. OK. It wasn't like that. Not like blackmail. But my little girl, she, uh, heard something she shouldn't. She was at a Halloween party at this insurance company, and she was hiding under this big dude's desk. Jen's kind of shy, you know, and sometimes she gets uncomfortable with groups of kids. So she's under this big dude's desk, and suddenly there are like people in the office. And the door slams so she can't sneak out. And she hears this big dude screaming - I mean, just screaming - at this lady she knew from her school. Jen really liked this gal from the school. She told the kids stories. And this big dude made the story lady cry - but even while she was crying, she told him he was cheating the government or something and that he ought to go to jail.

"Well, when I picked up my kid that night, she was like, scared to death. She had hidden under that desk for hours. She had missed the whole party, even the trick-or-treating. She didn't get any candy, not even a cookie. And I just thought - well, dammit, I just thought that it was time someone gave this guy a swift kick in the ass. This lady from the school, she had never hurt nobody in her whole life. She was a nice gal, always telling those kids stories and visiting her mom in the rest home. And here this asshole, this Chuck Thomas, is treating her like a dishrag. Like something he could wipe himself on. It pissed me off. And I'll admit, I was also in a spot where I needed the cash. I thought I'd give this Chuck character something to think about and maybe make a few bucks off it. So I left him a message late at night at the insurance company. I said I knew what he was doing, and I'd go to the cops unless I got twenty grand cash by the end of the week."

He stopped and took a deep breath. "I swear, it was mostly a prank - just to make him squirm. But I guess he didn't see it that way. The very next day, some broad shows up at the job site where I work. And she tells me that Chuck Thomas is having me investigated for child abuse and neglect, that he's trying to have the state take Jen away from me because I'm an unfit parent." Suddenly, his voice shook.

The streetwise defiance was gone. "I know I got some problems. I'm working on them. I'm off the junk. It's just the bud for me now. And I am a good dad. And Jen and I need each other. No way was I going to let this asshole take her away from me. No way in the world."

"Who was this woman?"

"Said she volunteered at the school. She looked kind of familiar. Said she heard Chuck talking it over with the principal there, and she knew that Chuck always got what he wanted. She said she knew I was a good father, and Jenny loved me. And she gave me a couple of bucks to get us both out of town."

"How much money?"

"A grand," Clifford said reluctantly. "And two one-way bus tickets to Vancouver."

"*A thousand dollars?*" Mark demanded. "A woman walks up to you on the street and gives you a thousand dollars, and you don't even get her name?"

"Hey, for that kind of money, I was not going to ask questions. And she looked like she could afford it. She was cool, actually. She apologized that it couldn't be more. She said that was the most she could take out of her checking account without her husband noticing. I thought, *some checking account.*"

Harmony and I looked at each other, puzzled. Maybe Didi really did love children. Maybe she had intervened to protect Jenny and Clifford from her husband. But why would she hire me to try to find her? Why would she be so frantic about it - unless Clifford had doublecrossed her, or unless she thought that maybe Chuck had found and silenced Jenny after all.

"Describe the woman you saw."

Clifford shrugged. "I don't know. Tall, blond, thin."

"Pretty?"

"Nope. And kinda old."

Mark slid a picture across the table. "This her?"

Clifford considered the picture. "Naw. That's the lady from the rest home across the street from where I was working."

Another picture. From my vantage point, I could tell it was Kit. "How about her?"

"No way. But I sure wish it had been. Can I keep this?"

Mark snatched it back and handed him the last picture. It was Didi's drawn and haggard mug shot. "Her?"

"Hey, that's more like it." Clifford considered. "Yeah, this could be her."

"*Could* be?"

"It was like, last year sometime. I only saw her for a few minutes. I can't be completely positive. But yeah, this could have been her."

Mark and Anthony didn't press the point. "So what have you been doing since you left Seattle?"

"Jen and I left for Vancouver that day. We've been here ever since. I work at the Mary Jane doing this and that - line cook, washing up, security. We have our own little room over the café. We like it here. We don't want to go back."

"What about April? What happened then?"

"What do you mean, what about April? Who's April?"

"What about the letter you sent to the Seattle police in April? The one about Chuck Thomas?"

"I didn't send you no letter. What are you talking about?"

Mark slid a copy of the document across the table. Clifford read a few lines, his lips moving, and dropped it. "This is disgusting! It's sick! I never wrote nothing like this!"

"You didn't decide to get back at Chuck Thomas by accusing him of molesting a little girl?"

"No! Absolutely not. That's horrible." Clifford sucked in his breath. "Wait - is someone saying that Chuck Thomas touched my baby? Is this letter saying that he hurt my Jen?"

"Do you have any reason to believe that he did?"

"No. But if he did - if he did, I swear I'll kill him."

"Let's not get ahead of ourselves," one of the Canadian detectives interjected. "Cliff, we've got to talk to your daughter."

"No way. Absolutely no fucking way. You're not filling her head with shit like this. I'm not going to let you scare her."

"We know how to do it so it's not scary. It's fine for you to be in the room." When Clifford balked, the detective went on, "Look, if something happened, she needs help. You've got to know."

A female detective came up from the sex crimes squad to conduct the interview. She brought a basket full of dolls and toys and arranged them around the room. When Jenny Walton came in - a sober seven-year-old with dark brown hair and huge grey eyes - she looked around in wonder, as if she had never seen so many toys.

The female detective took her time. First she confirmed Clifford's story about Jenny's overhearing Chuck Thomas scream at Carrie Mayer. Jenny recounted it almost word for word. Then she let Jenny pick out a doll, select an outfit, and begin to change its clothes. As Jenny played with her new toy, the detective slipped in subtle questions about the doll's body, about whether anyone had ever touched the doll's private parts.

"No," Jenny answered confidently.

"How can you be so sure?"

"Because it's gross. She wouldn't let anybody do that. And if anyone tried, she would have told me."

"Would you tell your daddy if someone had ever tried to touch you?"

"Sure I would. And they'd go to jail because it's gross. I wouldn't ever let anybody do that."

There were no red flags throughout the interview. Jenny answered questions without discomfort and played appropriately with her doll. When the detective told her she could keep it, she threw her arms around her neck, then rushed over to show her dad her new Barbie. Clifford had tears in his eyes.

So did Harmony. "I'm just relieved," she said.

We were all relieved - and puzzled. Clifford's account of his abortive blackmail attempt rang true - and it made sense that Didi would have tried to get Jenny out of the way if she thought Chuck might reach for a more permanent solution. But Clifford's vehement denial about the letter also rang true. He loved his daughter. He did not seem capable of writing down the kind of details that were in that letter.

So who wrote it? And why?

More than 40 little girls had passed through Children First between the dates of the alleged touching and the time the police received the letter. They were homeless; they slipped in and out of cities and shelters with no record of where they were going or where they had been. There was no way the police could find them.

"Who benefited from that letter?" Anthony asked as we were driving back to Seattle. This time, he was at the wheel, and we were progressing much more sedately along I-5. "Assuming it's a fake - and it's always sort of sounded like a fake - who had a reason to send it?"

"Well, Didi doesn't have any money of her own," Harmony said. "Just the allegation of molestation would give her a big club to use against Chuck in a divorce settlement."

"Who else?"

"Didi told me the Board of Directors kicked Chuck out when you got that letter," I said. "They called it a leave of absence, but they took his keys, his car, the whole bit. So they must have put someone in his place. I mean, someone got to be CEO because of that letter."

"That's a good point." Harmony said. "Who is running Puget Health right now? Who's in charge?"

Anthony caught my eyes in the rearview mirror.

"Wouldn't it be interesting if it was Donald Carter?"

CHAPTER 48

But it wasn't. The acting CEO of Puget Health partners was the former SVP over Carrie's Medicare unit, Jim Hunter. His fingerprints were all over the anonymous letter the police had received, the letter that accused Chuck Thomas of molesting a little girl at Children First.

Jim Hunter first denied all knowledge of the letter - then, confronted with the fingerprint evidence, claimed that he had received the letter anonymously in the mail, and had merely sent it on to the police in an act of civic duty. Apparently, there's an elective at Wharton called Dirty Tricks.

Gregerson wanted to arrest Jim Hunter for making a false report to the police, but Hunter was going to have enough problems. The Medicare fraud had continued unabated on his watch, and the SPD referred both Hunter and Chuck Thomas to the U.S. Attorney for federal prosecution. The Tadpole was on the federal case – and on TV at least three nights a week. Chuck and Didi Thomas were both charged with three counts of murder, and Didi was also charged with breaking and entering Megan Swenson's house.

Donald Carter wasn't charged at all - not in county court. It would be up to the U.S. Attorney to decide whether he was complicit in the Medicare fraud. The county prosecuting attorney's office granted Clifford Walton immunity from any blackmail charge in exchange for his and his daughter's testimony, and the Seattle police weren't going to pursue the drug warrants. If they wanted to, the Waltons could come home.

The prosecuting attorney passed on the mercy killing case, but the State Department of Health was still concerned. The Campbells and Tommie Pekins (aka Ian Lark, aka Trudy Hooks, aka Jane Doe) asked me to defend Evergreen in the license and disciplinary proceeding. It was going to be a hell of a conflicts check.

Chuck's and Didi's arraignments exploded on Seattle. In deference to Carrie Mayer, Mark tipped off The Stranger to the arraignments in time for the paper's weekly deadline. The Stranger hit the newsstands late Wednesday night with a major exposé of the Medicare scandal. Greg had a staff artist create a full-color portrait of Carrie Mayer, as she would have looked with her new figure, in her new clothes, and with her new makeup by Sedrique. The picture was stunning - a warm blonde with a sweet, dimpled face, blue-gray eyes, and a secret smile, all dolled up in the fake Prada suit.

Greg ran the portrait on the cover, with the caption "<u>Stranger</u> Reporter C.A. Mayer: The Story She Died to Bring You," and again inside, with a sidebar about Carrie, her courage, and her kind deeds. At the bagel place, I watched all the male customers gravitate toward the tabloid and check out the pretty girl on the front. They all took a paper with them. In death, Carrie Mayer had become a sex symbol.

As the criminal justice system cranked into high gear, we saw less and less of Mark. By day, he was tussling with the feds over information-sharing and jurisdiction, and whenever he had a few hours at night, he would slip away to visit Megan and Hannah. Things seemed to be moving fast on that front. Hannah had started questioning Mark about his position on important issues of the day - like spanking, bedtimes, and slumber parties - and he didn't even seem too freaked out that she seemed to be auditioning him for stepfather. Harmony and I were happy for him - but my yard was beginning to look distinctly seedy.

I sent Leah Batson a copy of <u>The Stranger</u>, with a final report concluding that Carrie Mayer had been murdered, and not by her sister. Because Melanie had outlived Carrie, and because Melanie had not played a role in her sister's death, American Fidelity paid Carrie's $250,000 life insurance policy to Melanie Mayer's estate. American Fidelity's Phoenix office found the local law firm that had done a simple will for Melanie. Leah called a few days later to report that under Melanie's will, everything passed to a battered women's shelter in Tucson. I rethought my impression of The Incredible Crying Melanie. Sometimes there's more to people than meets the eye.

And that was it. We boxed up the files on the case and sent them to archives. Todd's grand jury returned the expected indictments against Rockface and its prior management but disbanded without indicting Higuro or Yamashita, Inc. David orchestrated a joint press release with the U.S. Attorney's office, in which Higuro praised Todd's diligence, wisdom, and fairness and committed to a Corporate Integrity Agreement to restore trust in Rockface. The Tadpole got his publicity; Higuro stayed out of jail. Sometimes – slowly, strangely, *expensively* – the system sort of works.

Todd had recommended to Higuro that Harmony be Yamashita's Chief Compliance Officer, and Higuro had agreed. Harmony had politely declined. She explained that she had just launched her own firm, and that the Chief Compliance Officer probably shouldn't be related to the CEO. All very logical and sensible. But when she said it, I heard: She chose *me*. She chose Piper & Hart. After almost two years of running off to Japan whenever Higuro called, Harmony was finally re-establishing a life in Seattle – with me.

We began planning our wedding in earnest. At lunchtimes, we'd sample caterers' menus or tuck into tiny demonstration wedding cakes. I kept telling Harmony that I liked all cake, so long as it was chocolate, but she wanted me to try all of them with her and help make the decision. So I ate a lot of cake, and my new thin clothes from the Bon started to feel a bit snug. Harmony flew to San Francisco to find a seamstress to make her wedding dress. Her mom's gown fit in the waist but strained over the bust. I told her that if she started trying to lose weight up there, the wedding was off. After a short, stunned silence, she had burst out laughing and put her mom's fairytale dress back in its plastic bag.

The Mayer case rapidly receded to the past. New work surged in, and I was caught up defending a slew of fraud charges and Consumer Protection Act claims against a Wildwood horse breeder who did not - allegedly - supply his patrons' mares with the promised sperm of champions. The case was a loser, but it was fun to see the horses and trace their genealogy. And Mrs. Holbrook started coming to work in pert little Elizabeth Taylor riding caps.

Seattle slipped into the two-week period we fondly call summer - the end of July and beginning of August - when everything slows down, and the city focuses on the sea and the sky. The Seafair Festival was in full swing. Aircraft carriers and submarines pulled into port. White-suited sailors waved to screaming girls on shore. The Blue Angels thundered overhead - so fast that they were almost always gone by the time you looked up, leaving impossibly close trails of smoke. Truckloads of semi-comical Seafair Pirates swashbuckled up and down the streets, blocking traffic as they piled out to kiss passing women, fire their canons, and menace little kids with their very realistic-looking hooks and cutlasses.

Even in the depth of Seafair madness, the "Medicare Murders" were never far away. When the Seafair royalty was crowned, even the Lifestyles sections got into the act, running breathless stories about Melanie and Didi, one past Seafair queen slain by another.

It was moments like that - moments when the murders seemed to jump out from nowhere - that the few loose ends of the case nagged at me. Who had been outside my house the night before the FBI showed up to talk to Harmony? Who were those people coming out of the interview room at the courthouse, the ones who were so startled to see me? Where was Kit McCracken? And why, oh, why, had Didi hired me to find little Jenny Walton if she had engineered her disappearance? I could come up with any number of answers - Chuck had insisted that she track down the Waltons so he could finish the job; she thought Clifford had sent the anonymous letter and wanted him silenced; she really was afraid that Chuck might have found and murdered the little girl. The possibilities made intellectual sense, but none of them rang true inside. None of them quite explained the shaken, suffering woman who had shown up in my conference room.

It was no use asking her. While Chuck was trying to swing a plea bargain between the county and federal prosecutors - dismissal of the murder charges in exchange for a full confession to the Medicare fraud - Didi maintained her complete and total innocence. She wouldn't even admit to approaching Clifford Walton, even though Anthony explained to her that getting the Waltons out of town was actually a mitigating factor, an act that showed she didn't want them hurt. She had done nothing of the sort, she insisted. When the prosecutor offered her a sweetheart deal in exchange for testimony against her husband, she refused outright. You have to sort of admire somebody like that.

But it was out of my hands. A jury would decide whether Didi was guilty; if she was, a judge would set her sentence.

My small involvement in the life of Didi Thomas was over.

Or so I thought.

CHAPTER 49

I t was the hottest day of the year. Sunlight filtered through the warm, wet air like rock sugar swirling through steaming tea.

It was the day of the Seafair Torchlight Parade, when lighted floats stream down Fourth Avenue. The parade started at dusk, but the streets were already crowded.

I was baching it for a couple of days. Harmony was in San Francisco for the first fitting of her wedding dress. Mark was in Spokane for a serial killer task force. Betsy was under my desk.

When Harmony had returned from the grand jury, we had had a mandatory roommate meeting, with only one agenda item: Betsy. We had gone over the list on the fridge and had come to a quick consensus: We could no longer leave Betsy alone for the many, many hours we were all at work. I had suggested doggy daycare. Mark preferred a dog walker. Harmony bought our office building. As Mark had put it, rich-girl thinking.

Harmony wasn't the only owner, but she had a large enough share that our building was now dog-friendly. It was going surprisingly well. We had delivered a box of Mr. Barky's dog biscuits to all the tenants in advance of Betsy's arrival, just in case she gave us the slip and wandered into someone's office. There had been only one day of mayhem, when I thought Betsy was with Mrs. Holbrook, and Mrs. Holbrook thought she was with me. It turned out she was holding court in the elevator well, repeatedly swatting the button to call the elevator to our floor.

Since then, one of the key tasks in our law firm was keeping EOB: Eyes On Betsy. It was my turn. Every time I looked at her, Betsy smiled and wagged her tail, front paws down and ears up. The only bad part of taking your dog to work is that it reminds you how much more fun it would be to just say to hell with it and go out and play.

So, to hell with it. It was about 2 p.m. From my window, I could see children clustered around the Seafair balloon vendors and the carts with blue and pink cotton candy.   The only thing I absolutely had to do downtown was pick up Harmony's car from the shop. I would get it and head home. If I waited any later, I'd spend more than an hour just fighting my way out of the Torchlight traffic.

I shut off my computer, told Mrs. Holbrook she could leave early, and locked up the firm. On the way down to the lobby, I noticed Betsy studying the elevator's floor-selection buttons, enticingly located right at nose-level. Busted, she looked the other way. *Bad Things I'm Going to Do Tomorrow*, by Betsy Hart.

Olive Way was packed, even more crowded than normal for a Torchlight Parade. There was a campaign rally for our badass insurance commissioner, who was running for Senate. Standing on a large platform between our building and the car dealer, the insurance commissioner wore a black leather miniskirt and pumped her fist in the air. Her supporters cheered and waved hand-lettered signs as she denounced the evils of insurance companies like Puget Health.

A guitar throbbed from the center of the crowd. As people swayed to the music, I caught glimpses of Rat Cat Hogan up on the stage. They were playing "Board Meeting Minutes" - the best and possibly only rock song ever written about a state insurance commissioner. The commissioner herself bobbed up and down and clapped to the beat. The lyrics slipped across the warm air toward me:

The honorable insurance commissioner wears a leopard skin suit.
She's much cooler than all these uptight health plan executives.
She says, what gives? When will you give the people what they need?

The crowd roared the last line again with the band: *She says, what gives? When will you give the people what they need?*

A movement behind the insurance commissioner caught my eye. Donald Carter was standing on the other side of the makeshift podium, talking on his cellphone and watching the commissioner campaign.

I looked from the commissioner to Donald and back again. I remembered him telling me about the costume he wore to work on Halloween: *I usually come as the state insurance commissioner, which is the scariest character I can think of.*

At the time, I had chuckled at the thought of lean and lugubrious Donald dolled up as the short, pugnacious politician. Now I remembered Jenny's drawing, which showed Donald wearing a dress on Halloween.

What if Donald had dressed as a woman at other times?

The only reason we were focusing on Didi is that a woman – a well-dressed woman with "a face like an old tire" - had paid Clifford to leave town. And a woman matching the same description had tried to break into Megan Swenson's house. But what if that wasn't a woman after all, just Donald in a woman's suit?

Donald was not a handsome man.

Man or woman, "a face like an old tire" described him perfectly.

We had spent so much time figuring out how Chuck and Didi could have committed the crimes. Yet everything was also true of Donald Carter. Carrie would have let Donald into her apartment at a decent hour on December 28. She had known him since she was a little girl. She liked him. She trusted him. She considered him a hero. And he could have smacked her over the head with the aebleskiver pan, changed her clothes, searched her apartment, and messed up her bed before throwing her over her balcony at 3 a.m.

Who had talked to Megan Swenson not an hour before someone tried to break into her house? Donald Carter.

Who had steered me - with a pretty show of reluctance - toward suspecting Chuck Thomas of molesting Jenny Walton? Donald Carter.

Who had worked in two places - the elementary school and the insurance company - where a man had been dismissed because of anonymous accusations of child molestation? Donald Carter.

Who had come out of that interview room at the courthouse, then panicked when he saw me and dived back in? A tall, thin, bristly haired man like Donald Carter.

Who knew about Boyd's and Melanie's threats to expose the Medicare fraud? Chuck Thomas - *and Donald Carter.*

The more I thought about the Medicare fraud, the more certain I became. Donald was right that Boyd Tate was notoriously disorganized and unpredictable. There would be no reason for concern if Tate missed one meeting. But a demand for $10 million? Even Boyd would have made that a priority. And even if Boyd was a screw-up, Donald wasn't. I thought back to the stack of nastygrams - my own included - that had accumulated from exasperated opposing counsel while Tate lay dead in his ramshackle basement. I knew that Donald had at least one current case against Tate. Donald would have encountered the same sort of deadlines and frustrations with Tate's non-responsiveness, his failures to appear, that I had. But there hadn't been *any* reminder letters from Donald in that stack, any demands from Donald for Rule 37 conferences, any motions from Donald for default judgments. Why not? The answer hissed around my skull: *Because Donald knew Tate was already dead.*

I had been suspicious of Donald early on, when there had been a tall, thin man in my backyard the night that Melanie Mayer was found dead in her burnt-out house. But the early morning call to Donald's home number had convinced me that Donald was home in bed. I hadn't considered cellphones. It was easy enough to program your home or office phone to ring through to your cell. I had done it myself. That's how Megan reached me in the Central District. Could it have been Donald, after all, skulking out there in the dark, stealing toward my house?

One sure way to find out.

I just had to get Betsy close enough to smell Donald without spooking him – easier said than done in the olfactory crush of a pre-parade summer's day. Even my much less sensitive nose was almost overwhelmed – the sweat, the sunscreen, the softening asphalt, the hot dogs, the cotton candy, the peanuts, the balloons. We were going to have to get pretty damn close.

We angled through the crowd, keeping eyes on Donald. We were soon at the front of the rally. Only the platform with the band and the commissioner separated us from Donald. He was still talking on his cellphone and watching the band. He hadn't seen us emerge through the crowd.

Betsy was not reacting. Either we were still too far away, or Donald hadn't been the man in my yard. The crowd was thick around us, and maybe everything was just too distracting.

The commissioner caught sight of me and smiled. American Fidelity had a couple of matters before her office. I gave her the thumbs-up. A news photographer snapped my picture.

It was a small movement, but enough to catch Donald's eye on the other side of the platform. He nodded at me and pocketed his cellphone, as though he was going to come around to talk to me. Then he froze when he caught sight of Betsy.

It is correct to say that I am a big guy. It is an understatement to say that Betsy is a big dog. She is 95 pounds of muscle and teeth, and she moves with a coiled grace and intensity, like she might unleash her rage at any moment. I was used to people looking at Betsy with trepidation. But Donald was looking at Betsy with pure fear.

Either he was super-afraid of dogs – even dogs who were across a stage from him – or he was super-afraid that Betsy was going to recognize his scent.

Suddenly I saw the rear side of Donald. He was retreating, heading west fast toward Puget Health.

It was exactly the wrong move. The wind was coming from the west. As soon as he was behind us, Betsy would smell him.

I forced myself to try to look engrossed in the rally. The band had wrapped up to great applause, and now the insurance commissioner herself was stepping up to the mike.

The commissioner was still waving to the crowd and thanking everyone for coming when it happened.

Betsy growled.

We were close enough to the stage that the commissioner's mike picked up the growl. Betsy's deep, guttural snarl ripped from her throat and burst over the rally.

The crowd fell silent. No cheering. No speeches. No band. All you could hear was the roar of traffic from nearby I-5 and Betsy's growls – wet, menacing, rumbling like a train going full speed to run you down, throbbing like an angry hive ready to explode.

Betsy had smelled and spotted Donald Carter.

The crowd scattered as she lunged toward him. I was trying to keep hold of her leash.

Donald looked around, desperately. There were police cars parked along Olive and Stewart, probably as security for the commissioner. Donald pivoted and took off east, back toward the stage.

The stage was not going to keep Betsy from the man who had trespassed in her backyard. Nor was her leash, which burned through my hand as she leapt up on the platform. She knocked down the insurance commissioner as she plunged off the other side of the stage toward Capitol Hill.

The commissioner swore at me as she hit the ground. I helped her up, then tore off the stage after Betsy. If I survived this chase, I was going to have a lot of explaining to do – obviously to the insurance commissioner, definitely to American Fidelity, possibly to the Washington Office of Disciplinary Counsel. But at the moment, I had more pressing obligations. I had to keep Eyes On Betsy. She was hurtling after Donald, who swerved and ducked south up Boren toward the hospitals.

Betsy was a suburban dog. She spent most afternoons watching Mexican soap operas and redecorating my house. Downtown Seattle drivers are insane, even not on parade day. I was not letting any harm come to Betsy. So Betsy chased Donald, and I chased Betsy up Boren's steep hill.

As the caboose of this crazy train, I had a view of where Donald was headed. He seemed to be aiming for Freeway Park - a thicket of blind spots, dead ends, and overgrowth in the heart of the city – where anyone could just disappear.

Donald was about fifty yards ahead of me.

He was a sprinter - long and lean.

But you have to be a damned good sprinter to outrun my dog.

CHAPTER 50

Betsy was almost on top of him. Donald plunged wildly in and out of traffic. The bastard was trying to get my dog run over. I charged up the hill, yelling for Betsy to sit. Of course she didn't. But she got ahead of him. As he was zigzagging in and out of the street, dodging cars and looking back to try to spot her, she ran straight up. She was lying in wait for him at the top of the hill.

Donald suddenly skidded to a halt. As I neared Pike, I saw why. A truckload of Seafair Pirates had pulled onto the sidewalk near Four Columns Park, the tiny triangle of grass, trees, and ruined church columns that overlooks the Space Needle and Queen Anne Hill.

I caught up to him just as Betsy stepped from between the columns. Donald was surrounded. I blocked the way back down Boren; the Pirate truck blocked him from crossing Boren; and Betsy – a very angry Betsy – blocked his way to Pike. Donald was panting and sweating. He looked at me. He looked at Betsy, who had her back up, feet planted, and teeth bared. She looked like she was two-thirds teeth. Another look at me. Another look at Betsy.

And then Donald plunged through Four Columns Park, past the benches and over the fence separating the small park from the steeply pitched, overgrown incline high above I-5.

Betsy dived right after him. I went right after Betsy. I went over the fence; I slipped and teetered on the sheer drop-off to the freeway, stumbling over roots and weeds, getting tangled in the snarls of ivy and vines. I was trying to get a hand on Betsy. She was trying to get her teeth into Donald. Donald thrashed through the undergrowth, trying to hack his way to Pike Street on the southwest.

Donald lost his footing and slipped to the very edge of the precipice. I grabbed Betsy's collar before she could jump on him and accidentally topple over the ledge.

Donald struggled up. He was standing right by the ledge, trying to get and keep his footing on a mound of blackberry brambles and debris. The top of the ledge came only to his thigh. He was so tall and so thin. He couldn't center. The wind had shifted, pushing him toward the ledge. There was an updraft from I-5, tugging at him. His suit jacket billowed, pulling him into the air.

It was Larry Gregerson's ridiculous torque and thrust theory come to life. I owed that man an apology.

As Donald fought to keep upright, a sharp *boom* echoed above us. It was just the Seafair Pirates setting off their canon, but it took Donald by surprise.

He swayed, caught himself, then swayed again.

He tumbled over the ledge toward the concrete freeway far below.

I leapt. I caught his foot. I braced myself against the precipice and tried to pull him up. I couldn't. I was crunched in a sort of ditch next to the retaining wall. I didn't have the leverage. If I stood up to gain some footing, he could pull me over. And he was flailing and thrashing and screaming so bad that it was making everything worse.

I couldn't pull him up. I couldn't bring myself to drop him - however tempting it seemed. So I settled for shaking him over the freeway, shaking him like a cat shakes a mouse.

"Why did you do it?" I shouted at him. "Why did you kill Carrie Mayer?"

"Don't drop me!" he screamed. "Don't let me fall!"

I shook him again. "Tell me, or I swear I will let go."

Just more screaming. Maybe a few aspersions on my character and parentage.

"Why? She trusted you! She thought you were a hero." I leaned over the precipice to glower at him, and immediately regretted it. The view was dizzying. The whizzing cars made it look like he was dangling over a roaring sea.

"My hands are getting tired, Donald. No one would expect me to be able to hold on much longer."

A desperate, strangled cry broke from his throat. "She was going to the press. She had always wanted to be a journalist. She thought the Medicare fraud was her big break."

"What did you care? You agreed with her. You said you were trying to get Chuck Thomas to stop."

Donald sobbed out something. I couldn't catch it. It sounded like "resource."

"What? What did you say?"

"Original source. I had to be the original source."

I nearly dropped him in complete surprise. It took a moment for it to sink in.

Donald was talking about filing a *qui tam*. *Donald* was the one who wanted to file the *qui tam*, and he couldn't have done it if Carrie had published her story. The bounty for a *qui tam* plaintiff hinges on bringing a unique allegation to the courthouse. You can't expect a payout if you're basing your suit on allegations that are already in the press.

Once Carrie Mayer's story hit print, only someone who had been the original source of the public disclosure could have filed a *qui tam* based on those allegations. No one else could gotten a whack of those treble damages for the way Puget Health Partners had been defrauding the government.

"You killed Carrie Mayer so you could file a *qui tam*?"

The answer was faint and terrified. "I had to. She wouldn't wait. She wouldn't wait to go to the press until after I had filed my lawsuit."

And you killed Boyd and Melanie when they found out about the Medicare fraud? Because you were afraid they might file instead?"

"Yes."

"And you bribed Clifford and Jenny Walton to leave town?"

"I couldn't make sure they'd keep it quiet, even if I paid them off. I had to scare them away."

"And covered your tracks by dressing up like Didi, and then by making it look like Chuck was molesting Jenny Walton?"

"Yes. Jack, please. I admit it. Please, pull me up."

I ignored him. It was better he didn't know I *couldn't* pull him up.

"And what about me, Donald? Why were you in my backyard at 4 a.m. the night Melanie Mayer was killed?"

"I just wanted the pan. Sandstrom told me he gave it to you. I washed it that night, but when you kept asking questions, I was worried that it might still have bloodstains or hair or something."

My stomach convulsed at the thought of the aebleskiver cooked in that murderous pan. My hands were cold and sweaty. At any moment, my arms were going to give out. I braced my feet against the ledge.

"You tried to break into Megan's house because you knew if she told the police about the time capsule, they'd find your picture with the children. They'd know you lied about not knowing Carrie. And they'd know which sister died first - no matter how hard you tried to make it look like Carrie had passed herself off as Melanie and murdered her sister for the insurance. You cut off Melanie's head and her hands just to throw us off the trail. You were going to kill Megan. You were going to kill her little girl."

He didn't answer. I gave him such a shake that he smacked against the concrete wall of the freeway.

I was hurt and furious and betrayed. But I was also starting to worry. My hands and arms really were getting tired, and I didn't know how long I could hang on. Although I would have gladly dropped Donald at that point, I didn't want him to get off that easy. I wanted him to face what he had done.

Betsy wriggled beneath my arms. If I had to grab Betsy to keep her from going over the ledge, it was going to be goodbye, Donald.

Betsy's front paws were up on the precipice. She was peering over the ledge.

I was just about to let go of Donald when Betsy sank her teeth into Donald's leg.

Donald's howl drew some attention. I heard voices behind me. The Seafair Pirates had decided to investigate what happened to the two mad lawyers who had plunged over the wire fence.

I explained my predicament, which did not cause them undue concern.

"He killed three people," I said.

"Well, drop him, then," one advised.

I looked down at Donald, who was gibbering to himself. "I can't."

They yanked him up. They held him at cutlass-point while one of them pulled out a cellphone and dialed it, expertly, with a fake hook hand. The police arrived within minutes.

I sank down on the bench in Four Columns Park. I rubbed Betsy's ears and pressed my forehead against hers. She licked my nose. She leaned against me and let out a ceremonial and triumphant growl as the police handcuffed Donald and shoved him into the back of a squad car.

A shadow fell across us. One of the Seafair Pirates was standing a few feet away, decked out in a torn shirt, an eyepatch, and puffy pants, twiddling a mustache I devoutly hoped had come out of a box - and even more devoutly hoped would soon find its way back in.

"So, kid," he said, nodding to his companions, who were putting the canon back on the truck.

"We were talking. How'd you like to join the Pirates?"

CHAPTER 51

had always, secretly, somewhat wanted to be a Seafair Pirate. It looked like a month of non-stop fun - storming the beach at Alki, swaggering around town in costume, kissing any girl you pleased. But even though the Pirates did a lot of charity work and had been the symbol of Seafair for decades, they were not universally adored. Some folks saw the Pirates as overgrown juvenile delinquents with severe arrested development, who lived for the license to get liquored up and carouse. The Elks Club without the class.

So I was thinking it over.

Meanwhile, the police were working on nailing down additional evidence so Donald's conviction wouldn't depend on what he said while he was hanging upside down over the freeway. Apparently, some might consider that coercion. Donald had a new scar on his forearm that looked like a bite mark. That took some of the bluster out of his defense attorney. In Donald's closet, the police found strands of synthetic blond hair the length of a pageboy wig. There were black fibers that did not match any of his remaining clothes, and purple fibers that matched the shreds left behind from the man lurking in my back yard. He had the same size feet as the cast the police had taken of the footprints in my yard, although his one pair of running shoes was brand new, and the tread didn't match the cast. But there were traces of mud in his closet that typed to Mark's proprietary, penetrating blend of organic fertilizer – bat guano, fish emulsion, and molasses. No one else had that particular concoction in their yard. No one else would want to. And no wonder my neighbors all hated us.

Faced with the physical evidence and a prosecutor who was willing to take the death penalty off the table, Donald confessed. He told the police that Carrie had come to him in October with her evidence of Medicare fraud. He had confronted Chuck Thomas, who had ridiculed him and had tried to intimidate him and Carrie into dropping it. But this time, it didn't work.

For ten years, Donald had been Chuck Thomas's punching bag. Chuck wouldn't listen to legal advice if it went against what he had already decided, but when he got into trouble, he always blamed Donald. He made Donald do all his dirty work, including bribing Clifford Walton to leave town - although Donald never told Chuck he had gone dressed up as Didi so Clifford wouldn't be able to identify him. With so much baggage between them, with so much at stake, with his former student looking to him to make everything right, Donald decided that unless Chuck knuckled under and stopped the Medicare fraud, Donald was going to file a *qui tam*.

But he couldn't until Chuck told him that Puget Health was going to continue the Medicare fraud even knowing that what he was doing was illegal. Until Chuck made a statement in furtherance of an ongoing or future crime or fraud, the attorney-client privilege cloaked everything that Donald knew. Donald could have been disciplined or disbarred if he broke the privilege, and it wasn't guaranteed that he'd get any money out of the *qui tam*. Courts don't like rewarding attorneys who break the ethics rules. So he had to wait until Chuck crossed that line.

It happened right after Christmas. Chuck had been putting off dealing with the issue. He kept coming up with new questions for Donald to answer; new places for him to look. When Chuck said he wanted to bring in a consultant to give him an industry comparison of how other payors processed Medicare claims, Donald told him that fraud was fraud, whether or not other people did it. Chuck blew up at Donald and Carrie and said he didn't care if it was illegal: Puget Health was going to keep deleting overage Medicare claims. Donald was thrilled – that was exactly the sort of unprivileged statement he needed to allow him to file his *qui tam*. But Carrie told him she had already called The Stranger and was going to take the information to the press.   Donald pleaded with her to wait, but she was determined. He went over to her apartment that night to try to talk her out of it - and that was when he killed her.

He insisted it wasn't premeditated. They had argued, she had shown him the story she was going to publish, and he had seen his share of any *qui tam* recovery – potentially millions of dollars - evaporating before his eyes. Donald liked to gamble; he had debts; he had been counting on that money. When he couldn't get Carrie to see reason, he picked up the aebleskiver pan from the stove and smacked her on the head. And when he realized how badly he'd hurt her, he panicked, put her in her pajamas, messed up the bed, and tossed her over the balcony after everyone seemed to be asleep. He took her story with him, but he didn't search her car. He didn't know that another copy of the story was in her new portfolio under the seat – waiting for her trip to see Brad at The Stranger.

After Carrie's murder, things started to fall apart for Donald. The first blow was Chuck Thomas's change of heart. He stopped the Medicare fraud right after Carrie died. He thought she had killed herself because she was so upset over what was happening at the company, and he felt like he had her blood on his hands. So he called a halt to everything: no more deleting overage claims, no more fudging on timeliness standards. Everything by the book. Supervisors had to report claim and call timeliness directly to him, and employees who couldn't meet standards were let go. And Donald, who had murdered so he could file a *qui tam*, now found himself stuck - again.

So Donald decided to get rid of Chuck. There was an ambitious senior vice president - Jim Hunter - who wanted to keep up the skimming, so Donald had to get Jim in Chuck's place. Donald wrote the anonymous letter accusing Chuck of being a child molester. He knew the damage a letter like that could cause. Years before, he had undermined Carrie's fifth-grade teacher - his competition for school principal - by accusing him of molesting a student in his class. Donald sent his letter about Chuck Thomas to Jim Hunter, thinking Jim would take it to the company's board of directors. But Jim sent it to the police, and all hell broke loose. The board threw Chuck out of the company as soon as the allegations hit print.

Even as Donald was plotting to get rid of Chuck, another hurdle surfaced. Melanie had found her sister's story in the leather portfolio under the seat of Carrie's car. Boyd Tate demanded a $10 million settlement - or else Melanie would file a *qui tam* against Puget Health, Chuck Thomas, and Donald himself. They weren't bound by the privilege; they could have moved ahead when he couldn't. Donald went to Boyd's house under the pretense of negotiating the demand - and bludgeoned him to death when his back was turned.

Then he went to Melanie's house and told her he and Boyd had agreed on a settlement. While she was reviewing the fake release of claims, he came up behind her with a lamp. But Melanie sensed his approach, dodged the blow, and started screaming. He put his hand over her mouth. She bit and clawed him. He strangled her after a bloody struggle. He cut off her head and hands because his blood was in her mouth and under her fingernails, the marks of his hands and nails on her face and throat. It was only afterward - after he threw the head and hands into the Sound - that he realized the unintended benefit of the mutilation. It seemed such an extreme way of masking the body's identity that we couldn't help questioning whether the dead woman was actually Melanie Mayer. And when he saw us going down the wrong path, Donald was only too happy to suggest that the original corpse might not have been Carrie after all.

With Chuck out of the way, Jim Hunter took control of the company and reinstituted the Medicare fraud. Donald filed a secret *qui tam* complaint charging Puget Health Partners with defrauding the government. That was indeed Donald Carter I had seen at the courthouse, talking with the government investigators.

When Donald ran into Megan at Fred Meyer, seeing him jogged Megan's memory about the time capsule they had put together in elementary school. Donald knew that not only would the time capsule establish that it was Carrie - not Melanie - who had gone over the railing, it would reveal that he had known Carrie since second grade, that he had had a much deeper relationship with Carrie than he had disclosed to the police. He had left a cryptic message for Chuck and Didi to cast suspicion onto them, dressed up in the clothes he had worn to impersonate Didi with Clifford Walton, and tried to break into Megan's house. He had intended to bludgeon Megan before she could call the police.

"Ugh," Harmony said, putting down the confession. Mark had met us for lunch at the Cloud Room to bring us a copy.

"I know," Mark said. "Anthony had to hold me back when we got to the part about Meg. By the way, Jack, Anthony and Larry send their compliments on your interrogation technique. Shaking a dirtbag over the freeway while your dog mauls him; why didn't we think of that?"

I had been getting this sort of ribbing on a regular basis - from cops, other lawyers, clients, judges, even the friendly counterman at the bagel store. One of the Department of Transportation traffic cameras had captured me grabbing Donald's foot as he plunged over the precipice toward I-5. Unfortunately, it had also captured me shaking him and shouting at him while - I hadn't realized this part at the time - a semicircle of Seafair Pirates stood behind me, grinning hugely. The local TV stations had aired the tape almost every night. Then one of the networks picked it up, and it went nationwide. Wider. Higuro saw it in Japan - and called to ask Harmony what in the hell I thought I was doing. At least I had gotten them talking again.

"Do you think this means that Carrie wasn't really molested by her fifth-grade teacher?" Harmony asked Mark. "I mean, the letter Donald wrote about Chuck was a fake. Was the one he wrote about her teacher a fake too?"

Mark shrugged. "He swears it was for real. Just a coincidence that it helped him get the principal spot. But we can't really prove it either way. Carrie's dead. And the other teacher committed suicide, so we can't ask him."

Harmony had been wrapped up with the grand jury when Mark had discovered that Carrie's former teacher had killed himself. It was a bit of the story she hadn't heard. "He did?" she asked. "What was his name?"

"Jerry Iverson. Lived in our neighborhood. He jumped off the Aurora Bridge about six years ago."

"Oh," Harmony said. She pushed her plate away. Her sandwich was almost untouched - just two or three little bites around the edges. "Oh."

Mark and I looked at her curiously. "Why? What is it?"

"That Stranger article Carrie wrote. 'Jumpers.' It begins with a 54-year-old man named Jerry, a man from Green Lake who jumped from the Aurora Bridge. Given the timeframe of the article, it would have been about six years ago."

I whistled. I had forgotten the specifics of Carrie's "Jumpers" article. If Carrie had learned that her old teacher - maybe the man who molested her - had committed suicide, that explained why she would have written the story. Not because she herself was suicidal. But because it let her bury an old, horrible hurt - because it let her move on.

"You think Jerry Iverson is the guy in Carrie's suicide story?" Mark asked.

Harmony shook her head. "I don't know. But if it was her old teacher - and if he molested her - I can see why she wanted to write that article. When she learned he was dead, it would have been the first time since fifth grade that she would have felt safe. The first time she could have gone to sleep without worrying she'd wake up and find him standing over her."

I didn't know what to say. There was someone out there who had hurt Harmony, someone who had just about crushed her when she was sixteen, and a virgin, and on her second date. All Mark and I knew was that he had been two years older than she was and a Seattle Tennis Club member, which meant he probably had moved in the same rarified societal air. She wouldn't tell us his name. She wouldn't tell us whether he was still in Seattle. But I figured he was. I had watched her carefully on the few occasions when we went to social events, and I had seen the way she scanned the crowd the instant she stepped into a room. Some day she would spot him. And when she did, I would know she had spotted him. I would follow her eyes and know who he was. And then? Well, shaking him upside down over the freeway sprang to mind.

Mark excused himself to go back to work. Harmony and I lingered, savoring the break in our day. It was Mrs. Holbrook's turn for EOB, and the two of them were at that moment tooling around Lake Union in the Hat Mobile. Harmony and I took a moment to enjoy the view from the top of the Camlin. The doomed view. A forty-story office building was in the works right beside the hotel, and soon Cloud Room diners would look over rabbit warrens of cubicles instead of the sweep of the Olympic Mountains, the Space Needle, and glittering Queen Anne.

I beckoned for the check. The waiter looked me over nervously.

"A drink for you, sir," he said, bobbing back from the table. The tray held a frosty Coke and a folded napkin. "From that gentleman over there."

I followed his nod and looked across the restaurant to a tall, thin man with closely cropped black hair, a black goatee, a loose gray suit, and a scholarly appearance.

I opened the napkin and found a note:

"Hey, sailor," it read. "Buy me a drink?"

CHAPTER 52

The waiter was sweating. Apparently, he watched the evening news.

"Please give the 'gentleman' a Camlin Cosmo and tell him to stop being such a horse's ass," I instructed the waiter, who backed away to fetch the bright pink drink. Kit - because it had to be Kit - tipped the Cosmo toward me, downed it in a gulp, and started across the restaurant.

She – or, I guess, he - walked like a man. The female Kit had been all curves and sway, a bouncing, breathtaking vision on teetering heels. But this version of Kit - because it had to be Kit - was all angles, strides, and forward thrust. When he sat down opposite me, he even hitched up his pant legs to save the crease.

Harmony did not seem in the least disconcerted. "Hello," she said. "I'm Harmony Piper."

"Kit McCracken," Kit said, shaking hands. "Your secretary told me that you and Jack would be here. But she didn't mention how beautiful you are." He turned to me. "You are such a lucky man."

"Where in the hell have you been?" I demanded.

"Oh, I've been around. Can I have another drink?" He beckoned for the waiter.

"No, you cannot. You said you were Carrie's best friend, but you sure don't act like a best friend. You didn't help us try to solve her murder. You lied about not being at her place around Christmas. And when the police tried to talk to you, you got weepy and split. All the time we needed to ask you questions - all the time you could have been helping the police - you were in the wind. So that tells me that you were either in on it, or you are a selfish little bastard."

Kit's mouth was open. "I was scared!" he protested.

"Oh, bullshit. Scared of what?"

"Of Donald. Of you."

I was about to tell him he had only begun to be scared of me when Harmony intervened. "Maybe you should start at the beginning," she said to Kit. "We need to understand this better."

Kit paused, looking from one of us to the other. His huge eyes were gray, not green, but just as liquid and alive as when we had had our first drink at the Camlin.

"I did not - did *not* - have anything to do with what happened to Carrie. Or her sister. Or her attorney. But I knew what was going on at the insurance company. And I knew Carrie was trying to stop it. I knew she had told Donald she was going to The Stranger, and then suddenly, she was dead."

"Why in the hell didn't you tell me that in the first place?"

"You were Donald's friend. He was right there in the interview. And I kept seeing the two of you together - at the bagel store, getting coffee at Torrefazione. I thought you might be in on it. Honestly, until I saw you on the news shaking him upside down over the freeway, I thought you might be helping him."

I thought that over. I had run into Donald a lot - mostly because there just weren't that many places to eat around my office. We had been friends. And Donald had been in the interview where I first met Kit. We had exchanged a look that unnerved her. Him. In retrospect, I could see why Kit had been so leery of me.

"OK," I said. I signaled the waiter for another drink for Kit. "I understand why you thought I might be working with Donald. But why did you suspect Donald in the first place?"

"He was so insistent that Carrie not go to the press. And the day she tells him she's going no matter what he says, she ends up dead. What was I supposed to think? I couldn't prove anything, but he's always given me the creeps. I tried to warn Carrie, but she'd known him since she was a little girl. One of her teachers liked to play patty-cake with her, if you get my drift, and Donald got it stopped. Carrie told him everything about the Medicare fraud, kept believing he could fix that, too." Kit stopped. His eyes were suddenly bright and hot, his cheeks flushed with anger. "He fixed it all right," he said.

I was quiet a moment, watching him. It was plausible, but I wasn't convinced.

"And then there he was at your house the night Melanie was killed. I thought you guys were living together."

"Wait, what? Why did you come to my house that night?"

"Because I wanted to see whether you were there - or whether you had been off setting that fire. I was supposed to meet Melanie and her attorney that night. They wanted me to sign a declaration about the Medicare stuff at Puget Health. When I got there, the whole house was on fire. There were fire trucks, and ambulances, and I parked and watched until they brought out the body bag and put it in the coroner's van. I looked up your address at a gas station, and I went over to your house. I wanted to see whether you looked smudgy or smoky or bloody or anything like that. From the street, I could tell that you were sitting in your living room. When I went around to the alley to see if I could get a closer look, there was Donald Carter standing in your back yard. I thought I must be imagining things, just getting scared at tall shadows, but then he started walking toward your back door. And he's unmistakable, you know – so big, and thin, and flappy."

He shuddered and downed his new drink in a single gulp. Definitely Kit.

"And after that?"

"The whole thing was just too freaky for me. The cop who kept trying to question me lived with you; you were like best buddies with Donald; Donald kept offering to give me a ride home, like he was trying to get me alone; and I couldn't tell if you guys were a couple or a threesome or what. All I knew was that I wasn't getting in the middle of whatever the three of you might be cooking up." He tipped his glass toward Harmony. "Or the four of you, I guess. No offense."

"So, what did you do?"

"I left my apartment the day your cop roommate came to Puget Health to question me. I got another place up on Capitol Hill, and I've been living as a man ever since. I've been bartending, modeling, doing odd jobs. Anything to stay under the radar. To stay alive."

Harmony asked, "Had you dressed as a man before?"

Kit nodded. "Oh, yeah, lots of times, but just for fun. The Breakroom has a drag king contest now and then. I've won it twice in a row."

"I can see why." Harmony seemed genuinely interested. "You look wonderful. How do you make your figure so manly?"

"I just tape these girls down," Kit said, patting her chest. "I wear a little padding in the shoulders and waist, so it all evens out. And a couple of socks down the front. I used to wear a red wig to work, so it was actually a pretty quick transition. I just buzzed off the hair I had, took out the green contacts, and slapped on the beard. It itches a little, but it creates a masculine line in your jaw. Instant man. It was the best disguise I could think of."

"So you weren't worried that anyone would recognize you?" I asked. "Didn't anyone from Puget Health know you had dressed up as a guy?"

"Just Carrie. And she wouldn't have told anyone."

"What did she think about it?" Harmony asked.

"She thought it was cool. She was shy, but she wasn't sheltered. I mean, she lived by Capitol Hill for eight years. She was just fascinated with how different I looked - how I could slip from being a woman to a man with just a change of clothes. That you can be anything - really, anything you want - with the right clothes and the right hair and the right makeup. You can control the way people see you - or don't see you. It's in your hands. It's all up to you. Those are some of the things I was trying to teach her."

"Teach her?" Harmony prompted.

Kit looked out the window, looked out at the sharp, slate gray mountains, etched with snow even in Seattle's deep summer, looked out over the Space Needle and Queen Anne, looked over - finally - the building where he used to work.

"Carrie never wanted anyone to notice her - especially not men. Maybe it was because of what happened to her when she was little; I don't know. But she really wanted to be a reporter. And after the guy from <u>The Stranger</u> just brushed her off a couple of years ago, well, I was trying to get her ready to talk with him again. I gave her a couple of suits that I had bought thinking I would get them tailored - they didn't fit me, but they were a really good price; you know how that goes. And I took her over to a place on Capitol Hill where a friend of mine does makeovers. She looked fabulous. She had lost about fifty pounds in six months on some diet she'd started when her mom got sick."

"Why did she start trying to lose weight then?" Harmony asked.

"Her mom always wanted her to lose weight," Kit said. "Carrie was so pretty, and her mom didn't understand why she tried so hard to cover that up. So Carrie wanted her to know she'd be all right. She wanted her mom to see her pretty before she died."

He stopped and swallowed. "Poor Carrie," he said. "Poor little thing."

I couldn't think of anything else to do. I bought Kit another drink.

CHAPTER 53

"How'd it go with the insurance commissioner?" I asked Harmony after Kit had sauntered out of the restaurant. She had been in Olympia all morning pleading my case.

"Overall, good. Once I explained what you were doing and why, she was impressed that American Fidelity had tried so hard to execute Carrie's policy properly. And she loved that you were chasing down someone who had committed insurance fraud. If you would be willing to do a photo op with her to use in anti-fraud public service announcements – you and Betsy – I think all will be forgiven."

It would be up to American Fidelity, but they had everything to gain from my staying in favor with the insurance commissioner. American Fidelity itself had been amazingly cool about everything. Leah had told me her board was already well aware she had hired an odd duck, but an odd duck who got things done. I was going to put it on my résumé.

"Thanks for saving my butt."

"Thanks for saving *my* butt."

"It's such a good butt," I said to her – right as our geriatric waitperson walked by. She glowered at me with venerable disapproval, and Harmony flushed a deep and beautiful rose.

"Jack, you have a one-track mind."

"It's such a good track, Harmony."

I enjoyed watching her blush again, then turned back to the topic of Kit McCracken.

"So how did you know that she was actually a woman?"

"Little things. The way she shook my hand. The way she held her glass. The way she kept her knees together." She smiled at me. "The way you responded to her."

"I categorically deny that I responded to Kit in any revealing way," I insisted, realizing as I did so that my ears were red.

"And the way I didn't respond to her."

That was interesting. Harmony seemed so - well, not cold exactly, but at least non-warm - when it came to men. She barely seemed to respond to me. And she was *marrying* me. I had no idea that she responded to other guys, that there was anything switched on inside her. It was a heartening - but somewhat galling - thought.

"Really?"

"Really."

"So you, um, knew she wasn't a man because you weren't attracted to her?"

She looked confused, and then she laughed. Not a happy laugh. "Because I wasn't *afraid* of her," she said.

Oh.

I reached over the table and took her hand. "Are you afraid of me?"

"Yes."

Ow. That was all I could think of. Ow. Ow. *Ow.*

"Not because you would try to hurt me," Harmony said hastily. "But because I'm not sure I can give you what you want."

I had lost control of this conversation. But something - courage or cowardice or both - pushed me to follow it to the end. "Does that mean you don't want to get married?"

She shook her head. A double negative. What did that mean?

"No. I want to get married. I really do love you, Jack."

"But?"

"But I know I don't give you what you need. Even before the waitress incident I knew that, but when the waitress jumped you, it really brought it home. So after we're married, if you needed - well, if you needed to look outside our marriage for what I don't give you - I would understand."

A license to cheat. She was giving me a license to cheat. She was giving me what every red-blooded American man secretly - and not so secretly - dreams about. And if I hadn't worked with her so long, she would have gotten away with it. But I had negotiated hundreds of deals with Harmony. I knew the signs that she was about to put one over on some poor sucker - the serious angle of her head, the generous uplift of her open hands, the studied innocence of her still and watchful eyes. I knew how her slippery little brain worked. I knew how she would wait and watch until her opponent was most vulnerable, then make an offer that seemed to give him everything he wanted. An offer that always - *always* - served her client more than her opponent could ever guess.

You had to watch her. You just had to watch that girl.

"Oh, no," I said, rather to my own surprise. "Absolutely not. I'm not letting you get away with that."

She had the nerve to look affronted. "Get away with what? I'm just trying -"

"You're just trying to distract me. You're just trying to get me to agree that you don't have to sleep with me. You're just trying to send me to every other girl in the world so I won't come after you. Hell, Harmony, you're almost pimping for me."

She stared at me, aghast. I moved in before she could collect her thoughts.

"I don't want other women, Harmony. I want you. I want to go to bed with you, I want to wake up with you, and I want to do everything else in between with you."

She pulled her hand from mine. She crossed her arms in front of her chest. She looked simultaneously nettled, frightened, and abashed. I braced myself for another mind game.

It didn't come. Instead, she spoke in a very small voice. "What if I can't?"

"You can."

She shook her head. "You don't know that. How can you say that?"

I leaned in close. "Because I'm irresistible, Harmony."

There was a pause where everything really, really could have gone to hell. And then she started to laugh. But as she laughed, there was this little breaking sound, as if someone had shattered it before she ever got to enjoy it. Her eyes were wet, and her hands were shaking. She braced her fingertips against her temples and took a deep breath.

"Putting aside, for the moment, your alleged irresistibleness - and assuming I can't . . . ." Her voice trailed off. She tried again. "Not because I don't want to or because I don't love you, but because I just can't - I want to know what you're going to do about it. Because I want to be ready for that going in."

When I didn't answer, she tried to prompt me. "Are you going to leave me? Or cheat on me? Or get mad at me? Or are you just going to look at me the way you do sometimes, like I've been mutilated? Like you're so sorry for me you can hardly bear it? Because that's the worst thing, Jack. That look. I'd rather have you turn me upside down over the freeway than look at me like that."

I was probably looking at her like that right then. I bent in close again. I spoke so softly that she had to lean into me to catch the words. "Harmony, I am going to turn you upside down, and backwards and forwards, and inside out if I do it right. But I promise you that I'll never, ever let you fall."

Her hands were clasped in front of her - so tightly that her fingertips were white. I reached into my pocket and withdrew the small velvet box I had been carrying for weeks, carrying around trying to find the right time. If this wasn't it, I didn't know what would be.

I eased out the ring. It blazed hot and white in the amber light of the Camlin's chandeliers, something new and sharp and strong cutting through the gloom. I held out my hand and watched her fingers gradually uncurl, her left hand open like a leaf, like a flower.

She didn't exactly take my hand, but she let me take hers.

She let me slip the fiery ring on her finger, next to my mother's promise ring.

She let me interlace our fingers so the ring blazed between us, so you couldn't tell which one of us wore the spark.

"OK, Harmony?" was all I said.

She studied me. She studied the ring. Then she gave my hand a hard, long squeeze.

"OK, Jack."

- The End -

BOOK CLUB QUESTIONS

Spoiler: Some of these questions may reveal elements of the story.

Thank you for featuring *Dead Weight* at your book club. Here are some questions to get you started. Enjoy your discussion!

1. When were you sure you knew who the murderer was? Were you right?

2. What clues are given throughout the book? What was the most significant clue? Why?

3. Carrie Mayer is presumably dead from the first page. How is her character developed?

4. How are themes of identity and loss of identity explored and developed?

5. Would Carrie's life have been different if she had been the pretty sister? Why or why not?

6. How do the different characters react to weight and weight loss?

7. Discuss how the possibility of suicide was handled in the story. When were you sure whether Carrie Mayer had committed suicide? Why?

8. How does the Seattle setting affect the story? What is the importance of the different Seattle neighborhoods? Share examples.

9. How does the retro timeframe affect the story? Share examples.

10. What is the significance of food in the novel? Share examples.

11. How are themes of work and hurdles to work developed in this book?

12. What does the character of Betsy add to the story?

13. Discuss how themes of silencing are developed in the book. What are the different ways in which characters are silenced? For what purposes?

14. Discuss two of the novel's storylines. How do they relate to each other?

15. How does the author increase suspense?

16. Who has more leverage in the last chapter? Who negotiates the better deal? Why do you think so?

17. Would you like to read more books by this author?

If you have a question for me, you can reach me at:

https://www.goodreads.com/goodreadscomrosemary__reeve

"The best way to thank an author is to write a review."
-Nathan Bransford

Thank you so much for reading my book!
If you enjoyed it, please leave a review/rating online, and
please look for other Jack Hart mysteries on Amazon and
the Kindle Store.

All the best,

Rosemary Reeve

The Jack Hart Mystery Series:

All Good Things
No Good Deed
Only the Good
Dead Weight

amazon.com/author/rosemaryreeve
https://www.goodreads.com/goodreadscomrosemary__reeve